WOMEN RESURRECTED

Stories from Women Science Fiction Writers of the 50's

Edited by Greg Fowlkes

WOMEN RESURRECTED

Stories from Women Science Fiction Writers of the 50's

© 2011 Resurrected Press
www.ResurrectedPress.com

Published by Resurrected Press

This classic book was handcrafted by Resurrected Press. Resurrected Press is dedicated to bringing high quality classic books back to the readers who enjoy them. These are not scanned versions of the originals, but, rather, quality checked and edited books meant to be enjoyed!

Please visit ResurrectedPress.com to view our entire catalogue!

ISBN 13: 978-1-937022-06-8

Printed in the United States of America

FOREWORD

The decade of the 50's was a special period for the short story in science fiction. Numerous magazines provided outlets for both established and new writers. One of the results of this, was women entering the field in unprecedented numbers. While it is true that there had been women writers in the pulp era of the 30's and 40's, most notably Leigh Brackett and C. L. Moore, they had been the exception, not the rule. In the 50's, their numbers, if not exploded, at least increased dramatically.

A number of factors contributed to this. One was certainly the fact that women were attending college in much larger numbers than in the period before World War II. This provided a pool of educated and literate women with a desire to express themselves. A second factor was that the genre, itself had changed. Under editors such as John W, Campbell and H. L. Gold, science fiction had evolved from being dominated by action and adventure to being a genre of ideas. This helped to attract women to the field.

This is not to say that the eighteen authors presented in this volume formed some organized women's movement. They are much too varied a group of authors for that. They encompass a vast spread of ages and experience level. A few had been writing in other genres, primarily mysteries, for decades, while for others, the story included here is their first, and often only, offering in the field.

This latter fact is interesting in and of itself. A third of the writers in this group had long careers with a substantial body of work, another third only had published one or two stories, while the rest fell somewhere in between with seven to twenty stories published during their writing days. I don't think that these statistics are unique to women. It's always been a struggle to establish oneself as a working writer. No doubt many aspiring authors grew discouraged as the rejection slips piled up and dropped out of the field.

The subject matter and themes of the stories aren't that different than that of their male contemporaries. Several themes show up in a number of stories. One is that of the alien among us. This was, after all, the period of cold war paranoia and McCarthyism. Going from a "red menace" to a "green menace" is not a big stretch. Another idea is that of a post apocalypse world. Again, the cold war and the Bomb were on everyone's mind.

Several of the stories deal with the next step in human evolution and how the new species will interact with the old. If the new species is rare, they might not even realize that there are others of their kind. If the new species has become dominant, what happens to the few remaining individuals of the old?

The last, and perhaps most interesting theme is that of human-alien interaction, either with aliens arriving on Earth, or with Terrans exploring the Galaxy. It is a situation fraught with possibilities for error and misunderstanding; or humor.

This latter characteristic is certainly not missing from this volume. Indeed, it is the hallmark of several of the more successful writers, Evelyn E. Smith in particular, who had a talent for drawing out the humorous from the most dire situations.

If one can draw any generalities about the writers in this book, it is that their work is more likely to deal with domestic situations than would be true for a comparable group of male writers, but this is by no means true for all of the stories included here.

The 50's were an important era in the history of science fiction, and there is no question that women played an important part in that history. Unfortunately, with the passage of time, many of the lesser known authors, of either gender, tend to get forgotten and their works unavailable or hard to find. With this in mind, Resurrected Press has brought together this collection of the works of eighteen of the women writers of this period so that the reader may judge for themselves their contribution.

A brief note about the sources for the biographical material included with each stories. The bulk of it was drawn from either Wikipedia or the Internet Speculative Fiction Database (www.isfdb.org). The latter, in particular, was of great value in determining the course of each author's writing career. Unfortunately, for far too many of these authors, there is no information readily available other than the existence of the stories themselves.

Greg Fowlkes
Editor-In-Chief
Resurrected Press
www.ResurrectedPress.com

Table Of Contents

THE LOST KAFOOZALUM
BY PAULA ASHWELL

ORIGINALLY PUBLISHED IN *ANALOG SCIENCE FACT & FICTION*
OCTOBER 1950

Editor's Notes:
The Lost Kafoozalum
By Pauline Ashwell

Pauline Ashwell made a big start out of the box by winning a Hugo for her first published story and then followed it up with another Hugo for this story, "The Lost Kafoozalum." This is especially impressive considering she only had four stories published during this period. She later resumed writing science fiction in the 80's, with another fifteen published stories.

"The Lost Kafoozalum" is a great space romp in the best traditions of 50's vintage space opera, an action packed story of a young woman who as part of her final in a Cultural Engineering course finds herself part of a group of students trying to prevent a war between two factions on a primitive (relatively) planet. As can be imagined, many adventures and calamities ensue. It is just the kind of story that made the science fiction of the period fun and exciting to read.

Pauline Ashwell was the pen name of Pauline Whitby who also wrote under the name Paul Ash. She was born in 1928. She wrote a handful of stories in the late 50's and early 60's and then resumed writing science fiction in the 80's. She also wrote the novel *Project FarCry*. She has won two Hugo awards, one for best new author for her 1958 story "Unwilling to School," and one for best short story for "The Lost Kafoozalum" in 1960.

THE LOST KAFOOZALUM

One of the beautiful things about a delusion is that no matter how mad someone gets at it ... he can't do it any harm. Therefore a delusion can be a fine thing for prodding angry belligerents....

*   *   *   *   *

I remember some bad times, most of them back home on Excenus 23; the worst was when Dad fell under the reaping machine but there was also the one when I got lost twenty miles from home with a dud radio, at the age of twelve; and the one when Uncle Charlie caught me practicing emergency turns in a helicar round the main weather-maker; and the one on Figuerra being chased by a cyber-crane; and the time when Dad decided to send me to Earth to do my Education.

This time is bad in a different way, with no sharp edges but a kind of a desolation.

Most people I know are feeling bad just now, because at Russett College we finished our Final Examination five days ago and Results are not due for a two weeks.

My friend B Laydon says this is yet another Test anyone still sane at the end being proved tough enough to break a molar on; she says also The worst part is in bed remembering all the things she could have written and did not; The second worst is also in bed picturing how to explain to her parents when they get back to Earth that *someone* has to come bottom and in a group as brilliant as Russett College Cultural Engineering Class this is really no disgrace.

I am not worried that way so much, I cannot remember what I wrote anyway and I can think of one or two people I am pretty sure will come bottomer than me--or B either.

I would prefer to think it is just Finals cause me to feel miserable but it is not.

In Psychology they taught us The mind has the faculty of concealing any motive it is ashamed of, especially from itself; seems unfortunately mine does not have this gadget supplied.

I never wanted to come to Earth. I was sent to Russett against my will and counting the days till I could get back to Home, Father and Excensus 23, but the sad truth is that now the longed-for moment is nearly on top of me I do not want to go.

Dad's farm was a fine place to grow up, but now I had four years on Earth the thought of going back there makes me feel like a three-weeks' chicken got to get back in its shell.

B and I are on an island in the Pacific. Her parents are on Caratacus researching on local art forms, so she and I came here to be miserable in company and away from the rest.

It took me years on Earth to get used to all this water around, it seemed unnatural and dangerous to have it all lying loose that way, but now I shall miss even the Sea.

The reason we have this long suspense over Finals is that they will not use Reading Machines to mark the papers for fear of cutting down critical judgement; so each paper has to be read word by word by three Examiners and there are forty-three of us and we wrote six papers each.

What I think is I am sorry for the Examiners, but B says they were the ones who set the papers and it serves them perfectly right.

I express surprise because D. J. M'Clare our Professor is one of them, but B says He is one of the greatest men in the galaxy, of course, but she gave up thinking him perfect *years* ago.

One of the main attractions on this Island is swimming under water, especially by moonlight. Dad sent me a fish-boat as a birthday present two years back, but I never used it yet on account of my above-mentioned attitude to water. Now I got this feeling of Carpe Diem, make the most of Earth while I am on it because probably I shall not pass this way again.

The fourth day on the Island it is full moon at ten o'clock, so I pluck up courage to wriggle into the boat and go out under the Sea. B says Fish parading in and out of reefs just remind her of Cultural Engineering--crowd behavior--so she prefers to turn in early and find out what nightmares her subconscious will throw up *this* time.

The reefs by moonlight are everything they are supposed to be, why did I not do this often when I had the chance? I stay till my oxygen is nearly gone, then come out and sadly press the button that collapses the boat into a thirty-pound package of plastic hoops and oxygen cans. I sling it on my back and head for the chalet B and I hired among the coconut trees.

*   *   *   *   *

I am crossing an open space maybe fifty yards from it when a Thing drops on me out of the air.

I do not see the Thing because part of it covers my face, and the rest is grabbed round my arms and my waist and my hips and whatever, I cannot see and I cannot scream and I cannot find anything to kick. The Thing is strong and rubbery and many-armed and warmish, and less than a second after I first feel it I am being hauled up into the air.

I do not care for this at all.

I am at least fifty feet up before it occurs to me to bite the hand that gags me and then I discover it is plastic, not alive at all. Then I feel self and encumberance scraping through some kind of aperture; there is a sharp click as of a door closing and the Thing goes limp all round me.

I spit out the bit I am biting and it drops away so that I can see.

Well!

I am in a kind of a cup-shaped space maybe ten feet across but not higher than I am; there is a trap door in the ceiling; the Thing is lying all around me in a mess of plastic arms, with an extensible stalk connecting it to the wall. I kick free and it turns over exposing the label FRAGILE CARGO right across the back.

The next thing I notice is two holdalls, B's and mine, clamped against the wall, and the next after that is the opening of a trap door in the ceiling and B's head silhouetted in it remarking Oh there you are Liz.

I confirm this statement and ask for explanations.

B says She doesn't understand all of it but it is all right.

It is not all right I reply, if she has joined some Society such as for the Realization of Fictitious Improbabilities that is her privilege but no reason to involve me.

B says Why do I not stop talking and come up and see for myself?

There is a slight hitch when I jam in the trap door, then B helps me get the boat off my back and I drop it on the Fragile Cargo and emerge into the cabin of a Hopper, drop-shaped, cargo-carrying; I have been in its hold till now.

There are one or two peculiar points about it, or maybe one or two hundred, such as the rate at which we are ascending which seems to be bringing us right into the Stratosphere; but the main thing I notice is the pilot. He has his back to us but is recognizably Ram Gopal who graduated in Cultural Engineering last year, Rumor says next to top of his class.

I ask him what kind of a melodramatic shenanigan is this?

B says We had to leave quietly in a hurry without attracting attention so she booked us out at the Hotel *hours* ago and she and Ram have been hanging around waiting for me ever since.

I point out that the scope-trace of an Unidentified Flying Object will occasion a lot more remark than a normal departure even at midnight.

At this Ram smiles in an inscrutable Oriental manner and B gets nearly as cross as I do, seems she has mentioned this point before.

We have not gone into it properly when the cabin suddenly shifts through a right angle. B and I go sliding down the vertical floor and end sitting on a window. There is a jolt and a shudder and Ram mutters things in Hindi and then suddenly Up is nowhere at all.

B and I scramble off the window and grab fixtures so as to stay put. The stars have gone and we can see nothing except the dim glow over the instruments; then suddenly lights go on outside.

We look out into the hold of a ship.

Our ten-foot teardrop is sitting next to another one, like two eggs in a rack. On the other side is a bulkhead; behind, the curve of the hull; and directly ahead an empty space, then another bulkhead and an open door, through which after a few seconds a head pokes cautiously.

The head is then followed by a body which kicks off against the wall and sails slowly towards us. Ram presses a stud and a door slides open in the hopper; but the new arrival stops himself with a hand on either side of the frame, his legs trailing any old how behind him. It is Peter Yeng Sen who graduated the year I did my Field Work.

He says, Gopal, dear fellow, there was no need for the knocking, we heard the bell all right.

Ram grumbles something about the guide beam being miss-set, and slides out of his chair. Peter announces that we have only just made it as the deadline is in seven minutes time; he waves B and me out of the hopper, through the door and into a corridor where a certain irregular vibration is coming from the walls.

Ram asks what is that tapping? And Peter sighs and says The present generation of students has no discipline at all.

At this B brakes with one hand against the wall and cocks her head to listen; next moment she laughs and starts banging with her fist on the wall.

Peter exclaims in Mandarin and tows her away by one wrist like a reluctant kite. The rapping starts again on the far side of the wall and I suddenly recognize a primitive signaling system called Regret or something, I guess because it was used by people in situations they did not like such as Sinking ships or solitary confinement; it is done by tapping water pipes and such.

Someone found it in a book and the more childish element in College learned it up for signaling during compulsory lectures. Interest waning abruptly when the lecturers started to learn it, too.

I never paid much attention not expecting to be in Solitary confinement much; this just shows you; next moment Ram opens a door and pushes me through it, the door clicks behind me and Solitary confinement is what I am in.

I remember this code is really called Remorse which is what I feel for not learning when I had the chance.

However I do not have long for it, a speaker in the wall requests everyone to lie down as acceleration is about to begin. I strap down on the couch which fills half the compartment, countdown begins and at zero the floor is suddenly *down* once more.

I wait till my stomach settles, then rise to explore.

*   *   *   *   *

I am in an oblong room about eight by twelve, it looks as though it had been hastily partitioned off from a larger space. The walls are prefab plastic sheet, the rest is standard fittings slung in and bolted down with the fastenings showing.

How many of my classmates are on this ship? *Remorse* again as tapping starts on either side of me.

Discarding such Hypotheses as that Ram and Peter are going to hold us to ransom--which might work for me, since my Dad somehow got to be a millionaire, but not for B because her parents think money is vulgar--or that we are being carried off to found an ideal Colony somewhere--any first-year student can tell you why that won't work--only one idea seems plausible.

This is that Finals were not final and we are in for a Test of some sort.

After ten minutes I get some evidence; a Reading Machine is trundled in, the door immediately slamming shut so I do not see who trundles it.

I prowl round it looking for tricks but it seems standard; I take a seat in it, put on the headset and turn the switch.

Hypothesis confirmed, I suppose.

There is a reel in place and it contains background information on a problem in Cultural Engineering all set out the way we are taught to do it in Class. The Problem concerns developments on a planet got settled by two groups during the Exodus and been isolated ever since.

Well while a Reading Machine is running there is no time to think, it crams in data at full speed and evaluation has to wait. However my subconscious goes into action and when the reel stops it produces a Suspicion full grown.

The thing is too tidy.

When we were First Year we dreamed up situations like this and argued like mad over them, but they were a lot too neat for real life and too dramatic as well.

However one thing M'Clare said to us, and every other lecturer too, just before the Finals, was Do not spend time trying to figure what the examiner was after but answer the question as set; I am more than halfway decided this is some mysterious Oriental idea of a joke but I get busy thinking in case it is not.

*   *   *   *   *

The Problem goes like this:

The planet is called Incognita in the reel and it is right on the edge of the known volume of space, it got settled by two groups somewhere between three and three and a half centuries ago. The rest of the human race never heard of it till maybe three years back.

(Well it happens that way, inhabited planets are still turning up eight or ten a century, on account of during the Exodus some folk were willing to travel a year or more so as to get away from the rest).

The ship that spotted the planet as inhabited did not land, but reported to Central Government, Earth, who shipped observers out to take a look.

(There was a rumor circulating at Russett that the Terry Government might employ some of us on that kind of job, but it never got official. I do not know whether to believe this bit or not.)

It is stated the observers landed secretly and mingled with the natives unobserved.

(This is not physically impossible but sounds too like a Field Trip to be true.)

The observers are not named but stated to be graduates of the Cultural Engineering Class.

They put in a few months' work and sent home unanimous Crash Priority reports the situation is *bad*, getting worse and the prognosis is War.

Brother.

I know people had wars, I know one reason we do not have them now is just that with so many planets and cheap transportation, pressure has other outlets; these people scrapped their ships for factories and never built more.

But.

There are only about ten million of them and surely to goodness a whole planet gives room enough to keep out of each other's hair?

Well this is not Reasoning but a Reaction, I go back to the data for another look.

The root trouble is stated to be that two groups landed on the planet without knowing the others were there, when they met thirty years later they got a disagreeable shock.

I cannot see there was any basic difference between them, they were very similar, especially in that neither lot wanted anything to do with people they had not picked themselves.

So they divided the planet along a Great Circle which left two of the main land-masses in one hemisphere and two in another.

They agree each to keep to its own section and leave the other alone.

Twenty years later, trading like mad; each has certain minerals the other lacks; each has certain agricultural products the other finds it difficult to grow.

You think this leads to Co-operation Friendship and ultimate Federation?

I will not go into the incidents that make each side feel it is being gypped, it is enough that from time to time each has a scarcity or hold-up on deliveries that upsets the other's economy; and they start experimenting to become self-sufficient: and the exporter's economy is upset in turn. And each thinks the other did it on purpose.

This sort of situation reacts internally leading to Politics.

There are troubles about a medium-sized island on the dividing line, and the profits from interhemispherical transport, and the laws of interhemispherical trade.

It takes maybe two hundred years, but finally each has expanded the Police into an army with a whole spectrum of weapons not to be used on any account except for Defense.

This situation lasts seventy years getting worse all the time, now Rumors have started on each side that the other is developing an Ultimate Weapon, and the political parties not in power are agitating to move first before the thing is complete.

The observers report War not maybe this year or the next but within ten, and if neither side was looking for an Ultimate Weapon to begin with they certainly are now.

Taking all this at face value there seems an obvious solution.

I am thinking this over in an academic sort of way when an itchy trickle of sweat starts down my vertebrae.

Who is going to apply this solution? Because if this is anything but another Test, or the output of a diseased sense of humor, I would be sorry for somebody.

I dial black coffee on the wall servitor and wish B were here so we could prove to each other the thing is just an exercise; I do not do so well at spotting proofs on my own.

Most of our class exercises have concerned something that happened, once.

* * * * *

After about ninety minutes the speaker requests me to write not more than one thousand words on any scheme to improve the situation and the equipment required for it.

I spent ten minutes verbalizing the basic idea and an hour or so on "equipment"; the longer I go on the more unlikely it all seems. In the end I have maybe two hundred words which acting on instructions I post through a slit in the door.

Five minutes later I realize I have forgotten the Time Factor.

If the original ship took a year to reach Incognita, it will take at least four months now; therefore it is more than four months since that report was written and will be more than a year before anyone arrives and War may have started already.

I sit back and by transition of ideas start to wonder where this ship is heading? We are still at one gee and even on Mass-Time you cannot juggle apparent acceleration and spatial transition outside certain limits; we are not just orbiting but must be well outside the Solar System by now.

The speaker announces Everyone will now get some rest; I smell sleep-gas for one moment and have just time to lie down.

I guess I was tired, at that.

When I wake I feel more cheerful than I have for weeks; analysis indicates I am glad something is *happening* even if it is another Exam.

I dial breakfast but am too restless to eat; I wonder how long this goes on or whether I am supposed to show Initiative and break out; I am examining things with this in mind when the speaker comes to life again.

It says, "Ladies and gentlemen. You have not been told whether the problem that you studied yesterday concerned a real situation or an imaginary one. You have all outlined measures which you think would improve the situation described. Please consider, seriously, whether you would be prepared to take part yourself in the application of your plan."

Brother.

There is no way to tell whether those who say No will be counted cowardly or those who say Yes rash idiots or what, the owner of that voice has his inflections too well trained to give anything away except intentionally.

D. J. M'Clare.

Not in person but a recording, anyway M'Clare is on Earth surrounded by exam papers.

I sit back and try to think, honestly, if that crack-brained notion I wrote out last night were going to be tried in dead earnest, would I take a hand in it?

The trouble is, hearing M'Clare's voice has convinced me it is a Test, I don't know whether it is testing my courage or my prudence in fact I might as well toss for it.

Heads I am crazy, Tails a defaulter; Tails is what it is.

I seize my styler and write the decision down.

There is the slit in the door.

I twiddle the note and think Well nobody asked for it yet.

Suppose it is real, after all?

I remember the itchy, sweaty feeling I got yesterday and try to picture really embarking on a thing like this, but I cannot work up any lather today.

I begin to picture M'Clare reading my decision not to back up my own idea.

I pick up the coin and juggle it around.

The speaker remarks When I am quite ready will I please make a note of my decision and post it through the door.

I go on flipping the coin up and presently it drops on the floor, it is Heads this time.

Tossing coins is a pretty feeble way to decide.

I drop the note on the floor and take another sheet and write "YES. Lysistrata Lee."

Using that name seems to make it more legal.

I slip the paper in the slit and poke till it falls through on the other side of the door.

I am suddenly immensely hungry and dial breakfast all over again.

*   *   *   *   *

Just as I finish M'Clare's voice starts once more.

"It's always the minor matters that cause the most difficulty. The timing of this announcement has cost me as much thought as any aspect of the arrangements. The trouble is that however honest you are--and your honesty has been tested repeatedly-- and however strong your imagination--about half of your training has been devoted to developing it--you can't possibly be sure, answering a hypothetical question, that you are giving the answer you would choose if you knew it was asked in dead earnest.

"Those of you who answered the question in the negative are out of this. They have been told that it was a test, of an experimental nature, and have been asked to keep the whole thing a secret. They will be returning to Earth in a few hours' time. I ask the rest of you to think it over once again. Your decision is still private. Only the two people who gathered you together know which members of the class are in this ship. The list of possible helpers was compiled by a computer. I haven't seen it myself.

"You have a further half hour in which to make up your minds finally. Please remember that if you have any private reservations on the matter, or if you are secretly afraid, you may endanger us all. You all know enough psychology to realize this.

"If you still decide in favor of the project, write your name on a slip of paper and post it as before. If you are not absolutely certain about it, do nothing. Please think it over for half an hour."

Me, I had enough thinking. I write my name--just L. Lee--and post it straight away.

However I cannot stop thinking altogether. I guess I think very hard, in fact. My Subconscious insists afterwards that it did register the plop as something came through the slit, but my Conscious failed to notice it at all.

Hours later--my watch says twenty-five minutes but I guess the Mass-Time has affected it--anyway I had three times too much solitary confinement--when will they let me out of here?--there is a knock at the door and a second later it slides apart.

I am expecting Ram or Peter so it takes me an appreciable fraction of a moment to realize I am seeing D. J. M'Clare.

Then I remember he is back on Earth buried in Exam papers and conclude I am having a hallucination.

This figment of my imagination says politely, "Do you mind if I sit down?"

He collapses on the couch as though thoroughly glad of it.

It is a strange thing, every time I see M'Clare I am startled all over again at how good-looking he is; seems I forget it between times which is maybe why I never fell for him as most female students do.

However what strikes me this time is that he looks tired, three-days-sleepless tired with worries on top.

I guess he is real, at that.

He says, "Don't look so accusing, Lizzie, I only just got on this ship myself."

This does not make sense; you cannot just arrive on a ship twenty-four hours after it goes on Mass-Time; or can you?

M'Clare leans back and closes his eyes and inquires whether I am one of the Morse enthusiasts?

So that is the name; I say when we get back I will learn it first thing.

"Well," says he, "I did my best to arrange privacy for all of you; with so many ingenious idiots on board I'm not really surprised that they managed to circumvent me. I had to cheat and check that you really were on the list; and I knew that whoever backed out you'd still be on board."

So I should hope he might: Horrors there is my first answer screwed up on the floor and Writing side top-most.

However he has not noticed it, he goes on "Anyway you of all people won't be thought to have dropped out because you were afraid."

I have just managed to hook my heel over the note and get it out of sight, M'Clare has paused for an answer and I have to dredge my Sub-threshold memories for--

WHAT?

*   *   *   *   *

M'Clare opens his eyes and says like I am enacting Last Straw, "Have some sense, Lizzie." Then in a different tone, "Ram says he gave you the letter half an hour ago."

What letter?

My brain suddenly registers a small pale patch been occupying a corner of my retina for the last half hour; it turns out to be a letter postmarked Excenus 23.

I disembowel it with one jerk. It is from my Dad and runs like this:

My dear Liz,

Thank you for your last letter, glad you are keeping fit and so am I.

I just got a letter from your College saying you will get a degree conferred on you on September 12th and parents if on Earth will be welcome.

Well Liz this I got to see and Charlie says the same, but the letter says too Terran Authority will not give a permit to visit Earth just for this, so I wangled on to a Delegation which is coming to discuss trade with the Department of Commerce. Charlie and I will be arriving on Earth on August 24th.

Liz it is good to think I shall be seeing you again after four years. There are some things about your future I meant to write to Professor M'Clare about, but now I shall be able to talk it over direct. Please give him my regards.

Be seeing you Lizzie girl, your affectionate Dad

J. X. Lee.

Dear old Dad, after all these years farming with a weather-maker on a drydust planet I want to see his face the first time he sees real rain.

Hell's fires and shades of darkness, I shan't be there!

M'Clare says, "Your father wrote to me saying that he will be arriving on Earth on 24th August. I take it your letter says the same. I came on a dispatch boat; you can go back on it."

Now what is he talking about? Then I get the drift.

I say, "Look. So Dad will be on Earth before we get back. What difference does that make?"

"You can't let him arrive and find you missing."

Well I admit to a qualm at the thought of Dad let loose on Earth without me, but after all Uncle Charlie is a born Terrie and can keep him in line; Hell he is old enough to look after himself anyway.

"You met my Dad," I point out. "You think J. X. Lee would want any daughter of his backing out on a job so as to hold his hand? I can send him a letter saying I am off on a job or a Test or whatever I please and hold everything till I get back; what are you doing about people's families on Earth already?"

M'Clare says we were all selected as having families not on Earth at present, and I must go back.

I say like Hell I will.

He says he is my official guardian and responsible for me.

I say he is just as responsible for everyone else on this ship.

I spent years and years trying to think up a remark would really get home to M'Clare; well I have done it now.

I say, "Look. You are tired and worried and maybe not thinking so well just now.

"I know this is a very risky job, don't think I missed that at all. I tried hard to imagine it like you said over the speaker. I cannot quite imagine dying but I know how Dad will feel if I do.

"I did my level best to scare myself sick, then I decided it is just plain worth the risk anyway.

"To work out a thing like this you have to have a kind of arithmetic, you add in everybody's feelings with the other factors, then if you get a plus answer you forget everything else and go right ahead.

"I am not going to think about it any more, because I added up the sum and got the answer and upsetting my nerves won't help. I guess you worked out the sum, too. You decided four million people were worth risking twenty, even if they do have parents. Even if they are your students. So they are, too, and you gave us all a chance to say No.

"Well nothing has altered that, only now the values look different to you because you are tired and worried and probably missed breakfast, too."

Brother some speech, I wonder what got into me? M'Clare is wondering, too, or maybe gone to sleep sitting, it is some time before he answers me.

"Miss Lee, you are deplorably right on one thing at least. I don't know whether I was fit to make such a decision when I made it, but I'm not fit now. As far as you personally are concerned...." He trails off looking tireder than ever, then picks up again suddenly. "You are again quite right, I am every bit as responsible for the other people on board as I am for you."

He climbs slowly to his feet and walks out without another word.

The door is left open and I take this as an invitation to freedom and shoot through in case it was a mistake.

No because Ram is opening doors all along the corridor and ten of Russett's brightest come pouring out like mercury finding its own level and coalesce in the middle of the floor.

The effect of release is such that after four minutes Peter Yeng Sen's head appears at the top of a stairway and he says the crew is lifting the deck plates, will we for Time's sake go along to the Conference Room which is soundproof.

*   *   *   *   *

The Conference Room is on the next deck and like our cabins shows signs of hasty construction; the soundproofing is there but the acoustics are kind of muffled and the generator is not boxed in but has cables trailing all over, and the fastenings have a strong but temporary look.

Otherwise there is a big table and a lot of chairs and a small projection box in front of each with a note-taker beside.

It is maybe this very functional setup or maybe the dead flatness of our voices in the damped room, but we do not have so much to talk about any more. We automatically take places at the table, all at one end, leaving seven vacant chairs near the door.

Looking round, I wonder what principle we were selected on.

Of my special friends Eru Te Whangoa and Kirsty Lammergaw are present but Lily Chen and Likofo Komom'baratse and Jean LeBrun are not; we have Cray Patterson who is one of my special enemies but not Blazer Weigh or the Astral Cad; the rest are P. Zapotec, Nick Howard, Aro Mestah, Dillie Dixie, Pavel Christianovitch, Lennie DiMaggio and Shootright Crow.

Eru is at the end of the table, opposite the door, and maybe feels this position puts it up to him to start the discussion; he opens by remarking "So nobody took the opportunity to withdraw."

Cray Patterson lifts his eyebrows ceilingwards and drawls out that the decision was supposed to be a private one.

B says "Maybe but it did not work out that way, everyone who learned Morse knows who was on the ship, anyway they are all still here so what does it matter? And M'Clare would not have picked people who were going to funk it, after all."

My chair gets a kick on the ankle which I suppose was meant for B; Eru is six foot five but even his legs do not quite reach; he is the only one of us facing the door.

M'Clare has somehow shed his weariness; he looks stern but fresh as a daisy. There are four with him; Ram and Peter looking serious, one stranger in Evercleans looking determined to enjoy the party and another in uniform looking as though nothing would make him.

M'Clare introduces the strangers as Colonel Delano-Smith and Mr. Yardo. They all sit down at the other end of the table; then he frowns at us and begins like this:

"Miss Laydon is mistaken. You were not selected on any such grounds as she suggests. I may say that I was astonished at the readiness with which you all engaged yourselves to take part in such a desperate gamble; and, seeing that for the last four years

I have been trying to persuade you that it is worth while, before making a decision of any importance, to spend a certain amount of thought on it, I was discouraged as well."

Oh.

"The criterion upon which you were selected was a very simple one. As I told you, you were picked not by me but by a computer; the one in the College Office which registers such information as your home addresses and present whereabouts. You are simply that section of the class which could be picked up without attracting attention, because you all happened to be on holiday by yourselves or with other members of the class; and because your nearest relatives are not on Earth at present."

Oh, well.

All of us can see M'Clare is doing a job of deflation on us for reasons of his own, but it works for all that.

He now seems to feel the job is complete and relaxes a bit.

"I was interested to see that you all, without exception, hit on variations of the same idea. It is of course the obvious way to deal with the problem." He smiles at us suddenly and I get mad at myself because I know he is following the rules for introducing a desired state of mind, but I am responding as meant. "I'll read you the most succinct expression of it; you may be able to guess the author."

Business with bits of paper.

"Here it is. I quote: 'Drag in some outsider looks like he is going for both sides; they will gang up on him.'"

Yells of laughter and shouts of "Lizzie Lee!" even the two strangers produce sympathetic grins; I do not find it so funny as all that myself.

"Ideas as to the form the 'outsider' should take were more varied. This is a matter I propose to leave you to work out together, with the assistance of Colonel Delano-Smith and Mr. Yardo. Te Whangoa, you take the chair."

Exit M'Clare.

*   *   *   *   *

This leaves the two halves of the table eying one another. Ram and Peter have been through this kind of session in their time; now they are leaning back preparing to watch us work. It is plain we are supposed to impress the abilities of Russett near-graduates on the two strangers, and for some moments we are all occupied taking them in. Colonel Delano-Smith is a small, neat guy with a face that has all the muscular machinery for producing an expression; he just doesn't care to use it. Mr. Yardo is taller than any of us except Eru and flesh is spread very thin on his bones, including his face which splits now and then in a grin like an affable skeleton. Where the colonel fits is guessable enough, Mr. Yardo is presumably Expert at something but no data on *what*.

Eru rests his hands on the table and says we had better start; will somebody kindly outline an idea for making the Incognitans "gang up"? The simpler the better and it does not matter whether it is workable or not; pulling it to pieces will give us a start.

We all wait to see who will rush in; then I catch Eru's eye and see I am elected Clown again. I say "Send them a letter postmarked Outer Space signed BEM saying we lost our own planet in a nova and will take over theirs two weeks from Tuesday."

Mr. Yardo utters a sharp "Ha! Ha!" but it is not seconded; the colonel having been expressionless all along becomes more so; Eru says, "Thank you, Lizzie." He looks across at Cray who is opposite me; Cray says there are many points on which he might comment; to take only one, two weeks from Tuesday leaves little time for 'ganging up', and what happens when the BEMs fail to come?

We are suddenly back in the atmosphere of a seminar; Eru's glance moves to P. Zapotec sitting next to Cray, and he says, "These BEMs who lost their home planet in a nova, how many ships have they? Without a base they cannot be very dangerous unless their fleet is very large."

It goes round the table.

Pavel: "How would BEMs learn to write?"

Nick: "How are they supposed to know that Incognita is inhabited? How do they address the letter?"

The Crow: "Huh. Why write letters? Invaders just invade."

Kirsty: "We don't want to inflame these people against alien races. We might find one some day. It seems to me this idea might have all sorts of undesirable by-products. Suppose each side regards it as a ruse on the part of the other. We might touch off a war instead of preventing it. Suppose they turn over to preparations for repelling the invaders, to an extent that cripples their economy? Suppose a panic starts?"

Dilly: "Say, Mr. Chairman, is there any of this idea left at all? How about an interim summary?"

Eru coughs to get a moment for thought, then says:

"In brief, the problem is to provide a menace against which the two groups will be forced to unite. It must have certain characteristics.

"It must be sufficiently far off in time for the threat to last several years, long enough to force them into a real combination.

"It must obviously be a plausible danger and they must get to know of it in a plausible manner. Invasion from outside is the only threat so far suggested.

"It must be a limited threat. That is, it must appear to come from one well-defined group. The rest of the Universe should appear benevolent or neutral."

He just stops, rather as though there is something else to come; while the rest of us are waiting B sticks her oar in to the following effect.

"Yes, but look, suppose this goes wrong; it's all very well to make plans but suppose we get some of Kirsty's side-effects just the same, well what I mean is suppose it makes the mess worse instead of better we want some way we can sort of switch it off again.

"Look this is just an illustration, but suppose the Menace was pirates, if it went wrong we could have an Earth ship make official contact and they could just happen to say By the way have you seen anything of some pirates, Earth fleet wiped them up in this sector about six months ago.

"That would mean the whole crew conniving, so it won't do, but you see what I mean."

There is a bit of silence, then Aro says, "I think we should start fresh. We have had criticisms of Lizzie's suggestion, which was not perhaps wholly serious, and as Dilly says there is little of it left, except the idea of a threat of invasion. The idea of an alien intelligent race has objections and would be very difficult to fake. The invaders must be men from another planet. Another unknown one. But how do the people of Incognita come to know that they exist?"

More silence, then I hear my own voice speaking although it was my intention to keep quiet for once: it sounds kind of creaky and it says: "A ship. A crashed ship from Outside."

Whereupon another voice says, "Really! Am I expected to swallow this?"

*   *   *   *   *

We had just about forgotten the colonel, not to mention Mr. Yardo who contributes another "Ha! Ha!" so this reminder comes as a slight shock, nor do we see what he is talking about but this he proceeds to explain.

"I don't know why M'Clare thought it necessary to stage this discussion. I am already acquainted with his plan and have had orders to co-operate. I have expressed my opinion on using undergraduates in a job like this and have been overruled. If he, or you, imagine that priming you to bring out his ideas like this is going to reconcile me to the whole business you are mistaken. He might have chosen a more suitable mouthpiece than that child with the curly hair--"

Here everybody wishes to reply at once; the resulting jam produces a moment of silence and I get in first.

"As for curly hair I am rising twenty-four and I was only saying what we all thought, if we have the same ideas as M'Clare that is because he taught us for four years. How else would you set about it anyway?"

My fellow students pick up their stylers and tap solemnly three times on the table; this is the Russett equivalent of "Hear! Hear!" and the colonel is surprised.

Eru says coldly, "This discussion has not been rehearsed. As Lizzie ... as Miss Lee says, we have been working and thinking together for four years and have been taught by the same people."

"Very well," says Delano-Smith testily. "Tell me this, please: Do you regard this idea as practicable?"

Cray tilts his chair back and remarks to the ceiling, "This is rather a farce. I suppose we had to go through our paces for the colonel's benefit--and Mr. Yardo's of course--but can't we be briefed properly now?"

"What do you mean by that?" snaps the colonel.

"It's been obvious right along," says Cray, balancing his styler on one forefinger, "so obvious none of us has bothered to mention it, that accepting the normal limitations of Mass-Time, the idea of interfering in Incognita was doomed before it began. No conventional ship would have much hope of arriving before war broke out; and if it did arrive it couldn't do anything effective. Therefore I assume that this is not a conventional ship. I might accept that the Government has sent us out in a futile attempt to do the impossible, but I wouldn't believe that of M'Clare."

Cray is the only Terry I know acts like an Outsider's idea of one; many find this difficult to take and the colonel is plainly one of them. Eru intervenes quickly.

"I imagine we all realized that. Anyway this ship is obviously not a conventional model. If you accept the usual Mass-Time relationship between the rate of transition and the fifth power of the apparent acceleration, we must have reached about four times the maximum already."

"Ram!" says B suddenly, "What did you do to stop the Hotel scope registering the little ship you picked up me and Lizzie in?"

Everybody cuts in with something they have noticed about the capabilities of this ship or the hoppers, and Lenny starts hammering on the table and chanting! "Brief! Brief! Brief!" and others are just starting to join in when Eru bangs on the table and glares us all down.

Having got silence, he says very quietly, "Colonel Delano-Smith, I doubt whether this discussion can usefully proceed without a good deal more information; will you take over?"

The colonel looks round at all the eager earnest interested maps hastily put on for his benefit and decides to take the plunge.

"Very well. I suppose it is ... very well. The decision to use students from Russett was made at a very high level, and I suppose--" Instead of saying "Very well" again he shrugs his shoulders and gets down to it.

"The report from the planet we decided to call 'Incognita' was received thirty-one days ago. The Department of Spatial Affairs has certain resources which are not generally known. This ship is one of them. She works on a modified version of Mass-Time which enables her to use about a thousand channels instead of the normal limit of two hundred; for good and sufficient reasons this has not been generally released."

Pause while we are silently dared to doubt the Virtue and sufficiency of these reasons which personally I do not.

"To travel to Incognita direct would take about fifteen days by the shortest route. We shall take eighteen days as we shall have to make a detour."

But presumably we shall take only fifteen days back. Hurrah we can spend a week round the planet and still be back in time for Commemoration. We shall skip maybe a million awkward questions and I shall not disappoint Dad.

It is plain the colonel is not filled with joy; far from it, he did not enjoy revealing a Departmental secret however obvious, but he likes the next item even less.

"We shall detour to an uninhabited system twelve days' transit time from here and make contact with another ship, the *Gilgamesh*."

$$*\quad*\quad*\quad*\quad*$$

At which Lennie DiMaggio who has been silent till now brings his fist down on the table and exclaims, "You *can't*!"

Lennie is much upset for some reason; Delano-Smith gives him a peculiar look and says what does he know about it? and Lennie starts to stutter.

Cray remarks that Lennie's childhood hobby appears to have been spaceships and he suffers from arrested development.

B says it is well known Lennie is mad about the Space Force and why not? It seems to have uses Go on and tell us Lennie.

Lennie says "*G-Gilgamesh* was lost three hundred years ago!"

"The flaw in that statement," says Cray after a pause, "is that this may be another ship of the same name."

"No," says the colonel. "Explorer Class cruiser. They went out of service two hundred eighty years back."

The Space Force, I remember, does not re-use names of lost ships: some says Very Proper Feeling some say Superstitious Rot.

B says, "When was she found again?"

Lennie says it was j-just thirty-seven revolutions of his native planet which means f-f-fifty-three Terrestrial years ago, she was found by an Interplanetary scout called *Crusoe.*

Judging by the colonel's expression this data is Classified; he does not know that Lennie's family come from one of the oldest settled planets and are space-goers to a man, woman, and juvenile; they pick up ship gossip the way others hear about the relations of people next door.

Lennie goes on to say that the Explorer Class were the first official exploration ships sent out from Earth when the Terries decided to find out what happened to the colonies formed during the Exodus. *Gilgamesh* was the first to re-make contact with Garuda, Legba, Lister, Cor-bis and Antelope; she vanished on her third voyage.

"Where was she found?" asks Eru.

"Near the p-p-pole of an uninhabited planet--maybe I shouldn't say where because that may be secret, but the rest's History if you know where to look."

*   *   *   *   *

Maybe the colonel approves this discretion; anyway his face thaws very slightly unless I am Imagining it.

"*Gilgamesh* crashed," he says. "Near as we can make out from the log, she visited Seleucis system. That's a swarmer sun. Fifty-seven planets, three settled; and any number of fragments.

The navigator calculated that after a few more revolutions one of the fragments was going to crash on an inhabited planet. Might have done a lot of damage. They decided to tow it out of the way.

"Grappling-beams hadn't been invented. They thought they could use Mass-Time on it a kind of reverse thrust--throw it off course.

"Mass-Time wasn't so well understood then. Bit off more than they could chew. Set up a topological relation that drained all the free energy out of the system. Drive, heating system--everything.

"She had emergency circuits. When the engines came on again they took over--landed the ship, more or less, on the nearest planet. Too late, of course. Heating system never came on--there was a safety switch that had to be thrown by hand. She was embedded in ice when she was found. Hull breached at one point--no other serious damage."

"And the ... the crew?"

Dillie ought to know better than that.

"Lost with all hands," says the colonel.

"How about weapons?"

We are all startled. Cray is looking whitish like the rest of us but maintains his normal manner, i.e. offensive affection while pointing out that *Gilgamesh* can hardly be taken for a Menace unless she has some means of aggression about her.

Lennie says The Explorer Class were all armed--

Fine, says Cray, presumably the weapons will be thoroughly obsolete and recognizable only to a Historian--

Lennie says the construction of no weapon developed by the Space Department has ever been released; making it plain that anyone but a Nitwit knows that already.

Eru and Kirsty have been busy for some time writing notes to each other and she now gives a small sharp cough and having collected our attention utters the following Address.

"There is a point we seem to have missed. If I may recapitulate, the idea is to take this ship *Gilgamesh* to Incognita and make it appear as though she had crashed there while attempting to land. I understand that the ship has been buried in the polar cap; though she must have been melted out if the people on *Crusoe* examined the engines. Of course the cold--All the same there may have been ... well ... changes. Or when ... when we thaw the ship out again--"

I find I am swallowing good and hard, and several of the others look sick, especially Lennie. Lennie has his eyes fixed on the colonel; it is not prescience, but a slight sideways movement of the colonel's eye causes him to blurt out, "What is *he* doing here?"

Meaning Mr. Yardo who seems to have been asleep for some time, with his eyes open and grinning like the spikes on a dog collar. The colonel gives him another sideways look and says, "Mr. Yardo is an expert on the rehabilitation of space-packed materials."

This is stuff transported in un-powered hulls towed by grappling-beams; the hulls are open to space hence no need for refrigeration, and the contents are transferred to specially equipped orbital stations before being taken down to the planet. But--

Mr. Yardo comes to life at the sound of his name and his grin widens alarmingly.

"Especially meat," he says.

*   *   *   *   *

It is maybe two hours afterwards, Eru having adjourned the meeting abruptly so that we can ... er ... take in the implications of the new data. Lennie has gone off somewhere by himself; Kirsty has gone after him with a view to Mothering him; Eru, I suspect, is looking for Kirsty; Pavel and Aro and Dillie and the Crow are in a cabin arguing in whispers; Nick and P. Zapotec are exploring one of the Hoppers, cargo-carrying, drop-shaped, and I only hope they don't hop through the hull in it.

B and I having done a tour of the ship and ascertained all this have withdrawn to the Conference Room because we are tired of our cabins and this seems to be the only other place to sit.

B breaks a long silence with the remark that However often you see it M'Clare's technique is something to watch, like choosing my statement to open with, it broke the ice beautifully.

I say, "Shall I tell you something?"

B says Yes if it's interesting.

"My statement," I inform her, "ran something like this: The best hope of inducing a suspension of the aggressive attitude of both parties, long enough to offer hope of ultimate reconciliation, lies in the intrusion of a new factor in the shape of an outside force seen to be impartially hostile to both."

B says: "Gosh. Come to think of it Liz you have not written like that in years, you have gone all pompous like everyone else; well that makes it even *more* clever of M'Clare."

Enter Cray Patterson and drapes himself sideways on a chair, announcing that his own thoughts begin to weary him.

I say this does not surprise me, at all.

"Lizzie my love," says he, "you are twice blessed being not only witty yourself but a cause of wit in others; was that bit of Primitive Lee with which M'Clare regaled us really not from the hand of the mistress, or was it a mere pastiche?"

I say Whoever wrote that it was not me anyway.

"It seemed to me pale and luke-warm compared with the real thing," says Cray languidly, "which brings me to a point that, to quote dear Kirsty, seems to have been missed."

I say, "Yep. Like what language it was that these people wrote their log in that we can be *certain* the Incognitans won't know."

"More than that," says B, "we didn't decide who they are or where they were coming from or how they came to crash or anything."

"Come to think of it, though," I point out, "the language and a good many other things must have been decided already because of getting the right hypnotapes and translators on board."

B suddenly lights up.

"Yes, but look, I bet that's what we're here for, I mean that's why they picked us instead of Space Department people--the ship's got to have a past history, it has to come from a planet somewhere only no one must ever find out *where* it's supposed to be. Someone will have to fake a log, only I don't see how--"

"The first reel with data showing the planet of origin got damaged during the crash," says Cray impatiently.

"Yes, of course--but we have to find a reason why they were in that part of Space and it has to be a *nice* one, I mean so that the Incognitans when they finally read the log won't hate them any more--"

"Maybe they were bravely defending their own planet by hunting down an interplanetary raider," I suggest.

Cray says it will take only the briefest contact with other planets to convince the Incognitans that interplanetary raiders can't and don't exist, modern planetary alarm and defense systems put them out of the question.

"That's all he knows," says B, "some interplanetary pirates raided Lizzie's father's farm once. Didn't they, Liz?"

"Yes in a manner of speaking, but they were bums who pinched a spaceship from a planet not many parsecs away, a sparsely inhabited mining world like my own which had no real call for an alarm system, so that hardly alters the argument."

"Well," says B, "the alarm system on Incognita can't be so hot or the observation ships could not have got in, or out, for that matter, unless of course they have some other gadget we don't know about."

"On the other hand," she considers, "to mention Interplanetary raiders raises the idea of Menace in an Unfriendly Universe again, and this is what we want to cancel out.

"These people," she says at last with a visionary look in her eye, "come from a planet which went isolationist and abandoned space travel; now they have built up their civilization to a point where they can build ships of their own again, and the ones on Gilgamesh have cut loose from the ideas of their ancestors that led to their going so far afield--"

"How far afield?" says Cray.

"No one will ever know," I point out to him. "Don't interrupt."

"Anyway," says B, "they set out to rejoin the rest of the Human Race just like the people on *Gilgamesh really* did, in fact, a lot of this is the truth only kind of backwards--they were looking for the Cradle of the Race, that's what. Then there was some sort of disaster that threw them off course to land on an uninhabited section of a planet that couldn't understand their signals. And when Incognita finally does take to space flight again I bet the first thing the people do is to try and follow back to where *Gilgamesh* came from and make contact with them. It'll become a legend on Incognita--the Lost People ... the Lost ... Lost--"

"The Lost Kafoozalum," says Cray. "In other words we switch these people off a war only to send them on a wild goose chase."

At which a strange voice chimes in, "No, no, no, son, you've got it all *wrong*."

*   *   *   *   *

Mr. Yardo is with us like a well-meaning skeleton.

During the next twenty-five minutes we learn a lot about Mr. Yardo including material for a good guess at how he came to be picked for this expedition; doubtless there are many experts on Reversal Of Vacuum-Induced Changes in Organic Tissues but maybe only one of them a Romantic at heart.

Mr. Yardo thinks chasing the Wild Goose will do the Incognitans all the good in the galaxy, it will take their minds off controversies over interhemispherical trade and put them on to the quest of the Unobtainable; they will get to know something of the Universe outside their own little speck. Mr. Yardo has seen a good deal of the Universe in the course of advising on how to recondition space-packed meat and he found it an Uplifting Experience.

We gather he finds this desperate bit of damfoolery we are on now pretty Uplifting altogether.

Cray keeps surprisingly quiet but it is as well that the rest of the party start to trickle in about twenty minutes later the first arrivals remarking Oh *that's* where you've got to!

Presently we are all congregated at one end of the table as before, except that Mr. Yardo is now sitting between B and me; when M'Clare and the colonel come in he firmly stays where he is evidently considering himself One of Us now.

"The proposition," says M'Clare, "is that we intend to take *Gilgamesh* to Incognita and land her there in such a way as to suggest that she crashed. In the absence of evidence to the contrary the Incognitans are bound to assume that that was her intended destination, and the presence of weapons, even disarmed, will suggest that her mission was aggressive. Firstly, can anyone suggest a better course of action? or does anyone object to this one?"

We all look at Lennie who sticks his hands in his pockets and mutters "No."

Kirsty gives her little cough and says there is a point which has not been mentioned.

If a heavily-armed ship crashes on Incognita, will not the government of the hemisphere in which it crashes be presented with new ideas for offensive weapons? And won't this make it *more* likely that they will start aggression? And won't the fear of this make the other hemisphere even more likely to try and get in first before the new weapons are complete?

Hell, I ought to have thought of that.

From the glance of unwilling respect which the colonel bestows on M'Clare it is plain these points have been dealt with.

"The weapons on Gilgamesh were disarmed when she was rediscovered," he says. "Essential sections were removed. The Incognitans won't be able to reconstruct how they worked."

Another fact for which we shall have to provide an explanation. Well how about this: The early explorers sent out by these people--the people in Gilgamesh ... oh, use Cray's word and call them Lost Kafoozalum anyway their ships were armed, but they never found any enemies and the Idealists of B's story refused even to carry arms any more.

(Which is just about what happened when the Terries set out to rediscover the colonies, after all.)

So the Lost Kafoozalum could not get rid of their weapons completely because it would have meant rebuilding the ship; so they just partially dismantled them.

Mr. Yardo suddenly chips in, "About that other point, girlie, surely there must be some neutral ground left on a half-occupied planet like that?" He beams round, pleased at being able to contribute.

B says, "The thing is," and stops.

We wait.

We have about given up hope when she resumes, "The thing is, it will have to be neutral ground of course, only that might easily become a thingummy ... I mean a, a *casus belli* in itself. So the *other* thing is it ought to be a place which is very hard to get at, so difficult that neither side can really get to it first, they'll have to reach an agreement and co-operate."

"Yeah," says Dillie "that sounds fine, but what sort of place is that?"

I am sorting out in my head the relative merits of mountains, deserts, gorges, et cetera, when I an seized with inspiration at the same time as half the group; we say the same thing in different words and for a time there is Babel, then the idea emerges:

"Drop her into the sea!"

The colonel nods resignedly.

"Yes," he says, "that's what we're going to do."

He presses a button and our projection-screens light up, first with a map of one pole of Incognita, expanding in scale till finally we are looking down on one little bit of coast on one of the polar islands. A glacier descends on to it from mountains inland and there is a bay between cliffs. Then we get a stereo scene of approximately the least hospitable of scenery I ever did see-- except maybe when Parvati Lal Dutt's brother made me climb up what he swore was the smallest peak in the Himalayas.

It is a small bay backed by tumbled cliffs. A shelving beach can be deduced from contour and occasional boulders big enough to stick through the snow that smothers it all. A sort of mess of rocks and mud at the back may be glacial moraine. Over the sea the ice is split in all directions by jagged rifts and channels; the whole thing is a bit like Antarctica but nothing is high enough or white enough to uplift the spirit, it looks not only chilly but kind of mean.

"This place," says the colonel, "is the only one, about which we have any topographical information, that seems to meet the requirements. Got to know about it through an elementary planetography. One of the observers had the sense to see we might need something of the sort. This place"--the stereo jigs as he taps his projector--"seems it's the center of a rising movement in the crust ... that's not to the point. Neither side has bothered to claim the land at the poles...."

I see their point if it's all like this--

"... And a ship trying to land on those cliffs might very well pitch over into the sea. That is, if she were trying to land on emergency rockets."

Rockets--that brings home the ancientness of this ship *Gilgamesh*--but after all the ships that settled Incognita probably carried emergency rockets, too.

This settled, the meeting turns into a briefing session and merges imperceptibly with the beginning of the job.

*   *   *   *   *

The job of course is Faking the background of the crash; working out the past history and present aims of the Lost Kafoozalum. We have to invent a planet and what's more difficult convey all the essential information about it by the sort of sideways hints you gather among peoples' personal possessions; diaries, letters et cetera; and what is even *more* difficult we have to leave out anything that could lead to definite identification of our unknown world with any known one.

We never gave that world a name; it might be dangerous. Who speaks of their world by name, except to strangers? They call it "home"--or "Earth," as often as not.

Some things have been decided for us. Language, for instance--one of two thousand or so Earth tongues that went out of use late enough to be plausible as the main language of a colonized planet. The settlers on Incognita were not of the sort to take along dictionaries of the lesser-known tongues, so the computers at Russett had a fairly wide choice.

We had to take a hypnocourse in that language. Ditto the script, one of several forgotten phonetic shorthands. (Designed to enable the tongues of Aliens to be written down; but the Aliens have never been met. It is plausible enough that some colony might have kept the script alive; after all Thasia uses something of the sort to this day.)

The final result of our work looks pretty small. Twenty-three "Personal Background Sets"--a few letters, a diary in some, an assortment of artifacts. Whoever stocked this ship we are on supplied wood, of the half-dozen kinds that have been taken wherever men have gone; stocks of a few plastics--known at the time of the Exodus, or easily developed from those known, and not associated with any particular planet. Also books on Design, a Form-writer for translating drawings into materials, and so on. Someone put in a lot of work before this voyage began.

Most of the time it is like being back on Russet doing a group Project. What we are working on has no more and no less reality than that. Our work is all read into a computer and checked against everybody else's. At first we keep clashing. Gradually a consistent picture builds up and gets translated finally into the Personal Background Kits. The Lost Kafoozalum start to exist like people in a History book.

Fifteen days hard work and we have just about finished; then we reach--call it Planet Gilgamesh.

I wake in my bunk to hear that there will be brief cessation of weight; strap down, please.

We are coming off Mass-Time to go on planetary drive.

Colonel Delano-Smith is in charge of operations on the planet, with Ram and Peter to assist. None of the rest of us see the melting out of fifty years' accumulation of ice, the pumping away of the water, the fitting and testing of the holds for the grappling-beams. We stay inside the ship, on five-eighths gee which we do not have time to get used to, and try to work, and discard the results before the computer can do so. There is hardly any work left to do, anyway.

It takes nearly twelve hours to get the ship free, and caulked, and ready to lift. (Her hull has to be patched because of Mr. Yardo's operations which make use of several sorts of vapors). Then there is a queer blind period with Up now one way, now another, and sudden jerks and tugs that upset everything not in gimbals or tied down; interspersed with periods when weightlessness supervenes with no warning at all. After an hour or two of this it would be hard to say whether Mental or physical discomfort is more acute; B consulted, however, says my autonomic system must be quite something, after five minutes *her* thoughts were with her viscera entirely.

Then, suddenly, we are back on Mass-Time again.

Two days to go.

*   *   *   *   *

At first being on Mass-Time makes everything seem normal again. By sleep time there is a strain, and next day it is everywhere. I know as well as any that on Mass-Time the greater the mass the faster the shift; all the same I cannot help feeling we are being slowed, dragged back by the dead ship coupled to our live one.

When you stand by the hull *Gilgamesh* is only ten feet away.

I should have kept something to work on like B and Kirsty who have not done their Letters for Home in Case of Accidents; mine is signed and sealed long ago. I am making a good start on a Neurosis when Delano-Smith announces a Meeting for one hour ahead.

Hurrah! now there is a time-mark fixed I think of all sorts of things I should have done before; for instance taking a look at the controls of the Hoppers.

I have been in one of them half an hour and figured out most of the dials--Up down and sideways are controlled much as in a helicar, but here a big viewscreen has been hooked in to the autopilot--when across the hold I see the air lock start to move.

Gilgamesh is on the other side.

It takes forever to open. When at last it swings wide on the dark tunnel what comes through is a storage rack, empty, floating on antigrav.

What follows is a figure in a spacesuit; modern type, but the windows of the hopper are semipolarized and I cannot make out the face inside the bubble top.

He slings the rack upon the bulkhead, takes off the helmet and hangs that up, too. Then he just stands. I am beginning to muster enough sense to wonder why when he comes slowly across the hold.

Reaching the doorway he says: "Oh it's you, Lizzie. You'll have to help me out of this. I'm stuck."

M'Clare.

The outside of the suit is still freezing cold; maybe this is what has jammed the fastening. After a few minutes tugging it suddenly gives away. M'Clare climbs out of the suit, leaving it standing, and says, "Help me count these, will you?"

These are a series of transparent containers from a pouch slung at one side of the suit. I recognize them as the envelopes in which we put what are referred to as Personal Background Sets.

I say, "There ought to be twenty-three."

"No," says M'Clare dreamily, "twenty-two, we're saving one of them."

"What on earth is the use of an extra set of faked documents and oddments--"

He seems to wake up suddenly and says: "What are you doing here, Lizzie?"

I explain and he wanders over to the hopper and starts to explain the controls.

There is something odd about all this. M'Clare is obviously dead tired, but kind of relaxed; seeing that the hour of Danger is only thirty-six hours off I don't understand it. Probably several of his students are going to have to risk their lives--

I am on the point of seeing something important when the speaker announces in the colonel's voice that Professor M'Clare and Miss Lee will report to the Conference Room at once please.

M'Clare looks at me and grins. "Come along, Lizzie. Here's where we take orders for once, you and I."

It is the colonel's Hour. I suppose that having to work with Undergraduates is something he could never quite forget, but from the way he looks at us we might almost be Space Force personnel,--low-grade of course but respectable.

Everything is at last worked out and he has it on paper in front of him; he puts the paper four square on the table, gazes into the middle distance and proceeds to recite.

"One. This ship will go off Mass-Time on 2nd August at 11.27 hours ship's time....

"Thirty-six hours from now.

"... At a point one thousand miles vertically above Co-ordinates 165OE, 7320S, on Planet Incognita, approximately one hour before midnight local time.

"Going on planetary drive as close as that will indicate that something is badly wrong to begin with.

"Two. This ship will descend, coupled to *Gilgamesh* as at present, to a point seventy miles above the planetary surface. It will then uncouple, discharge one hopper, and go back on Mass-Time. Estimated time for this stage of descent forty minutes.

"Three. The hopper will then descend on its own engines at the maximum speed allowed by the heat-disposal system; estimated at thirty-seven minutes. *Gilgamesh* will complete descent in thirty-three minutes. Engines of *Gilgamesh* will not be used except for the heat-disposal and gyro auxiliaries. The following installations have been made to allow for the control of the descent; a ring of eight rockets in peltathene mounts around the tail and, and one outsize antigrav unit inside the nose. "Sympathizer" controls hooked up with a visiscreen and a computer have also been installed in the nose.

"Four. *Gilgamesh* will carry one man only. The hopper will carry a crew of three. The pilot of *Gilgamesh* will establish the ship on the edge of the cliff, supported on antigrav a foot or so above the ground and leaning towards the sea at an angle of approximately 20° with the vertical. Except for this landing will be automatic.

"Five."

The colonel's voice has lulled us into passive acceptance; now we are jerked into sharper attention by the faintest possible check in it.

"The greatest danger attaching to the expedition is that the Incognitans may discover that the crash has been faked. This would be inevitable if they were to capture (a) the hopper; (b) any of the new installations in Gilgamesh, especially the antigrav; (c) any member of the crew.

"The function of the hopper is to pick up the pilot of *Gilgamesh* and also to check that ground appearances are consistent. If not, they will produce a landslip on the cliff edge, using power tools and explosives carried for the purpose. That is why the hopper has a crew of three, but the chance of their having to do this is slight."

So I should think; ground appearances are supposed to show that *Gilgamesh* landed using emergency rockets and then toppled over the cliff and this will be exactly what happened.

"The pilot will carry a one-frequency low-power transmitter activated by the change in magnetic field on leaving the ship. The hopper will remain at five hundred feet until this signal is received. It will then pick up the pilot, check ground appearances, and rendezvous with this ship at two hundred miles up at 18.27 hours."

The ship and the hopper both being radar-absorbent will not register on alarm systems, and by keeping to planetary nighttime they should be safe from being seen.

"Danger (b) will be dealt with as follows. The rocket-mounts being of peltathene will be destroyed by half an hour's immersion in water. The installations in the nose will be destroyed with Andite."

Andite produces complete colecular disruption in a very short range, hardly any damage outside it; the effect will be as though the nose broke off on impact; I suppose the Incognitans will waste a lot of time looking for it on the bed of the sea.

"Four ten-centimeter cartridges will be inserted within the nose installations. The fuse will have two alternative settings. The first will be timed to act at 12.50 hours, seven minutes after the estimated time of landing. It will not be possible to deactivate it before 12.45 hours. This takes care of the possibility of the pilot's becoming incapacitated during the descent.

"Having switched off the first fuse the pilot will get the ship into position and then activate a second, timed to blow in ten minutes. He will then leave the ship. When the antigrav is destroyed the ship will, of course, fall into the sea.

"Six. The pilot of *Gilgamesh* will wear a spacesuit of the pattern used by the original crew and will carry Personal Background Set number 23. Should he fail to escape from the ship the crew of the hopper will on no account attempt to rescue him."

The colonel takes up the paper, folds it in half and puts it down one inch further away.

"The hopper's crew," he says, "will give the whole game away should one of them fall into Incognitan hands, alive or dead. Therefore they don't take any risks of it."

He lifts his gaze ceilingwards. "I'm asking for three volunteers."

Silence. Manning the hopper is definitely second best. Then light suddenly bursts on me and I lift my hand and hack B on the ankle.

"I volunteer," I say.

B gives me a most dubious glance and then lifts her hand, too.

Cray on the other side of the table is slowly opening his mouth when there is an outburst of waving on the far side of B.

"Me too, colonel! I volunteer!"

Mr. Yardo proceeds to explain that his special job is over and done, he can be more easily spared than anybody, he may be too old to take charge of *Gilgamesh* but will back himself as a hopper pilot against anybody.

The colonel cuts this short by accepting all three. He then unfolds his paper again.

"Piloting *Gilgamesh*," he says. "I'm not asking for volunteers now. You'll go to your cabins in four hours' time and those who want to will volunteer, secretly. To a computer hookup, Computer will select on a random basis and notify the one chosen. Give him his final instructions, too. No one need know who it was till it's all over. He can tell anyone he likes, of course."

A very slight note of triumph creeps into the next remark. "One point. Only men need volunteer."

Instant outcry from Kirsty and Dilly: B turns to me with a look of awe.

"Nothing to do with prejudice," says the colonel testily. "Just facts. The crew of *Gilgamesh* were all men. Can't risk one solitary woman being found on board. Besides--spacesuits, personal background sets--all designed for men."

Kirsty and Dilly turn on me looks designed to shrivel and B whispers "Lizzie how wonderful you are."

*　*　*　*　*

The session dissolves. We three get an intensive session course of instruction on our duties and are ordered off to sleep. After breakfast next morning I run into Cray who says, Before I continue about what is evidently pressing business would I care to kick him, hard?

Not right now I reply, what for anyway?

"Miss Lee," says Cray, dragging it out longer than ever, "although I have long realized that your brain functions in a way much superior to logic I had not sense enough yesterday to follow my own instinct and do what you do as soon as you did it; therefore that dessicated meat handler got in first."

I say: "So you weren't picked for pilot? It was only one chance in ten."

"Oh," says Cray, "did you really think so?" He gives me a long look and goes away.

I suppose he noticed that when the colonel came out with his remarks about No women in Gilgamesh I was as surprised as any.

Presently the three of us are issued with protective clothing; we just might have to venture out on the planet's surface and therefore we get white one-piece suits to protect against Cold, heat, moisture, dessication, radioactivity, and mosquitoes, and they are quite becoming, really.

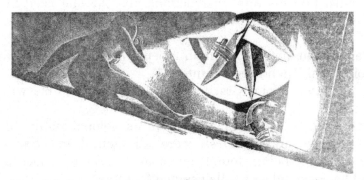

B and I drag out dressing for thirty minutes; then we just sit while Time crawls asymptotically towards the hour.

Then the speaker calls us to go.

We are out of the cabin before it says two words and racing for the hold; so that we are just in time to see a figure out of an Historical movie--padded, jointed, tin bowl for head and blank reflecting glass where the face should be--stepping through the air lock.

The colonel and Mr. Yardo are there already. The colonel packs us into the hopper and personally closes the door, and for once I know what he is thinking; he is wishing he were not the only pilot in this ship who could possibly rely on bringing the ship off and on Mass-Time at one particular defined spot of Space.

Then he leaves us; half an hour to go.

The light in the hold begins to alter. Instead of being softly diffused it separates into sharp-edged beams, reflecting and crisscrossing but leaving cones of shadow between. The air is being pumped into store.

Fifteen minutes.

The hull vibrates and a hatch slides open in the floor so that the black of Space looks through; it closes again.

Mr. Yardo lifts the hopper gently off its mounts and lets it back again.

Testing; five minutes to go.

I am hypnotized by my chronometer; the hands are crawling through glue; I am still staring at it when, at the exact second, we go off Mass-Time.

No weight. I hook my heels under the seat and persuade my esophagus back into place. A new period of waiting has begun. Every so often comes the impression we are falling head-first; the colonel using ship's drive to decelerate the whole system. Then more free fall.

The hopper drifts very slowly out into the hold and hovers over the hatch, and the lights go. There is only the glow from the visiscreen and the instrument board.

One minute thirty seconds to go.

The hatch slides open again. I take a deep breath.

I am still holding it when the colonel's voice comes over the speaker: "Calling *Gilgamesh*. Calling the hopper. Good-by and Good luck. You're on your own."

The ship is gone.

Yet another stretch of time has been marked off for us. Thirty-seven minutes, the least time allowable if we are not to get overheated by friction with the air. Mr. Yardo is a good pilot; he is concentrating wholly on the visiscreen and the thermometer. B and I are free to look around.

I see nothing and say so.

I did not know or have forgotten that Incognita has many small satellites; from here there are four in sight.

*   *   *   *   *

I am still looking at them when B seizes my arm painfully and points below us.

I see nothing and say so.

B whispers it was there a moment ago, it is pretty cloudy down there--Yes Lizzie there it is *look*.

And I see it. Over to the left, very faint and far below, a pin-prick of light.

Light in the polar wastes of a sparsely inhabited planet, and since we are still five miles up it is a very powerful light too.

No doubt about it, as we descend farther; about fifty miles from our objective there are men, quite a lot of them.

I think it is just then that I understand, *really* understand, the hazard of what we are doing. This is not an exercise. This is in dead earnest, and if we have missed an essential factor or calculated something wrong the result will be not a bad mark or a failed exam, or even our personal deaths, but incalculable harm and misery to millions of people we never even heard of.

Dead earnest. How in Space did we ever have cheek enough for this?

The lights might be the essential factor we have missed, but there is nothing we can do about them now.

Mr. Yardo suddenly chuckles and points to the screen.

"There you are, girlies! He's down!"

There, grayly dim, is the map the colonel showed us; and right on the faint line of the cliff-edge is a small brilliant dot.

The map is expanding rapidly, great lengths of coastline shooting out of sight at the edge of the screen. Mr. Yardo has the cross-hairs centered on the dot which is *Gilgamesh*. The dot is changing shape; it is turning into a short ellipse, a longer one. The gyros are leaning her out over the sea.

I look at my chronometer; 12.50 hours exactly. B looks, too, and grips my hand.

Thirty seconds later the Andite has not blown; first fuse safety turned off. Surely she is leaning far enough out by now?

We are hovering at five hundred feet. I can actually see the white edge of the sea beating at the cliff. Mr. Yardo keeps making small corrections; there is a wind out there trying to blow us away. It is cloudy here: I can see neither moons nor stars.

Mr. Yardo checks the radio. Nothing yet.

I stare downwards and fancy I can see a metallic gleam.

Then there is a wordless shout from Mr. Yardo; a bright dot hurtles across the screen and at the same time I see a streak of blue flame tearing diagonally downwards a hundred feet away.

The hopper shudders to a flat concussion in the air, we are all thrown off balance, and when I claw my way back to the screen the moving dot is gone.

So is *Gilgamesh*.

B says numbly, "But it wasn't a meteor. It can't have been."

"It doesn't matter what it was," I say. "It was some sort of missile, I think. They must be even nearer to war than we thought."

We wait. What for, I don't know. Another missile, perhaps. No more come.

At last Mr. Yardo stirs. His voice sounds creaky.

"I guess," he says, then clears his throat, and tries again. "I guess we have to go back up."

B says, "Lizzie, who was it? Do you know?"

Of course I do. "Do you think M'Clare was going to risk one of us on that job? The volunteering was a fake. He went himself."

B whispers, "You're just guessing."

"Maybe," says Mr. Yardo, "but I happened to see through that face plate of his. It was the professor all right."

He has his hand on the controls when my brain starts working again. I utter a strangled noise and dive for the hatch into the cargo hold. B tries to grab me but I get it open and switch on the light.

Fifty-fifty chance--I've lost.

No, this is the one we came in and the people who put in the new cargo did not clear out my fish-boat, they just clamped it neatly to the wall.

I dive in and start to pass up the package. B shakes her head.

"No, Lizzie. We can't. Don't you remember? If we got caught, it would give everything away. Besides ... there isn't any chance--"

"Take a look at the screen," I tell her.

Sharp exclamation from Mr. Yardo. B turns to look, then takes the package and helps me back.

*   *   *   *   *

Mr. Yardo maneuvers out over the sea till the thing is in the middle of the screen; then drops to a hundred feet. It is sticking out of the water at a fantastic angle and the waves are hardly moving it. The nose of a ship.

"The antigrav," whispers B. "The Andite hasn't blown yet."

"Ten minutes," says Mr. Yardo thoughtfully. He turns to me with sudden briskness. "What's that, Lizzie girl? A fish-boat? Good. We may need it. Let's have a look."

"It's mine," I tell him.

"Now look--"

"Tailor made," I say. "You might get into it, though I doubt it. You couldn't work the controls."

It takes him fifteen seconds to realize there is no way round it; he is six foot three and I am five foot one. Even B would find it hard.

His face goes grayish and he stares at me helplessly. Finally he nods.

"All right, Lizzie. I guess we have to try it. Things certainly can't be much worse than they are. We'll go over to the beach there."

On the beach there is wind and spray and breakers but nothing unmanageable; the cliffs on either side keep off the worst of the force. It is queer to feel moving air after eighteen days in a ship. It takes six minutes to unpack and expand the boat and by that time it is ten minutes since the missile hit and the Andite has not blown.

I crawl into the boat. In my protective clothing it is a fairly tight fit. We agree that I will return to this same point and they will start looking for me in fifty minutes' time and will give up if I have not returned in two hours. I take two Andite cartridges to deal with all eventualities and snap the nose of the boat into place. At first I am very conscious of the two little white cigars in the pouch of my suit, but presently I have other things to think about.

I use the "limbs" to crawl the last few yards of shingle into the water and on across the sea bottom till I am beyond the line of breakers; then I turn on the motor. I have already set the controls to "home" on *Gilgamesh* and the radar will steer me off any obstructions. This journey in the dark is as safe as my trip around the reefs before all this started--though it doesn't feel that way.

It takes twelve minutes to reach *Gilgamesh,* or rather the fragment that antigrav is supporting; it is about half a mile from the beach.

The radar stops me six feet from her and I switch it off and turn to Manual and inch closer in.

Lights, a very small close beam. The missile struck her about one third of her length behind the nose. I know, because I can see the whole of that length. It is hanging just above the water, sloping at about 30° to the horizontal. The ragged edge where it was torn from the rest is just dipping into the sea.

If anyone sees this, I don't know what they will make of it but no one could possibly think an ordinary spaceship suffered an ordinary crash, and very little investigation would show up the truth.

I reach up with the forward set of "limbs" and grapple on to the break. I now have somehow to get the hind set of "limbs" up without losing my grip. I can't.

It takes several minutes to realize that I can just open the nose and crawl out.

Immediately a wave hits me in the face and does its best to drag me into the sea. However the interior of the ship is relatively sheltered and presently I am inside and dragging the boat up out of reach.

I need light. Presently I manage to detach one of the two from the boat. I turn it down to minimum close beam and hang it round my neck; then I start up the black jag-edged tunnel of the ship.

I have to get to the nose, find the fuse, change the setting to twenty minutes--maximum possible--and get out before it blows--out of the water I mean. The fish-boat is not constructed to take explosions even half a mile away. But the first thing is to find the fuse and I cannot make out how *Gilgamesh* is lying and therefore cannot find the door through this bulkhead; everything is ripped and twisted. In the end I find a gap between the bulkhead itself and the hull, and squeeze through that.

In the next compartment things are more recognizable and I eventually find the door. Fortunately ships are designed so that you can get through doors even when they are in the ceiling; actually here I have to climb up an overhang, but the surface is provided with rungs which make it not too bad. Finally I reach the door. I shall have to use antigrav to get down ... why didn't I just turn it on and jump? I forgot I had it.

The door was a little way open when the missile struck; it buckled in its grooves and is jammed fast. I can get an arm through. No more. I switch on antigrav and hang there directing the light round the compartment. No rents anywhere, just buckling. This compartment is divided by a partition and the door through that is open. There will be another door into the nose on the other side.

I bring back my feet ready to kick off on a dive through that doorway.

Behind me, something stirs.

*   *   *   *   *

My muscles go into a spasm like the one that causes a falling dream, my hold tears loose and I go tumbling through the air, rebound from a wall, twist, and manage to hook one foot in the frame of the door I was aiming for. I pull myself down and turn off the antigrav; then I just shake for a bit.

The sound was--

This is stupid, with everything torn to pieces in this ship there is no wonder if bits shake loose and drop around--

But it was not a metallic noise, it was a kind of soft dragging, very soft, that ended in a little thump.

Like a--

Like a loose piece of plastic dislodged from its angle of rest and slithering down, pull yourself together Lizzie Lee.

I look through the door into the other half of this level. Shambles. Smashed machinery every which way, blocking the door, blocking everything. No way through at all.

Suddenly I remember the tools. Mr. Yardo loaded the fish-boat with all it would take. I crawl back and return with a fifteen inch expanding beam-lever, and overuse it; the jammed trap door does not slide back in its grooves but flips right out of them, bent double; it flies off into the dark and clangs its way to rest.

I am halfway through the opening when I hear the sound again. A soft slithering; a faint defeated thump.

I freeze where I am, and then I hear the sigh; a long, long weary sound, almost musical.

An air leak somewhere in the hull and wind or waves altering the air pressure below.

All the same I do not seem able to come any farther through this door.

Light might help; I turn the beam up and play it cautiously around. This is the last compartment, right in the nose; a sawn-off cone-shape. No breaks here, though the hull is buckled to my left and the "floor"--the partition, horizontal when the ship is in the normal operating position, which holds my trap door--is torn up; some large heavy object was welded to a thin surface skin which has ripped away leaving jagged edges and a pattern of girders below.

There is no dust here; it has all been sucked out when the ship was open to space; nothing to show the beam except the sliding yellow ellipse where it touches the wall. It glides and turns, spiraling down, deformed every so often where it crosses a projection or a dent, till it halts suddenly on a spoked disk, four feet across and standing nearly eighteen inches out from the wall. The antigrav.

I never saw one this size, it is like the little personal affairs as a giant is like a pigmy, not only bigger but a bit different in proportion. I can see an Andite cartridge fastened among the spokes.

The fuse is a "sympathizer" but it is probably somewhere close. The ellipse moves again. There is no feeling that I control it; it is hunting on its own. To and fro around the giant wheel. Lower. It halts on a small flat box, also bolted to the wall, a little way below. This is it, I can see the dial.

The ellipse stands still, surrounding the fuse. There is something at the very edge of it.

When *Gilgamesh* was right way up the antigrav was bolted to one wall, about three feet above the floor. Now the lowest point is the place where this wall joins what used to be the floor. Something has fallen down to that point and is huddled there in the dark.

The beam jerks suddenly up and the breath whoops out of me; a round thing sticking out of the wall--then I realize it is an archaic space-helmet, clamped to the wall for safety when the wearer took it off.

I take charge of the ellipse of light and move it slowly down, past the fuse, to the thing below. A little dark scalloping of the edge of the light. The tips of fingers. A hand.

I turn up the light.

When the missile struck the big computer was wrenched loose from the floor. It careened down as the floor tilted, taking with it anything that stood in its way.

M'Clare was just stooping to the fuse, I think. The computer smashed against his legs and pinned him down in the angle between the wall and the floor. His legs are hidden by it.

Because of the spacesuit he does not looked crushed; the thick clumsy joints have kept their roundness, so far as they are visible; only his hands and head are bare and vulnerable looking.

I am halfway down, floating on minimum gravity, before it really occurs to me that he may be still alive.

I switch to half and drop beside him. His face is colorless but he is breathing all right.

First-aid kit. I will never make fun of Space Force thoroughness again. Rows and rows of small plastic ampoules. Needles.

Pain-killer, first. I read the directions twice, sweating. Emergencies only--this is. One dose *only* to be given and if patient is not in good health use--never mind that. I fit on the longest needle and jab it through the suit, at the back of the thigh, as far towards the knee-joint as I can get because the suit is thinner. Half one side, half the other.

Now to get the computer off. At a guess it weighs about five hundred pounds. The beam-lever would do it but it would probably fall back.

Antigrav; the personal size is supposed to take up to three times the weight of the average man. I take mine off and buckle the straps through a convenient gap. I have my hands under the thing when M'Clare sighs again.

He is lying on his belly but his head is turned to one side, towards me. Slowly his eyelids open. He catches the sight of my hand; his head moves a little, and he says, "Lizzie. Golden Liz."

I say not to worry, we will soon be out of here.

His body jumps convulsively and he cries out. His hand reaches my sleeve and feels. He says, "Liz! Oh, God, I thought ... what--"

I say things are under control and just keep quiet a bit.

His eyes close. After a moment he whispers, "Something hit the ship."

"A homing missile, I think."

I ought not to have said that; but it seems to make no particular impression, maybe he guessed as much.

*   *   *   *   *

I was wrong in wanting to shift the computer straight away, the release of pressure might start a hemorrhage; I dig out ampoules of blood-seal and inject them into the space between the suit and the flesh, as close to the damage as I can.

M'Clare asks how the ship is lying and I explain, also how I got here. I dig out the six-by-two-inch packet of expanding stretcher and read the directions. He is quiet for a minute or two, gathering strength; then he says sharply: "Lizzie. Stop that and listen.

"The fuse for the Andite is just under the antigrav. Go and find it. Go now. There's a dial with twenty divisions. Marked in black--you see it. Turn the pointer to the last division. Is that done?

"Now you see the switch under the pointer? Is your boat ready? I beg your pardon, of course you left it that way. Then turn the switch and get out."

I come back and see by my chrono that the blood-seal should be set; I get my hands under the computer. M'Clare bangs his hand on the floor.

"Lizzie, you little idiot, don't you realize that even if you get me out of this ship, which is next to impossible, you'll be delayed all the way--and if the Incognitans find either of us the whole plan's ruined? Much worse than ruined, once they see it's a hoax--"

I tell him I have two Andite sticks and they won't find us and on a night like this any story of explosions will be put down to sudden gusts or to lightning.

He is silent for a moment while I start lifting the computer, carefully; its effective weight with the antigrav full on is only about twenty pounds but is has all its inertia. Then he says quietly, "Please, Lizzie--can't you understand that the worst nightmare in the whole affair has been the fear that one of you might get injured? Or even killed? When I realized that only one person was needed to pilot *Gilgamesh*--it was the greatest relief I ever experienced. Now you say...." His voice picks up suddenly. "Lizzie, you're beaten anyway. The ... I'm losing all feeling. Even pain. I can't feel anything behind my shoulders ... it's creeping up--"

I say that means the pain-killer I shot him with is acting as advertised, and he makes a sound as much like an explosive chuckle as anything and it's quiet again.

The curvature between floor and wall is not helpful, I am trying to find a place to wedge the computer so it cannot fall back when I take off the antigrav. Presently I get it pushed on to a sort of ledge formed by a dent in the floor, which I think will hold it. I ease off the antigrav and the computer stays put, I don't like the looks of it so let's get out of here.

I push the packaged stretcher under his middle and pull the tape before I turn the light on to his legs to see the damage. I cannot make out very much; the joints of the suit are smashed some, but as far as I can see the inner lining is not broken which means it is still air-and-water-tight.

I put a hand under his chest to feel how the stretcher is going; it is now expanded to eighteen inches by six and I can feel it pushing out, but it is *slow*, what else have I to do--oh yes, get the helmet.

I am standing up to reach for it when M'Clare says, "What are you doing? Yes ... well, don't put it on for a minute. There's something I would like to tell you, and with all respect for your obstinacy I doubt very much whether I shall have another chance. Keep that light off me, will you? It hurts my eyes.

"You know, Lizzie, I dislike risking the lives of any of the students for whom I am responsible, but as it happens I find the idea of you--blowing yourself to atoms particularly objectionable because ... I happen to be in love with you. You're also one of my best students, I used to think that ... was why I'd been so insistent on your coming to Russett, but I rather think ... my motives were mixed even then. I meant to tell you this after you graduated, and to ask you to marry me, not that ... I thought you would, I know quite well ... you never quite forgave me, but I don't-want-to-have-to remember ... I didn't ... have the guts to--"

His voice trails off, I get a belated rush of sense to the head and turn the light on his face. His head is turned sideways and his fist is clenched against the side of his neck. When I touch it his hand falls open and five discharged ampoules fall out.

Pain-killer.

Maximum dose, one ampoule.

All that talk was just to hold my attention while he fixed the needles and--

I left the kit spread out right next to him.

While I am taking this in some small cold corner of my mind is remembering the instructions that are on the pain-killer ampoule; it does not say, outright, that it is the last refuge for men in the extremity of pain and despair; therefore it cannot say, outright, that they sometimes despair too soon; but it does tell you the name of the antidote.

There are only three ampoules of this and they also say, maximum dose one ampoule. I try to work it out but lacking all other information the best I can do is inject two and keep one till later. I put that one in my pocket.

The stretcher is all expanded now; a very thin but quite rigid grid, six feet by two; I lash him on it without changing his position and fasten the helmet over his head.

Antigrav; the straps just go round him and the stretcher.

I point the thing up towards the trap door and give it a gentle push; then I scramble up the rungs and get there just in time to guide it through. It takes a knock then and some more while I am getting it down to the next partition, but he can't feel it.

This time I find the door, because the roar of noise behind it acts as a guide. The sea is getting up and is dashing halfway to the door as I crawl through. My boat is awash, pivoting to and fro on the grips of the front "limbs."

I grab it, release the limbs and pull it as far back as the door. I maneuver the stretcher on top and realize there is nothing to fasten it with ... except the antigrav, I get that undone, holding the stretcher in balance, and manage to put it under the stretcher and pass the straps between the bars of the grid ... then round the little boat, and the buckle just grips the last inch. It will hold, though.

*   *   *   *   *

I set the boat to face the broken end of the ship, but I daren't put it farther back than the doorway; I turn the antigrav to half, fasten the limb-grips and rush back towards the nose of the ship. Silver knob under the dial. I turn it down, hear the thing begin a fast, steady ticking, and turn and run.

Twenty minutes.

One and a half to get back to the boat, four to get inside it without overturning. Nearly two to get down to the sea--balance difficult. One and a half to lower myself in.

Thirty seconds' tossing before I sink below the wave layer; then I turn the motor as high as I dare and head for the shore.

In a minute I have to turn it down; at this speed the radar is bothered by water currents and keeps steering me away from them as though they were rocks; I finally find the maximum safe speed but it is achingly slow. What happens if you are in water when Andite blows half a mile away? A moment's panic as I find the ship being forced up, then I realize I have reached the point where the beach starts to shelve, turn off radar and motor and start crawling. Eternal slow reach out, grab, shove, haul, with my heart in my mouth; then suddenly the nose breaks water and I am hauling myself out with a last wave doing its best to overbalance me.

I am halfway out of the boat when the Andite blows behind me. There is a flat slapping sound; then an instant roar of wind as the air receives the binding energies of several tons of matter; then a long wave comes pelting up the beach and snatches at the boat.

I huddle into the shingle and hold the boat; I have just got the antigrav turned off, otherwise I think it would have been carried away. There are two or three more big waves and a patter of spray; then it is over.

The outlet valve of the helmet is working, so M'Clare is still breathing; very deep, very slow.

I unfasten the belt of the antigrav, having turned it on again, and pull the belt through the buckle. No time to take it off and rearrange it; anyway it will work as well under the stretcher as on top of it. I drag the boat down to the water, put in an Andite cartridge with the longest fuse I have, set the controls to take it straight out to sea at maximum depth the radar control will allow--six feet above bottom--and push it off. The other Andite cartridge starts burning a hole in my pocket; I would have liked to put that in too, but I must keep it, in case.

I look at my chrono and see that in five minutes the hopper will come.

Five minutes.

I am halfway back to the stretcher when I hear a noise further up the beach. Unmistakable. Shingle under a booted foot.

I stand frozen in mid-stride. I turned the light out after launching the boat but my eyes have not recovered yet; it is murkily black. Even my white suit is only the faintest degree paler than my surroundings.

Silence for a couple of minutes. I stand still. But it can't have gone away. What happens when the hopper comes? They will see whoever it is on the infrared vision screen. They won't come--

Footsteps again. Several.

Then the clouds part and one of those superfluous little moons shines straight through the gap.

The bay is not like the stereo the colonel showed because that was taken in winter; now the snow is melted, leaving bare shingle and mud and a tumble of rocks; more desolate than the snow. Fifty feet off is a man.

He is huddled up in a mass of garments but his head is bare, rising out of a hood which he has pushed back, maybe so as to listen better; he looks young, hardly older than me. He is holding a long thin object which I never saw before, but it must be a weapon of some sort.

This is the end of it. All the evidence of faking is destroyed; except M'Clare and me. Even if I use the Andite he has seen me--and that leaves M'Clare.

I am standing here on one foot like a dancer in a jammed movie, waiting for Time to start again or the world to end--

Like the little figure in the dance-instruction kit Dad got when I was seven, when you switched her off in the middle.

*   *   *   *   *

Like a dancer--

My weight shifts on to the forward foot. My arms swing up, forwards, back. I take one step, another.

Swing. Turn. Kick. Sideways.

Like the silly little dancer who could not get out of the plastic block; but I am moving forward little by little, even if I have to take three steps roundabout for every one in advance.

Arms, up. Turn, round. Leg, up. Straighten, out. Step.

Called the Dance of the Little Robot, for about three months Dad thought it was no end cute, till he caught on I was thinking so, too.

It is just about the only kind of dance you could do on shingle, I guess.

When this started I thought I might be going crazy, but I just had not had time to work it out. In terms of Psychology it goes like this; to shoot off a weapon a man needs a certain type of Stimulus like the sight of an enemy over the end of it. So if I do my best not to look like an enemy he will not get that Stimulus. Or put it another way most men think twice before shooting a girl in the middle of a dance. If I should happen to get away with this, nobody will believe his story, he won't believe it himself.

As for the chance of getting away with it, i.e., getting close enough to grab the gun or hit him with a rock or something, I know I would become a Stimulus to shooting before I did that but there are always the clouds, if one will only come back over the moon again.

I have covered half the distance.

Twenty feet from him, and he takes a quick step back.

Turn, kick, out, step. I am swinging round away from him, let's hope he finds it reassuring. I dare not look up but I think the light is dimming. Turn, kick, out, step. Boxing the compass. Coming round again.

And the cloud is coming over the moon, out of the corner of my eye I see darkness sweeping towards us--and I see his face of sheer horror as he sees it, too; he jumps back, swings up the weapon, and fires straight in my face.

And it is dark. So much for Psychology.

There is a clatter and other sounds--

Well, quite a lot for Psychology maybe, because at twenty feet he seems to have missed me.

*　　*　　*　　*　　*

I pick myself up and touch something which apparently is his weapon, gun or whatever. I leave it and hare back to the stretcher, next-to fall over it but stop just in time, and switch on the antigrav. Up; level it; now where to? The cliffs enclosing the bay are about thirty yards off to my left and they offer the only cover.

The shingle is relatively level; I make good time till I stumble against a rock and nearly lose the stretcher. I step up on to the rock and see the cliff as a blacker mass in the general darkness, only a yard away. I edge the stretcher round it.

It is almost snatched out of my hand by a gust of wind. I pull it back and realize that in the bay I have been sheltered; there is pretty near half a gale blowing across the face of the cliff.

Voices and footsteps, away back among the rocks where the man came from.

If the clouds part again they will see me, sure as shooting.

I take a hard grip on the stretcher and scramble round the edge of the cliff.

After the first gust the wind is not so bad; for the most part it is trying to press me back into the cliff. The trouble is that I can't see. I have to shuffle my foot forward, rubbing one shoulder against the cliff to feel where it is because I have no hand free.

After a few yards I come to an impasse; something more than knee high; boulder, ridge, I can't tell.

I weigh on the edge of the stretcher and tilt it up to get it over the obstacle. With the antigrav full on it keeps its momentum and goes on moving up. I try to check it, but the wind gets underneath.

It is tugging to get away; I step blindly upwards in the effort to keep up with it. One foot goes on a narrow ledge, barely a toe hold. I am being hauled upwards. I bring the other foot up and find the top of a boulder, just within reach. Now the first foot--

And now I am on top of the boulder, but I have lost touch with the cliff and the full force of the wind is pulling the stretcher upwards. I get one arm over it and fumble underneath for the control of the antigrav; I must give it weight and put it down on this boulder and wait for the wind to drop.

Suddenly I realize that my weight is going; bending over the stretcher puts me in the field of the antigrav. A moment later another gust comes, and I realize I am rising into the air.

Gripping the edge of the stretcher with one hand I reach out the other, trying to grasp some projection on the face of the cliff. Not being able to see I simply push farther away till it is out of reach.

We are still rising.

I pull myself up on the stretcher; there is just room for my toes on either side of M'Clare's legs. The wind roaring in my ears makes it difficult to think.

Rods of light slash down at me from the edge of the cliff. For a moment all I can do is duck; then I realize we are still well below them, but rising every moment. The cliff-face is about six feet away; the wind reflecting from it keeps us from being blown closer.

I must get the antigrav off. I let myself over the side of the stretcher, hanging by one hand, and fumble for the controls. I can just reach. Then I realize this is no use. Antigrav controls are not meant to go off with a click of the finger; they might get switched off accidentally. To work the switch and the safety you must have two hands, or one hand in the optimum position. My position is about as bad as it could be. I can stroke the switch with one finger; no more.

I haul myself back on to the stretcher and realize we are only about six feet under the beam of light. Only one thing left. I feel in my pocket for the Andite. Stupidly, I am still also bending over the outlet valve of the helmet, trying to see whether M'Clare is still breathing or not.

The little white cigar is not fused. I have to hold on with one hand. In the end I manage to stick the Andite between thumb and finger-roots of that hand while I use the other to find the fuse and stick it over the Andite. The shortest; three minutes.

I think the valve is still moving--

Then something drops round me; I am hauled tight against the stretcher; we are pulled strongly downwards with the wind buffeting and snatching, banged against the edge of something, and pulled through into silence and the dark.

For a moment I do not understand; then I recognize the feel of Fragile Cargo, still clamping me to the stretcher, and I open my mouth and scream and scream.

Clatter of feet. Hatch opens. Fragile Cargo goes limp.

I stagger to my feet. Faint light through the hatch; B's head. I hold out the Andite stick and she turns and shouts; and a panel slides open in the wall so that the wind comes roaring in.

I push the stick through and the wind snatches it away and it is gone.

After that--

*   *   *   *   *

After that, for a while, nothing, I suppose, though I have no recollection of losing consciousness; only without any sense of break I find I am flat on my back on one of the seats in the cabin of the hopper.

I sit up and say "How--"

B who is sitting on the floor beside me says that when the broadcaster was activated of course they came at once, only while they were waiting for the boat to reach land whole squads of land cars arrived and started combing the area, and some came up on top of the cliff and shone their headlights out over the sea so Mr. Yardo had to lurk against the cliff face and wait till I got into a position where he could pick me up and it was *frightfully* clever of me to think of floating up on antigrav--

I forgot about the broadcaster.

I forgot about the hopper come to that, there seemed to be nothing in the world except me and the stretcher and the enemy.

Stretcher.

I say, "Is M'Clare--"

At which moment Mr. Yardo turns from the controls with a wide smile of triumph and says "Eighteen twenty-seven, girls!" and the world goes weightless and swings upside down.

Then still with no sense of any time-lapse I am lying in the big lighted hold, with the sound of trampling all round: it is somehow filtered and far off and despite the lights there seems to be a globe of darkness around my head. I hear my own voice repeating, "M'Clare? How's M'Clare?"

A voice says distantly, without emphasis, "M'Clare? He's dead."

The next time I come round it is dark. I am vaguely aware of having been unconscious for quite a while.

There is a single thread of knowledge connecting this moment with the last: M'Clare's dead.

This is the central factor: I seem to have been debating it with myself for a very long time.

I suppose the truth is simply that the Universe never guarantees anything; life, or permanence, or that your best will be good enough.

The rule is that you have to pick yourself up and go on; and lying here in the dark is not doing it.

I turn on my side and see a cluster of self-luminous objects including a light switch. I reach for it.

How did I get into a hospital?

On second thoughts it is a cabin in the ship, or rather two of them with the partition torn out, I can see the ragged edge of it. There is a lot of paraphernalia around; I climb out to have a look.

Holy horrors what's happened? Someone borrowed my legs and put them back wrong; my eyes also are not functioning well, the light is set at Minimum and I am still dazzled. I see a door and make for it to get Explanations from somebody.

Arrived, I miss my footing and stumble against the door and on the other side someone says "Hello, Lizzie. Awake at last?"

I think my heart stops for a moment. I can't find the latch. I am vaguely aware of beating something with my fists, and then the door gives, sticks, gives again and I stumble through and land on all fours the other side of it.

Someone is calling: "Lizzie! Are you hurt? Where the devil have they all got to? Liz!"

I sit up and say, "They said you were *dead*!"

"*Who* did?"

"I ... I ... someone in the hold. I said How's M'Clare? and they said you were dead."

M'Clare frowns and says gently, "Come over here and sit down quietly for a bit. You've been dreaming."

Have I? Maybe the whole thing was a dream--but if so how far does it go? Going down in the heli? The missile? The boat? Crawling through the black tunnel of a broken ship?

No, because he is sitting in a sort of improvised chaise longue and his legs are evidently strapped in place under the blanket; he is fumbling with the fastening or something.

*   *   *   *   *

I say "Hey! Cut that out!"

He straightens up irritably.

"Don't you start that, Lysistrata. I've been suffering the attentions of the damnedest collection of amateur nurses who ever handled a thermocouple, for over a week. I don't deny they've been very efficient, but when it comes to--"

Over a *week*?

He nods. "My dear Lizzie, we left Incognita ten days ago. Amateur nursing again! They have some unholy book of rules which says that for Exposure, Exhaustion and Shock the best therapy is sleep. I don't doubt it, but it goes on to say that in extreme cases the patient has been known to benefit by as much as two weeks of it. I didn't find out that they were trying it on you until about thirty-six hours ago when I began inquiring why you weren't around. They kept me under for three days--in fact until their infernal Handbook said it was time for my leg muscles to have some exercise. Miss Lammergaw was the ring-leader."

No wonder my legs feel as though someone exchanged the muscles for cotton wool, just wait till I get hold of Kirsty.

If it hadn't been for her, I shouldn't have spent ten days remembering, even in my sleep, that--

I say, "Hell's feathers, it was *you*!"

M'Clare makes motions as though to start getting out of his chair, looking seriously alarmed. I say, "It was your voice! When I asked--"

M'Clare, quite definitely, starts to blush. Not much, but some.

"Lizzie, I believe you're right. I have a sort of vague memory of someone asking how I was--and I gave what I took to be a truthful answer. I remember it seemed quite inconceivable that I could be alive. In fact I still don't understand it. Neither Yardo nor Miss Laydon could tell me. How *did* you get me out of that ship?"

Well, I do my best to explain, glossing over one or two points; at the finish he closes his eyes and says nothing for a while.

Then he says, "So except for this one man who saw you, you left no traces at all?"

Not that I know of, but--

"Do you know, five minutes later there were at least twenty men in that bay, most of them scientists? They don't seem to have found anything suspicious. Visibility was bad, of course, and you can't leave foot-prints in shingle--"

Hold on, what *is* all this?

M'Clare says, "We've had two couriers while you were asleep. Yes, I know it's not ordinarily possible for a ship on Mass-Time to get news. One of these days someone will have an interesting problem in Cultural Engineering, working out how to integrate some of these Space Force secrets into our economic and social structure without upsetting the whole of the known volume. Though courier boats make their crews so infernally sick I doubt whether the present type will ever come into common use. Anyway, we've had transcripts of a good many broadcasts from Incognita, the last dated four days ago; and as far as we can tell they're interpreting *Gilgamesh* just as we meant them to.

"The missile, by the way, was experimental, waiting to be test-fired the next day. The man in charge saw *Gilgamesh* on the alarm screens and got trigger-happy. The newscasters were divided as to whether he should be blamed or praised; they all seem to feel he averted a menace, at least temporarily, but some of them think the invaders could have been captured alive.

"The first people on the scene came from a scientific camp; you and Miss Laydon saw their lights on the way down. You remember that area is geophysically interesting? Well, by extraordinary good luck an international group was there studying it. They rushed straight off to the site of the landing-- they actually saw *Gilgamesh,* and she registered on some of their astronomical instruments, too. They must be a reckless lot. What's more, they started trying to locate her on the sea bottom the next day. Found both pieces; they're still trying to locate the nose. They were all set to try raising the smaller piece when their governments both announced in some haste that they were sending a properly equipped expedition. Jointly.

"There's been no mention in any newscast of anyone seeing fairies or sea maidens--I expect the poor devil thinks you were a hallucination."

So we brought it off.

*   *   *   *   *

I am very thankful in a distant sort of way, but right now the Incognitans have no more reality for me than the Lost Kafoozalum.

M'Clare came through alive.

I could spend a good deal of time just getting used to that fact, but there is something I ought to say and I don't know how.

I inquire after his injuries and learn they are healing nicely.

I look at him and he is frowning.

He says, "Lizzie. Just before my well-meant but ineffective attempt at suicide--"

Here it comes.

I say quick If he is worrying about all that nonsense he talked in order to distract my attention, forget it; I have.

Silence, then he says wearily, "I talked nonsense, did I?"

I say there is no need to worry, under the circumstances anyone would have a perfect right to be raving off his Nut.

I then find I cannot bear this conversation any longer so I get up saying I expect he is tired and I will call someone.

I get nearly to the door when

"*No,* Lizzie! you can't let that crew loose on me just in order to change the conversation. Come back here. I appreciate your wish to spare my feelings, but it's wasted. We'll have this out here and now.

"I remember quite well what I said, and so do you: I said that I loved you. I also said that I had intended to ask you to marry me as soon as you ceased to be one of my pupils. Well, the results of Finals were officially announced three days ago.

"Oh, I suppose I always knew what the answer would be, but I didn't want to spend the rest of my life wondering, because I never had the guts to ask you.

"You don't dislike me as you used to--you've forgiven me for making you come to Russett--but you still think I'm a cold-blooded manipulator of other people's minds and emotions. So I am; it's part of the job.

"You're quite right to distrust me for that, though. It is the danger of this profession, that we end up by looking on everybody and everything as a subject for manipulation. Even in our personal lives. I always knew that: I didn't begin to be afraid of it until I realized I was in love with you.

"I could have made you love me, Lizzie. I could! I didn't try. Not that I didn't want love on those terms, or any terms. But to use professional ... tricks ... in private life, ends by destroying all reality. I always treated you exactly as I treated my other students--I think. But I could have made you think you loved me ... even if I am twice your age--"

This I cannot let pass, I say "Hi! According to College rumor you cannot be more than thirty-six; I'm twenty-three."

M'Clare says in a bemused sort of way He will be thirty-seven in a couple of months.

I say, "I will be twenty-four next week and your arithmetic is still screwy; and here is another datum you got wrong. I do love you. Very much."

He says, "Golden Liz."

Then other things which I remember all right, I shall keep them to remember any time I am tired, sick, cold, hungry Hundred-and-ninety--; but they are not for writing down.

Then I suppose at some point we agreed it is time for me to go, because I find myself outside the cabin and there is Colonel Delano-Smith.

He makes me a small speech about various matters ending that he hears he has to congratulate me.

Huh?

Oh, Space and Time did one of those unimitigated so-and-sos, my dear classmates, leave M'Clare's communicator on?

The colonel says he heard I did very well in my Examinations.

Sweet splitting photons I forgot all about Finals.

It is just as well my Education has come to an honorable end, because ... well, shades of ... well, Goodness gracious and likewise Dear me, I am going to marry a *Professor*.

Better just stick to it I am going to marry M'Clare, it makes better sense that way.

But Gosh we are going to have to do some re-adjusting to a changed Environment. Both of us.

Oh, well, M'Clare is a Professor of Cultural Engineering and I just past my Final Exams in same; surely if anyone can we should be able to work out how you live Happily Ever After?

Year of the Big Thaw
By Marion Zimmer Bradley

Originally Published in *Fantastic Universe*
May 1953

Editor's Notes:
Year of the Big Thaw
By Marion Zimmer Bradley

This is an early, fairly conventional, story from a writer who was to become a leader in the feminist fantasy wave of the 70's and 80's. In the forward to one of her early novels, she describes how she had determined to follow in the footsteps of such early women science fiction writers as C. L. Moore and Leigh Brackett only to discover that when she actually started writing in the 50's science fiction had become much more "scientific." She spent most of the 50's writing the typical technology based fiction of the era only to return to the blend of fantasy and science that she was to become so well known for.

In "Year of the Big Thaw," despite the subject matter, a crashed space ship with an alien survivor, Bradley takes a soft approach. There is no menace, no violence except that of nature. There is only humanity, exhibited in its most expansive form.

Marion Zimmer Bradley (June 3, 1930-September 25, 1999) was born in upstate New York near Albany. She began writing in the late 40's with her first story and continued during a prolific career until her death. Much of her fiction has a distinct feminist tone to it. She is best known for her series of novels and stories that take place on the planet Darkover. She was the long time editor of the series of anthologies, *Sword and Sorceress*. She also was a founding member of the Society for Creative Anachronism.

Year of the Big Thaw

Mr. Emmett did his duty by the visitor from another world--
never doubting the right of it.

You say that Matthew is your own son, Mr. Emmett?

Yes, Rev'rend Doane, and a better boy never stepped, if I do
say it as shouldn't. I've trusted him to drive team for me since he
was eleven, and you can't say more than that for a farm boy.
Way back when he was a little shaver so high, when the war
came on, he was bounden he was going to sail with this Admiral
Farragut. You know boys that age--like runaway colts. I couldn't
see no good in his being cabin boy on some tarnation Navy ship
and I told him so. If he'd wanted to sail out on a whaling ship, I
'low I'd have let him go. But Marthy--that's the boy's Ma--took on
so that Matt stayed home. Yes, he's a good boy and a good son.

We'll miss him a powerful lot if he gets this scholarship
thing. But I 'low it'll be good for the boy to get some learnin'
besides what he gets in the school here. It's right kind of you,
Rev'rend, to look over this application thing for me.

*Well, if he is your own son, Mr. Emmett, why did you write
'birthplace unknown' on the line here?*

Rev'rend Doane, I'm glad you asked me that question. I've
been turnin' it over in my mind and I've jest about come to the
conclusion it wouldn't be nohow fair to hold it back. I didn't lie
when I said Matt was my son, because he's been a good son to
me and Marthy. But I'm not his Pa and Marthy ain't his Ma, so
could be I stretched the truth jest a mite. Rev'rend Doane, it's a
tarnal funny yarn but I'll walk into the meetin' house and swear
to it on a stack o'Bibles as thick as a cord of wood.

You know I've been farming the old Corning place these past
seven year? It's good flat Connecticut bottom-land, but it isn't
like our land up in Hampshire where I was born and raised. My
Pa called it the Hampshire Grants and all that was King's land
when *his* Pa came in there and started farming at the foot of
Scuttock Mountain. That's Injun for fires, folks say, because the
Injuns used to build fires up there in the spring for some of their

heathen doodads. Anyhow, up there in the mountains we see a tarnal power of quare things.

You call to mind the year we had the big thaw, about twelve years before the war? You mind the blizzard that year? I heard tell it spread down most to York. And at Fort Orange, the place they call Albany now, the Hudson froze right over, so they say. But those York folks do a sight of exaggerating, I'm told.

Anyhow, when the ice went out there was an almighty good thaw all over, and when the snow run off Scuttock mountain there was a good-sized hunk of farmland in our valley went under water. The crick on my farm flowed over the bank and there was a foot of water in the cowshed, and down in the swimmin' hole in the back pasture wasn't nothing but a big gully fifty foot and more across, rushing through the pasture, deep as a lake and brown as the old cow. You know freshet-floods? Full up with sticks and stones and old dead trees and somebody's old shed floatin' down the middle. And I swear to goodness, Parson, that stream was running along so fast I saw four-inch cobblestones floating and bumping along.

I tied the cow and the calf and Kate--she was our white mare; you mind she went lame last year and I had to shoot her, but she was just a young mare then and skittish as all get-out--but she was a good little mare.

Anyhow, I tied the whole kit and caboodle of them in the woodshed up behind the house, where they'd be dry, then I started to get the milkpail. Right then I heard the gosh-awfullest screech I ever heard in my life. Sounded like thunder and a freshet and a forest-fire all at once. I dropped the milkpail as I heard Marthy scream inside the house, and I run outside. Marthy was already there in the yard and she points up in the sky and yelled, "Look up yander!"

We stood looking up at the sky over Shattuck mountain where there was a great big--shoot now, I d'no as I can call its name but it was like a trail of fire in the sky, and it was makin' the dangdest racket you ever heard, Rev'rend. Looked kind of like one of them Fourth-of-July skyrockets, but it was big as a house. Marthy was screaming and she grabbed me and hollered, "Hez! Hez, what in tunket is it?" And when Marthy cusses like that, Rev'rend, she don't know what she's saying, she's so scared.

I was plumb scared myself. I heard Liza--that's our young-un, Liza Grace, that got married to the Taylor boy. I heard her crying on the stoop, and she came flying out with her pinny all black and hollered to Marthy that the pea soup was burning. Marthy let out another screech and ran for the house. That's a woman for you. So I quietened Liza down some and I went in and told Marthy it weren't no more than one of them shooting stars. Then I went and did the milking.

But you know, while we were sitting down to supper there came the most awful grinding, screeching, pounding crash I ever heard. Sounded if it were in the back pasture but the house shook as if somethin' had hit it.

Marthy jumped a mile and I never saw such a look on her face.

"Hez, what was that?" she asked.

"Shoot, now, nothing but the freshet," I told her.

But she kept on about it. "You reckon that shooting star fell in our back pasture, Hez?"

"Well, now, I don't 'low it did nothing like that," I told her. But she was jittery as an old hen and it weren't like her nohow. She said it sounded like trouble and I finally quietened her down by saying I'd saddle Kate up and go have a look. I kind of thought, though I didn't tell Marthy, that somebody's house had floated away in the freshet and run aground in our back pasture.

So I saddled up Kate and told Marthy to get some hot rum ready in case there was some poor soul run aground back there. And I rode Kate back to the back pasture.

It was mostly uphill because the top of the pasture is on high ground, and it sloped down to the crick on the other side of the rise.

Well, I reached the top of the hill and looked down. The crick were a regular river now, rushing along like Niagary. On the other side of it was a stand of timber, then the slope of Shattuck mountain. And I saw right away the long streak where all the timber had been cut out in a big scoop with roots standing up in the air and a big slide of rocks down to the water.

It was still raining a mite and the ground was sloshy and squanchy under foot. Kate scrunched her hooves and got real balky, not likin' it a bit. When we got to the top of the pasture she started to whine and whicker and stamp, and no matter how loud I whoa-ed she kept on a-stamping and I was plumb scared she'd pitch me off in the mud. Then I started to smell a funny smell, like somethin' burning. Now, don't ask me how anything could burn in all that water, because I don't know.

When we came up on the rise I saw the contraption.

Rev'rend, it was the most tarnal crazy contraption I ever saw in my life. It was bigger nor my cowshed and it was long and thin and as shiny as Marthy's old pewter pitcher her Ma brought from England. It had a pair of red rods sticking out behind and a crazy globe fitted up where the top ought to be. It was stuck in the mud, turned halfway over on the little slide of roots and rocks, and I could see what had happened, all right.

The thing must have been--now, Rev'rend, you can say what you like but that thing must have *flew* across Shattuck and landed on the slope in the trees, then turned over and slid down the hill. That must have been the crash we heard. The rods weren't just red, they were *red-hot*. I could hear them sizzle as the rain hit 'em.

In the middle of the infernal contraption there was a door, and it hung all to-other as if every hinge on it had been wrenched halfway off. As I pushed old Kate alongside it I heared somebody hollering alongside the contraption. I didn't nohow get the words but it must have been for help, because I looked down and there was a man a-flopping along in the water.

He was a big fellow and he wasn't swimming, just thrashin' and hollering. So I pulled off my coat and boots and hove in after him. The stream was running fast but he was near the edge and I managed to catch on to an old tree-root and hang on, keeping his head out of the water till I got my feet aground. Then I hauled him onto the bank. Up above me Kate was still whinnying and raising Ned and I shouted at her as I bent over the man.

Wal, Rev'rend, he sure did give me a surprise--weren't no proper man I'd ever seed before. He was wearing some kind of red clothes, real shiny and sort of stretchy and not wet from the water, like you'd expect, but dry and it felt like that silk and India-rubber stuff mixed together. And it was such a bright red that at first I didn't see the blood on it. When I did I knew he were a goner. His chest were all stove in, smashed to pieces. One of the old tree-roots must have jabbed him as the current flung him down. I thought he were dead already, but then he opened up his eyes.

A funny color they were, greeny yellow. And I swear, Rev'rend, when he opened them eyes I *felt* he was readin' my mind. I thought maybe he might be one of them circus fellers in their flying contraptions that hang at the bottom of a balloon.

He spoke to me in English, kind of choky and stiff, not like Joe the Portygee sailor or like those tarnal dumb Frenchies up Canady way, but--well, funny. He said, "My baby--in ship. Get--baby ..." He tried to say more but his eyes went shut and he moaned hard.

I yelped, "Godamighty!" 'Scuse me, Rev'rend, but I was so blame upset that's just what I did say, "Godamighty, man, you mean there's a baby in that there dingfol contraption?" He just moaned so after spreadin' my coat around the man a little bit I just plunged in that there river again.

Rev'rend, I heard tell once about some tomfool idiot going over Niagary in a barrel, and I tell you it was like that when I tried crossin' that freshet to reach the contraption.

I went under and down, and was whacked by floating sticks and whirled around in the freshet. But somehow, I d'no how except by the pure grace of God, I got across that raging torrent and clumb up to where the crazy dingfol machine was sitting.

Ship, he'd called it. But that were no ship, Rev'rend, it was some flying dragon kind of thing. It was a real scarey lookin' thing but I clumb up to the little door and hauled myself inside it. And, sure enough, there was other people in the cabin, only they was all dead.

There was a lady and a man and some kind of an animal looked like a bobcat only smaller, with a funny-shaped rooster-comb thing on its head. They all--even the cat-thing--was wearing those shiny, stretchy clo'es. And they all was so battered and smashed I didn't even bother to hunt for their heartbeats. I could see by a look they was dead as a doornail.

Then I heard a funny little whimper, like a kitten, and in a funny, rubber-cushioned thing there's a little boy baby, looked about six months old. He was howling lusty enough, and when I lifted him out of the cradle kind of thing, I saw why. That boy baby, he was wet, and his little arm was twisted under him. That there flying contraption must have smashed down awful hard, but that rubber hammock was so soft and cushiony all it did to him was jolt him good.

I looked around but I couldn't find anything to wrap him in. And the baby didn't have a stitch on him except a sort of spongy paper diaper, wet as sin. So I finally lifted up the lady, who had a long cape thing around her, and I took the cape off her real gentle. I knew she was dead and she wouldn't be needin' it, and that boy baby would catch his death if I took him out bare-naked like that. She was probably the baby's Ma; a right pretty woman she was but smashed up something shameful.

So anyhow, to make a long story short, I got that baby boy back across that Niagary falls somehow, and laid him down by his Pa. The man opened his eyes kind, and said in a choky voice, "Take care--baby."

I told him I would, and said I'd try to get him up to the house where Marthy could doctor him. The man told me not to bother. "I dying," he says. "We come from planet--star up there--crash here--" His voice trailed off into a language I couldn't understand, and he looked like he was praying.

I bent over him and held his head on my knees real easy, and I said, "Don't worry, mister, I'll take care of your little fellow until your folks come after him. Before God I will."

So the man closed his eyes and I said, *Our Father which art in Heaven,* and when I got through he was dead.

I got him up on Kate, but he was cruel heavy for all he was such a tall skinny fellow. Then I wrapped that there baby up in the cape thing and took him home and give him to Marthy. And the next day I buried the fellow in the south medder and next meetin' day we had the baby baptized Matthew Daniel Emmett, and brung him up just like our own kids. That's all.

All? Mr. Emmett, didn't you ever find out where that ship really came from?

Why, Rev'rend, he said it come from a star. Dying men don't lie, you know that. I asked the Teacher about them planets he mentioned and she says that on one of the planets--can't rightly remember the name, March or Mark or something like that--she says some big scientist feller with a telescope saw canals on that planet, and they'd hev to be pretty near as big as this-here Erie canal to see them so far off. And if they could build canals on that planet I d'no why they couldn't build a flying machine.

I went back the next day when the water was down a little, to see if I couldn't get the rest of them folks and bury them, but the flying machine had broke up and washed down the crick.

Marthy's still got the cape thing. She's a powerful saving woman. We never did tell Matt, though. Might make him feel funny to think he didn't really b'long to us.

But--but--Mr. Emmett, didn't anybody ask questions about the baby--where you got it?

Well, now, I'll 'low they was curious, because Marthy hadn't been in the family way and they knew it. But up here folks minds their own business pretty well, and I jest let them wonder. I told Liza Grace I'd found her new little brother in the back pasture, and o'course it was the truth. When Liza Grace growed up she thought it was jest one of those yarns old folks tell the little shavers.

And has Matthew ever shown any differences from the other children that you could see?

Well, Rev'rend, not so's you could notice it. He's powerful smart, but his real Pa and Ma must have been right smart too to build a flying contraption that could come so far.

O'course, when he were about twelve years old he started reading folks' minds, which didn't seem exactly right. He'd tell Marthy what I was thinkin' and things like that. He was just at the pesky age. Liza Grace and Minnie were both a-courtin' then, and he'd drive their boy friends crazy telling them what Liza Grace and Minnie were a-thinking and tease the gals by telling them what the boys were thinking about.

There weren't no harm in the boy, though, it was all teasing. But it just weren't decent, somehow. So I tuk him out behind the woodshed and give his britches a good dusting just to remind him that that kind of thing weren't polite nohow. And Rev'rend Doane, he ain't never done it sence.

Bride of the Dark One
By Florence Verbell Brown

Originally Published in *Planet Stories*
July 1952

Editor's Notes:
Bride of the Dark One
By Florence Verbell Brown

"Bride of the Dark Ones" follows in the footsteps of writers such as C. L. Moore and Leigh Bracket who began their careers writing for the Pulps in the 30's. In particular, it bears a strong resemblance to the "Northwest Smith" stories that Moore wrote for *Weird Tales*. The world it explores is a shadowy mix of spaceships and vengeful gods, blasters and priests, where illicit business is conducted in dimly lit bars whose denizens imbibe exotic beverages and drugs from a dozen different planets. When this story was published in 1952, it was already a throwback to an earlier era, which doesn't limit its appeal.

Other than the existence of the single story "Bride of the Dark One" there is no biographical information available.

Bride of the Dark One

The outcasts; the hunted of all the brighter worlds, crowded onto Yaroto. But even here was there salvation for Ransome, the jinx-scarred acolyte, when tonight was the night of Bani-tai ... the night of expiation by the photo-memoried priests of dark Darion?

*   *   *   *   *

The last light in the Galaxy was a torch. High in the rafters of Mytor's Cafe Yaroto it burned, and its red glare illuminated a gallery of the damned. Hands that were never far from blaster or knife; eyes that picked a hundred private hells out of the swirling smoke where a woman danced.

She was good to look at, moving in time to the savage rhythm of the music. The single garment she wore bared her supple body, and thighs and breasts and a cloud of dark hair wove a pattern of desire in the close room.

Fat Mytor watched, and his little crafty eyes gleamed. The Earth-girl danced like a she-devil tonight. The tables were crowded with the outcast and the hunted of all the brighter worlds. The woman's warm body, moving in the torchlight, would stir memories that men had thought they left light years behind. Gold coins would shower into Mytor's palm for bad wine, for stupor and forgetfulness.

Mytor sipped his imported amber kali, and the black eyes moved with seeming casualness, penetrating the deep shadows where the tables were, resting briefly on each drunken, greedy or fear-ridden face.

It was an old process with Mytor, nearly automatic. A glance told him enough, the state of a man's mind and senses and wallet. This trembling wreck, staring at the woman and nursing a glass of the cheapest green Yarotian wine, had spent his last silver. Mytor would have him thrown out. Another, head down and muttering over a tumbler of raw whiskey, would pass out before the night was over, and wake in an alley blocks away, with his gold in Mytor's pocket. A third wanted a woman, and Mytor knew what kind of a woman.

When the dance was nearly over Mytor heaved out of his chair, drew the rich folds of his native Venusian tarab about his bulk, and padded softly to a corner of the room, where the shadows lay deepest. Smiling, he rested a moist, jeweled paw on the table at which Ransome, the Earthman, sat alone.

Blue eyes looked up coldly out of a weary, lean face. The voice was bored.

"I've paid for my bottle and I have nothing left for you to steal. We have nothing in common, no business together. Now, if you don't mind, you're in my line of vision, and I'd like to watch the finish of the dance."

The fat Venusian's smile only broadened.

"May I sit down, Mr. Ransome?" he persisted. "Here, out of your line of vision?"

"The chair belongs to you," Ransome observed flatly.

"Thank you."

Covertly, as he had done for hours now, Mytor studied the gaunt, pale Earthman in the worn space harness. Ransome had apparently dismissed the Venusian renegade already, and his cold blue eyes followed the woman's every movement with fixed intensity.

The music swept on toward its climax and the woman's body was a storm of golden flesh and tossing black hair. Mytor saw the Earthman's pale lips twist in the faint suggestion of a bitter smile, saw the long fingers tighten around the glass.

Every man had his price on Yaroto, and Ransome would not be the first Mytor had bought with a woman. For a moment, Mytor watched the desire brighten in Ransome's eyes, studied the smile that some men wear on the way to death, in the last moment when life is most precious.

*   *   *   *   *

In this moment Ransome was for sale. And Mytor had a proposition.

"You were not surprised that I knew your name, Mr. Ransome?"

"Let's say that I wasn't interested."

Mytor flushed but Ransome was looking past him at the woman. The Venusian wiped his forehead with a soiled handkerchief, drummed fat fingers on the table for a moment, tried a different tack.

"Her name is Irene. She's lovely, isn't she, Mr. Ransome? Surely the inner worlds showed you nothing like her. The eyes, the red mouth, the breasts like--"

"Shut up," Ransome grated, and the glass shattered between his clenched fingers.

"Very well, Mr. Ransome." Whiskey trickled from the edge of the table in slow, thick drops, staining Mytor's white tarab. Ice was in the Venusian's voice. "Get out of my place--now. Leave the whiskey, and the woman. I have no traffic with fools."

Ransome sighed.

"I've told you, Mytor that you're wasting your time. But make your pitch, if you must."

"Ah, Mr. Ransome, you do not care to go out into the starless night. Perhaps there are those who wait for you, eh? With very long knives?"

Reflex brought Ransome's hand up in a lightning arc to the blaster bolstered under his arm, but Mytor's damp hand was on his wrist, and Mytor's purr was in his ear, the words coming quickly.

"You would die where you sit, you fool. You would not live even to know the sharpness of the long knives, the sacred knives of Darion, with the incantations inscribed upon their blades against blasphemers of the Temple."

Ransome shuddered and was silent. He saw Mytor's guards, vigilant in the shadows, and his hand fell away from the blaster.

When the dance was ended, and the blood was running hot and strong in him, he turned to face Mytor. His voice was impatient now, but his meaning was shrouded in irony.

"Are you trying to sell me a lucky charm, Mytor?"

The Venusian laughed.

"Would you call a space ship a lucky charm, Mr. Ransome?"

"No," Ransome said grimly. "If it were berthed across the street I'd be dead before I got halfway to it."

"Not if I provided you with a guard of my men."

"Maybe not. But I wouldn't have picked you for a philanthropist, Mytor."

"There are no philanthropists on Yaroto, Mr. Ransome. I offer you escape, it is true; you will have guessed that I expect some service in return."

"Get to the point." Ransome's eyes were weary now that the woman's dancing no longer held them. And there was little hope in his voice.

A man can put off a date across ten years, and across a hundred worlds, and there can be whiskey and women to dance for him. But there was a ship with burned-out jets lying in the desert outside this crumbling city, and it was the night of Banitai, the night of expiation in distant Darion, and Ransome knew that for him, this was the last world.

After tonight the priests would proclaim the start of a new Cycle, and the old debts, if still unpaid, would be canceled forever.

Ransome shrugged, a hopeless gesture. Enough of the cult of the Dark One lingered in the very stuff of his nerves and brain to tell him that the will of the Temple would be done.

But Mytor was speaking again, and Ransome listened in spite of himself.

"All the scum of the Galaxy wash up on Yaroto at last," the fat Venusian said. "That is why you and I are here, Mr. Ransome. It is also why a certain pirate landed his ship on the desert out there three days ago. *Callisto Queen*, the ship's name is, though it has borne a dozen others. Cargo--Jovian silks and dyestuffs from the moons of Mars, narco-vin from the system of Alpha Centauri."

Mytor paused, put the tips of fat fingers together, and looked hard at Ransome.

"Is all of that supposed to mean something to me?" Ransome asked. A waiter had brought over a glass to replace the broken one, and he poured a drink for himself, not inviting Mytor. "It doesn't."

"It suggests a course, nothing more. In toward Sol, out to Yaroto by way of Alpha Centauri. Do you follow the courses of pirate ships, Mr. Ransome?"

"One," Ransome said savagely. "I've lost track of her."

"Perhaps you know the *Callisto Queen* better under her former name, then."

Again Ransome's hand moved toward the blaster, and this time Mytor made no attempt to stop him. Ransome's thin lips tightened with some powerful emotion, and he half rose to look hard at Mytor.

"The name of the ship?"

"Her captain used to call her *Hawk of Darion*."

Ransome understood. *Hawk of Darion*, hell ship driving through black space under the command of a man he had once sworn to kill. Eight years rolled back and he saw them together, laughing at him: the Earthman-captain and the woman who had been Ransome's.

"Captain Jareth," Ransome said slowly. "Here--on Yaroto."

The Venusian nodded, pushing the bottle toward Ransome. The Earthman ignored the gesture.

"Is the woman with him?"

Mytor smiled his feline smile. "You would like to see her blood run under the knives of the priests, no?"

"No."

Ransome meant it. Somewhere, in the years of flight, he had lost his love for the blonde, red-lipped Dura-ki, and with it had gone his bitter hatred and his desire for revenge.

He jerked his mind back to the present, to Mytor.

"And if I told you that it must be her life or yours?" Mytor was asking him.

Ransome's eyes widened. He sensed that Mytor's last question was not, an idle one. He leaned forward and asked:

"How do you fit into this at all, Mytor?"

"Easily. Once, ten years ago, you and the woman now aboard the *Hawk of Darion* blasphemed together against the Temple of the Dark One, in Darion."

"Go on," Ransome said.

"When you landed here this afternoon the avenging priests were not far behind you."

"How did you--"

"I have many contacts," Mytor purred. "I find them invaluable. But you are growing impatient, Mr. Ransome. I will be brief. I have contracted with the priests of Darion to deliver you to them tonight for a considerable sum."

"How did you know you would find me?"

"I was given your description." He made a gesture that took in all the occupants of the torch-lit room. "So many of the hunted, and the haunted, come here to forget for an hour the things that pursue them. I was expecting you, Mr. Ransome."

"If there is a large sum of money involved, I'm sure you'll make every effort to carry out your part of the bargain," Ransome observed ironically.

"I am a businessman, it is true. But in my dealings with the master of the *Hawk of Darion* I have seen the woman and I have heard stories. It occurred to me that the priests would pay much more for the woman than they would for you, and it seemed to me that a message from you might coax her off the ship. After all, when one has been in love--"

"That's enough." Ransome had risen to his feet. "I wonder if I could kill you before your guards got to me."

"Are you then so in love with death, Ransome?" The Venusian spoke quickly. "Don't be a fool. It is a small thing, a woman's life--a woman who has betrayed you."

Ransome stood silent, his arm halfway to his blaster. The woman had begun to dance again in the red glare of the torch.

"There will be other women," the Venusian was murmuring. "The woman who dances now, I will give her to you, to take with you in your new ship."

Ransome looked slowly from the glowing body of the woman to the guards around the walls, down into Mytor's confident face. His arm dropped away from the blaster.

"Any man--for a price." The Venusian's murmur was lost in the blare of the music. Ransome had eased his lean body back into the chair.

*   *   *   *   *

The night air was cold against Ransome's cheek when he went out an hour later, surrounded by Mytor's men. Yaroto's greenish moon was overhead now, but its pale light did not help him to see more clearly. It only made shadows in every doorway and twisting alley.

Mytor's car was only a few feet away but before he could reach it he was shoved aside by one of the Venusian's guards. At the same moment the night flamed with the blue-yellow glare from a dozen blasters. Ransome raised his own weapon, staring into the shadows, seeking his attackers.

"That's our job. Get in," said one of the guards, wrenching open the car door.

Then the firing was over as suddenly as it had begun. The guards clustered at the opening of an alley down the street. Mytor's driver sat impassively in the front seat.

When the guards returned one of them thrust something at Ransome, something hard and cold. He glanced at it. A long knife.

There was no need to read the inscription on the hilt. He knew it by heart.

"Death to him who defileth the Bed of the Dark One. Life to the Temple and City of Darion."

Once Ransome would have pocketed the knife as a kind of grim keepsake. Now he only let it fall to the floor.

In the brief, ghostly duel just over he had neither seen nor heard his attackers. That added, somehow, to the horror of the thing.

He shrugged off the thought, turning his mind to the details of the plan by which he would save his life.

It was quite simple. Ransome had been in space long enough to know where the crewmen went on a strange world. Half an hour later he sat with a gunner from the *Hawk of Darion*, in one of the gaudy pleasure houses clustered on the fringe of the city near the spaceport and the desert beyond.

"Will you take the note to the Captain's woman?"

The man squirmed, avoiding Ransome's ice-blue stare.

"Captain killed the last man who looked at his woman," the gunner muttered sullenly. "Flogged him to death."

"I'm not asking you to look at her," Ransome reminded him.

The gunner sat looking at the stack of Mytor's money piled on the table before him. A woman drifted over.

"Go away," Ransome said, without raising his eyes. He added another bill to the stack.

"Let me see the note before I take it," the gunner demanded.

"It would mean nothing to you." Ransome pushed a half-empty bottle toward the man, poured him out another drink.

The man's hands were trembling with inner conflict as he measured the killing lash against the stack of yellow Yarotian kiroons, and the pleasures it would buy him. He drank, dribbling a little of the wine down his grimy chin, and then returned to the subject of seeing the note, with drunken persistence.

"I got to see it first."

"It's in a language you wouldn't--"

"Let him see it," a new voice cut in. "Translate it for him, Mr. Ransome."

*   *   *   *   *

It was a woman's voice, cold and contemptuous. Ransome looked up quickly, and at first he didn't recognize her. The gunner never took his eyes from the stack of kiroons on the table.

"Let him see how a man murders a woman to save his own neck."

"You're supposed to be dancing at Mytor's place," Ransome said. "That's your business; this is mine."

He closed his hand over the gunner's wrist as the man reached convulsively for the money, menaced now by the angry woman.

"Half now, the rest later." Ransome's eyes burned into the crewman's. The latter looked away. Ransome tightened his grip, and pain contorted the gunner's features.

"Look at me," Ransome said. "If you cross me you'll wish you could die by flogging."

The woman Mytor had called Irene was still standing by the table when the gunner had left with the note and his money.

"Aren't you going to ask me to sit down?"

"Certainly. Sit down."

"I'd like a drink."

She sipped her wine in silence and Ransome studied her by the flickering light of the candle burning on the table between them.

She wore a simple street dress now, in contrast to the gaudy, revealing garments of the pleasure house women. The beauty of her soft, unpainted lips, her golden skin and wide-set green eyes was more striking now, seen at close range, than it had been in the smoky cavern of Mytor's place.

"What are you thinking now, Ransome?"

The question was unexpected, and Ransome answered without forethought: "The Temple."

"You studied for the priesthood of the Dark One yourself."

"Did Mytor tell you that?"

Irene nodded. The candlelight gave luster to her dark hair and revealed the contours of her high, firm breasts.

Ransome's pulse speeded up just looking at her. Then he saw that she was regarding him as if he were something crawling in damp stone, and there was bitterness in him.

"There are things that even Mytor doesn't know, even omniscient Mytor--"

He checked himself.

"Well?"

"Nothing."

"You were going to tell me about how you are really a very honorable man. Why don't you? You have an hour before it will be time to betray the woman from the *Hawk of Darion*."

Ransome shrugged, and his voice returned her mockery.

"If I told you that I had been an acolyte in the Temple of the Dark One, and that I was condemned to death for blasphemy, committed for love of a woman, would you like me better?"

"I might."

"Ten years ago," Ransome said. He talked, and the mighty walls of the Temple reared themselves around his mind, and the music of the pleasure house became the chanting of the priests at the high altar.

*   *   *   *   *

He stood at the rear of the great Temple, and he had the tonsure and the black robes, and his name was not Ransome, but Ra-sed.

He had almost forgotten his Terran name. Forgotten, too, were his parents, and the laboratory ship that had been his home until the crash landing that had left him an orphan and Ward of the Temple.

Red candles burned before the high altar, but terror began just beyond their flickering light. It was dark where Ra-sed stood, and he could hear the cries of the people in the courtyard outside, and feel the trembling of the pillars, the very pillars of the Temple, and the groaning of stone on massive stone in the great, shadowed arches overhead. Above all, the chanting before the altar of the Dark One, rising, rising toward hysteria.

And then, like a knife in the darkness, the scream, and the straining to see which of the maidens the sacred lots cast before the altar had chosen; and the sudden, sick knowledge that it was Dura-ki. Dura-ki, of the soft golden hair and bright lips.

In stunned silence, Ra-sed, acolyte, listened to the bridal chant of the priests; the ancient words of the Dedication to the Dark One.

The chant told of the forty times forty flights of onyx steps leading downward behind the great altar to the dwelling place of the Dark One and of the forty terrible beasts couched in the pit to guard His slumber.

In the beginning, Dalir, the Sire, God of the Mists, had gone down wrapped in a sea fog, and had stolen the Sacred Fire while the Dark One slept. All life in Darion had come from Dalir's mystic union with the Sacred Fire.

Centuries passed before a winter of bitter frosts came, and the Dark One awakened cold in His dwelling place and found the Sacred Fire stolen. His wrath moved beneath the city then, and Darion crashed in shattered ruin and death.

Those who were left had hurled a maiden screaming into the greatest of the clefts in the earth, that the bed of the Idol might be warmed by an ember of the stolen Fire. Later, they had raised His awful Temple on the spot.

So it had been, almost from the beginning. When the pillars of the Temple shook, a maiden was chosen by the Sacred Lots to go down as a bride to the Dark One, lest He destroy the city and the people.

The chant had come to an end. The legend had been told once more.

They led her forth then--Dura-ki, the chosen one. Shod in golden sandals, and wearing the crimson robe of the ritual, she moved out of Ra-sed's sight, behind the high altar. No acolyte was permitted to approach that place.

The chanting was a thing of wild delirium now, and Ra-set placed a cold hand to steady himself against a trembling pillar. He heard the drawing of the ancient bolts, the booming echo as the great stone was drawn aside, and he closed his eyes, as though that could shut out the vision of the monstrous pit.

But his ears he could not close, and he heard the scream of Dura-ki, his own betrothed, as they threw her to the Idol.

*   *   *   *   *

At the table in the Yarotian pleasure house, Ransome's thin lips were pale. He swallowed his drink.

The woman opposite him was nearly forgotten now, and when he went on, it was for himself, to rid himself of things that had haunted him down all the bleak worlds to his final night of betrayal and death. His eyes were empty, fixed on another life. He did not see the change that crossed Irene's face, did not see the cold contempt fade away, to be replaced slowly with understanding. She leaned forward, lips slightly parted, to hear the end of his story.

For the love of golden-haired Dura-ki, the acolyte, Ra-sed, had gone down into the pit of the Dark one, where no mortal had gone before, except as a sacrifice.

He had hidden himself in the gloom of the pillars when the others left in chanting procession after the ceremony. Now he was wrenching at the rusted bolts that held the stone in place. It seemed to him that the rumbling grew in the earth beneath his feet and in the blackness of the vaulting overhead. Terror was in him, for his blasphemy would bring death to Darion. But the vision of Dura-ki was in him too, giving strength to tortured muscles. The bolts came away with a metallic screech, piercing against the mutter of shifting stone.

He was turning to the heavy ring set in the stone when he caught a glimmer of reflected light in an idol's eye. Swiftly he crouched behind the great stone, waiting.

The priests came, two of them, bearing torches. Knives flashed as Ra-sed sprang, but he wrenched the blade from the hand of the first, buried it in the throat of the second. The man fell with a cry, but a stunning blow from behind sent Ra-sed sprawling across the fallen body. The other priest was on him, choking out his life.

The last torch fell; and Ra-sed twisted savagely, lashed out blindly with the long knife. There was a sound of rending cloth, a muttered curse in the darkness, and the fingers ground harder into Ra-sed's throat. Black tides washed over his mind, and he never remembered the second and last convulsive thrust of the knife that let out the life of the priest.

He did remember straining against the ring of the great stone. The echo boomed out for the second time that night, as the stone moved away at last, to lay bare the realm of the Dark One.

Bitterness touched Ransome's eyes as he spoke now, the bitterness of a man who has lost his God.

"There were no onyx steps, no monsters waiting beneath the stone. The legends were false."

Ransome turned his glass slowly, staring into its amber depths. Then he became aware of Irene, waiting for him to go on.

"I got her out," Ransome said shortly. "I went down into that stinking pit and I got Dura-ki out. The air was nearly unbreathable where I found her. She was unconscious on a ledge at the end of a long slope. Hell itself might have been in the pit that opened beneath it. A geologist would have called it a major fault, but it was hell enough. When I picked her up, I found the bones of all those others...."

Irene's green eyes had lost their coldness. She let her hand rest on his for a moment. But her voice was puzzled.

"This Dura-ki--she is the woman on the *Hawk of Darion?*"

Ransome nodded. He stood up. His lips were a hard, thin line.

"My little story has an epilogue. Something not quite so romantic. I lived with Dura-ki in hiding near Darion for a year, until a ship came in from space. A pirate ship, with a tall, good-looking Earthman for a master. I took passage for Dura-ki, and signed on myself as a crewman. A fresh start in a bright, new world." Ransome laughed shortly. "I'll spare you the details of that happy voyage. At the first port of call, on Jupiter, Dura-ki stood at the top of the gangway and laughed when her Captain Jareth had me thrown off the ship."

"She betrayed you for the master of the *Hawk of Darion*," Irene said softly.

"And tonight she'll pay," Ransome finished coldly. He threw down a few coins to pay for their drinks. "It's been pleasant telling you my pretty little story."

"Ransome, wait. I--"

"Forget it," Ransome said.

*   *   *   *   *

Mytor's car was waiting, and Ransome could sense the presence of the guards lurking in the dark, empty street.

"The spaceport," Ransome told his driver. "Fast."

He thought of the note he had given the crewman to deliver:

"Ra-sed would see his beloved a last time before he dies."

"Faster," Ransome grated, and the powerful car leapt forward into the night.

*   *   *   *   *

Ships, like the men who drove them, came to Yaroto to die. Three quarters of the spaceport was a vast jungle of looming black shapes, most of them awaiting the breaker's hammer. Ransome dismissed the car and threaded his way through the deserted yards with the certainty of a man used to the ugly places of a hundred worlds.

Mytor had suggested the meeting place, a hulk larger than most, a cruiser once in the fleet of some forgotten power.

Ransome had fought in the ships of half a dozen worlds. Now the ancient cruiser claimed his attention. Martian, by the cut of her rusted braking fins. Ransome tensed, remembering the charge of the Martian cruisers in the Battle of Phoebus. Since then he had called himself an Earthman, because, even if his parentage had not given him claim to that title already, a man who had been in the Earth ships at Phoebus had a right to it.

He was running a hand over the battered plate of a blast tube when Dura-ki found him. She was a smaller shadow moving among the vast, dark hulls. With a curious, dead feeling in him, Ransome stepped away from the side of the cruiser to meet her.

"Ra-sed, I could not let you die alone--"

Because her voice was a ghost from the past, because it stirred things in him that had no right to live after all the long years that had passed, Ransome acted before Dura-ki could finish speaking. He hit her once, hard; caught the crumpling body in his arms, and started back toward Mytor's car. If he remembered another journey in the blackness with this woman in his arms, he drove the memory back with the savage blasphemies of a hundred worlds.

*   *   *   *   *

On the rough floor of Mytor's place, Dura-ki stirred and groaned.

Ransome didn't like the way things were going. He hadn't planned to return to the Cafe Yaroto, to wait with Mytor for the arrival of the priests.

"There are a couple of my men outside," Mytor told him. "When the priests are spotted you can slip out through the rear exit."

"Why the devil do I have to be here now?"

"As I have told you, I am a businessman. Until I have turned the girl over to the priests I cannot be sure of my payment. This girl, as you know, is not without friends. If Captain Jareth knew that she was here he would tear this place apart, he and his crew. Those men have rather an impressive reputation as fighters, and while my guard here--"

"You've been drinking too much of your own rotten liquor, Mytor. Why should I try to save her at the eleventh hour? To hand her back to her lover?"

"I never drink my own liquor, Mr. Ransome." He took a sip of his kali in confirmation. "I have seen love take many curious shapes."

Ransome stood up. "Save your memoirs. I want a guard to get me to the ship you promised me. And I want it now."

Mytor did not move. The guards, ranged around the walls, stood silent but alert.

"Mytor."

"Yes, Mr. Ransome?"

"There isn't any ship. There never was."

The Venusian shrugged. "It would have been easier for you if you hadn't guessed. I'm really sorry."

"So you'll make a double profit on this deal. I was the bait for Dura-ki, and Irene was bait for me. You are a good businessman, Mytor."

"You are taking this rather better than I had expected, Mr. Ransome."

Ransome slumped down into his chair again. He felt no fear, no emotion at all. Somewhere, deep inside, he had known from the beginning that there would be no more running away after tonight, that the priests would have their will with him. Perhaps he had been too tired to care. And there had been Irene, planted by Mytor to fill his eyes, to make him careless and distracted.

He wondered if Irene had known of her role, or had been an unconscious tool, like himself. With faint surprise, he found himself hoping that she had not acted against him intentionally.

*   *   *   *   *

Dura-ki was unconscious when the priests came. She had looked at Ransome only once, and he had stared down at his hands.

Now she stood quietly between two of the black-robed figures, watching as others counted out gold coins into Mytor's grasping palm. Her eyes betrayed neither hope nor fear, and she did not shrink from the burning, fanatical stares of the priests, nor from their long knives. The pirate's consort was not the girl who had screamed in the dimness of the Temple when the Sacred Lots were cast.

A priest touched Ransome's shoulder and he started in spite of himself. He tried to steady himself against the sudden chill that seized him.

And then Dura-ki, who had called him once to blasphemy, now called him to something else.

"Stand up, Ra-sed. It is the end. The game is played out and we lose at last. It will not be worse than the pit of the Dark One."

Ransome got to his feet and looked at her. He no longer loved this woman but her quiet courage stirred him.

With an incredibly swift lunge he was on the priest who stood nearest Dura-ki. The man reeled backward and struck his skull against the wall. It was a satisfying sound, and Ransome smiled tightly, a half-forgotten oath of Darion on his lips.

He grabbed the man by the throat, spun him around, and sent him crashing into another.

A knife slashed at him, and he broke the arm that held it, then sprang for the door while the world exploded in blaster fire.

Dura-ki moved toward him. He wrenched at the door, felt the cold night air rash in. A hand clawed at the girl's shoulder, but Ransome freed her with a hard, well-aimed blow.

When she was outside, Ransome fought to give her time to get back to the *Hawk of Darion*. Also, he fought for the sheer joy of it. The air in his lungs was fresh again, and the taste of treachery was out of his mouth.

It took all of Mytor's guards and the priests to overpower him, but they were too late to save Mytor from the knife that left him gasping out his life on the floor.

Ransome did not struggle in the grip of the guards. He stood quietly, waiting.

"Your death will not be made prettier by what you have done," a priest told him. The knife was poised.

"That depends on how you look at it," Ransome answered.

"Does it?"

"Absolutely," a hard, dry voice answered from the doorway.

Ransome turned his head and had a glimpse of Irene. With her, a blaster level in his hand, and his crew at his back, was Captain Jareth. It was he who had answered the priest's last question.

Mytor had said that Jareth's crew had an impressive reputation as fighters, and he lived just long enough to see the truth of his words. The priests and the guards went down before the furious attack of the men from the *Hawk of Darion*. Ransome fought as one of them.

When it was over, it was not to Captain Jareth that he spoke, but to Irene.

"Why did you do this? You didn't know Dura-ki, and you despised me."

"At first I did. That's why I agreed to Mytor's plan. But when I had spoken to you, I felt differently. I--"

Jareth came over then, holstering his blaster. Irene fell silent.

The big spaceman shifted uneasily, then spoke to Ransome.

"I found Dura-ki near here. She told me what you did."

Ransome shrugged.

"I sent her back to the ship with a couple of my men."

Abruptly, Jareth turned and stooped over the still form of Mytor. From the folds of the Venusian's stained tarab he drew a ring of keys. He tossed them to Ransome.

"This will be the first promise that Mytor ever kept."

"What do you mean?"

"Those are the keys to his private ship. I'll see that you get to it."

It was Irene who spoke then. "That wasn't all that Mytor promised him."

The two men looked at her in surprise. Then Ransome understood.

"Will you come with me, Irene?" he asked her.

"Where?" Her eyes were shining, and she looked very young.

Ransome smiled at her. "The Galaxy is full of worlds. And even the Dark One cancels his debts when the night of Bani-tai is over."

"Let's go and look at some of those worlds," Irene said.

THE SOUND OF SILENCE
BY BARBARA CONSTANT

ORIGINALLY PUBLISHED IN *ANALOG*
JUNE 1962

Editor's Notes:
The Sound of Silence
By Barbara Constant

Psychic powers were a frequent subject in science fiction stories of the time. The experiments by the Rhine Institute seemed to give some credibility to the possibility of such powers as telepathy, clairvoyance and telekinesis existing, and science fiction authors were quick to exploit the concept as a plot device. "The Sound of Silence" explores the effect such powers might have on the life of a young woman. Constant was not alone in concluding that such powers might well be a mixed blessing.

The only available information on the author is that she had two stories published, "Ugly Duckling" (1955) and "The Sound of Silence" (1962).

The Sound of Silence

Most people, when asked to define the ultimate in loneliness, say it's being alone in a crowd. And it takes only one slight difference to make one forever alone in the crowd....

*   *   *   *   *

Nobody at Hoskins, Haskell & Chapman, Incorporated, knew jut why Lucilla Brown, G.G. Hoskins' secretary, came to work half an hour early every Monday, Wednesday, and Friday. Even G.G. himself, had he been asked, would have had trouble explaining how his occasional exasperated wish that just once somebody would reach the office ahead of him could have caused his attractive young secretary to start doing so three times a week ... or kept her at it all the months since that first gloomy March day. Nobody asked G.G. however--not even Paul Chapman, the very junior partner in the advertising firm, who had displayed more than a little interest in Lucilla all fall and winter, but very little interest in anything all spring and summer. Nobody asked Lucilla why she left early on the days she arrived early--after all, eight hours is long enough. And certainly nobody knew where Lucilla went at 4:30 on those three days--nor would anybody in the office have believed it, had he known.

"Lucky Brown? seeing a psychiatrist?" The typist would have giggled, the office boy would have snorted, and every salesman on the force would have guffawed. Even Paul Chapman might have managed a wry smile. A real laugh had been beyond him for several months--ever since he asked Lucilla confidently, "Will you marry me?" and she answered, "I'm sorry, Paul--thanks, but no thanks."

Not that seeing a psychiatrist was anything to laugh at, in itself. After all, the year was 1962, and there were almost as many serious articles about mental health as there were cartoons about psychoanalysts, even in the magazines that specialized in poking fun. In certain cities--including Los Angeles--and certain industries--especially advertising--"I have an appointment with my psychiatrist" was a perfectly acceptable excuse for leaving work early. The idea of a secretary employed by almost the largest advertising firm in one of the best-known suburbs in the sprawling City of the Angels doing so should not, therefore, have seemed particularly odd. Not would it have, if the person involved had been anyone at all except Lucilla Brown.

The idea that she might need aid of any kind, particularly psychiatric, was ridiculous. She had been born twenty-two years earlier in undisputed possession of a sizable silver spoon--and she was, in addition, bright, beautiful, and charming, with 20/20 vision, perfect teeth, a father and mother who adored her, friends who did likewise ... and the kind of luck you'd have to see to believe. Other people entered contests--Lucilla won them. Other people drove five miles over the legal speed limit and got caught doing it--Lucilla out-distanced them, but fortuitously slowed down just before the highway patrol appeared from nowhere. Other people waited in the wrong line at the bank while the woman ahead of them learned how to roll pennies-- Lucilla was always in the line that moved right up to the teller's window.

"Lucky" was not, in other words, just a happenstance abbreviation of "Lucilla"--it was an exceedingly apt nickname. And Lucky Brown's co-workers would have been quite justified in laughing at the very idea of her being unhappy enough about anything to spend three precious hours a week stretched out on a brown leather couch staring miserably at a pale blue ceiling and fumbling for words that refused to come. There were a good many days when Lucilla felt like laughing at the idea herself. And there were other days when she didn't even feel like smiling.

Wednesday, the 25th of July, was one of the days when she didn't feel like smiling. Or talking. Or moving. It had started out badly when she opened her eyes and found herself staring at a familiar blue ceiling. "I don't know," she said irritably. "I tell you, I simply don't know what happens. I'll start to answer someone and the words will be right on the tip of my tongue, ready to be spoken, then I'll say something altogether different. Or I'll start to cross the street and, for no reason at all, be unable to even step off the curb...."

"For no reason at all?" Dr. Andrews asked. "Are you sure you aren't withholding something you ought to tell me?"

She shifted a little, suddenly uncomfortable ... and then she was fully awake and the ceiling was ivory, not blue. She stared at it for a long moment, completely disoriented, before she realized that she was in her own bed, not on Dr. Andrews' brown leather couch, and that the conversation had been another of the interminable imaginary dialogues she found herself carrying on with the psychiatrist, day and night, awake and asleep.

"Get out of my dreams," she ordered crossly, summoning up a quick mental picture of Dr. Andrews' expressive face, level gray eyes, and silvering temples, the better to banish him from her thoughts. She was immediately sorry she had done so, for the image remained fixed in her mind; she could almost feel his eyes as she heard his voice ask again, "For no reason at all, Lucilla?"

*   *   *   *   *

The weatherman had promised a scorcher, and the heat that already lay like a blanket over the room made it seem probable the promise would be fulfilled. She moved listlessly, showering patting herself dry, lingering over the choice of a dress until her mother called urgently from the kitchen.

She was long minutes behind schedule when she left the house. Usually she rather enjoyed easing her small car into the stream of automobiles pouring down Sepulveda toward the San Diego Freeway, jockeying for position, shifting expertly from one lane to another to take advantage of every break in the traffic. This morning she felt only angry impatience; she choked back on the irritated impulse to drive directly into the side of a car that cut across in front of her, held her horn button down furiously when a slow-starting truck hesitated fractionally after the light turned green.

When she finally edged her Renault up on the "on" ramp and the freeway stretched straight and unobstructed ahead, she stepped down on the accelerator and watched the needle climb up and past the legal 65-mile limit. The sound of her tires on the smooth concrete was soothing and the rush of wind outside gave the morning an illusion of coolness. She edged away from the tangle of cars that had pulled onto the freeway with her and momentarily was alone on the road, with her rear-view mirror blank, the oncoming lanes bare, and a small rise shutting off the world ahead.

That was when it happened. "Get out of the way!" a voice shrieked "out of the way, out of the way, OUT OF THE WAY!" Her heart lurched, her stomach twisted convulsively, and there was a brassy taste in her mouth. Instinctively, she stamped down on the brake pedal, swerved sharply into the outer lane. By the time she had topped the rise, she was going a cautious 50 miles an hour and hugging the far edge of the freeway. Then, and only then, she heard the squeal of agonized tires and saw the cumbersome semitrailer coming from the opposite direction rock dangerously, jackknife into the dividing posts that separated north and south-bound traffic, crunch ponderously through them, and crash to a stop, several hundred feet ahead of her and squarely athwart the lane down which she had been speeding only seconds earlier.

The highway patrol materialized within minutes. Even so, it was after eight by the time Lucilla gave them her statement, agreed for the umpteenth time with the shaken but uninjured truck driver that it was indeed fortunate she hadn't been in the center lane, and drove slowly the remaining miles to the office. The gray mood of early morning had changed to black. Now there were two voices in her mind, competing for attention. "I knew it was going to happen," the truck driver said, "I couldn't see over the top of that hill. All I could do was fight the wheel and pray that if anybody was coming, he'd get out of the way." She could almost hear him repeating the words, "Get out of the way, out of the way...." And right on the heel of his cry came Dr. Andrews' soft query, "For no reason at all, Lucilla?"

She pulled into the company parking lot, jerked the wheel savagely to the left, jammed on the brakes. "Shut up!" she said. "Shut up, both of you!" She started into the building, then hesitated. She was already late, but there was something.... (Get out of the way, the way.... For no reason at all, at all....) She yielded to impulse and walked hurriedly downstairs to the basement library.

"That stuff I asked you to get together for me by tomorrow, Ruthie," she said to the gray-haired librarian. "You wouldn't by any chance have already done it, would you?"

"Funny you should ask." The elderly woman bobbed down behind the counter and popped back up with an armload of magazines and newspapers. "Just happened to have some free time last thing yesterday. It's already charged out to you, so you just go right ahead and take it, dearie."

*   *   *   *   *

It was 8:30 when Lucilla reached the office.

"When I need you, where are you?" G.G. asked sourly. "Learned last night that the top dog at Karry Karton Korporation is in town today, so they've pushed that conference up from Friday to ten this morning. If you'd been here early--or even on time--we might at least have gotten some of the information together."

Lucilla laid the stack of material on his desk. "I haven't had time to flag the pages yet," she said, "but they're listed on the library request on top. We did nineteen ads for KK last year and three of premium offers. I stopped by Sales on my way in-- Susie's digging out figures for you now."

"Hm-m-m," said G.G. "Well. So that's where you've been. You could at least have let me know." There was grudging approval beneath his gruffness. "Say, how'd you know I needed this today, anyhow?"

"Didn't," said Lucilla, putting her purse away and whisking the cover off her typewriter. "Happenstance, that's all." (Just happened to go down to the library ... for no reason at all ... withholding something ... get out of the way....) The telephone's demand for attention overrode her thoughts. She reached for it almost gratefully. "Mr. Hoskins' office," she said. "Yes. Yes, he knows about the ten o'clock meeting this morning. Thanks for calling, anyway." She hung up and glanced at G.G., but he was so immersed in one of the magazines that the ringing telephone hadn't even disturbed him. Ringing? The last thing she did before she left the office each night was set the lever in the instrument's base to "off," so that the bell would not disturb G.G. if he worked late. So far today, nobody had set it back to "on."

*   *   *   *   *

"It's getting worse," she said miserably to the pale blue ceiling. "The phone didn't ring this morning--it couldn't have--but I answered it." Dr. Andrews said nothing at all. She let her eyes flicker sidewise, but he was outside her range of vision. "I don't LIKE having you sit where I can't see you," she said crossly. "Freud may have thought it was a good idea, but I think it's a lousy one." She clenched her hands and stared at nothing. The silence stretched thinner and thinner, like a balloon blown big, until the temptation to rupture it was too great to resist. "I didn't see the truck this morning. Nor hear it. There was no reason at all for me to slow down and pull over."

"You might be dead if you hadn't. Would you like that better?"

The matter-of-fact question was like a hand laid across Lucilla's mouth. "I don't want to be dead," she admitted finally. "Neither do I want to go on like this, hearing words that aren't spoken and bells that don't ring. When it gets to the point that I pick up a phone just because somebody's thinking...." She stopped abruptly.

"I didn't quite catch the end of that sentence," Dr. Andrews said.

"I didn't quite finish it. I can't."

"Can't? Or won't? Don't hold anything back, Lucilla. You were saying that you picked up the phone just because somebody was thinking...." He paused expectantly. Lucilla reread the ornate letters on the framed diploma on the wall, looked critically at the picture of Mrs. Andrews--whom she'd met--and her impish daughter--whom she hadn't--counted the number of pleats in the billowing drapes, ran a tentative finger over the face of her wristwatch, straightened a fold of her skirt ... and could stand the silence no longer.

"All right," she said wearily. "The girl at Karry Karton thought about talking to me, and I heard my phone ring, even though the bell was disconnected. G.G. thought about needing backup material for the conference and I went to the library. The truck driver thought about warning people and I got out of his way. So I can read people's minds--some people's minds, some of the time, anyway ... only there's no such thing as telepathy. And if I'm not telepathic, then...." She caught herself in the brink of time and bit back the final word, fighting for self-control.

"Then what?" The peremptory question toppled Lucilla's defenses.

"I'm crazy," she said. Speaking the word released all the others dammed up behind it. "Ever since I can remember, things like this have happened--all at once, in the middle of doing something or saying something, I'd find myself thinking about what somebody else was doing or saying. Not thinking--knowing. I'd be playing hide-and-seek, and I could see the places where the other kids were hiding just as plainly as I could see my own surroundings. Or I'd be worrying over the answers to an exam question, and I'd know what somebody in the back of the room had decided to write down, or what the teacher was expecting us

to write. Not always--but it happened often enough so that it bothered me, just the way it does now when I answer a question before it's been asked, or know what the driver ahead of me is going to do a split second before he does it, or win a bridge game because I can see everybody else's hand through his own eyes, almost."

"Has it always ... bothered you, Lucilla?"

"No-o-o-o." She drew the word out, considering, trying to think when it was that she hadn't felt uneasy about the unexpected moments of perceptiveness. When she was very little, perhaps. She thought of the tiny, laughing girl in the faded snaps of the old album--and suddenly, inexplicably, she was that self, moving through remembered rooms, pausing to collect a word from a boyish father, a thought from a pretty young mother. Reluctantly, she closed her eyes against that distant time. "Way back," she said, "when I didn't know any better, I just took it for granted that sometimes people talked to each other and that sometimes they passed thoughts along without putting them into words. I was about six, I guess, when I found out it wasn't so." She slipped into her six-year-old self as easily as she had donned the younger Lucilla. This time she wasn't in a house, but high on a hillside, walking on springy pine needles instead of prosaic carpet.

"Talk," Dr. Andrews reminded her, his voice so soft that it could almost have come from inside her own mind.

"We were picnicking," she said. "A whole lot of us. Somehow, I wandered away from the others...." One minute the hill was bright with sun, and the next it was deep in shadows and the wind that had been merely cool was downright cold. She shivered and glanced around expecting her mother to be somewhere near, holding out a sweater or jacket. There was no one at all in sight. Even then, she never thought of being frightened. She turned to retrace her steps. There was a big tree that looked familiar, and a funny rock behind it, half buried in the hillside. She was trudging toward it, humming under her breath, when the worry thoughts began to reach her. (... only a little creek so I don't think she could have fallen in ... not really any bears around here ... but she never gets hurt ... creek ... bear ... twisted ankle ... dark ... cold....) She had veered from her course and started in the direction of the first thought, but now they were coming from all sides and she had no idea at all which way to go. She ran wildly then, first one way, then the other, sobbing and calling.

"Lucilla!" The voice sliced into the night, and the dark mountainside and the frightened child were gone. She shuddered a little, reminiscently, and put her hand over her eyes.

"Somebody found me, of course. And then Mother was holding me and crying and I was crying, too, and telling her how all the different thought at once frightened me and mixed me up. She ... she scolded me for ... for telling fibs ... and said that nobody except crazy people thought they could read each other's minds."

"I see," said Dr. Andrews, "So you tried not to, of course. And anytime you did it again, or thought you did, you blamed it on coincidence. Or luck."

"And had that nightmare again."

"Yes, that, too. Tell me about it."

"I already have. Over and over."

"Tell me again, then."

"I feel like a fool, repeating myself," she complained. Dr. Andrew's made no comment. "Oh, all right. It always starts with me walking down a crowded street, surrounded by honking cars and yelling newsboys and talking people. The noise bothers me and I'm tempted to cover my ears to shut it out, but I try to ignore it, instead, and walk faster and faster. Bit by bit, the buildings I pass are smaller, the people fewer, the noise less. All at once, I discover there's nothing around at all but a spreading carpet of gray-green moss, years deep, and a silence that feels as old as time itself. There's nothing to frighten me, but I am frightened ... and lonesome, not so much for people, but for a sound ... any sound. I turn to run back toward town, but there's nothing behind me now but the same gray moss and gray sky and dead silence."

*　　*　　*　　*　　*

By the time she reached the last word, her throat had tightened until speaking was difficult. She reached out blindly for something to cling to. Her groping hand met Dr. Andrews' and his warm fingers closed reassuringly around hers. Gradually the panic drained away, but she could think of nothing to say at all, although she longed to have the silence broken. As if he sensed her longing, Dr. Andrews said, "You started having the dream more often just after you told Paul you wouldn't marry him, is that right?"

"No. It was the other way around. I hadn't had it for months, not since I fell in love with him, then he got assigned to that "Which Tomorrow?" show and he started calling me "Lucky," the way everybody does, and the dream came back...." She stopped short, and turned on the couch to stare at the psychiatrist with startled eyes. "But that can't be how it was," she said. "The lonesomeness must have started after I decided not to marry him, not before."

"I wonder why the dream stopped when you fell in love with him."

"That's easy," Lucilla said promptly, grasping at the chance to evade her own more disturbing question. "I felt close to him, whether he was with me or not, the way I used to feel close to people back when I was a little girl, before ... well, before that day in the mountains ... when Mother said...."

"That was when you started having the dream, wasn't it?"

"How'd you know? I didn't--not until just now. But, yes, that's when it started. I'd never minded the dark or being alone, but I was frightened when Mother shut the door that night, because the walls seemed so ... so solid, now that I knew all the thoughts I used to think were with me there were just pretend. When I finally went to sleep, I dreamed, and I went on having the same dream, night after night after night, until finally they called a doctor and he gave me something to make me sleep."

"I wish they'd called me," Dr. Andrews said.

"What could you have done? The sleeping pills worked, anyway, and after a while I didn't need them any more, because I'd heard other kids talking about having hunches and lucky streaks and I stopped feeling different from the rest of them, except once in a while, when I was so lucky it ... bothered me."

"And after you met Paul, you stopped being ... too lucky ... and the dream stopped?"

"No!" Lucilla was startled at her own vehemence. "No, it wasn't like that at all, and you'd know it, if you'd been listening. With Paul, I felt close to him all the time, no matter how many miles or walls or anything else there were between us. We hardly had to talk at all, because we seemed to know just what the other one was thinking all the time, listening to music, or watching the waves pound in or just working together at the office. Instead of feeling ... odd ... when I knew what he was thinking or what he was going to say, I felt good about it, because I was so sure it was the same way with him and what I was thinking. We didn't talk about it. There just wasn't any need to." She lapsed into silence again. Dr. Andrews straightened her clenched hand out and stroked the fingers gently. After a moment, she went on.

"He hadn't asked me to marry him, but I knew he would, and there wasn't any hurry, because everything was so perfect, anyway. Then one of the company's clients decided to sponsor a series of fantasy shows on TV and wanted us to tie in the ads for next year with the fantasy theme. Paul was assigned to the account, and G.G. let him borrow me to work on it, because it was such a rush project. I'd always liked fairy stories when I was little and when I discovered there were grown-up ones, too, like those in *Unknown Worlds* and the old *Weird Tales*, I read them, too. But I hadn't any idea how much there was, until we started buying copies of everything there was on the news-stands, and then ransacking musty little stores for back issues and ones that had gone out of publication, until Paul's office was just full of teetery piles of gaudy magazines and everywhere you looked there were pictures of strange stars and eight-legged monsters and men in space suits."

"So what do the magazines have to do with you and Paul?"

"The way he felt about them changed everything. He just laughed at the ones about space ships and other planets and robots and things, but he didn't laugh when came across stories about ... well, mutants, and people with talents...."

"Talents? Like reading minds, you mean?"

She nodded, not looking at him. "He didn't laugh at those. He acted as if they were ... well, indecent. The sort of thing you wouldn't be caught dead reading in public. And he thought that way, too, especially about the stories that even mentioned telepathy. At first, when he brought them to my attention in that disapproving way, I thought he was just pretending to sneer, to tease me, because he--we--knew they could be true. Only his thoughts matched his remarks. He hated the stories, Dr. Andrews, and was just determined to have me hate them, too. All at once I began to feel as if I didn't know him at all and I began to wonder if I'd just imagined everything all those months I felt so close to him. And then I began to dream again, and to think about that lonesome silent world even when I was wide awake."

"Go on, Lucilla," Dr. Andrews said, as she hesitated.

"That's all, just about. We finished the job and got rid of the magazines and for a little while it was almost as if those two weeks had never been, except I couldn't forget that he didn't know what I was thinking at all, even when everything he did, almost, made it seem as if he did. It began to seem wrong for me to know what he was thinking. Crazy, like Mother had said, and worse, somehow. Not well, not even nice, if you know what I mean."

"Then he asked you to marry him."

"And I said no, even when I wanted, oh, so terribly, to say yes and yes and yes." She squeezed her eyes tight shut to hold back a rush of tears.

*   *   *   *   *

Time folded back on itself. Once again, the hands of her wristwatch pointed to 4:30 and the white-clad receptionist said briskly, "Doctor will see you now." Once again, from some remote vantage point, Lucilla watched herself brush past Dr. Andrews and cross to the familiar couch, heard herself say, "It's getting worse," watched herself move through a flickering montage of scenes from childhood to womanhood, from past to present.

She opened he eyes to meet those of the man who sat patiently beside her. "You see," he said, "telling me wasn't so difficult, after all." And then, before she had decided on a response, "What do you know about Darwin's theory of evolution, Lucilla?"

His habit of ending a tense moment by making an irrelevant query no longer even startled her. Obediently, she fumbled for an answer. "Not much. Just that he thought all the different kinds of life on earth today evolved from a few blobs of protoplasm that sprouted wings or grew fur or developed teeth, depending on when they lived, and where." She paused hopefully, but met with only silence. "Sometimes what seemed like a step forward wasn't," she said, ransacking her brain for scattered bits of information. "Then the species died out, like the saber-tooth tiger, with those tusks that kept right on growing until they locked his jaws shut, so he starved to death." As she spoke, she remembered the huge beast as he had been pictured in one of her college textbooks. The recollection grew more and more vivid, until she could see both the picture and the facing page of text. There was an irregularly shaped inkblot in the upper corner and several heavily underlined sentences that stood out so distinctly she could actually read the words. "According to Darwin, variations in general are not infinitesimal, but in the nature of specific mutations. Thousands of these occur, but only the fittest survive the climate, the times, natural enemies, and their own kind, who strive to perpetuate themselves unchanged." Taken one by one, the words were all familiar--taken as a whole, they made no sense at all. She let the book slip unheeded from her mind and stared at Dr. Andrews in bewilderment.

"Try saying it in a different way."

"You sound like a school teacher humoring a stupid child." And then, because of the habit of obedience was strong, "I guess he meant that tails didn't grow an inch at a time, the way the dog's got cut off, but all at once ... like a fish being born with legs as well as fins, or a baby saber-tooth showing up among tigers with regular teeth, or one ape in a tribe discovering he could swing down out of the treetops and stand erect and walk alone."

He echoed her last words. "And walk alone...." A premonitory chill traced its icy way down Lucilla's backbone. For a second she stood on gray moss, under a gray sky, in the midst of a gray silence. "He not only could walk alone, he had to. Do you remember what your book said?"

"Only the fittest survive," Lucilla said numbly. "Because they have to fight the climate ... and their natural enemies ... and their own kind." She swung her feet to the floor and pushed herself into a sitting position. "I'm not a ... a mutation. I'm not, I'm not, I'm NOT, and you can't say I am, because I won't listen!"

"I didn't say you were." There was the barest hint of emphasis on the first word. Lucilla was almost certain she heard a whisper of laughter, but he met her gaze blandly, his expression completely serious.

"Don't you dare laugh!" she said, nonetheless. "There's nothing funny about ... about...."

"About being able to read people's minds," Dr Andrews said helpfully. "You'd much rather have me offer some other explanation for the occurrences that bother you so--is that it?"

"I guess so. Yes, it is. A brain tumor. Or schizophrenia. Or anything at all that could maybe be cured, so I could marry Paul and have children and be like everybody else. Like you." She looked past him to the picture on his desk. "It's easy for you to talk."

He ignored the last statement. "Why can't you get married, anyway?"

"You've already said why. Because Paul would hate me--everybody would hate me--if they knew I was different."

"How would they know? It doesn't show. Now if you had three legs, or a long bushy tail, or outsized teeth...."

Lucilla smiled involuntarily, and then was furious at herself for doing so and at Dr Andrews for provoking her into it. "This whole thing is utterly asinine, anyhow. Here we are, talking as if I might really be a mutant, and you know perfectly well that I'm not."

"Do I? You made the diagnosis, Lucilla, and you've given me some mighty potent reasons for believing it ... can you give me equally good reasons for doubting that you're a telepath?"

*   *   *   *   *

The peremptory demand left Lucilla speechless for a moment. She groped blindly for an answer, then almost laughed aloud as she found it.

"But of course. I almost missed it, even after you practically drew me a diagram. If I could read minds, just as soon as anybody found it out, he'd be afraid of me, or hate me, like the book said, and you said, too. If you believed it, you'd do something like having me locked up in a hospital, maybe, instead of...."

"Instead of what, Lucilla?"

"Instead of being patient, and nice, and helping me see how silly I've been." She reached out impulsively to touch his hand, then withdrew her own, feeling somewhat foolish when he made no move to respond. Her relief was too great, however, to be contained in silence. "Way back the first time I came in, almost, you said that before we finished therapy, you'd know me better than I knew myself. I didn't believe you--maybe I didn't want to--but I begin to think you were right. Lot of times, lately, you've answered a question before I even asked it. Sometimes you haven't even bothered to answer--you've just sat there in your big brown chair and I've lain here on the couch, and we've gone through something together without using words at all...." She had started out almost gaily, the words spilling over each other in their rush to be said, but bit by bit she slowed down, then faltered to a stop. After she had stopped talking altogether, she could still hear her last few phrases, repeated over and over, like an echo that refused to die. (Answered ... before I even asked ... without using words at all ... without using words....)

She could almost taste the terror that clogged her throat and dried her lips. "You do believe it. And you could have me locked up. Only ... only...." Fragments of thought, splinters of words, and droplets of silence spun into a kaleidoscopic jumble, shifted infinitesimally, and fell into an incredible new pattern. Understanding displaced terror and was, in turn, displaced by indignation. She stared accusingly at her interrogator. "But you look just like ... just like anybody."

"You expected perhaps three legs or a long bushy tail or teeth like that textbook tiger?"

"And you're a psychiatrist!"

"What else? Would you have talked to me like this across a grocery counter, Lucilla? Or listened to me, if I'd been driving a bus or filling a prescription? Would I have found the others in a bowling alley or a business office?"

"Then there are ... others?" She let out her breath on a long sigh involuntarily glancing again at the framed picture. "Only I love Paul, and he isn't ... he can't...."

"Nor can Carol." His eyes were steady on hers, yet she felt as if he were looking through and beyond her. For no reason at all, she strained her ears for the sound of footsteps or the summons of a voice. "Where do you suppose the second little blob of protoplasm with legs came from?" Dr. Andrews asked. "And the third? If that ape who found he could stand erect had walked lonesomely off into the sunset like a second-rate actor on a late, late show, where do you suppose you'd be today?"

He broke off abruptly and watched with Lucilla as the office door edged open. The small girl who inched her way around it wore blue jeans and a pony tail rather than an organdy frock and curls, but her pixie smile matched that of the girl in the photograph Lucilla had glanced at again and again.

"You wanted me, Daddy?" she asked, but she looked toward Lucilla.

"I thought you'd like to meet someone with the same nickname as yours," Dr. Andrews said, rising to greet her. "Lucky, meet Lucky."

"Hello," the child said, then her smile widened. "Hello!" (But I don't have to say it, do I? I can talk to you just the way I talk to Daddy and Uncle Whitney and Big Bill).

"Hello yourself," said Lucilla. This time when the corners of her mouth began to tick upward, she made no attempt to stop them. (Of course you can, darling. And I can answer you the same way, and you'll hear me.)

Dr. Andrews reached for the open pack of cigarettes on his deck. (Is this strictly a private conversation, girls, or can I get in on it, too?)

(It's unpolite to interrupt, Daddy.)

(He's not exactly interrupting--it was his conversation to begin with!)

Dr. Andrews' receptionist paused briefly beside the still-open office door. None of them heard either her gentle rap or the soft click of the latch slipping into place when she pushed the door shut.

Nor did she hear them.

THE TRAP
BY BETSY CURTIS

ORIGINALLY PUBLISHED IN *GALAXY*
AUGUST 1953

Editor's Notes:
The Trap
By Betsy Curtis

A door to door salesman and an old woman who never leaves her house; through in rejuvenation and immortality, and it sounds like the setup for a typical tale of horror. But Curtis puts a spin on the premise in "The Trap" that is both surprising and innovative, while posing the question "What does it mean to be immortal?"

One of the things that sets the science fiction of the 50's apart from stories of an earlier period is the tendency to take conventional story lines and stand them on their heads, often with a touch of humor. Mere horror was no longer good enough. This tendency was to become a regular feature of the best science fiction TV show to come out of the era, "The Twilight Zone," which often adapted stories for its screen plays. Betsy Curtis was not a prolific writer, but as "The Trap" demonstrates, she was capable of telling an entertaining story.

Elizabeth M. Curtis was born in Toledo, Ohio September 17, 1917 and died April 17, 2002. She wrote a little over a dozen stories, mostly in the early 50's, though she did continue to publish sporadically into the 70's. She won a Hugo award for her short story "The Steiger Effect."

THE TRAP

She had her mind made up--the one way they'd make her young again was over her dead body!

*　　*　　*　　*　　*

Old Miss Barbara Noble twitched aside the edge of the white scrim curtain to get a better look at the young man coming down the street. He might be the one.

The young man bent a little under the weight of the battered black suitcase as he crossed Maple and started up Prospect on Miss Noble's side. She could see him set the case down on the wide porch of the Raney house and wipe his forehead with a handkerchief. Then she lost sight of him as he advanced to the door. He could be a visitor to the Raney's, but they were out of town on vacation. He could be a salesman.

Miss Barbara shifted her rocker to the other side of the window where she could watch without having to disturb the curtain. This second-floor sitting room made an excellent lookout. She quickly scanned the street in the other direction, but there was no sign of movement in the hot sunlight. She settled down to watch the black suitcase sitting uncommunicatively at the edge of the porch.

It must have been all of two minutes before the young man appeared from under the over-hanging roof and picked up the case. A persistent fellow. He went down to the sidewalk and approached her own house, came up on her own front doorstep, tried to set the case down on the narrow stoop, couldn't, straightened up and rang the bell. A raucous buzz filled the sitting room.

*　　*　　*　　*　　*

Barbara Noble leaned toward the window, pulled back the curtain a scant inch, and studied his back as he looked at the windows on the other side of the front door. Limp yellow hair and a big perspiration stain in the middle of a dark sport shirt were her chief impressions. He could be a bona fide salesman working hard at it. She wouldn't let him in, of course; but she felt a little sorry for him lugging that big case around in this weather. Then he turned and looked straight at the window behind which she was hiding, and she let the curtain go suddenly. Had he seen it move? The buzzer sounded again, imperiously.

Miss Barbara got up stiffly, moved to the big vizer screen in the nearest corner, and switched it on. The man might have something interesting and she couldn't get out to shop the way she used to. She smoothed her lilac housedress and left the room to descend the stairs to the front door.

In the tiny front hall she hesitated, then opened the door inward about eight inches. Deftly the man stuck the broad brown toe of his shoe into the opening and looked down at her. She grinned as she saw his expression of shock.

She was old, really old. Her sparse white hair was pulled so tightly into a knob on top of her head that the plentiful wrinkles on her forehead and around her eyes seemed to run vertically, giving her an oriental look. The hand she rested on the door jamb was a waxy-white claw, a blue vein standing up prominently under the skin tight-drawn over gnarly finger joints. He had probably never seen a woman much past middle age.

"Well?" Her croak was high and rough.

*   *   *   *   *

The young man recovered himself and began his spiel. "Madame, I represent one of the best-known and most reputable firms in the country. Our products have received three international medals for purity and effective performance. They...."

"What are you selling, young man?"

"I have the privilege of being a field representative for Taffeta Beauty Aids. Please accept this generous ten-ounce bottle of our Diamond Dew Refreshest Lotion...." He reached into his side pocket and brought it out, offered it with the most appreciative smile, his 'you hardly need this' smile.

Her hand did not reach out. "I don't want any. Goodbye!" The door tightened against his foot.

"But madame," his foot did not budge and his smile became both engaging and pleading, "all I ask is a chance to show you our line. Our products sell themselves. Besides, I'm paid on a demonstration basis--so much for every potential customer who receives our free sample and so much for every home demonstration. You wouldn't want me to lose two-fifty when it would take only six and a third minutes of your time exactly to look over one of the most amazing displays ever...."

"Well, I don't know...."

"I know you'll enjoy watching our Tissue Cleanser in action and seeing the new simplicity of our Home Re--...." (oops, he'd almost said it) "... Hair Relustrification Kit. I promise you that your few minutes won't be wasted."

"Yours would be, young man. I don't buy that stuff."

"You may be one of the lucky few women who don't need our products, but I don't think you can say that before you've seen them."

"I never did see such persistence, honest to goodness!" Her face assumed a crabbed smile. "Come along then."

*   *   *   *   *

She moved back from the door into the darkness of the house; and the salesman shifted his case back to his left hand, pushed the front door wide and took a quick long step inside. He was just in time to hear the slight click of the closing of a second door in front of him. He reached for the knob, turned it; but the door was locked. The outside door still stood open, caught by the end of the sample case.

The July daylight from outside showed him that he was in a tiny entrance hall not more than forty inches each way. He pulled the case in and by squeezing against the inner door allowed the front door to close. Anyhow, he was inside the house. He rapped sharply on the inner door.

The latch on the front door snapped to and instantly the hall was flooded with light from a tremendous bulb in the ceiling, which, surprisingly, was twenty feet above him.

A harsh voice, tinny with tremendous amplification but unmistakably that of the old woman, filled the hall, "ALL RIGHT, YOUNG MAN. I HAVE THE VIZER TURNED ON YOU. LET'S SEE THE DEMONSTRATION. I BELIEVE YOU SAID SIX MINUTES. GET ON WITH IT."

Screening his eyes with his fingers, the salesman scanned the walls and ceiling for the vizer lens, found it beside the five-hundred watt bulb pouring blindingly down on him, on the other side of a speaker grille.

"C-certainly, madame." What a layout. As he automatically laid his case on the floor and opened back the top against the front door, his eyes searched the walls for indications of openings which might mean unexpected defenses such as anesthetic tanks. The only breaks in the two smooth white plaster surfaces which he could see as he squatted before the case were a horizontal row of glass bosses on each side at about the height of his knees.

"Now, since my face," he closed his eyes and flashed a toothy smile, like a video actor, up at the vizer lens, "is subjected to the daily care of Taffeta Products," he turned his face down to the case and gritted his teeth, "I must smear facial muscle softener into the left half to show the action and appearance of muscles which have lost their tonus." He whipped the cover off a small ivorine jar and rubbed his cheek vigorously with a brownish salve. "You will note that this softener also contains a percentage of grime which lodges in the pores."

He heard a gasp from the speaker grille when he displayed a face whose left cheek and brow were sagged, wrinkled and hideously brown speckled. From somewhere behind the gasp, he heard a continuous tinkle of tiny bells.

His hands moved among the bottles and jars, raised a round silver box which he held up. "The delicately perfumed applicator pads for all applications of Taffeta Preparations are pre-saturated with Firmol Tone Charger. I dip the pad into this solution of Enhancing Hyssop," he did so, "and work it gently into the pores. The results are instantaneous!" He turned up his original video star appearance.

*   *   *   *   *

While bending his body forward to reach the articles strapped to the top of the case, he noticed that the tone of the distant bells was raised. Screwing a circular hairbrush to the thread of a collapsible tube, he sank back on his haunches. The bell tones were lower. He placed a hand on one of the glass bosses nearest the inner door, apparently to steady himself. An even lower tone was added to the bell notes. Obviously electric eyes with a set of bell signals in the old woman's present location. He smiled down at the floor--to himself.

"Now I want you to notice closely this object which I will show you." He held up the brush with the tube screwed on its back and turned it about. "Do you know what this is?"

There was no answer from the speaker but its own hum and the tinkle of the bells. "What does it look like?" He spoke rapidly, pleasantly. There was still no answer.

He rose quickly and tried the knob of the inner door again. He could hear the bell notes lower in pitch as he pressed against the door.

"LET ME SEE THE THING AGAIN, YOUNG MAN. HONEST TO GOODNESS, WHAT DIFFERENCE DOES IT MAKE WHETHER OR NOT I KNOW WHAT IT IS? IT LOOKS LIKE A HAIRBRUSH WITH SOME DO-JIGGER ON THE TOP."

He jumped back to the center of the hall. "This brush is the essential feature of our sensational Hair Relustrifier Kit. The tube screwed to the top feeds the specially developed Brilliancette directly through each hollow bristle to reach every part of the hair." He ran or rather scrubbed the brush through the right side of his long fair pompadour with small rotary motions. When he removed the brush, that side of his head was covered with crisp yellow ringlets which shone under the light like sculptured gold.

"THAT'S SOME SORT OF A TRICK! DO IT ON THE OTHER...." Her voice was interrupted by a syncopated clicking. A telephone signal. "JUST A MOMENT, YOUNG MAN." The hum of the speaker cut off and the sudden silence seemed full of the echoes of the bells.

*   *   *   *   *

Instantly the man dropped the gadget into the case and grabbed a handful of cleansing tissues from a box in it. He snapped down the top of the case and whipped the straps through the buckles. Then he shoved the case against one of the side walls and sat on it to flip off his shoes and socks. Shoving his back tightly against the wall, he bent his knees up and pushed his bare feet flat against the other. After placing the wad of tissues in his lap, he put his hands against the wall below his buttocks and, like an experienced mountain climber, inched his way rapidly up the 'chimney' of the hall. When his head touched the ceiling, he braced himself firmly with his left hand and reached with his right for the tissues in his lap. Protecting his hand with several of the white papers, he felt above him for the base of the light bulb, unscrewed it, and dropped it gently onto the rest of the tissues still in his lap. The sudden blackness was smothering.

Heat seeped through the tissues more rapidly than he had expected; and the effort to keep his knees from contracting and spilling him in the utter darkness to the floor fifteen feet below was agony.

When he finally reached the floor, he placed the bulb on it beside the sample case. Then he opened the front door and closed it again, leaving the door caught open a fraction of an inch by the latch against the frame. Taking an anesthetic cartridge out of his pants pocket, he broke the seal, taking care not to trigger it, and returned to his crevice-climbing posture. He lifted himself again above the row of electric eyes and waited, cartridge in hand, leg muscles cramping painfully.

*   *   *   *   *

After Miss Noble had turned off the speakphone, she pulled herself away from the fascinating view of golden curls and scuttled over to a stiff ladder-back chair beside the telephone stand. She lifted the antique cradle phone (none of these modern invasions of privacy like the vizerphone) and spoke warily into the mouthpiece.

"Who is it? What do you want?"

"Barbara?" A man's voice was urgent.

"This is Miss Noble speaking," she replied haughtily.

The voice was savage. "Well, this is *Doctor* Harris, then. Have you looked at the mail today? I got my directors' meeting notice this morning."

"Yes, I got one. The fifth of August," she said impatiently.

"And this seems to be our year. There's been a girl here already this morning with some story about my having advertised for a housekeeper. She told it to the doorphone and wouldn't leave when I said I didn't want anybody--but it only took one drop of skunk oil in the hallway to send her packing." The horrid chuckle that came from the receiver was so raucous that Miss Noble held it away from her ear.

"Blonde or brunette?" she asked noncommittally.

"Blonde--and really young, not a damn rejuvenee!"

"Rod Harris! You actually went and peeked at her, you old goat!"

"Only through the one-way."

"Well, since the company knows that a pretty girl is still good bait for an old ninny, you're as good as a goner. They'll have *you* rejuvenated before long."

"They won't get a chance to! And I'm going to get old enough so I can't even lift a hand to thumb my nose at the company. Then I'm going to go and die and the Juvine Perpetual Youth Corporation will scream in agony as it disbands and makes public property of its hallowed formulas as per the original articles of incorporation ... and *you* will probably get a new set of false teeth and take the treatment again since you could get it real cheap when the monopoly's finished and not have to disturb your millions salted away in the sugar bowl."

This mixture of facetiousness and downright sarcasm was only surpassed by Miss Noble, who snapped back, "Don't you sneer at me, Doctor Roland Harris, when you know perfectly well that the *only* reason I have to go on living this long is to make sure that you are really dead first. You didn't invent rejuvenation all by yourself without the aid of Barbara Noble, Ph.D., and the company has the sole right to the process until we're *both* dead. And, if you start peeking at plump blonde wenches at this point, I suppose I'll have to live till Los Alamos freezes over!"

"All right, all right. But she wasn't plump. She wasn't any bigger than you are. Besides, you know I'd rather have dinner with you. My man Marko could give us roast beef with all the fixings and afterward I want you to hear my latest discovery. It's the best damn extempore-singer you've ever heard, Jeery Wade-- fellow in his first late fifties, no fluff-brain of a juvenee--a blood and thunder baritone that'll lift that knob of hair clean off your scalp. Let's say you get here about six-thirty and I'll phone him we'll be over at his place for a session of hollering about eight."

*   *   *   *   *

Miss Noble's scorn needed no vizer to carry it over the wire in full force. "I'm not going to budge out of this house until after the director's meeting and then only if the shops stop all delivery service. This time I'm not taking any chances. Life is too much of a bore to have to put up with it for another eighty years even for your marvelous singer who would probably go and get rejuvenated just as I got to enjoy him. And *nothing* could induce me to listen to an evening of your stories for the nine hundredth time. If there's one thing I'm thankful for in this scatter-brained age, it's the marriage dissolution law that's got me free from your anecdotes after three separate terms of fifty years each."

"Now, Barbara, was it that bad?" Roland Harris sounded distressed.

"Do you really think I could be honestly grateful to the Corporation for a hundred and fifty years of listening to that disgraceful old thing about the Martian, the Venusian, and the robot?"

"Well, if you feel that way about it, I'll keep my discoveries to myself. I hope your fancy hallway keeps you safe till you rot."

"It's doing all right," replied the old woman smugly. "I have a young pup down there right now cooling his number thirteens and waiting to pretend to interest me in some new face paint and hair gik. My electric eye set and vizer are less repulsive than your skunk oil and *twice* as effective."

"They're not going to stop me from having a good time while I last, anyhow. I think they're through with me for today; and I'm going to hear Jeery Wade, anyhow. He'll make up a hooting good song about all this when I tell him."

"Take care of yourself, Rod ... goodbye," said Miss Noble, almost concernedly.

She dropped the phone into its cradle, rose, and went back to the vizer screen, switching on the speaker as she sat down. Only then did she notice that the screen was entirely dark except for a vague sliver of gray.

"Are you still there, young man?" she asked the microphone.

There was silence from the speaker. The hammer on each bar of the long metal xylophone of the electric eye signal hung motionless.

"He's gone ... and left the front door unlatched too. And I thought he was persistent." She was disappointed. "He owes me four more minutes of fun."

She got up slowly and started for the door. "That curly hair stuff is new since my last sixties, too. I wonder if it would work on white hair ... I'd better go down and close the door. Can't have just anybody coming into one's house."

*   *   *   *   *

She descended the stairs, opened the door from the front room, then took one step forward into the hall. Before she could interpret the soft bump of the salesman's bare feet as they struck the floor, she was encircled by his strong arm; and the hiss of the anesthetic gun was loud in the small area of the hall. Limply she sagged against his arm.

The hissing of the gun stopped. The young man slipped it into his pocket and, turning, thrust the inner door wide open with his now free hand. Entering the tidy front room, he kicked the door shut behind him and gulped in the good air before he headed for the back of the house, cradling the small body easily in his arms. Failing to find there what he was looking for, he went up the narrow white-railed stairway to the second floor. Across the landing, the gleam of porcelain showed through a half-open door.

He laid his burden carefully on the vari-colored braided rug by the tub and began to draw a warm bath, testing the temperature frequently with his hand. When water reached the overflow outlet, he turned off the tap and sprinted downstairs for his sample case. The hall was still chokingly full of gas; and after grabbing out the case, he slammed the door again. He brought the case up to the bathroom, where he opened it on the floor beside the form of the old woman. He lifted out the tray, revealing masses of silvery tubing and a number of flasks of iridescent solutions nestling among loops of rubber insulated wiring. One flask he emptied into the bath, making the water seethe and turn a cloudy green.

Then, dashing down the stairs again, he began looking for the telephone. His search became more and more hurried, as he opened cupboards and drawers in front room and kitchen with no success. Returning upstairs, he almost missed the instrument in the sitting-room because he was expecting the familiar sight of a round vizer screen. He stood over the phone and dialed.

"Hey, Alice!"

"What luck, Riggy?"

"I'm in. The old lady's out cold on the bathroom floor. Primer solution's in the bath at five above tepid. I'm shoving her in now--with all her clothes on, of course--and I've wasted a lot of time already looking for this hypoblastic phone, so beat it on over here with Margy and get to work."

"Are you ordering me around, Rigel O'Maffey?"

"You know I never did this job on a woman. And don't forget, honey, we'll get enough out of this to get a new copter together. C'mon now." He put the phone back in, the cradle before she could answer.

*　　*　　*　　*　　*

Back in the bathroom, he drew a long thermometer from the case, took a careful reading on the water, ran in a little more hot from the faucet and left it running the slightest dribble.

Carefully lifting the small body of Barbara Noble, Ph.D., he slid it gently into the water feet first over the end, smoothing down with one hand the percale housedress which ballooned as she went into the water. Finally he knelt beside the tub, holding her head out of the water in the crook of his elbow.

A banging on the inner door downstairs some fifteen minutes later reminded him of the force with which he had slammed it in his hurry to reach the uncontaminated air of the front room. He looked longingly across the bathroom at the racks of towels on the other side, but finally, as the banging stopped and a feminine voice began yelling, "Hey, Riggy! Let us in!" he grabbed up the bright rug and wadded it under the scrawny neck.

The girls scolded him all the way up the stairs for not leaving the door unlocked, while he tried to explain, at the same time, that he had to hold up the woman's head.

"Screepers, Riggy, what do you think the perfectly good pair of water-wings in your case is for?"

Humbled, he departed as the girls took over the beginning of the complicated, fortnight-long process of the rejuvenation of Barbara Noble.

*   *   *   *   *

The receptionist behind the ebony desk, whose gold plate proclaimed it as the headquarters of the Juvine Perpetual Youth Corporation, crammed shut the drawer before her. A metallic clink from within was the fall of a mirror with which she had been assisting the application of scarlet which now fluoresced gently on her full lips.

Tossing her head (which showed the crop of glistening black curls to the fullest advantage) in a preoccupied manner, she addressed the man who stood before her desk. "How can the Juvine Perpetual Youth Corporation serve you?" Her hastily assumed look of efficient importance was replaced by melting eagerness as she took in the chiselled perfection of features and the broad shoulders of the young man in knife-creased bronze spunlon.

"I'm Harris. For the directors' meeting." His voice was curt.

"*You're* Doctor Harris? The Director? Oh, do come in." She rose from the desk and went around the end of it to open the high wrought-gold gate and hold it wide for him. "You're a little early. I'll take you down to the Board Room." Eager willingness to help was apparent in her every gesture.

"Thanks, I know the way," he informed her, brushing past.

She followed him, however, across the patio-like reception room, with its exotically gardened borders and splashing fountain, down the long corridor past glowing murals of men and women swimming, dancing and playing tennis, past tapestry shielded doorways to the great bright arch at the end. Before he went through, she caught his sleeve.

"I should be pleased to steno for you today, if you need me."

He turned and looked at her as if he had not known she was behind him. "Thanks, but I sha'n't need one. It'll be a short meeting." He smiled down and patted her cheek. "But if I'm not entirely satisfied with the proceedings, maybe I can dictate a little afterward."

She laughed as if that were a special joke between them and retreated rapidly down the corridor before he had time to turn and miss the splendor of her graceful carriage.

His eyebrows were still raised and the corners of his mouth curved in appreciation when he passed through the arch and into the vast room under the clear bubble of a tremendous skydome.

*   *   *   *   *

A girl was sitting there, her back to him, looking out over the simmering city streets to the cool rise of mountains beyond. He recognized at once the slight figure, the sheen of the long curling auburn bob, the poise of her head and slim hand resting on the arm of the chair.

"Babs!"

She turned half around. "Hello, Rod."

He grinned and sank down in the next chair. "Here we are again."

"Knocked out by your own skunk oil?" she asked pointedly.

"No. Company copter man got me leaving Jeery Wade's. What happened to you? I thought you were walled up neatly for the declining years."

"The cosmetic man ambushed me in the hall. But I've got another fifty years to figure out something better ... if I still need it."

"What do you mean *if* you still need it? Are you changing your mind about rejuvenation?"

She smiled. "Well, you know it's always fun at first. But I'm having my lawyer come to this meeting. I've got an idea we can change the articles of agreement so that the process can finally become public property at the end of another fifty years instead of only after our deaths. Then if we want to go on and die, nobody" (she waved her hand around the great room at the little group of athletic men and glamorous, expensively gowned women moving in through the arch) "nobody will have any financial interest in rejuvenating us. Then, too, our own fat incomes will lapse; and since that's the reason we set up the articles the way they are--so we'd never be in danger of starving, that is--we'd have the more interesting choice of whether to die off or get young again and go back to work. Would you sign a fifty-year termination, Rod?"

"Would you marry me for the fifty years, Babs?" His voice was gentle, pleading.

"Honest to goodness, now, aren't you really pretty tired of me?" she asked earnestly, turning to face him.

"No, I can't say I am. You're pretty special, doctor, and you're special pretty." It was a ritual.

"You know you're the only man. I'll marry you. Will you sign?"

"Of course I'll sign. I would have anyhow when I knew you wanted me to. And Babs--maybe we could get some sort of jobs now--sort of to get in practice. I'll bet we could rent a lab somewhere and do commercial analyses for a while until we got hit by another idea for research."

"Rod, that's the best idea you've had in the last hundred and fifty years. But we could have a honeymoon first, couldn't we?"

"That's your best suggestion in the last seventy years. And maybe we could get Jeery Wade and his wife to rejuvenate and go with us. After the first couple of weeks, that is."

*   *   *   *   *

They left the meeting arm in arm, somewhat ahead of the rather disgruntled group of directors, who stayed behind to lament the end of a good thing. In the garden room, Barbara stopped to choose an orchid.

Rod Harris wandered on to the receptionist's desk, where the girl of the black curls waited, smiling.

He looked back at Barbara, then smiled down at the girl. "Just like I said ... a short meeting. No need for any dictating. Lucky you."

"Oh, I don't know," she countered coyly.

"Say, I heard a story the other day you might like. Do you like stories?"

"What kind of story?"

"You'd have to be the judge of that."

Suddenly Barbara was with them, pinning on a bronze and green blossom. "C'mon along, dear. We've got a good many things to do before we leave."

He opened the golden wicket for her and followed her out. Turning back toward the desk, he called to the girl, "I may be back in a few weeks to see about a job. Remind me then to tell you the one about the Martian, the Venusian and the robot."

Foundling on Venus

By Dorothy de Courcy

Originally Published in *Fantastic Universe*
March 1954

Editor's Notes
Foundling on Venus
By Dorothy de Courcy

When this story was written, there was still very little information on what the conditions were like on the planets of the solar system. Venus was typically portrayed as a swampy, cloud-shrouded jungle with a ecology that was unpleasant at best and deadly at its worst. This convention had originated in the 20's and 30's and really didn't change until the scientific information was irrefutable, so it's no surprise that the de Courcys chose to follow the "Venus is Hell" theme.

The other theme that was popular was that of the alien amongst us, sometimes as a menace, sometimes benign, and sometimes as just accidental visitors. It is certainly possible to draw parallels with the fear of the "communist menace" and McCarthyism that was part of the politics of the time, but it is probably a much deeper human trait, the same trait that produced the witch scares of a few centuries previous. The aliens of this tale are of the benign sort, but the idea that they could live amongst us mimicking our behavior still creates a feeling of unease.

Dorothy de Courcy wrote twenty some stories with her husband John de Courcy from the late 40's into the middle 50's.

FOUNDLING ON VENUS

Venus was the most miserable planet in the system, peopled by miserable excuses for human beings. And somewhere among this conglomeration of boiling protoplasm there was a being unlike the others, a being who walked and talked like the others but who was different--and afraid the difference would be discovered. You'll remember this short story.

*   *   *   *   *

The foundling could not have been more than three years old. Yet he held a secret that was destined to bring joy to many unhappy people.

Unlike Gaul, the north continent of Venus is divided into *four* parts. No Caesar has set foot here either, nor shall one--for the dank, stinging, caustic air swallows up the lives of men and only Venus may say, *I conquered.*

This is colonized Venus, where one may walk without the threat of sudden death--except from other men--the most bitterly fought for, the dearest, bloodiest, most worthless land in the solar system.

Separated by men into East and West at the center of the Twilight Zone, the division across the continent is the irregular, jagged line of Mud River, springing from the Great Serpent Range.

The African Republic holds one quarter which the Negroes exploit as best they can, encumbered by filter masks and protective clothing.

The Asians still actually try to colonize their quarter, while the Venusian primitives neither help nor hinder the bitter game of power-politics, secret murder, and misery--most of all, misery.

The men from Mars understand this better, for their quarter is a penal colony. Sleepy-eyed, phlegmatic Martians, self-condemned for minute violations of their incredible and complex mores--without guards save themselves--will return to the subterranean cities, complex philosophies, and cool, dry air of Mars when they have declared their own sentences to be at an end.

Meanwhile, they labor to extract the wealth of Venus without the bitterness and hate, without the savagery and fear of their neighbors. Hence, they are regarded by all with the greatest suspicion.

The Federated States, after their fashion, plunder the land and send screaming ships to North America laden with booty and with men grown suddenly rich--and with men who will never care for riches or anything else again. These are the fortunate dead. The rest are received into the sloppy breast of Venus where even a tombstone or marker is swallowed in a few, short weeks. And they die quickly on Venus, and often.

From the arbitrary point where the four territories met, New Reno flung its sprawling, dirty carcass over the muddy soil and roared and hooted endlessly, laughed with the rough boisterousness of miners and spacemen, rang with the brittle, brassy laughter of women following a trade older than New Reno. It clanged and shouted and bellowed so loudly that quiet sobbing was never heard.

But a strange sound hung in the air, the crying of a child. A tiny child, a boy, he sat begrimed by mud at the edge of the street where an occasional ground car flung fresh contamination on his small form until he became almost indistinguishable from the muddy street. His whimpering changed to prolonged wailing sobs. He didn't turn to look at any of the giant passers-by nor did they even notice him.

But finally one passer-by stopped. She was young and probably from the Federated States. She was not painted nor was she well-dressed. She had nothing to distinguish her, except that she stopped.

"Oh, my!" she breathed, bending over the tiny form. "You poor thing. Where's your mama?"

The little figure rubbed its face, looked at her blankly and heaved a long, shuddering sigh.

"I can't leave you sitting here in the mud!" She pulled out a handkerchief and tried to wipe away some of the mud and then helped him up. His clothes were rags, his feet bare. She took him by the hand and as they walked along she talked to him. But he seemed not to hear.

Soon they reached the dirty, plastic front of the Elite Cafe. Once through the double portals, she pulled the respirator from her face. The air inside was dirty and smelly but it was breathable. People were eating noisily, boisterously, with all the lusty, unclean young life that was Venus. They clamored, banged and threw things for no reason other than to throw them.

She guided the little one past the tables filled with people and into the kitchen. The door closed with a bang, shutting out much of the noise from the big room. Gingerly she sat him down on a stool, and with detergent and water she began removing the mud. His eyes were horribly red-rimmed.

"It's a wonder you didn't die out there," she murmured. "Poor little thing!"

"Hey! Are you going to work or aren't you, Jane?" a voice boomed.

A large ruddy man in white had entered the kitchen and he stood frowning at the girl. Women weren't rare on Venus, and she was only a waitress ...

"What in the blue blazes is that!" He pointed to the child.

"He was outside," the girl explained, "sitting in the street. He didn't have a respirator."

The ruddy man scowled at the boy speculatively. "His lungs all right?"

"He isn't coughing much," she replied.

"But what are you going to do with him?" the man asked Jane.

"I don't know," she said. "Something. Tell the Patrol about him, I guess."

The beefy man hesitated. "It's been a long time since I've seen a kid this young on Venus. They always ship 'em home. Could have been dumped. Maybe his parents left him on purpose."

The girl flinched.

He grunted disgustedly, his face mirroring his thoughts. *Stringy hair ... plain face ... and soft as Venus slime clear through!* He shrugged. "Anyway, he's got to eat." He looked at the small figure. "Want to eat, kid? Would you like a glass of milk?" He opened a refrigerator, took out a plastic bottle and poured milk in a glass.

Chubby hands reached out for the glass.

"There, that's better," the cook said. "Pete will see that you get fed all right." He turned to the girl. "Could he belong to someone around here?"

Jane shook her head. "I don't know. I've never seen him before."

"Well, he can stay in the kitchen while you work the shift. I'll watch him."

She nodded, took an apron down from a hook and tied it around her waist. Then she patted the sober-faced youngster on his tousled head and left.

The beefy man studied the boy. "I think I'll put you over there," he said. He lifted him, stool and all, and carried him across the kitchen. "You can watch through that panel. See? That's Jane in there. She'll come back and forth, pass right by here. Is that all right?"

The little one nodded.

"Oh?" Pete raised his eyebrows. "So you *do* know what I'm saying." He watched the child for a few minutes, then turned his attention to the range. The rush hour was on and he soon forgot the little boy on the stool ...

Whenever possible during the lunch-hour rush, Jane stopped to smile and talk to the child. Once she asked, "Don't you know where your mama and daddy are?"

He just stared at her, unblinking, his big eyes soft and sad-looking.

The girl studied him for a moment, then she picked up a cookie and gave it to him. "Can you tell me your name?" she asked hopefully.

His lips parted. Cookie crumbs fell off his chin and from the corners of his mouth, but he spoke no words.

She sighed, turned, and went out to the clattering throng with laden plates of food.

For a while Jane was so busy she almost forgot the young one. But finally people began to linger more over their food, the clinking of dishes grew quieter and Pete took time for a cup of coffee. His sweating face was haggard. He stared sullenly at the little boy and shook his head.

"Shouldn't be such things as kids," he muttered. "Nothing but a pain in the neck!"

Jane came through the door. "It gets worse all the time," she groaned. She turned to the little boy. "Did you have something to eat?"

"I didn't know what to fix for him," Pete said. "How about some beef stew? Do you think he'd go for that?"

Jane hesitated. "I--I don't know. Try it."

Pete ladled up a bowl of steaming stew. Jane took it and put it on the table. She took a bit on a spoon, blew on it, then held it out. The child opened his mouth. She smiled and slowly fed him the stew.

"How old do you think he is?" Pete asked.

The girl hesitated, opened her mouth, but said nothing.

"About two and a half, I'd guess," Pete answered himself. "Maybe three." Jane nodded and he turned back to cleaning the stove.

"Don't you want some more stew?" Jane asked as she offered the small one another spoonful.

The little mouth didn't open.

"Guess you've had enough," she said, smiling.

Pete glanced up. "Why don't you leave now, Jane. You're going to have to see the Patrol about that kid. I can take care of things here."

She stood thinking for a moment. "Can I use an extra respirator?"

"You can't take him out without one!" Pete replied. He opened a locker and pulled out a transparent facepiece. "I think this'll tighten down enough to fit his face."

She took it and walked over to the youngster. His large eyes had followed all her movements and he drew back slightly as she held out the respirator. "It won't hurt," she coaxed. "You have to wear it. The air outside stings."

The little face remained steady but the eyes were fearful as Jane slid the transparent mask over his head and tightened the elastic. It pulsed slightly with his breathing.

"Better wrap him in this," Pete suggested, pulling a duroplast jacket out of the locker. "Air's tough on skin."

The girl nodded, pulling on her own respirator. She stepped quickly into her duroplast suit and tied it. "Thanks a lot, Pete," she said, her voice slightly muffled. "See you tomorrow."

Pete grunted as he watched her wrap the tiny form in the jacket, lift it gently in her arms, then push through the door.

The girl walked swiftly up the street. It was quieter now, but in a short time the noise and stench and garishness of New Reno would begin rising to another cacophonous climax.

The strange pair reached a wretched metal structure with an askew sign reading, "El Grande Hotel." Jane hurried through the double portals, the swish of air flapping her outer garments as the air conditioning unit fought savagely to keep out the rival atmosphere of the planet.

There was no one at the desk and no one in the lobby. It was a forlorn place, musty and damp. Venus humidity seemed to eat through everything, even metal, leaving it limp, faded, and stinking.

She hesitated, looked at the visiphone, then impulsively pulled a chair over out of the line of sight of the viewing plate and gently set the little boy on it. She pulled the respirator from her face, pressed the button under the blank visiphone disk. The plate lit up and hummed faintly.

"Patrol Office," Jane said.

There was a click and a middle-aged, square-faced man with blue-coated shoulders appeared. "Patrol Office," he repeated.

"This is Jane Grant. I work at the Elite Cafe. Has anyone lost a little boy?"

The patrolman's eyebrows raised slightly. "Little boy? Did you find one?"

"Well--I--I saw one earlier this evening," she faltered. "He was sitting at the edge of the street and I took him into the cafe and fed him."

"Well, there aren't many children in town," he replied. "Let's see." He glanced at a record sheet. "No, none's reported missing. He with you now?"

"Ah--no."

He shook his head again, still looking downward. He said slowly, "His parents must have found him. If he was wandering we'd have picked him up. There is a family that live around there who have a ten-year-old kid who wanders off once in a while. Blond, stutters a little. Was it him?"

"Well, I--" she began. She paused, said firmly, "No."

"Well, we don't have any reports on lost children. Haven't had for some time. If the boy was lost his parents must have found him. Thank you for calling." He broke the connection.

Jane stood staring at the blank plate. No one had reported a little boy missing. In all the maddening confusion that was New Reno, no one had missed a little boy.

She looked at the small bundle, walked over and slipped off his respirator. "I should have told the truth," she murmured to him softly. "But you're so tiny and helpless. Poor little thing!"

He looked up at her, then around the lobby, his brown eyes resting on first one object, then another. His little chin began to quiver.

The girl picked him up and stroked his hair. "Don't cry," she soothed. "Everything's going to be all right."

She walked down a hall, fumbling inside her coveralls for a key. At the end of the hall she stopped, unlocked a door, and carried him inside. As an afterthought she locked the door, still holding the small bundle in her arms. Then she placed him on a bed, removed the jacket and threw it on a chair.

"I don't know why I should go to all this trouble," she said, removing her protective coveralls. "I'll probably get picked up by the Patrol. But *somebody's* got to look after you."

She sat down beside him. "Aren't you even a bit sleepy?"

He smiled a little.

"Maybe now you can tell me your name," she said. "Don't you know your name?"

His expression didn't change.

She pointed to herself. "Jane." Then she hesitated, looked downward for a moment. "Jana, I was called before I came here."

The little face looked up at her. The small mouth opened. "Jana." It was half whisper, half whistle.

"That's right," she replied, stroking his hair. "My, but your throat must be sore. I hope you won't be sick from breathing too much of that awful air."

She regarded him quizzically. "You know, I've never seen many little boys. I don't quite know how to treat one. But I know you should get some sleep."

She smiled and reached over to take off the rags. He pulled away suddenly.

"Don't be afraid," she said reassuringly. "I wouldn't hurt you."

He clutched the little ragged shirt tightly.

"Don't be afraid," she repeated soothingly. "I'll tell you what. You lie down and I'll put this blanket over you," she said, rising. "Will that be all right?"

She laid him down and covered the small form with a blanket. He lay there watching her with his large eyes.

"You don't look very sleepy," she said. "Perhaps I had better turn the light down." She did so, slowly, so as not to alarm him. But he was silent, watchful, never taking his eyes from her.

She smiled and sat down next to him. "Now I'll tell you a story and then you must go to sleep," she said softly.

He smiled--just a little smile--and she was pleased.

"Fine," she cried. "Well--once upon a time there was a beautiful planet, not at all like this one. There were lovely flowers and cool-running streams and it only rained once in a while. You'd like it there for it's a very nice place. But there were people there who liked to travel--to see strange places and new things, and one day they left in a great big ship."

She paused again, frowning in thought. "Well, they traveled a long, long way and saw many things. Then one day something went wrong."

Her voice was low and soft. It had the quality of a dream, the texture of a zephyr, but the little boy was still wide awake.

"Something went very, very wrong and they tried to land so they could fix it. But when they tried to land they found they couldn't--and they fell and just barely managed to save themselves. The big, beautiful ship was all broken. Well, since they couldn't fix the ship at all now, they set out on foot to find out where they were and to see if they could get help. Then they found that they were in a land of great big giants, and the people were very fierce."

The little boy's dark eyes were watching her intently but she went on, hardly noticing.

"So they went back to the broken ship and tried to decide what to do. They couldn't get in touch with their home because the radio part of the ship was all broken up. And the giants were horrible and wanted everything for themselves and were cruel and mean and probably would have hurt the poor ship-wrecked people if they had known they were there.

"So--do you know what they did? They got some things from the ship and they went and built a giant. And they put little motors inside and things to make it run and talk so that the giants wouldn't be able to tell that it wasn't another giant just like themselves."

She paused, straightening slightly.

"And then they made a space inside the giant where somebody could sit and run this big giant and talk and move around--and the giants wouldn't ever know that she was there. They made it a *she*. In fact, she was the only person who could do it because she could learn to talk all sorts of languages--that's what she could do best. So she went out in the giant suit and mingled with the giants and worked just like they did.

"But every once in a while she'd go back to the others, bringing them things they needed. And she would bring back news. That was their only hope--news of a ship which might be looking for them, which might take them home--"

She broke off. "I wonder what the end of the story will be?" she murmured.

For some time she had not been using English. She had been speaking in a soft, fluid language unlike anything ever heard on Venus. But now she had stopped speaking entirely.

After a slight pause--another voice spoke--in the same melodious, alien tongue! It said, "I think I know the end of the story. I think someone has come for you poor people and is going to take you home."

She gasped--for she realized it had not been her voice. Her artificial eyes watched, stunned, as the little boy began peeling off a skin-tight, flexible baby-faced mask, revealing underneath the face of a little man.

One Way

By Miriam Allen deFord

Originally Published in *Galaxy*
March 1955

Editor's Notes:
One Way
By Miriam Allen deFord

Miriam Allen deFord was a prolific and versatile writer, having achieved success in a number of genres. Her body of work also shows that the art of writing science fiction story is not that different than that of writing a mystery. This was particularly true in the era when magazines and short stories were the principle outlets for writers in both genres. Any number of writers during the period had successful careers writing both types of stories, Frederic Brown comes to mind particularly, but there were many others. Writing a good mystery of science fiction short story requires an economy of language to describe a premise and characters as efficiently as possible before delivering the punch line.

It should also be noted, that though this story was written when the author was in her sixties, she has no problem dealing with such matters as genetics, space travel, and interstellar colonization, evidence of a still agile and adaptable mind. Further proof of this is demonstrated by the fact that she won an Edgar in her seventies.

Miriam Allen deFord (August 21, 1888-February 22, 1975) was born in Philadelphia, PA. and worked as a reporter before turning to fiction. She wrote numerous mystery and science fiction stories as well as true crime stories up until her death. She received an Edgar Award for Best Fact Crime Book for *The Overbury Affair* in 1961. She had two collections of her science fiction published, *Elsewhere, Elsewhen, Elsehow* and *Xenogenesis* and edited the anthology of science fiction mysteries *Space, Time, and Crime*. She was also a follower of Charles Fort and did fieldwork for him.

One Way

We had the driver let us off in the central district and took a copter-taxi back to Homefield. There's no disgrace about it, of course; we just didn't feel like having all the neighbors see the big skycar with LYDNA PROJECT painted on its side, and then having them drop in casually to express what they would call interest and we would know to be curiosity.

There are people who boast that their sons and daughters have been picked for Lydna. What is there to boast about? It's pure chance, within limits.

And Hal is our only child and we love him.

Lucy didn't say a word all the way back from saying good-by to him. Lucy and I have been married now for 27 years and I guess I know her about as well as anybody on Earth does. People who don't know her so well think she's cold. But I knew what feelings she was crushing down inside her.

Besides, I wasn't feeling much like talking myself. I was remembering too many things:

Hal at about two, looking up at me--when I would come home dead-tired from a hard day of being chewed at by half a dozen bosses right up to the editor-in-chief whenever anything went the least bit out of kilter--with a smile that made all my tiredness disappear. Hal, when I'd pick him up at school, proudly displaying a Cybernetics Approval Slip (and ignoring the fact that half the other kids had one, too). Hal the day I took him to the Beard Removal Center, certain that he was a man, now that he was old enough for depilation. Hal that morning two weeks ago, setting out to get his Vocational Assignment Certificate....

That's when I stopped remembering.

It had been five years after our marriage before they let us start a child: some question about Lucy's uncle and my grandmother. Most parents aren't as old as we are when they get the news and usually have other children left, so it isn't so bad.

*   *   *   *   *

When we got home, Lucy still was silent. She took off her scarf and cloak and put them away, and then she pushed the button for dinner without even asking me what I wanted. I noticed, though, that she was ordering all the things I like. We both had the day off, of course, to go and say good-by to Hal-- Lucy is a technician at Hydroponics Center.

I felt awkward and clumsy. Her ways are so different from mine; I explode and then it's over--just a sore place where it hurts if I touch it. Lucy never explodes, but I knew the sore place would be there forever, and getting worse instead of better.

We ate dinner in silence, though neither of us felt hungry, and had the table cleared. Then it was nearly 19 o'clock and I had to speak.

"The takeoff will be at 19:10," I said. "Want me to tune in now? Last year, when Mutro was Solar President, he gave a good speech before the kids left."

"Don't turn it on at all!" she said sharply. Then, in a softer voice, she added: "Of course, Frank, turn it on whenever you like. I'll just go to my room and open the soundproofing."

There were still no tears in her eyes.

I thought of a thousand things to say: Don't you want to catch a glimpse of Hal in the crowd going up the ramp? Mightn't they let the kids wave a last farewell to their folks listening and watching in? Mightn't something in the President's speech make us feel a little better?

But I heard myself saying, "Never mind, Lucy. Don't go. I'll leave the thing off."

I didn't want to be alone. I wanted Lucy there with me.

So we sat out the whole time of the visicast, side by side on the window-couch, holding hands. I'll say this for the neighbors-- they must all have known, for Hal was the first to be selected from Homefield in nearly 40 years, and the newscast must have announced it over and over, but not a single person on the whole 62 floors of the house butted in on us. Not even that snoopy student from Venus in 47-14, who's always dropping in on other tenants and taking notes on "the mores of Earth Aboriginals." People can be very decent sometimes. We needn't have worried about coming home in the Lydna Project bus.

It was no good trying to keep my mind on anything else. Whether I wanted to or not, I had to relive the two last hours we'd ever have with Hal.

It couldn't mean to him what it meant to us. We were losing; he was both losing and gaining. We were losing our whole lives for 21 years past; he was, too, but he was entering a new life we would never know anything about. No word ever comes from Lydna; that's part of the project. Nobody even knows where it is for sure, though it's supposed to be one of the outer asteroids.

Both boys and girls are sent and there must be marriages and children--though probably the death-rate is pretty high, for every year they have to select 200 more from Earth to keep the population balanced. We would never know if our son married there, or whom, or when he died. We would never see our grandchildren, or even know if we had any.

*   *   *   *   *

Hal was a good son and I think we were fairly good parents and had made his childhood happy. But at 21, faced with a great, mysterious adventure and an unknown and exciting future, a boy can't be expected to be drowned in grief at saying good-by to his humdrum old father and mother. It might have been tougher for him 200 years ago, when they hadn't learned to decondition children early from parental fixations. But no youngster today would possess that kind of unwholesome dependency. If he did, he would never have been selected for Lydna in the first place.

That's one comfort we have--it's a sort of proof we had reared a child far above the average.

It was just weakness in me to half wish that Hal hadn't been so healthy, so handsome, so intelligent, so fine in character.

They were a wonderful lot. We said our good-bys in an enormous room of the spaceport, with this year's 200 selectees there from all over Earth, each with the relatives and whoever else had permission to make the last visit. I suppose it's a matter of accommodations and transportation, for nobody's allowed more than three. So it was mostly parents, with a few brothers, sisters and sweethearts or friends. The selectees themselves choose the names. After all, they've had two weeks after they were notified to say good-by to everyone else who matters to them.

Most of the time, all I could keep my mind on was Hal, trying to fix forever in my memory every last detail of him. We have dozens of sound stereos, of course, but this was the last time.

Still, it's my business at the News Office, and has been for 30 years, to observe people and form conclusions about them, so I couldn't help noticing with a professional eye some of the rest of the selectees. (This farewell visit is a private affair, and the press is barred, which is why I'd never been there before.)

There were two kinds of selectees that stood out, in my mind. One was those who had nobody at all to see them off. Completely alone, poor kids--orphans, doubtless, with no families and apparently not even friends near enough to matter. But, in a way, they would be the happiest; life on Earth couldn't have been very rewarding for them, and on Lydna they might find companionship. (If only companionship in misery, I thought--but I shied away from that. In our business, there are always leaks; we know--or guess--a few things about Lydna nobody else does, outside the authorities themselves. But we keep our mouths shut.)

The ones that tore my hearts were the boys and girls in love. They never take married people for Lydna, but a machine can't tell what a boy or girl is feeling about another girl or boy, and it's a machine that does the selecting. There's no use putting up an argument, for, once made, the choice is inexorable and unchangeable. In my work as a newsgatherer, I've heard some terrible stories. There have been suicide pacts and murders.

*   *   *   *   *

You could tell the couples in love. Not that there were any scenes. If there had been any in the two weeks past, they were over. But anybody who has learned to read human reactions, as I have, could recognize the agony those youngsters were going through.

I felt a deep gratitude that Hal wasn't one of them. He'd had his share of adolescent affairs, of course, but I was sure he was still just playing around. He'd seen a lot of Bet Milen, a girl a class ahead of him in school and college, but I didn't think she meant more to him than any of the others. If she had, she'd have been along to say good-by, but he'd asked for only the two of us. She was now a laboratory assistant in our hospital and could easily have gotten the time off.

It was growing late, almost midnight, and Lucy and I had to be at work tomorrow, no matter how we felt. I forced myself to talk, with Lucy's silent pain smothering me like a force-blanket. I made an effort and cleared my throat.

"Lucy, go to bed and turn on the hypno and try to get some sleep."

Lucy stood up obediently, but she shook her head. "You go, dear," she said, her voice firm. "I can't. I--"

The roof buzzer sounded. Somebody had landed in a copter and wanted us.

"Don't answer," I said quickly. "There's nobody we want to see--"

But she had already pushed the button to open the door.

It was Bet Milen, the girl Hal used to go around with.

I braced myself. This might be bad. She might have cared more for Hal than we had guessed.

But she didn't look grief-stricken. She looked excited, and determined, and a little bit frightened.

She scarcely glanced at me. She went right up to Lucy and took both Lucy's hands in hers.

"Well," she said in a clipped, tense voice, "we made it."

Then Lucy broke for the first time. The tears ran down her face and she didn't even wipe them away. "Are you *certain*?"

"Positive. And I got word to him. We'd agreed on a code. That's why he didn't want me there today--we couldn't trust ourselves not to betray it, either way."

I stood there staring at them, bewildered.

"What's this all about?" I demanded. "Have you two cooked up some crazy scheme to rescue Hal? I hope to heaven not! It would ruin all of us, including him!"

*   *   *   *   *

The wild daydreams I'd had myself flashed through my mind--the drug that would seem to kill him and wouldn't, the anonymous false accusation of subversion, the previous secret marriage. All impossible, all fatal.

Lucy disengaged her hands from the girl's and slipped her arm through mine.

"You tell him, Bet," she said gently. "You're the one who should."

I'd never noticed how pretty the girl was till then, when she stood there with her face flushed and her eyes straight on mine. A pang went through me; if only she and Hal could have--

"No, Mr. Sturt," she said, "we haven't rescued Hal. He's gone. But we've rescued part of him. I'm going to have his baby."

"Bet's going to live with us and be our daughter, Frank," Lucy explained. "Hal and she and I worked it out in these two weeks, after they came to me and told me how they felt about each other. We couldn't tell you till we were sure; I couldn't bear to have you hope and then be disappointed--it would be enough for me to have to suffer that."

"That is, I'll come if you want me here, Mr. Sturt," said Bet.

I had to sit down before I could speak. "Of course I want you. But what about your own family?"

"I haven't any. My mother's dead and my father's an engineer on Ganymede and gets home on leave about once in three years. I've been living in a youth hostel."

"But look here--" I turned to Lucy--"how on Earth can you know? Two weeks or less is no time--"

Lucy gave me a look I recognized, the patient one of the scientist for the layman.

"The Chow-Visalius test, dear. One day after the fertilized ovum starts dividing--"

"And I ran it myself every day for over a week. That's one of my jobs in the lab and it was easy to slip in another specimen. And it didn't, and it didn't and I went nearly out of my mind--"

"Every time Hal entered the apartment, I'd look at him and he'd shake his head," Lucy interrupted. "It meant everything to him. And it would just have broken my heart--"

"Mine, too," Bet said softly. "And his. And today was the last chance. I was scared to try it. This afternoon at 14:30, just before the farewell visits, was the deadline for viz messages to any of them. If I'd had to send mine without the word we'd agreed on that would tell him it was all right--But it was, at last! And now he knows, even if I never--even if we never--Excuse me, please, it's been a strain. I'm afraid I'm going to bawl."

* * * * *

We let her alone. Kids nowadays hate to be fussed over.

Us, we'd lost our son, and that was going to stay with us forever. But now we would have his child to love and--

An appalling thought struck me suddenly. I can't imagine why I hadn't realized it sooner. All this emotion, I suppose.

"Good God!" I cried. "An illegal child! We can't keep it!"

"Nobody's going to know," Lucy replied calmly. "Bet's going to live with us, and when it starts to show, she's going to take her allowed leave. We'll take ours, too, and we'll all go on a trip--to Mars, maybe, or Venus--one of the settled colonies where we can rent a house. Babies don't *have* to be born in hospitals, you know; our ancestors had them right at home. She's strong and healthy and I know what to do. Then we'll come back here and we'll have a baby with us that we adopted wherever we were. Nobody will ever know."

"Look," I said in a voice I tried to keep from rising. "There are four billion people on Earth and about 28 billion in the colonized Solar planets. Every one of those people is on record at Central Cybernetics. How do you suppose you're going to get away with the phony adoption of a non-existent child? The first time you have to take it to a baby clinic, they'll find it has no card."

"I thought of that," Lucy said, "and it can be done, because it must. Frank, for heaven's sake, use your wits! You're a newsgatherer. You know all sorts of people everywhere."

"I don't know any machines. And it's machines that handle the records."

"Machines under the supervision of humans."

"Sure," I said sarcastically. "I just go to my ex-newsgatherer pal who feeds the records to Io or Ceres and say, 'Look, old fellow, do me a favor, will you? My wife wants to adopt a baby from your colony, so just make up the names of two people and give them a life-check, invent their ancestors back to the time Central Cybernetics was established, and then slip in cards for their marriage, and the birth of their child--I'll let you know later whether to make it a boy or a girl--and then their deaths; and then my wife and I can adopt that made-up baby.'

"What kind of blackmailing hold do you think I have on any record official," I asked angrily, "to make him do a thing like that and keep his mouth shut about it? I could be eliminated for treason for even making such a suggestion."

"Frank, *think*! Surely there must be *some* way!"

*   *   *   *   *

And then it struck me. "Wait! I just got an idea. When I said 'treason,' just now--It might barely be possible--"

"Oh, what?"

"It would have to be Mars, the North Polar Cap colony. The K-Alph Conspiracy messed things up there badly."

"I remember, Mr. Sturt!" Bet said excitedly. "They wrecked everything in the three months before the rebellion was crushed, didn't they?"

"Everything including their cybernetics equipment. Central doesn't want it known, but I have inside information that it's still not in going condition. That colony is full of children who have never been registered. And I doubt if it will be in 100 per cent shape for the best part of another year. Those hellions really did a job. Let's see--this is the end of Month Two. We'd have to get away around Month Eight at the latest and the baby would be born--when exactly, Bet?"

"Early in Month Twelve. We could all be back here again by the first of next year, or even by the end of Month Thirteen."

"Well, I have enough accumulated leave for that and I guess you have too, Lucy; neither of us has taken more than two or three weeks for years. But what about you, Bet? You've been working less than a year."

"I can borrow it. Our director is crazy about travel and she'll be all for it when I tell her I have a chance to go to Mars for a long visit. Besides, she knows about Hal and me--I mean the way we are about each other--and she'll understand that I'd want to get away for a while now."

Asher, my editor-in-chief, would feel the same way, I thought, and so would Lucy's boss.

"I knew you'd find a way," remarked my wife complacently.

I looked at the telechron.

"We've all got to be at work in seven hours," I said, "if we expect to get through before the end of the afternoon. What say we turn in?"

"You stay here with us, Bet," said Lucy. "You parked your copter in our port, didn't you? Frank, I think we need a drink."

I pushed the buttons. Nobody said anything, but somehow it was a toast to Hal. I know the liquor had to get past a lump in my throat and the women were both crying. It wasn't like my self-contained Lucy. I guess she thought so herself, for she braced herself. But her voice was still trembling when she turned to Bet.

"A year from now," she said, "we'll all be back here in this room and, this time, part of Hal will be here with us--his son, our little Hal."

"It might be our little Hallie." Bet smiled through her tears. "It will be ten weeks before I can run the Schuster test to find out."

"It won't make any difference. Hal will never know that, but he'll know, way out there on Lydna, that his baby has been born. He'll know, even though he can never see it--or us."

*   *   *   *   *

Lucy blinked, then went on bravely. "Every time he looks in a mirror there, he'll say to himself, 'Well, back on Earth, there's a little tyke with my blue eyes and my curly hair and my mouth and nose and chin, who's going to grow up to be tall and straight like me--or maybe like Bet, but also a lot like me.'

"And as he grows older, he can think back to the way he was as a child and a boy and a man, and know that his son, or his daughter, will be feeling and thinking and looking some day just about the way he himself is then, and it will be a link with Earth and with us--"

That was when I had to go to the window and look out for a long time to pull myself together before I could face them again.

Lydna is top-top secret, but as I've said before, we newsgatherers get inside information.

I have a pretty shrewd idea of what the mysterious Lydna Project is. It's to alter human beings so they can adapt to the colonization of outer space.

The medics do things to them to enable them and their descendants to resist every possible condition of temperature and radiation and gravity. They have to alter the genes-- acquired characters would be of use only in a short-term project, and this is long-term. But you can't alter genes without affecting the individual.

We'd have Hal's normal child.

But when Hal got to Lydna, he and the rest of them would be shocked and sick for a while at sight of some of the inhabitants. And if he had any children on Lydna, we, back here, would scarcely recognize them as human. Some of them might have extra limbs. Some might have eyes and ears in odd places. Some might have lungs outside their bodies, or brains without a skull.

By that time, Hal himself would have got over being sick-- unless, some time, he got hold of a mirror and remembered the boy he used to be.

I'll Kill You Tomorrow
By Helen Huber

Originally Published in *If Worlds of Science Fiction*
November 1953

Editor's Notes:
I'll Kill You Tomorrow
By Helen Huber

This story is one of horror where you'd least expect it, amongst newborn babies in a hospital. Tales of horror have always been popular, and the 50's were no exception, except that the origins of the horror had become more varied with the addition of aliens, radioactive mutants, creatures from another dimension and so on. In "I'll Kill You Tomorrow," one of the oldest sources of horror, the changeling, is given an updated spin and multiplied by thirty.

Other than the existence of the single story "I'll Kill You Tomorrow" there is no biographical information available.

I'll Kill You Tomorrow

It was not a sinister silence. No silence is sinister until it acquires a background of understandable menace. Here there was only the night quiet of Maternity, the silence of noiseless rubber heels on the hospital corridor floor, the faint brush of starched white skirts brushing through doorways into darkened and semi-darkened rooms.

But there was something wrong with the silence in the "basket room" of Maternity, the glass-walled room containing row on row, the tiny hopes of tomorrow. The curtain was drawn across the window through which, during visiting hours, peered the proud fathers who did the hoping. The night-light was dim.

The silence should not have been there.

Lorry Kane, standing in the doorway, looked out over the rows of silent baskets and felt her blonde hair tighten at the roots. The tightening came from instinct, even before her brain had a chance to function, from the instincts and training of a registered nurse.

Thirty-odd babies grouped in one room and--*complete silence.*

Not a single whimper. Not one tiny cry of protest against the annoying phenomenon of birth.

Thirty babies--*dead?* That was the thought that flashed, unbidden, into Lorry's pretty head. The absurdity of it followed swiftly, and Lorry moved on rubber soles between a line of baskets. She bent down and explored with practiced fingers.

A warm, living bundle in a white basket.

The feeling of relief was genuine. Relief, even from an absurdity, is a welcome thing. Lorry smiled and bent closer.

Staring up at Lorry from the basket were two clear blue eyes. Two eyes, steady and fixed in a round baby face. An immobile, pink baby face housing two blue eyes that stared up into Lorry's with a quiet concentration that was chilling.

Lorry said, "What's the matter with you?" She spoke in a whisper and was addressing herself. She'd gone short on sleep lately--the only way, really, to get a few hours with Pete. Pete was an interne at General Hospital, and the kind of a homely grinning carrot-top a girl like Lorry could put into dreams as the center of a satisfactory future.

But all this didn't justify a case of jitters in the "basket room."

Lorry said. "Hi, short stuff," and lifted Baby Newcomb--Male, out of his crib for a cuddling.

Baby Newcomb didn't object. The blue eyes came closer. The week-old eyes with the hundred-year-old look. Lorry laid the bundle over her shoulder and smiled into the dimness.

"You want to be president, Shorty?" Lorry felt the warmth of a new life, felt the little body wriggle in snug contentment. "I wouldn't advise it. Tough job." Baby Newcomb twisted in his blanket. Lorry stiffened.

Snug contentment?

Lorry felt two tiny hands clutch and dig into her throat. Not just pawing baby hands. Little fingers that reached and explored for the windpipe.

She uncuddled the soft bundle, held it out. There were the eyes. She chilled. No imagination here. No spectre from lack of sleep.

Ancient murder-hatred glowing in new-born eyes.

*   *   *   *   *

"Careful, you fool! You'll drop this body." A thin piping voice. A shrill symphony in malevolence.

Fear weakened Lorry. She found a chair and sat down. She held the boy baby in her hands. Training would not allow her to drop Baby Newcomb. Even if she had fainted, she would not have let go.

*   *   *   *   *

The shrill voice: "It was stupid of me. Very stupid."

Lorry was cold, sick, mute.

"Very stupid. These hands are too fragile. There are no muscles in the arms. I couldn't have killed you."

"Please--I ..."

"Dreaming? No. I'm surprised at--well, at your surprise. You have a trained mind. You should have learned, long ago, to trust your senses."

"I don't understand."

"Don't look at the doorway. Nobody's coming in. Look at me. Give me a little attention and I'll explain."

"Explain?" Lorry pulled her eyes down to the cherubic little face as she parroted dully.

"I'll begin by reminding you that there are more things in existence than your obscene medical books tell you about."

"Who are you? What are you?"

"One of those things."

"You're not a baby!"

"Of course not. I'm ..." The beastly, brittle voice drifted into silence as though halted by an intruding thought. Then the thought voiced--voiced with a yearning at once pathetic and terrible: "It would be nice to kill you. Someday I will. Someday I'll kill you if I can find you."

"Why? Why?" Insane words in an insane world. But life had not stopped even though madness had taken over. "Why?"

The voice was matter-of-fact again. No more time for pleasant daydreams. "I'm something your books didn't tell you about. Naturally you're bewildered. Did you ever hear of a bodyless entity?"

Lorry shuddered in silence.

"You've heard of bodyless entities, of course--but you denied their existence in your smug world of precise tidy detail. I'm a bodyless entity. I'm one of a swarm. We come from a dimension your mind wouldn't accept even if I explained it, so I'll save words. We of the swarm seek unfoldment--fulfillment--even as you in your stupid, blind world. Do you want to hear more?"

"I ..."

"You're a fool, but I enjoy practicing with these new vocal chords, just as I enjoyed flexing the fingers and muscles. That's why I revealed myself. We are, basically of course, parasites. In the dimension where we exist in profusion, evolution has provided for us. There, we seek out and move into a dimensional entity far more intelligent than yourself. We destroy it in a way you wouldn't understand, and it is not important that you should. In fact, I can't see what importance there is in your existing at all."

"You plan to--kill all these babies?"

"Let me congratulate you. You've finally managed to voice an intelligent question. The answer is, no. We aren't strong enough to kill them. We dwelt in a far more delicate dimension than this one and all was in proportion. That was our difficulty when we came here. We could find no entities weak enough to take possession of until we came upon this roomful of infants."

"Then, if you're helpless ..."

"What do we plan to do? That's quite simple. These material entities will grow. We will remain attached--ingrained, so to speak. When the bodies enlarge sufficiently ..."

"*Thirty potential assassins....*" Lorry spoke again to herself, then hurled the words back into her own mind as her sickness deepened.

The shrill chirping: "What do you mean, potential? The word expresses a doubt. Here there is none." The entity's chuckle sounded like a baby, content over a full bottle. "Thirty certain assassins."

"But why must you kill?"

Lorry was sure the tiny shoulders shrugged. "Why? I don't know. I never thought to wonder. Why must you join with a man and propagate some day? Why do you feel sorry for what you term an unfortunate? Explain your instincts and I'll explain mine."

Lorry felt herself rising. Stiffly, she put Baby Newcomb back into his basket. As she did so, a ripple of shrill, jerky laughter crackled through the room. Lorry put her hands to her ears. "You know I can't say anything. You'd keep quiet. They'd call me mad."

"Precisely."

Malicious laughter, like driven sleet, cut into her ears as she fled from the room.

*   *   *   *   *

Peter Larchmont, M.D., was smoking a quick cigarette by an open fire-escape door on the third floor. He turned as Lorry came down the corridor, flipped his cigarette down into the alley and grinned. "Women shouldn't float on rubber heels," he said. "A man should have warning."

Lorry came close. "Kiss me. Kiss me--hard."

Pete kissed her, then held her away. "You're trembling. Anticipation, pet?" He looked into her face and the grin faded. "Lorry, what is it?"

"Pete--Pete. I'm crazy. I've gone mad. Hold me."

He could have laughed, but he had looked closely into her eyes and he was a doctor. He didn't laugh. "Tell me. Just stand here. I'll hang onto you and you tell me."

"The babies--they've gone mad." She clung to him. "Not exactly that. Something's taken them over. Something terrible. Oh, Pete! Nobody would believe me."

"I believe the end result," he said, quietly. "That's what I'm for, angel. When you shake like this I'll always believe. But I'll have to know more. And I'll hunt for an answer."

"There isn't any answer, Pete. I *know*."

"We'll still look. Tell me more, first."

"There isn't any more." Her eyes widened as she stared into his with the shock of a new thought. "Oh, Lord! One of them talked to me, but maybe he--or it--won't talk to you. Then you'll never know for sure! You'll think I'm ..."

"Stop it. Quit predicting what I'll do. Let's go to the nursery."

They went to the nursery and stayed there for three-quarters of an hour. They left with the tinny laughter filling their minds-- and the last words of the monstrous entity.

"We'll say no more, of course. Perhaps even this incident has been indiscreet. But it's in the form of a celebration. Never before has a whole swarm gotten through. Only a single entity on rare occasions."

Pete leaned against the corridor wall and wiped his face with the sleeve of his jacket. "We're the only ones who know," he said.

"Or ever will know." Lorry pushed back a lock of his curly hair. She wanted to kiss him, but this didn't seem to be the place or the time.

"We can never tell anyone."

"We'd look foolish."

"We've got a horror on our hands and we can't pass it on."

"What are we going to do?" Lorry asked.

"I don't know. Let's recap a little. Got a cigarette?"

They went to the fire door and dragged long and deep on two from Lorry's pack. "They'll be quiet from now on. No more talking--just baby squalls."

"And thirty little assassins will go into thirty homes," Lorry said. "All dressed in soft pink and blue, all filled with hatred. Waiting, biding their time, growing more clever." She shuddered.

"The electric chair will get them all, eventually."

"But how many will they get in the meantime?"

Pete put his arms around her and drew her close and whispered into her ear. "There's nothing we can do--nothing."

"We've got to do something." Lorry heard again the thin, brittle laughter following her, taunting her.

"It was a bad dream. It didn't happen. We'll just have to sleep it off."

She put her cheek against his. The rising stubble of his beard scratched her face. She was grateful for the rough touch of solid reality.

Pete said, "The shock will wear out of our minds. Time will pass. After a while, we won't believe it ourselves."

"That's what I'm afraid of."

"It's got to be that way."

"We've got to do something."

Pete lowered his arm wearily. "Yeah--we've got to do something. Where there's nothing that can be done. What are we--miracle workers?"

"We've got to do something."

"Sure--finish out the watch and then get some sleep."

*   *   *   *   *

Lorry awoke with the lowering sun in her window. It was a blood red sun. She picked up the phone by her bedside. "Room 307 Resident's extension."

Pete answered drowsily. Lorry said, "Tell me--did I dream, or did it really happen."

"I was going to ask you the same thing. I guess it happened. What are you doing?"

"Lying in bed."

"So am I. But two different beds. Things are done all wrong."

"Want to take a chance and sneak over? I've got an illegal coffee pot."

"Leave the door unlocked."

Lorry put on the coffee. She showered and got into her slip. She was brushing her hair when Pete came in. He looked at her and extended beckoning, clutching fingers. "The hell with phantoms. Come here."

After a couple of minutes, Lorry pulled away and poured the coffee. She reached for her uniform. Pete said, "Don't put it on yet."

"Too dangerous--leaving it off."

He eyed her dreamily. "I'll dredge up will power. I'll also get scads of fat rich clients. Then we'll get married so I can assault you legally."

Lorry studied him. "You're not even listening to yourself. What is it, Pete? What have you dreamed up?"

"Okay. I've got an idea. You said something would have to be done."

"What?"

"A drastic cure for a drastic case. With maybe disaster as the end product."

"Tell me."

"I'll tell you a little, but not too much."

"Why not all?"

"Because if we ever land in court. I want you to be able to say under oath, 'He didn't tell me what he planned to do.'"

"I don't like that."

"I don't care if you like it or not. Tell me, what's the one basic thing that stands out in your mind about these--entities?"

"That they're ..."

"Fragile?"

"Yes--fragile."

"Give me some more coffee."

*   *   *   *   *

Lorry demanded to know what was in Pete's mind. All she got was kissed, and she did not see Pete again until eleven o'clock that night. He found her in the corridor in Maternity and motioned her toward the nursery. He carried a tray under a white towel. He said, "You watch the door. I'm going inside. I'll be about a half an hour."

"What are you going to do?"

"You stay out here and mind your business. Your business will be to steer any nosey party away. If you can't, make noise coming in."

Doc Pete turned away and entered the nursery. Lorry stood at the doorway, in the silence, under the brooding night-light, and prayed.

Twenty-five minutes later, Pete came out. His face was white and drawn. He looked like a man who had lately had a preview of Hell's inverted pleasures. His hands trembled. The towel still covered the tray. He said, "Watch them close. Don't move ten steps from here." He started away--turned back. "All hell is scheduled to break loose in this hospital shortly. Let's hope God remains in charge."

Lorry saw the sick dread of his heart underneath his words.

*   *   *   *   *

It could have been a major scandal. An epidemic of measles on the maternity floor of a modern hospital indicates the unforgivable medical sin--carelessness. It was hushed up as much as possible, pending the time when the top people could shake off the shock and recover their wits. The ultimate recovery of thirty babies was a tribute to everyone concerned.

Wan, done-in, Doc Pete drank coffee in Lorry's room. Lorry gave him three lumps of sugar and said, "But are you sure the sickness killed the entities?"

"Quite sure. Somehow they *knew* when I made the injections. They screamed. They knew they were done for."

"It took courage. Tell me: why are you so strong, so brave? Why are you so wonderful?"

"Cut it out. I was scared stiff. If *one* baby had died, I'd have gone through life weighing the cure against the end. It isn't easy to risk doing murder--however urgent the need."

She leaned across and kissed him. "And you were all alone. You wouldn't let me help. Was that fair?"

He grinned, then sobered. "But I can't help remembering what that--that invisible monster said: '*Never before has a whole swarm gotten through. Only a single entity on rare occasions.*'

"I can't help wondering what happens to those single entities. I think of the newspaper headlines I've seen: Child Kills Parents in Sleep. Youth Slays Father. I'll probably always wonder--and I'll always remember...."

Lorry got up and crossed to him and put her arms around him. "Not always," she whispered. "There will be times when I'll make you forget. For a little while, anyhow."

ROUGH TRANSLATION
BY JEAN M. JANIS

ORIGINALLY PUBLISHED IN *GALAXY*
DECEMBER 1954

Editor's Notes:
Rough Translation
By Jean M. Janis

In the fifties, when it looked like we might actually travel to meet aliens, or they would come to meet us, the theme of communication was a common one. There were many variations, as the difficulties of establishing understanding are great, the possibilities for misunderstanding many, and the consequences of that misunderstanding might be humorous or dire depending on the whim of the author. Janis, in "Rough Translation," raises another question, what would really understanding aliens do to us?

Jean M. Janis wrote two stories "Rough Translation" 1954 and "Queen's Mate" 1954. There is an obituary for a Jean M. Janis who was born on March 3, 1920 and died on January 11, 2010 in Wyncote, Pennsylvania, but it is not clear whether this is the same person.

Rough Translation

"Shurgub," said the tape recorder. "Just like I told you before, Dr. Blair, it's krandoor, so don't expect to vrillipax, because they just won't stand for any. They'd sooner framish."

"Framish?" Jonathan heard his own voice played back by the recorder, tinny and slightly nasal. "What is that, Mr. Easton?"

"*You* know. Like when you guttip. Carooms get awfully bevvergrit. Why, I saw one actually--"

"Let's go back a little, shall we?" Jonathan suggested. "What does shurgub mean?"

There was a pause while the machine hummed and the recorder tape whirred. Jonathan remembered the look on Easton's face when he had asked him that. Easton had pulled away slightly, mouth open, eyes hurt.

"Why--why, I *told* you!" he had shouted. "Weeks ago! What's the matter? Don't you blikkel English?"

Jonathan Blair reached out and snapped the switch on the machine. Putting his head in his hands, he stared down at the top of his desk.

You learned Navajo in six months, he reminded himself fiercely.

You are a highly skilled linguist. What's the matter? Don't you blikkel English?

*   *   *   *   *

He groaned and started searching through his briefcase for the reports from Psych. Easton must be insane. He must! Ramirez says it's no language. Stoughton says it's no language. And *I*, Jonathan thought savagely, say it's no language.

But--

Margery tiptoed into the study with a tray.

"But Psych," he continued aloud to her, "Psych says it *must* be a language because, they say, Easton is *not* insane!"

"Oh, dear," sighed Margery, blinking her pale blue eyes. "That again?" She set his coffee on the desk in front of him. "Poor Jonathan. Why doesn't the Institute give up?"

"Because they can't." He reached for the cup and sat glaring at the steaming coffee.

"Well," said his wife, settling into the leather chair beside him, "*I* certainly would. My goodness, it's been over a month now since he came back, and you haven't learned a thing from him!"

"Oh, we've learned some. And this morning, for the first time, Easton himself began to seem puzzled by a few of the things he was saying. He's beginning to use terms we can understand. He's coming around. And if I could only find some clue--some sort of--"

Margery snorted. "It's just plain foolish! I knew the Institute was asking for trouble when they sent the *Rhinestead* off. How do they know Easton ever got to Mars, anyway? Maybe he did away with those other men, cruised around, and then came back to Earth with this made-up story just so he could seem to be a hero and--"

"That's nonsense!"

"Why?" she demanded stubbornly. "Why is it?"

"Because the *Rhinestead* was tracked, for one thing, on both flights, to and from Mars. Moonbase has an indisputable record of it. And besides, the instruments on the ship itself show--" He found the report he had been searching for. "Oh, never mind."

"All right," she said defiantly. "Maybe he did get to Mars. Maybe he did away with the crew after he got there. He knew the ship was built so that one man could handle it in an emergency. Maybe he--"

"Look," said Jonathan patiently. "He didn't do anything of the sort. Easton has been checked so thoroughly that it's impossible to assume anything except, (a) he is sane, (b) he reached Mars and made contact with the Martians, (c) this linguistic barrier is a result of that contact."

*   *   *   *   *

Margery shook her head, sucking in her breath. "When I think of all those fine young men," she murmured. "Heaven only knows what happened to them!"

"You," Jonathan accused, "have been reading that columnist--what's-his-name? The one that's been writing such claptrap ever since Easton brought the *Rhinestead* back alone."

"Cuddlehorn," said his wife. "Roger Cuddlehorn, and it's not claptrap."

"The other members of the crew are all alive, all--"

"I suppose Easton told you that?" she interrupted.

"Yes, he did."

"Using double-talk, of course," said his wife triumphantly. At the look on Jonathan's face, she stood up in guilty haste. "All right, I'll go!" She blew him a kiss from the door. "Richie and I are having lunch at one. Okay? Or would you rather have a tray in here?"

"Tray," he said, turning back to his desk and his coffee. "No, on second thought, call me when lunch is ready. I'll need a break."

He was barely conscious of the closing of the door as Margery left the room. Naturally he didn't take her remarks seriously, but--

He opened the folder of pictures and studied them again, along with the interpretations by Psych, Stoughton, Ramirez and himself.

Easton had drawn the little stick figures on the first day of his return. The interpretations all checked--and they had been done independently, too. There it is, thought Jonathan. Easton lands the *Rhinestead.* He and the others meet the Martians. They are impressed by the Martians. The others stay on Mars. Easton returns to Earth, bearing a message.

Question: What is the message?

Teeth set, Jonathan put away the pictures and went back to the tape on the recorder. "Yes," said his own voice, in answer to Easton's outburst. "I do--er--blikkel English. But tell me, Mr. Easton, do you understand me?"

"Under-stand?" The man seemed to have difficulty forming the word. "You mean--" Pause. "Dr. Blair, I murv you. Is that it?"

"Murv," repeated Jonathan. "All right, you murv me. Do you murv this? I do not always murv what you say."

A laugh. "Of course not. How could you?" Suppressed groan. "Carooms," Easton had murmured, almost inaudibly. "Just when I almost murv, the kwakut goes freeble."

Jonathan flipped the switch on the machine. "Murv" he wrote on his pad of paper. He added "Blikkel," "Carooms" and "Freeble." He stared at the list. He should understand, he thought. At times it seemed as if he did and then, in the next instant, he was lost again, and Easton was angry, and they had to start all over again.

*   *   *   *   *

Sighing, he took out more papers, notes from previous sessions, both with himself and with other linguists. The difficulty of reaching Easton was unlike anything he had ever before tackled. The six months of Navajo had been rough going, but he had done it, and done it well enough to earn the praise of Old Comas, his informant. Surely, he thought, after mastering a language like that, one in which the student must not only learn to imitate difficult sounds, but also learn a whole new pattern of thought--

Pattern of thought. Jonathan sat very still, as though movement would send the fleeting clue back into the corner from which his mind had glimpsed it.

A whole new frame of reference. Suppose, he toyed with the thought, suppose the Martian language, whatever it was, was structured along the lines of Navajo, involving clearly defined categories which did not exist in English.

"Murv," he said aloud. "I murv a lesson, but I blikkel a language."

Eagerly, Jonathan reached again for the switch. Categories clearly defined, yes! But the categories of the Martian language were not those of the concrete or the particular, like the Navajo. They were of the abstract. Where one word "understand" would do in English, the Martian used two--

Good Lord, he realized, they might use hundreds! They might--

Jonathan turned on the machine, sat back and made notes, letting the recorder run uninterrupted. He made his notes, this time, on the feelings he received from the words Easton used. When the first tape was done, he put on the second.

Margery tapped at the door just as the third tape was ending. "In a minute," he called, scribbling furiously. He turned off the machine, put out his cigarette and went to lunch, feeling better than he had in weeks.

Richie was at the kitchen sink, washing his hands.

"And next time," Margery was saying, "you wash up before you sit down."

Richie blinked and watched Jonathan seat himself. "Daddy didn't wash his hands," he said.

Margery fixed the six-year-old with a stern eye. "Richard, don't be rude."

"Well, he didn't." Richie sat down and reached for his glass of milk.

"Daddy probably washed before he came in," said Margery. She took the cover off a tureen, ladled soup into bowls and passed sandwiches, pretending not to see the ink-stained hand Jonathan was hiding in his lap.

Jonathan, elated by the promise of success, ate three or four sandwiches, had two bowls of soup and finally sat back while Margery went to get coffee.

Richie slid part way off his chair, remembered, and slid back on again. "Kin I go?" he asked.

"Please may I be excused," corrected his father.

*   *   *   *   *

Richie repeated, received a nod and ran out of the dinette and through the kitchen, grabbing a handful of cookies on the way. The screen door banged behind him as he raced into the backyard.

"Richie!" Margery started after him, eyes ablaze. Then she stopped and came back to the table with the coffee. "That boy! How long does it take before they get to be civilized?" Jonathan laughed. "Oh, sure," she went on, sitting down opposite him. "It's funny to you. But if you were here all day long--" She stirred sugar into her cup. "We should have sent him to camp, even if it would have wrecked the budget!"

"Oh? Is it that bad?"

Margery shuddered. "Sometimes he's a perfect angel, and then--It's unbelievable, the things that child can think of! Sometimes I'm convinced children are another species altogether! Why, only this morning--"

"Well," Jonathan broke in, "next summer he goes to camp." He stood up and stretched.

Margery said wistfully, "I suppose you want to get back to work."

"Ummmm." Jonathan leaned over and kissed her briefly. "I've got a new line of attack," he said, picking up his coffee. He patted his wife's shoulder. "If things work out well, we might get away on that vacation sooner than we thought."

"Really?" she asked, brightening.

"Really." He left the table and went back to his den.

Putting the next tape on the machine, he settled down to his job. Time passed and finally there were no more tapes to listen to.

He stacked his notes and began making lists, checking through the sheets of paper for repetitions of words Easton had used, listing the various connotations which had occurred to Jonathan while he had listened to the tapes.

As he worked, he was struck by the similarity of the words he was recording to the occasional bits of double-talk he had heard used by comedians in theaters and on the air, and he allowed his mind to wander a bit, exploring the possibilities.

Was Martian actually such a close relative to English? Or had the Martians learned English from Easton, and had Easton then formed a sort of pidgin-English-Martian of his own?

Jonathan found it difficult to believe in the coincidence of the two languages being alike, unless--

He laughed. Unless, of course, Earthmen were descended from Martians, or vice versa. Oh, well, not my problem, he thought jauntily.

*   *   *   *   *

He stared at the list before him and then he started to swear, softly at first, then louder. But no matter how loudly he swore, the list remained undeniably and obstinately the same:

Freeble--Displeasure (Tape 3)

Freeble--Elation (Tape 4)

Freeble--Grief (Tape 5)

"How," he asked the empty room, "can a word mean grief and elation at the same time?"

Jonathan sat for a few moments in silence, thinking back to the start of the sessions with Easton. Ramirez and Stoughton had both agreed with him that Easton's speech was phonemically identical to English. Jonathan's trained ear remembered the pronunciation of "Freeble" in the three different connotations and he forced himself to admit it was the same on all three tapes in question.

Stuck again, he thought gloomily.

Good-by, vacation!

He lit a cigarette and stared at the ceiling. It was like saying the word "die" meant something happy and something sad at one and the same, like saying--

Jonathan pursed his lips. Yes, it could be. If someone were in terrible pain, death, while a thing of sorrow, could also mean release from suffering and so become a thing of joy. Or it could mean sorrow to one person and relief to another. In that case, what he was dealing with here was not only--

The crash of the ball, as it sailed through the window behind his desk, lifted Jonathan right from his chair. Furious, his elusive clue shattered as surely as the pane of glass, he strode to the window.

"Richie!"

His son, almost hidden behind the lilac bush, did not answer.

"I see you!" Jonathan bellowed. "Come here!"

The bush stirred slightly and Richie peeped through the leaves. "Did you call me, Daddy?" he asked politely.

Jonathan clamped his lips shut and pointed to the den. Richie tried a smile as he sidled around the bush, around his father, and into the house.

"My," he marveled, looking at the broken glass on the floor inside. "My goodness!" He sat down in the leather chair to which Jonathan motioned.

"Richie," said his father, when he could trust his voice again, "how did it happen?"

His son's thin legs, brown and wiry, stuck out straight from the depths of the chair. There was a long scratch on one calf and numerous black-and-blue spots around both knees.

"I dunno," said Richie. He blinked his eyes, deeper blue than Margery's, and reached up one hand to push away the mass of blond hair tumbling over his forehead. He was obviously trying hard to pretend he wasn't in the room at all.

*   *   *   *   *

Jonathan said, "Now, son, that is not a good answer. What were you doing when the ball went through the window?"

"Watching," said Richie truthfully.

"How did it *go* through the window?"

"Real fast."

Jonathan found his teeth were clamped. No wonder he couldn't decode Easton's speech--he couldn't even talk with his own son!

"I mean," he explained, his patience wavering, "you threw the ball so that it broke the window, didn't you?"

"I didn't mean it to," said Richie.

"All right. That's what I wanted to know." He started on a lecture about respect for other people's property, while Richie sat and looked blankly respectful. "And so," he heard himself conclude, "I hope we'll be more careful in the future."

"Yes," said Richie.

A vague memory came to Jonathan and he sat and studied his son, remembering him when he was younger and first starting to talk. He recalled the time Richie, age three, had come bustling up to him. "Vransh!" the child had pleaded, tugging at his father's hand. Jonathan had gone outside with him to see a baby bird which had fallen from its nest. "Vransh!" Richie had crowed, exhibiting his find. "Vransh!"

"Do I get my spanking now?" asked Richie from the chair. His eyes were wide and watchful.

Jonathan tore his mind from still another recollection: the old joke about the man and woman who adopted a day-old French infant and then studied French so they would be able to understand their child when he began to talk. Maybe, thought Jonathan, it's no joke. Maybe there *is* a language--

"Spanking?" he repeated absentmindedly. He took a fresh pencil and pad of paper. "How would you like to help with something, Richie?"

The blue eyes watched carefully. "Before you spank me or after?"

"No spanking." Jonathan glanced at the Easton notes, vaguely aware that Richie had suddenly relaxed. "What I'm going to do," he went on, "is say some words. It'll be a kind of game. I'll say a word and then you say a word. You say the first word you think after you hear my word. Okay?" He cleared his throat. "Okay! The first word is--house."

"*My* house."

"Bird," said Jonathan.

"Uh--tree." Richie scratched his nose and stifled a yawn.

* * * * *

Disappointed, Jonathan reminded himself that Richie at six could not be expected to remember something he had said when he was three. "Dog."

"Biffy." Richie sat up straight. "Daddy, did you know Biffy had puppies? Steve's mother showed me. Biffy had four puppies, Daddy. *Four!*"

Jonathan nodded. He supposed Richie's next statement would be an appeal to go next door and negotiate for one of the pups, and he hurried on with, "Carooms."

"Friends," said Richie, eyes still shining. "Daddy, do you suppose we could have a pup--" He broke off at the look on Jonathan's face. "Huh?"

"Friends," repeated Jonathan, writing the word slowly and unsteadily. "Uh--vacation."

"Beach," said Richie cautiously, still looking scared.

Jonathan went on with more familiar terms and Richie slowly relaxed again in the big chair. From somewhere in the back of his mind, Jonathan heard Margery say, "Sometimes I think they're a different species altogether." He kept his voice low and casual, uncertain of what he was thinking, but aware of the fact that Richie was hiding something. The little mantel clock ticked drowsily, and Richie began to look sleepy and bored as they went through things like "car" and "school" and "book." Then--

"Friend," said Jonathan.

"Allavarg," yawned Richie. "No!" He snapped to, alert and wary. "I mean *Steve*."

His father looked up sharply. "What's that?"

"What?" asked Richie.

"Richie," said Jonathan, "what's a Caroom?"

The boy shrugged and muttered, "*I* dunno."

"Oh, yes, you do!" Jonathan lit a cigarette. "What's an Allavarg?" He watched the boy bite his lips and stare out the window. "He's a friend, isn't he?" coaxed Jonathan. "*Your* friend? Does he play with you?"

The blond head nodded slowly and uncertainly.

"Where does he live?" persisted Jonathan. "Does he come over here and play in your yard? Does he, Richie?"

The boy stared at his father, worried and unhappy. "Sometimes," he whispered. "Sometimes he does, if I call him."

"How do you call him?" asked Jonathan. He was beginning to feel foolish.

"Why," said Richie, "I just say 'Here, Allavarg!' and he comes, if he's not too busy."

"What keeps him busy?" Such nonsense! Allavarg was undoubtedly an imaginary playmate. This whole hunch of his was utter nonsense. He should be at work on Easton instead of--

"The nursery keeps him busy," said Richie. "Real busy."

*   *   *   *   *

Jonathan frowned. Did Richie mean the greenhouse down the road? Was there a Mr. Allavarg who worked there? "Whose nursery?"

"Ours." Richie wrinkled his face thoughtfully. "I think I better go outside and play."

"*Our* nursery?" Jonathan stared at his son. "Where is it?"

"I think I better go play," said Richie more firmly, sliding off the chair.

"Richard! *Where* is the nursery?"

The full lower lip began to tremble. "I can't tell you!" Richie wailed. "I promised!"

Jonathan slammed his fist on the desk. "Answer me!" He knew he shouldn't speak this way to Richie; he knew he was frightening the boy. But the ideas racing through his mind drove him to find out what this was all about. It might be nothing, but it also might be--"Answer me, Richard!"

The child stifled a sob. "Here," he said weakly.

"*Here*? Where?"

"In my house," said Richie. "And Steve's house and Billy's and all over." He rubbed his eyes, leaving a grimy smear.

"All right," soothed Jonathan. "It's all right now, son. Daddy didn't mean to scare you. Daddy has to learn these things, that's all. Just like learning in school."

The boy shook his head resentfully. "*You* know," he accused. "You just forgot."

"What did I forget, Richie?"

"You forgot all about Allavarg. He told me! It was a different Allavarg when you were little, but it was almost the same. You used to play with *your* Allavarg when you were little like me!"

Jonathan took a deep breath. "Where did Allavarg come from, Richie?"

But Richie shook his head stubbornly, lips pressed tight. "I promised!"

"Richie, a promise like that isn't a good one," pleaded Jonathan. "Allavarg wouldn't want you to disobey your father and mother, would he?"

The child sat and stared at him.

This was a very disturbing thought and Jonathan could see Richie did not know how to deal with it.

He pressed his momentary advantage. "Allavarg takes care of little boys and girls, doesn't he? He plays with them and he looks after them, I'll bet."

Richie nodded uncertainly.

"And," continued Jonathan, smiling what he hoped was a winning, comradely smile at his son, "I'll bet that Allavarg came from some place far, far away, didn't he?"

"Yes," said Richie softly.

"And it's his job to be here and look after the--the nursery?" Jonathan bit his lip. Nursery? Earth? Carooms--Martians? His head began to ache. "Son, you've got to help me understand. Do you--do you murv me?"

*   *   *   *   *

Richie shook his head. "No. But I *will* after--"

"After what?"

"After I grow up."

"Why not now?" asked Jonathan.

The blond head sank lower. "Because you framish, Daddy."

His father nodded, trying to look wise, wincing inwardly as he pictured his colleagues listening in on this conversation. "Well--why don't you help me so I *don't* framish?"

"I can't." Richie glanced up, his eyes stricken. "Some day, Allavarg says, *I'm* going to framish, too!"

"Grow up, you mean?" hazarded Jonathan, and this time his smile was real as he looked at the smudged eyes and soft round cheeks. "Why, Richie," he went on, his voice suddenly husky, "it's fun to be a little boy, but there'll be lots to do when you grow up. You--"

"I wish I was Mr. Easton!" Richie said fiercely.

Jonathan held his breath. "What about Mr. Easton?"

Richie squirmed out of the chair and clutched Jonathan's arm. "Please, Daddy! If you let Mr. Easton go back, can I go, too? Please? Can I?"

Jonathan put his hands on his son's shoulders. "Richie! What do you know about Mr. Easton?"

"Please? Can I go with him?" The shining blue eyes pleaded up at him. "If you don't let him go back pretty soon, he's going to framish again! Please! Can I?"

"He's going to framish," nodded Jonathan. "And what then?" he coaxed. "What'll happen after he framishes? Will he be able to tell me about his trip?"

"*I* dunno," said Richie. "I dunno how he *could*. After you framish, you don't remember lots of things. I don't think he's even gonna remember he *went* on a trip." The boy's hands shook Jonathan's arm eagerly. "Please, Daddy! Can I go with him?"

"No!" Jonathan glared and released his hold on Richie. Didn't he have troubles enough without Richie suggesting--"About the nursery," he said briskly. "Why is there a nursery?"

"To take care of us." Richie looked worried. "Why can't I go?"

"Because you can't! Why don't they have the nursery back where Allavarg came from?"

"There isn't any room." The blue eyes studied the man, looking for a way to get permission to go with Mr. Easton.

"No room? What do you mean?"

Richie sighed. Obviously he'd have to explain first and coax later. "Well, you know my school? You know my teacher in school? You know when my teacher was different?" He peered anxiously at Jonathan, and suddenly the man caught on.

"Of course! You mean when they split the kindergarten into two smaller groups because there were too many--"

*   *   *   *   *

His voice trailed off. Too many. Too many what? Too many Martians on Mars? Growing population? No way to cut down the birth rate? He pictured the planet with too many people. What to do? Move out. Take another planet. Why didn't they just do that? He put the question to Richie.

"Oh," said his son wisely, "they couldn't because of the framish. They *did* go other places, but everywhere they went, they framished. And after you framish, you ain't--*aren't* a Caroom any more. You're a Gunderguck and of course--"

"Huh?"

"--and a Caroom doesn't like to framish and be a Gunderguck," continued Richie happily, as though reciting a lesson learned in school. "He wants to be a Caroom *all* the time because it's better and more fun and you know lots of things you don't remember after you get to be a Gunderguck. Only--" he paused for a gulp of air--"only there wasn't room for *all* the Carooms back home and they couldn't find any place where they could be Carooms all the time, because of the framish. So after a long time, and after they looked all over all around, they decided maybe it wouldn't be so bad if they sent some of their little boys and girls--the ones they didn't have room for--to some place where they could be Carooms longer than most other places. And *that* place," Richie said proudly, "was right here! 'Cause *here* there's almost as much gladdisl as back home and--"

"Gladdisl?" Jonathan echoed hoarsely. "What's--"

"--and after they start growing up--"

"Gladdisl," Jonathan repeated, more firmly. "Richie, what is it?"

The forehead puckered momentarily. "It's something you breathe, sort of." The boy shied away from the difficult question, trying to remember what Allavarg had said about gladdisl. "Anyway, after the little boys and girls start to grow up and after they framish and be Gundergucks, like you and Mommy, the

Carooms back home send some *more* to take their places. And the Gundergucks who used to be Carooms here in the nursery look after the new little--"

"Wait a minute! Wait a minute!" Jonathan interrupted suspiciously. "I thought you said Allavarg looks after them."

"He does. But there's so many little Carooms and there aren't many Allavargs and so the Gundergucks have to help. You help," Richie assured his father. "You and Mommy help a little bit."

Big of you to admit it, old man, thought Jonathan, suppressing a smile. "But aren't you *our* little boy?" he asked. He had a sudden vision of himself addressing the scientists at the Institute: "And so, gentlemen, our babies--who, incidentally, are really Martians--*are* brought by storks, after all. Except in those cases where--"

"The doctor brought me in a little black bag," said Richie.

*　　*　　*　　*　　*

The boy stood silent and studied his father. He sort of remembered what Allavarg had said, too. Things like You *mustn't ever tell* and *It's got to be a secret* and *They'd only laugh at you, Richie, and if they didn't laugh, they might believe you and try to go back home and there just isn't any room.*

"I think," said Richie, "I think I better--" He took a deep breath. "Here, Allavarg," he called in a soft, piping voice.

Jonathan raised his head. "Just what do you think you're doing--"

There was a sound behind him, and Jonathan turned startledly.

"Shame on you," said Allavarg, coming through the broken window.

Jonathan's words dropped away in a faint gurgle.

"I'm sorry," said Richie. "Don't be dipplefit."

"It's a mess," Allavarg replied. "It's a krandoor mess!" He waved his arm in the air over Jonathan's head. "And don't think I'm going to forget it!" The insistent hiss of escaping gas hovered over the moving pellet in his hand. "Jivis boy!"

Jonathan coughed suddenly. He got as far as "Now look here" and then found that he could neither speak nor move. The gas or whatever it was stung his eyes and burned in his throat.

"Why don't you just freeble him?" Richie asked unhappily. "You're using up all your gladdisl! Why don't you freeble him and get me another one?"

"Freeble, breeble," grumbled Allavarg, shoving the capsule directly under Jonathan's nose. "Just like you youngsters, always wanting to take the easy way out! Gundergucks don't grow on blansercots, you know."

Jonathan felt tears start in his eyes, partly from the fumes and partly from a growing realization that Allavarg was sacrificing precious air for him. He tried to think. If this was gladdisl and if this would keep a man in the state of being a Caroom, then--

"There," said Allavarg, looking unhappily at the emptied pellet. He shook it, sniffed it and finally returned it to the container at his side.

"I'm sorry," Richie whispered. "But he kept askin' me and askin' me."

"There, there," said Allavarg, going to the window. "Don't fret. I know you won't do it again." He turned and looked thoughtfully at Jonathan. He winked at Richie and then he was gone.

*　　*　　*　　*　　*

Jonathan rubbed his eyes. He could move now. He opened his mouth and waggled his jaws. Now that the room was beginning to be cleared of the gas, he realized that it had had a pleasant odor. He realized--

Why, it was all so simple! Remembering his sessions with Easton, Jonathan laughed aloud. So simple! The message? *Stay away from Mars! No room there! They said I could come back if I gave you the message, but I have to come back alone because there's no room for more people!*

No room? Nonsense! Jonathan reached for the phone, dialled the Institute and asked for Dr. Stoughton. No room? On the paradise that was Mars? Well, they'd just have to make room! They couldn't keep that to themselves!

"Hello, Fred?" He leaned back in his chair, feeling a surge of pride and power. Wait till they heard about this! "Just wanted to tell you I solved the Easton thing. Just a simple case of hapsodon. You see, Allavarg came and gave me a tressimox of gladdisl and now that I'm a Caroom again--What? What do you mean, what's the matter? I said I'm not a Gunderguck any more." He stared at the phone. "Why, you spebberset moron! What's the matter with you? Don't you blikkel English?"

From the depths of the big chair across the room, Richie giggled.

Know Thy Neighbor

By Elisabeth R. Lewis

Originally Published in *Galaxy*
February 1953

EDITOR'S NOTES:
KNOW THY NEIGHBOR
BY ELISABETH R. LEWIS

EDITOR'S NOTES:
KNOW THY NEIGHBOR
BY ELISABETH R. LEWIS

How well does any apartment dweller know their neighbors? Other than chance encounters in hallways and elevators they are rarely seen, and what goes on behind the closed doors remains terra incognita. The person next door could be anyone– or anything. Lewis plays on this fear in "Know Thy Neighbor," a tale of urban terror.

Other than the existence of the single story "Know Thy Neighbor" there is no biographical information available.

KNOW THY NEIGHBOR

It began with the dead cat on the fire escape and ended with the green monster in the incinerator chute, but still, it wouldn't be quite fair to blame it all on the neighborhood....

The apartment house was in the heart of the district that is known as "The Tenderloin"--that section of San Francisco from Ellis to Market and east from Leavenworth to Mason Street. Not the best section.

To Ellen's mind, it was an unsavory neighborhood, but with apartments so hard to get and this one only $38.00 a month and in a regular apartment building with an elevator and all--well, as she often told the girls at the office, you can't be too particular these days.

Nevertheless, it was an ordeal to walk up the two blocks from Market Street, particularly at night when the noise of juke boxes dinned from the garish bars, when the sidewalks spilled over with soldiers and sailors, with peroxided, blowsy-looking women and the furtive gamblers who haunted the back rooms of the innocent-appearing cigar stores that lined the street. She walked very fast then, never looking to left or right, and her heart would pound when a passing male whistled.

But once inside the apartment house lobby, she relaxed. In spite of its location, the place seemed very respectable. She seldom met anyone in the lobby or the elevator and, except on rare occasions like last night, the halls were as silent as those in the swanky apartment houses on Nob Hill.

She knew by sight only two of her neighbors--the short, stocky young man who lived in 410, and Mrs. Moffatt, in 404. Mrs. Moffatt was the essence of lavender and old lace, and the young man--he was all right, really; you couldn't honestly say he was shady-looking.

*   *   *   *   *

On this particular morning, the man from 410 was waiting for the elevator when Ellen came out to get her paper. He glanced up at the sound of the door and stared. Quickly, she shut the door again. She didn't like the way he looked at her. She was wearing a housecoat over her nightgown, and a scarf wrapped around her head to cover the bobbypins--a costume as unrevealing as a nun's--but she felt as though he had invaded her privacy with his stare, like surprising her in the bathtub.

She waited until she heard the elevator start down before opening her door again. The boy must have aimed from the stairs; her paper was several yards down the hall, almost in front of 404. She went down to get it.

Mrs. Moffatt must have heard Ellen's footsteps in the hall. An old lady with a small income (from her late husband, as she had explained to Ellen) and little to do, she was intensely interested in her neighbors. She opened the door of her apartment and peered out. Her thin white hair was done up in tight kid curlers. With her round faded-blue eyes and round wrinkled-apple cheeks, she looked like an inquisitive aged baby.

"Good morning," said Ellen pleasantly.

"Good morning, my dear," the old lady answered. "You're up early for a Saturday."

"Well, I thought I might as well get up and start my house-cleaning. I didn't sleep a wink after four o'clock this morning anyway. Did you hear all that racket in the hall?"

"Why, no, I didn't." The old lady sounded disappointed. "I don't see how I missed it. I guess because I went to bed so late. My nephews--you've seen them, haven't you?--They're such nice boys. They took me to a movie last night."

"Well, I'm surprised you didn't hear it," said Ellen. "Thumping and scratching, like somebody was dragging a rake along the floor. I just couldn't get back to sleep."

The old lady clicked her tongue. "I'll bet somebody came home drunk. Isn't that terrible? I wonder who it was."

"I don't know," said Ellen, "but it was certainly a disgrace. I was going to call Mrs. Anderson."

With the door open, the hall seemed filled with the very odd odor of Mrs. Moffatt's apartment--not really unpleasant, but musty, with the smell of antiques. The apartment itself was like a museum. Ellen had been inside once when the old lady invited her in for a cup of tea. Its two rooms were crammed with a bizarre assortment of furniture, bric-a-brac and souvenirs.

"Oh, how's your bird this morning?" Ellen asked.

In addition to being a collector, Mrs. Moffatt was an animal fancier. She owned three cats, a pair of love-birds, goldfish, and even a cage of white mice. One of the love-birds, she had informed Ellen yesterday, was ailing.

"Oh, Buzzy's much better today," she beamed. "The doctor told me to feed him whisky every three hours--with an eyedropper, you know--and you'd be surprised how it helped the little fellow. He even ate some bird-seed this morning."

"I'm so glad," said Ellen. She picked up her paper and smiled at Mrs. Moffatt. "I'll see you later."

The old woman closed her door, shutting off the musty smell, and Ellen walked back to her own apartment. She filled the coffee pot with water and four tablespoons of coffee, then dressed herself while the coffee percolated. Standing in front of the medicine cabinet mirror, she took the bobbypins out of her hair. Her reflection looked back at her from the mirror, and she felt that unaccountable depression again. I'm not bad-looking, she thought, and young, and not too dumb. What have other women got that I haven't? She thought of the days and years passing, the meals all alone, and nothing ever happening.

That kind of thinking gets you nowhere; forget it. She combed her hair back, pinned it securely behind her ears, ran a lipstick over her mouth. Then she went into the kitchenette, turned off the gas flame under the coffee pot, and raised the window shade to let in the sun that was just beginning to show through morning fog.

A dead cat lay on the fire escape under the window.

* * * * *

She stared at it, feeling sick to her stomach. It was an ordinary gray cat, the kind you see in every alley, but its head was twisted back so that its open eyes and open mouth leered at her.

She pulled the blind down, fast.

Sit down, light a cigarette. It's nothing, just a dead cat, that's all. But how did it get on the fire escape? Fell, maybe, from the roof? And how did it get on the roof? Besides, I thought cats never got hurt falling. Isn't there something about landing on your feet like a cat? Maybe that's just a legend, like the nonsense about nine lives.

Well, what do I do, she thought. I can't sit here and drink coffee with *that* under the window. And God knows I can't take it away myself. She shuddered at the thought. Call the manager.

She got up and went to the telephone in the foyer. She found the number scribbled on the back of the phone book. Her hand was shaking when she dialed.

"This is Ellen Tighe in 402. Mrs. Anderson, there's a dead cat on the fire escape outside my window. You'll have to do something about it."

Mrs. Anderson sounded half-asleep. "What do you mean, a dead cat? Are you sure it's dead? Maybe it's sleeping."

"Of course I'm sure it's dead! Can't you send Pete up to take it away? It's a horrible thing to have under my window."

"All right, I'll tell Pete to go up. He's washing down the lobby now. As soon as he's finished, I'll send him up."

Ellen set the phone back on its stand. She felt a little silly. What a fuss to make over a dead cat. But really, outside one's window--and before breakfast--who could blame me?

She went back into the kitchenette, carefully not looking toward the window, even though the shade was drawn, and poured herself a cup of coffee. Then she sat at the table in the little nook, drinking coffee, smoking a cigarette and leafing through the paper.

The front page was all about a flying saucer scare in Marin County. She read the headline, then thumbed on through the paper, stopping to read the movie reviews and the comic page.

*   *   *   *   *

At the back section, she was attracted by a headline that read: "Liquor Strong These Days--Customer Turns Green, Says Bartender." It was a brief item, consciously cute. "John Martin, 38, a bartender of 152 Mason Street, was arrested early this morning, charged with drunkenness and disturbing the peace, after firing several shots from a .38 revolver on the sidewalk in front of his address. No one was injured. Martin's defense, according to police records, was that he was attempting to apprehend a 'pale-green, claw-handed' customer who fled after eating a live mouse and threatening Martin.

"Upon questioning, Martin admitted that the unidentified customer had been in the bar for several hours and appeared perfectly normal. But he insisted, 'When I refused to serve him after he ate the mouse, he turned green and threatened to claw me to death.' Martin has a permit to carry the gun and was dismissed with a fifty dollar fine and a warning by Judge Greely against sampling his own stock too freely."

Drunken fool, thought Ellen. With fresh indignation, she remembered the disturbance in her own hall this morning. Nothing but drunks and gangsters in this neighborhood. She thought vaguely of looking at the "For Rent" section of the want ads.

There was a noise on the fire escape. Ellen reached over and lifted up the shade. The janitor was standing there with a big paper sack in his hand.

Ellen opened the window and asked, "How do you think it got there, Pete?"

"I dunno. Maybe fall offa the roof. Musta been in a fight."

"What makes you think so?"

"Neck's all torn. Big teeth marks. Maybe dog get him."

"Up here?"

"Somebody find, maybe throw here--I dunno." Pete scratched his head. "You don't worry any more, though. I take away now. No smell, even."

He grinned at her and scuttled to the other end of the fire escape where he climbed through the window to the fourth floor corridor.

Ellen poured herself a second cup of coffee and lighted another cigarette, then turned to the woman's page in the paper. She read the Advice Column and the Psychology and glanced through the "Help Wanted--Women" in the classifieds. That finished the morning's reading. She looked at her watch. Almost ten.

She carried her coffee cup to the sink, rinsed it out and set it on the drainboard. There was still a cup or more coffee left in the pot. That could be warmed over later, but she took out the filler and dumped the grounds into the paper bag that held garbage. The bag was almost full.

I'll throw it in the incinerator now, she thought, before I straighten the apartment.

She emptied the ashtrays--the one beside her bed and the other on the breakfast table--then started down the hall with the garbage bag in her hand.

*   *   *   *   *

The incinerator chute was at the rear of the hall, next to the service stairs. Ellen could see the door standing slightly open. She hesitated. 410 might be there. It was bad enough to ride in the elevator with him, feeling his eyes on her, but there was something unbearably intimate about standing beside him, emptying garbage.

The door seemed to move a little, but nobody came out. She waited another minute. Oh, well, maybe the last person out there just forgot to shut the door tight. She opened it wider, stepped out on the stair landing. No one was there.

The chute was wide, almost three feet around. Ellen opened the top and started to throw the bag down. Something was stuck in there. Her eyes saw it, but her brain refused to believe.

What was there, blocking the chute, looked like--looked like--a chicken's foot, gnarled, clawed, but as large as a human foot--and an ugly, sickly green!

Automatically, she reached in and clutched it. Her stomach turned at the cold feel of the thing, but still she tugged at it, trying to work it loose. It was heavy. She pulled with all her strength, felt it start to slide back up the chute. Then it was free!

She gaped in sick horror at the thing she held. Her hand opened weakly and she sat down on the floor, her head swimming and her throat muscles retching. Dimly, she heard the thing rattle and bump down to the incinerator in the basement.

The full horror of it gradually hit home. Ellen stood up, swaying, and ran blindly down the hall. Her feet thudded on the carpeted floor. As she passed 404, she was vaguely conscious of Mrs. Moffatt's concerned face poking around the door.

"Is there something wrong, Miss Tighe?"

"No," Ellen managed to gasp "It's all right--really--all right."

She kept on running, burst through the apartment door, slammed it behind her, fell on her knees in the bathroom and became thoroughly, violently ill.

She continued to kneel, unable to think, her head against the cool porcelain bowl. Finally, she stood up weakly, ran cold water, washed her face and streaming eyes. Thank God the wall bed was still down! She fell on it, shaking.

*   *   *   *   *

What was that unbelievable ghastly, impossible thing? It was the size of a man, but thin, skeleton thin, and the color of brackish water. It had two legs, two arms, like a man ... but ending with those huge, birdlike claws. Heaven alone knew what its face was like. She had let go before it was that far clear of the chute.

She thought of the story in the paper. So that was what the bartender saw! He wasn't drunk at all, and what happened when he told the police? They laughed at him. They'd laugh at me, too, she thought. The proof is gone, burned up in the incinerator. Why did this happen to me? Dead cats on the fire escape, dead monsters in the incinerator chute ... it's this terrible neighborhood!

She tried to think coherently. Maybe the cat had something to do with it. The bartender said the thing ate a mouse--maybe it had tried to eat the cat, too. A monster like that might eat anything. Her stomach started churning again at the thought.

But what was it doing in the incinerator chute? Someone in the building must have put it there, thinking it would slide all the way down and be burned up. Who? One of *them*, probably. But there couldn't be any more green monsters around. They can't live in an apartment house, walk the streets like anyone else, not even in this neighborhood.

She remembered something else in the bartender's story. He said it looked perfectly normal at first. That meant they could look like humans if they wanted to. Hypnotism? Then any man could be....

Suddenly another thought struck her. Supposing they find out I saw--what will they do to me?

She jumped up from the bed, white with fear, her faintness forgotten in the urge to escape. She snatched her bag from the dresser, threw on her brown coat.

At the door, she hesitated, afraid to venture into the hall, yet afraid to stay inside. Finally, she eased open the door, peered out into the corridor. It was deserted. She ran to the elevator, punched the bell, heard the car begin its creaky, protesting ascent.

The elevator door had an automatic spring closing. The first time she tried it, her hands shook and the door sprang closed before she got in. She tried it again. This time she managed to hold it open long enough to get inside. She pushed the button, felt the elevator shake and grind and move slowly down.

Out into the lobby.

Out into the street.

$$*\qquad*\qquad*\qquad*\qquad*$$

The fog was completely gone now. The sun shone on the still-damp street. There were very few people around--The Tenderloin sleeps late. She went into the restaurant next door, sat down at the white-tiled counter. She was the only customer. A sleepy-eyed waitress, her black hair untidily caught into a net, waited, pad in hand.

"Just coffee," Ellen mumbled.

She drank it black and it scalded her throat going down. The waitress put a nickel in the juke box and then Bing Crosby was singing "Easter Parade." Everything was so normal. Listening to Bing Crosby, how could you believe in things like green monsters? In this sane, prosaic atmosphere, Ellen thought, I must be batty.

She said to herself, "I'm Ellen Tighe, bookkeeper, and I just saw the body of a green man with claws on his feet...." No, that didn't help a bit. Put it this way: "I'm Ellen Tighe and I'm 27 years old and I'm not married. Let's face it, any psychiatrist will tell you that's enough cause for neurosis. So I'm having delusions."

It made more sense that way. I read that story in the paper, Ellen thought, and it must have registered way down in my subconscious. That had to be it. Any other way, it was too horrible, too impossible to be borne.

I'll go back to the apartment and call Dr. Clive, thought Ellen. She had the feeling, no doubt held over from the days of measles and mumps, that a doctor could cure anything, even green monsters on the brain.

She drank the last of the coffee and fished in her coin purse for change. Picking up the check, she walked over to the cash register at the end of the counter, facing the street. The untidy waitress came from the back of the restaurant to take the money.

Ellen looked out at the street through the glass front. The man from 410 was standing out there, smoking a cigarette, watching her. When their eyes met, he abruptly threw away the cigarette and started walking toward the apartment house. Again she felt that faint dread she had experienced in the hall earlier.

The waitress picked up her quarter, gave her back a nickel and a dime. Ellen put the change into her purse, got out her key chain and held it in her hand while she walked quickly next door. 410 was just ahead of her in the lobby; he held the front door open for her.

She kept her head down, not looking at his face, and they walked, Indian file, across the lobby to the elevator. He opened the elevator doors, too, and she stepped in ahead of him.

*   *   *   *   *

When the doors clanged shut, she had a feeling of panic. Alone with him ... cut off from help. He didn't pretend not to know her floor, but silently pressed the proper button. While the car moved slowly upward, her heart was beating wildly.

I'm not convinced, she thought, I'm not convinced. I saw it so plainly ... I felt it, cold in my hands.

The elevator stopped. The man held the door open and for a moment she thought he was going to say something. His free hand made a swift, involuntary movement as though he were going to catch her arm. She shrank away, but he stepped back and let her through.

Ellen almost ran down the hall. Behind her, she heard his footsteps going in the opposite direction toward his apartment. She was panting when she reached her door. She fumbled for the right key--front door, office--and then she froze. There was a scratching sound in the apartment.

She put her ear close to the door, listened. There was a rasping noise, like somebody dragging a rake ... or like claws, great heavy claws, moving over the hardwood floors!

Ellen backed away from the door. It was true, then. She retreated, inch by inch, silently. Get away, leave before it catches you! She turned, ready to make a dash for the elevator ... and faced the man from 410.

Down at the end of the hall, in front of his apartment, he was watching her. The way he lingered outside the restaurant, the way he looked at her. One of *them* ... maybe underneath that homely, ordinary face, his skin was green and clammy. Maybe there were long, sharp claws on his feet.

She was breathing unevenly now. Trapped! The thing in the apartment, the man in the hall. Her eyes darted to the elevator, then back, down the hall, past the door marked 404 ... the door marked 404! She covered the few yards in a mad dash, flung herself at the door, pounding wildly.

"Please, please!" she sobbed. "Mrs. Moffatt, open, please!"

The door opened at once. Mrs. Moffatt's round, wrinkled face beamed at her.

"Come in, my dear, come in."

She almost fell over the landing. The door closed behind her.

She stumbled to the davenport, sank down, gasping. Two cats rubbed against her legs, purring. Two cats?

She heard herself say stupidly, "Mrs. Moffatt, where's the other cat?" and wondered why she said it.

Then she understood.

The old lady's face quivered, altered, melted into something ... something green.

*   *   *   *   *

Outside in the hall, the man from 410 slowly returned to his apartment. Pushing open the door, he thought, I'll never get the nerve to ask her out.

Well, probably wasn't a chance, anyhow. What would a girl like her have to do with a lousy cop like me?

GAMES
BY KATHERINE MACLEAN

ORIGINALLY PUBLISHED IN *GALAXY*
MARCH 1953

Editor's Notes:
Games
By Katherine MacLean

The concept that the next step in human evolution might involve the development of psychic powers was a common topic during the 50's. How the new species might react with the old provided plenty of fodder for the authors of the period. "Games" mixes telepathy with bio-weapons and a bit of paranoia about the government in a short, but potent story about a little boy and his imagination.

Unlike many of the authors in this book, and in science fiction in general, MacLean had a long and productive career, producing as many stories after the 50's as during it. She also collaborated with such well known authors in the genre such as Harry Harrison, Charles De Vet, and her husband Charles Dye. Having held a number of positions as a research and medical technician she was familiar with current biomedical ideas and often used them in her stories. Her ability to incorporate real science into her works was admired by authors Brian Aldiss and Theodore Sturgeon.

Katherine MacLean was born in Glen Ridge, New Jersey on January 22, 1925. She received a B. A. degree in economics from Barnard. She wrote or co-wrote five novels and nearly fifty short stories. Her first story appeared in 1949 and her most recent in 1997. In 1971 she received a Nebula award and was named an Author Emeritus by the Science Fiction Writers of America. She has taught literature at the University of Maine and creative writing at the Free University of Portland. She was briefly married to science fiction author Charles Dye with whom she wrote several stories.

GAMES

Ronny was playing by himself, which meant he was two tribes of Indians having a war.

"Bang," he muttered, firing an imaginary rifle. He decided that it was a time in history before the white people had sold the Indians any guns, and changed the rifle into a bow. "Wizz*thunk*," he substituted, mimicking from an Indian film on TV the graphic sound of an arrow striking flesh.

"Oof." He folded down onto the grass, moaning, "Uhhhooh ..." and relaxing into defeat and death.

"Want some chocolate milk, Ronny?" asked his mother's voice from the kitchen.

"No, thanks," he called back, climbing to his feet to be another man. "Wizzthunk, wizzthunk," he added to the flights of arrows as the best archer in the tribe. "Last arrow. Wizzzz," he said, missing one enemy for realism. He addressed another battling brave. "Who has more arrows? They are coming too close. No time--I'll have to use my knife." He drew the imaginary knife, ducking an arrow as it shot close.

*   *   *   *   *

Then he was the tribal chief standing somewhere else, and he saw that the warriors left alive were outnumbered.

"We must retreat. We cannot leave our tribe without warriors to protect the women."

Ronny decided that the chief was heroically wounded, his voice wavering from weakness. He had been propping himself against a tree to appear unharmed, but now he moved so that his braves could see he was pinned to the trunk by an arrow and could not walk. They cried out.

He said, "Leave me and escape. But remember...." No words came, just the feeling of being what he was, a dying old eagle, a chief of warriors, speaking to young warriors who would need advice of seasoned humor and moderation to carry them through their young battles. He had to finish the sentence, tell them something wise.

Ronny tried harder, pulling the feeling around him like a cloak of resignation and pride, leaning indifferently against the tree where the arrow had pinned him, hearing dimly in anticipation the sound of his aged voice conquering weakness to speak wisely of what they needed to be told. They had many battles ahead of them, and the battles would be against odds, with so many dead already.

They must watch and wait, be flexible and tenacious, determined and persistent--but not too rash, subtle and indirect--not cowardly, and above all be patient with the triumph of the enemy and not maddened into suicidal direct attack.

His stomach hurt with the arrow wound, and his braves waited to hear his words. He had to sum a part of his life's experience in words. Ronny tried harder to build the scene realistically. Then suddenly it was real. He was the man.

He was an old man, guide and adviser in an oblique battle against great odds. He was dying of something and his stomach hurt with a knotted ache, like hunger, and he was thirsty. He had refused to let the young men make the sacrifice of trying to rescue him. He was hostage in the jail and dying, because he would not surrender to the enemy nor cease to fight them. He smiled and said, "Remember to live like other men, but--remember to remember."

And then he was saying things that could not be put into words, complex feelings that were ways of taking bad situations that made them easier to smile at, and then sentences that were not sentences, but single alphabet letters pushing each other with signs, with a feeling of being connected like two halves of a swing, one side moving up when the other moved down, or like swings or like cogs and pendulums inside a clock, only without the cogs, just with the push.

It wasn't adding or multiplication, and it used letters instead of numbers, but Ronny knew it was some kind of arithmetic.

And he wasn't Ronny.

He was an old man, teaching young men, and the old man did not know about Ronny. He thought sadly how little he would be able to convey to the young men, and he remembered more, trying to sum long memories and much living into a few direct thoughts. And Ronny was the old man and himself, both at once.

*   *   *   *   *

It was too intense. Part of Ronny wanted to escape and be alone, and that part withdrew and wanted to play something. Ronny sat in the grass and played with his toes like a much younger child.

Part of Ronny that was Doctor Revert Purcell sat on the edge of a prison cot, concentrating on secret unpublished equations of biogenic stability which he wanted to pass on to the responsible hands of young researchers in the concealed-research chain. He was using the way of thinking which they had told him was the telepathic sending of ideas to anyone ready to receive. It was odd that he himself could never tell when he was sending. Probably a matter of age. They had started trying to teach him when he was already too old for anything so different.

The water tap, four feet away, was dripping steadily, and it was hard for Purcell to concentrate, so intense was his thirst. He wondered if he could gather strength to walk that far. He was sitting up and that was good, but the struggle to raise himself that far had left him dizzy and trembling. If he tried to stand, the effort would surely interrupt his transmitting of equations and all the data he had not sent yet.

Would the man with the keys who looked in the door twice a day care whether Purcell died with dignity? He was the only audience, and his expression never changed when Purcell asked him to point out to the authorities that he was not being given anything to eat. It was funny to Purcell to find that he wanted the respect of any audience to his dying, even of a man without response who treated him as if he were already a corpse.

Perhaps the man would respond if Purcell said, "I have changed my mind. I will tell."

But if he said that, he would lose his own respect.

At the biochemists' and bio-physicists' convention, the reporter had asked him if any of his researches could be applied to warfare.

He had answered with no feeling of danger, knowing that what he did was common practice among research men, sure that it was an unchallengeable right.

"Some of them can, but those I keep to myself."

The reporter remained dead-pan. "For instance?"

"Well, I have to choose something that won't reveal how it's done now, but--ah--for example, a way of cheaply mass-producing specific antitoxins against any germ. It sounds harmless if you don't think about it, but actually it would make germ warfare the most deadly and inexpensive weapon yet developed, for it would make it possible to prevent the backspread of contagion into a country's own troops, without much expense. There would be hell to pay if anyone ever let that out." Then he had added, trying to get the reporter to understand enough to change his cynical unimpressed expression, "You understand, germs are cheap--there would be a new plague to spread every time some pipsqueak biologist mutated a new germ. It isn't even expensive or difficult, as atom bombs are."

The headline was: "Scientist Refuses to Give Secret of Weapon to Government."

*   *   *   *   *

Government men came and asked him if this was correct, and on having it confirmed pointed out that he had an obligation. The research foundations where he had worked were subsidized by government money. He had been deferred from military service during his early years of study and work so he could become a scientist, instead of having to fight or die on the battlefield.

"This might be so," he had said. "I am making an attempt to serve mankind by doing as much good and as little damage as possible. If you don't mind, I'd rather use my own judgment about what constitutes service."

The statement seemed too blunt the minute he had said it, and he recognized that it had implications that his judgment was superior to that of the government. It probably was the most antagonizing thing that could have been said, but he could see no other possible statement, for it represented precisely what he thought.

There were bigger headlines about that interview, and when he stepped outside his building for lunch the next day, several small gangs of patriots arrived with the proclaimed purpose of persuading him to tell. They fought each other for the privilege.

The police had rescued him after he had lost several front teeth and had one eye badly gouged. They then left him to the care of the prison doctor in protective custody. Two days later, after having been questioned several times on his attitude toward revealing the parts of his research he had kept secret, he was transferred to a place that looked like a military jail, and left alone. He was not told what his status was.

When someone came and asked him questions about his attitude, Purcell felt quite sure that what they were doing to him was illegal. He stated that he was going on a hunger strike until he was allowed to have visitors and see a lawyer.

The next time the dinner hour arrived, they gave him nothing to eat. There had been no food in the cell since, and that was probably two weeks ago. He was not sure just how long, for during part of the second week his memory had become garbled. He dimly remembered something that might have been delirium, which could have lasted more than one day.

Perhaps the military who wanted the antitoxins for germ warfare were waiting quietly for him either to talk or die.

*   *   *   *   *

Ronny got up from the grass and went into the kitchen, stumbling in his walk like a beginning toddler.

"Choc-mil?" he said to his mother.

She poured him some and teased gently, "What's the matter, Ronny--back to baby-talk?"

He looked at her with big solemn eyes and drank slowly, not answering.

In the cell somewhere distant, Dr. Purcell, famous biochemist, began waveringly trying to rise to his feet, unable to remember hunger as anything separate from him that could ever be ended, but weakly wanting a glass of water. Ronny could not feed him with the chocolate milk. Even though this was another himself, the body that was drinking was not the one that was thirsty.

He wandered out into the backyard again, carrying the glass.

"Bang," he said deceptively, pointing with his hand in case his mother was looking. "Bang." Everything had to seem usual; he was sure of that. This was too big a thing, and too private, to tell a grownup.

On the way back from the sink, Dr. Purcell slipped and fell and hit his head against the edge of the iron cot. Ronny felt the edge gashing through skin and into bone, and then a relaxing blankness inside his head, like falling asleep suddenly when they are telling you a fairy story while you want to stay awake to find out what happened next.

"Bang," said Ronny vaguely, pointing at a tree. "Bang." He was ashamed because he had fallen down in the cell and hurt his head and become just Ronny again before he had finished sending out his equations. He tried to make believe he was alive again, but it didn't work.

You could never make-believe anything to a real good finish. They never ended neatly--there was always something unfinished, and something that would go right on after the end.

It would have been nice if the jailers had come in and he had been able to say something noble to them before dying, to show that he was brave.

"Bang," he said randomly, pointing his finger at his head, and then jerked his hand away as if it had burned him. He had become the wrong person that time. The feel of a bullet jolting the side of his head was startling and unpleasant, even if not real, and the flash of someone's vindictive anger and self-pity while pulling a trigger.... *My wife will be sorry she ever....* He didn't like that kind of make-believe. It felt unsafe to do it without making up a story first.

Ronny decided to be Indian braves again. They weren't very real, and when they were, they had simple straightforward emotions about courage and skill and pride and friendship that he would like.

*   *   *   *   *

A man was leaning his arms on the fence, watching him. "Nice day." *What's the matter, kid, are you an esper?*

"Hul-lo." Ronny stood on one foot and watched him. *Just making believe. I only want to play. They make it too serious, having all these troubles.*

"Good countryside." The man gestured at the back yards, all opened in together with tangled bushes here and there to crouch behind, when other kids were there to play hide and seek, and with trees to climb. *It can be the Universe if you pick and choose who to be, and don't let wrong choices make you shut off from it. You can make yourself learn from this if you are strong enough. Who have you been?*

Ronny stood on the other foot and scratched the back of his leg with his toes. He didn't want to remember. He always forgot right away, but this grownup was confident and young and strong-looking, and meant something when he talked, not like most grownups.

"I was playing Indian." *I was an old chief, captured by enemies, trying to pass on to other warriors the wisdom of my life before I died.* He made believe he was the chief a little to show the young man what he was talking about.

"Purcell!" The man drew in his breath between his teeth, and his face paled. He pulled back from reaching Ronny with his feelings, like holding his breath in. "Good game." *You can learn from him. Don't leave him shut off, I beg you. You can let him influence you without being pulled off your own course. He was a good man. You were honored, and I envy the man you will be if you contacted him on resonant similarities.*

The grownup looked frightened. *But you are too young. You'll block him out and lose him. Kids have to grow and learn at their own speed.*

Then he looked less afraid, but uncertain, and his thoughts struggled against each other. *Their own speed. But there should be someone alive with Purcell's pattern and memories. We loved him. Kids should grow at their own speed, but.... How strong are you, Ronny? Can you move ahead of the normal growth pattern?*

Grownups always want you to do something. Ronny stared back, clenching his hands and moving his feet uneasily.

The thoughts were open to him. *Do you want to be the old chief again, Ronny? Be him often, so you can learn to know what he knew? (And feel as he felt. It would be a stiff dose for a kid.) It will be rich and exciting, full of memories and skills. (But hard to chew. I'm doing this for Purcell, Ronny, not for you. You have to make up your own mind.)*

"That was a good game. Are you going to play it any more?"

*   *   *   *   *

His mother would not like it. She would feel the difference in him, as much as if he had read one of the books she kept away from him, books that were supposed to be for adults only. The difference would hurt her. He was being bad, like eating between meals. But to know what grownups knew....

He tightened his fists and looked down at the grass. "I'll play it some more."

The young man smiled, still pale and holding half his feelings back behind a dam. *Then mesh with me a moment. Let me in.*

He was in with the thought, feeling Ronny's confused consent, reassuring him by not thinking or looking around inside while sending out a single call, *Purcell, Doc,* that found the combination key to Ronny's guarded yesterdays and last nights and ten minutes agos. *Ronny, I'll set that door, Purcell's memories, open for you. You can't close it, but feel like this about it*--and he planted in a strong set, *questioning, cool, open, a feeling of absorbing without words ... it will give information when you need it, like a dictionary.*

The grownup straightened away from the fence, preparing to walk off. Behind a dam pressed grief and anger for the death of the man he called Purcell.

"And any time you want to *be* the old chief, at any age he lived, just make believe you are him."

Grief and anger pressed more strongly against the dam, and the man turned and left rapidly, letting his thoughts flicker and scatter through private memories that Ronny did not share, that no one shared, breaking thought contact with everyone so that the man could be alone in his own mind to have his feelings in private.

*   *   *   *   *

Ronny picked up the empty glass that had held his chocolate milk from the back steps where he had left it and went inside. As he stepped into the kitchen, he knew what another kitchen had looked like for a five-year-old child who had been Purcell ninety years ago. There had been an iron sink, and a brown-and-green-spotted faucet, and the glass had been heavier and transparent, like real glass.

Ronny reached up and put the colored plastic tumbler down.

"That was a nice young man, dear. What did he say to you?"

Ronny looked up at his mamma, comparing her with the remembered mamma of fifty years ago. He loved the other one, too.

"He tol' me he's glad I play Indian."

EXILE FROM SPACE
BY JUDITH MERRIL

ORIGINALLY PUBLISHED IN *FANTASTIC UNIVERSE*
NOVEMBER 1956

EDITOR'S NOTES:
EXILE FROM SPACE
BY JUDITH MERRIL

In this story, a young woman, born on Earth, but raised by aliens on a spaceship, returns to Earth to rediscover what it means to be human--and a woman. "Exile From Space" raises questions about the nature of love and ones identity, and is an example of a type of introspection that was absent in science fiction of earlier decades.

Judith Merril may well have been more influential as an editor than as a writer. Her long running series of anthologies "The Year's Greatest Science Fiction" was the anthology to appear in during its tenure and introduced many of the brightest new authors to a wider audience.

Judith Merril was the pen name of Josephine Juliet Grossman (January 21, 1923-September 12, 1997) born in Boston. She also wrote under the names Cyril Judd (with C.M. Kornbluth) and Rose Sharon. She wrote a number of novels and several dozen short stories and edited a number of anthologies. She worked to promote literary standards in science fiction and wrote numerous reviews of science fiction books. She was married for a time to the science fiction author Frederick Pohl and lived with Walter M. Miller. Active politically she moved to Canada in the 60's as a response to the Vietnam War and eventually became a Canadian citizen.

Exile From Space

I don't know where they got the car. We made three or four stops before the last one, and they must have picked it up one of those times. Anyhow, they got it, but they had to make a license plate, because it had the wrong kind on it.

They made me some clothes, too--a skirt and blouse and shoes that looked just like the ones we saw on television. They couldn't make me a lipstick or any of those things, because there was no way to figure out just what the chemical composition was. And they decided I'd be as well off without any driver's license or automobile registration as I would be with papers that weren't exactly perfect, so they didn't bother about making those either.

They were worried about what to do with my hair, and even thought about cutting it short, so it would look more like the women on television, but that was one time I was way ahead of them. I'd seen more shows than anyone else, of course--I watched them almost every minute, from the time they told me I was going--and there was one where I'd seen a way to make braids and put them around the top of your head. It wasn't very comfortable, but I practiced at it until it looked pretty good.

They made me a purse, too. It didn't have anything in it except the diamonds, but the women we saw always seemed to carry them, and they thought it might be a sort of superstition or ritual necessity, and that we'd better not take a chance on violating anything like that.

They made me spend a lot of time practicing with the car, because without a license, I couldn't take a chance on getting into any trouble. I must have put in the better part of an hour starting and stopping and backing that thing, and turning it around, and weaving through trees and rocks, before they were satisfied.

Then, all of a sudden, there was nothing left to do except *go*. They made me repeat everything one more time, about selling the diamonds, and how to register at the hotel, and what to do if I got into trouble, and how to get in touch with them when I wanted to come back. Then they said good-bye, and made me promise not to stay *too* long, and said they'd keep in touch the best they could. And then I got in the car, and drove down the hill into town.

I knew they didn't want to let me go. They were worried, maybe even a little afraid I wouldn't want to come back, but mostly worried that I might say something I shouldn't, or run into some difficulties they hadn't anticipated. And outside of that, they knew they were going to miss me. Yet they'd made up their minds to it; they planned it this way, and they felt it was the right thing to do, and certainly they'd put an awful lot of thought and effort and preparation into it.

If it hadn't been for that, I might have turned back at the last minute. Maybe they were worried; but *I* was petrified. Only of course, I wanted to go, really. I couldn't help being curious, and it never occurred to me then that I might miss them. It was the first time I'd ever been out on my own, and they'd promised me, for years and years, as far back as I could remember, that some day I'd go back, like this, by myself. But....

Going back, when you've been away long enough, is not so much a homecoming as a dream *deja vu*. And for me, at least, the dream was not entirely a happy one. Everything I saw or heard or touched had a sense of haunting familiarity, and yet of *wrongness*, too--almost a nightmare feeling of the oppressively inevitable sequence of events, of faces and features and events just not-quite-remembered and not-quite-known.

I was born in this place, but it was not my home. Its people were not mine; its ways were not mine. All I knew of it was what I had been told, and what I had seen for myself these last weeks of preparation, on the television screen. And the dream-feeling was intensified, at first, by the fact that I did not know *why* I was there. I knew it had been planned this way, and I had been told it was necessary to complete my education. Certainly I was aware of the great effort that had been made to make the trip possible. But I did not yet understand just *why*.

Perhaps it was just that I had heard and watched and thought and dreamed too much about this place, and now I was actually there, the reality was--not so much a disappointment as--just sort of *unreal*. Different from what I knew when I *didn't* know.

The road unwound in a spreading spiral down the mountainside. Each time I came round, I could see the city below, closer and larger, and less distinct. From the top, with the sunlight sparkling on it, it had been a clean and gleaming pattern of human civilization. Halfway down, the symmetry was lost, and the smudge and smoke began to show.

Halfway down, too, I began to pass places of business: restaurants and gas stations and handicraft shops. I wanted to stop. For half an hour now I had been out on my own, and I still hadn't seen any of the people, except the three who had passed me behind the wheels of their cars, going up the road. One of the shops had a big sign on it, "COME IN AND LOOK AROUND." But I kept going. One thing I understood was that it was absolutely necessary to have money, and that I must stop nowhere, and attempt nothing, till after I had gotten some.

Farther down, the houses began coming closer together, and then the road stopped winding around, and became almost straight. By that time, I was used to the car, and didn't have to think about it much, and for a little while I really enjoyed myself. I could see into the houses sometimes, through the windows, and at one, a woman was opening the door, coming out with a broom in her hand. There were children playing in the yards. There were cars of all kinds parked around the houses, and I saw dogs and a couple of horses, and once a whole flock of chickens.

But just where it was beginning to get really interesting, when I was coming into the little town before the city, I had to stop watching it all, because there were too many other people driving. That was when I began to understand all the fuss about licenses and tests and traffic regulations. Watching it on television, it wasn't anything like being in the middle of it!

Of course, what I ran into there was really nothing; I found that out when I got into the city itself. But just at first, it seemed pretty bad. And I still don't understand it. These people are pretty bright mechanically. You'd think anybody who could *build* an automobile--let alone an atom bomb--could *drive* one easily enough. Especially with a lifetime to learn in. Maybe they just like to live dangerously....

It was a good thing, though, that I'd already started watching out for what the other drivers were doing when I hit my first red light. That was something I'd overlooked entirely, watching street scenes on the screen, and I guess they'd never noticed either. They must have taken it for granted, the way I did, that people stopped their cars out of courtesy from time to time to let the others go by. As it was, I stopped because the others did, and just happened to notice that they began again when the light changed to green. It's really a very good system; I don't see why they don't have them at all the intersections.

*　　*　　*　　*　　*

From the first light, it was eight miles into the center of Colorado Springs. A sign on the road said so, and I was irrationally pleased when the speedometer on the car confirmed it. Proud, I suppose, that these natives from my own birth-place were such good gadgeteers. The road was better after that, too, and the cars didn't dart in and out off the sidestreets the way they had before. There was more traffic on the highway, but most of them behaved fairly intelligently. Until we got into town, that is. After that, it was everybody-for-himself, but by then I was prepared for it.

I found a place to park the car near a drugstore. That was the first thing I was supposed to do. Find a drugstore, where there would likely be a telephone directory, and go in and look up the address of a hock shop. I had a little trouble parking the car in the space they had marked off, but I could see from the way the others were stationed that you were supposed to get in between the white lines, with the front of the car next to the post on the sidewalk. I didn't know what the post was for, until I got out and read what it said, and then I didn't know what to do, because I didn't *have* any money. Not yet. And I didn't dare get into any trouble that might end up with a policeman asking to see my license, which always seemed to be the first thing they did on television, when they talked to anybody who was driving a car. I got back in the car and wriggled my way out of the hole between the other cars, and tried to think what to do. Then I remembered seeing a sign that said "Free Parking" somewhere, not too far away, and went back the way I'd come.

There was a sort of park, with a fountain spraying water all over the grass, and a big building opposite, and the white lines here were much more sensible. They were painted in diagonal strips, so you could get in and out quite easily, without all that backing and twisting and turning. I left the car there, and remembered to take the keys with me, and started walking back to the drugstore.

*   *   *   *   *

That was when it hit me.

Up to then, beginning I guess when I drove that little stretch coming into Manitou, with the houses on the hills, and the children and yards and dogs and chickens, I'd begun to feel almost as if I belonged here. The people seemed so *much* like me--as long as I wasn't right up against them. From a little distance, you'd think there was no difference at all. Then, I guess, when I was close enough to notice, driving through town, I'd been too much preoccupied with the car. It didn't really get to me till I got out and started walking.

They were all so *big*....

They were big, and their faces and noses and even the pores of their skin were too big. And their voices were too loud. And they *smelled*.

I didn't notice that last much till I got into the drugstore. Then I thought I was going to suffocate, and I had a kind of squeezing upside-down feeling in my stomach and diaphragm and throat, which I didn't realize till later was what they meant by "being sick." I stood over the directory rack, pretending to read, but really just struggling with my insides, and a man came along and shouted in my ear something that sounded like, "Vvvm trubbb lll-lll-lll ay-dee?" (I didn't get that sorted out for hours afterwards, but I don't think I'll ever forget just the way it sounded at the time. Of course, he meant, "Having trouble, little lady?") But all I knew at the time was he was too big and smelled of all kinds of things that were unfamiliar and slightly sickening. I couldn't answer him. All I could do was turn away so as not to breathe him, and try to pretend I knew what I was doing with the directory. Then he hissed at me ("Sorry, no offense," I figured out later), and said clearly enough so I could understand even then, "Just trying to help," and walked away.

As soon as he was gone, I walked out myself. Directory or no directory, I had to get out of that store. I went back to where I'd left the car, but instead of getting in it, I sat down on a bench in the park, and waited till the turmoil inside me began to quiet down.

I went back into that drugstore once before I left, purposely, just to see if I could pin down what it was that had bothered me so much, because I never reacted that strongly afterwards, and I wondered if maybe it was just that it was the first time I was inside one of their buildings. But it was more than that; that place was a regular snake-pit of a treatment for a stranger, believe me! They had a tobacco counter, and a lunch counter and a perfume-and-toiletries section, and a nut-roasting machine, and just to top it off, in the back of the store, an open-to-look-at (*and* smell) pharmaceutical center! Everything, all mixed together, and compounded with stale human sweat, which was also new to me at the time. And no air conditioning.

Most of the air conditioning they have is bad enough on its own, with chemical smells, but those are comparatively easy to get used to ... and I'll take them *any* time, over what I got in that first dose of *Odeur d'Earth*.

*   *   *   *   *

Anyhow, I sat on the park bench about fifteen minutes, I guess, letting the sun and fresh air seep in, and trying to tabulate and memorize as many of the components of that drugstore smell as I could, for future reference. I was simply going to have to adjust to them, and next time I wanted to be prepared.

All the same, I didn't feel prepared to go back into the same place. Maybe another store wouldn't be quite as bad. I started walking in the opposite direction, staying on the wide main street, where all the big stores seemed to be, and two blocks down, I ran into luck, because there was a big bracket sticking out over the sidewalk from the front of a store halfway down a side street, and it had the three gold balls hanging from it that I knew, from television, meant the kind of place I wanted. When I walked down to it, I saw too that they had a sign painted over the window: "We buy old gold and diamonds."

Just *how* lucky that was, I didn't realize till quite some time later. I was going to look in the Classified Directory for "Hock Shops." I didn't know any other name for them then.

Inside, it looked exactly like what I expected, and even the smell was nothing to complain about. Camphor and dust and mustiness were strong enough to cover most of the sweaty smell, and those were smells of a kind I'd experienced before, in other places.

The whole procedure was reassuring, because it all went just the way it was supposed to, and I knew how to behave. I'd seen it in a show, and the man behind the grilled window even *looked* like the man on the screen, and talked the same way.

"What can we do for you, girlie?"

"I'd like to sell a diamond," I told him.

He didn't say anything at first, then he looked impatient. "You got it with you?"

"Oh ... yes!" I opened my purse, and took out one of the little packages, and unwrapped it, and handed it to him. He screwed the lens into his eye, and walked back from the window and put it on a little scale, and turned back and unscrewed the lens and looked at me.

"Where'd you get this, lady?" he asked me.

"It's mine," I said. I knew just how to do it. We'd gone over this half a dozen times before I left, and he was behaving exactly the way we'd expected.

"I don't know," he said. "Can't do much with an unset stone like this...." He pursed his lips, tossed the diamond carelessly in his hand, and then pushed it back at me across the counter. I had to keep myself from smiling. It was just the way they'd said it would be. The people here were still in the Mech Age, of course, and not nearly conscious enough to communicate anything at all complex or abstract any way except verbally. But there is nothing abstract about avarice, and between what I'd been told to expect, and what I could feel pouring out of him, I knew precisely what was going on in his mind.

"You mean you don't *want* it?" I said. "I thought it was worth quite a lot...."

"Might have been once." He shrugged. "You can't do much with a stone like that any more. Where'd you get it, girlie?"

"My mother gave it to me. A long time ago. I wouldn't sell it, except.... Look," I said, and didn't have to work hard to sound desperate, because in a way I was. "Look, it must be worth *some*thing?"

He picked it up again. "Well ... what do you want for it?"

That went on for quite a while. I knew what it was supposed to be worth, of course, but I didn't hope to get even half of that. He offered seventy dollars, and I asked for five hundred, and after a while he gave me three-fifty, and I felt I'd done pretty well--for a greenhorn. I put the money in my purse, and went back to the car, and on the way I saw a policeman, so I stopped and asked him about a hotel. He looked me up and down, and started asking questions about how old I was, and what was my name and where did I live, and I began to realize that being so much smaller than the other people was going to make life complicated. I told him I'd come to visit my brother in the Academy, and he smiled, and said, "Your *brother*, is it?" Then he told me the name of a place just outside of town, near the Academy. It wasn't a hotel; it was a *mo*tel, which I didn't know about at that time, but he said I'd be better off there. A lot of what he said went right over my head at the time; later I realized what he meant about "a nice respectable couple" running the place. I found out later on, too, that he called them up to ask them to keep an eye on me; he thought I was a nice girl, but he was worried about my being alone there.

By this time, I was getting hungry, but I thought I'd better go and arrange about a place to stay first. I found the motel without much trouble, and went in and registered; I knew how to do that, at least--I'd seen it plenty of times. They gave me a key, and the man who ran the place asked me did I want any help with my bags.

"Oh, no," I said. "No, thanks. I haven't got much."

I'd forgotten all about that, and they'd never thought about it either! These people always have a lot of different clothes, not just one set, and you're supposed to have a suitcase full of things when you go to stay anyplace. I said I was hungry anyway, and wanted to go get something to eat, and do a couple of other things--I didn't say what--before I got settled. So the woman walked over with me, and showed me which cabin it was, and asked was everything all right?

It looked all right to me. The room had a big bed in it, with sheets and a blanket and pillows and a bedspread, just like the ones I'd seen on television. And there was a chest of drawers, and a table with more small drawers in it, and two chairs and a mirror and one door that went into a closet and one that led to the bathroom. The fixtures in there were a little different from the ones they'd made for me to practice in, but functionally they seemed about the same.

I didn't look for any difficulty with anything there except the bed, and that wasn't *her* fault, so I assured her everything was just fine, and let her show me how to operate the gas-burner that was set in the wall for heat. Then we went out, and she very carefully locked the door, and handed me the key.

"You better keep that door locked," she said, just a little sharply. "You never know...."

I wanted to ask her *what* you never know, but had the impression that it was something *every*body was supposed to know, so I just nodded and agreed instead.

"You want to get some lunch," she said then, "there's a place down the road isn't too bad. Clean, anyhow, and they don't cater too much to those ... well, it's clean." She pointed the way; you could see the sign from where we were standing. I thanked her, and started the car, and decided I might as well go there as anyplace else, especially since I could see she was watching to find out whether I did or not.

*   *   *   *   *

These people are all too big. Or almost all of them. But the man behind the counter at the diner was enormous. He was tall and fat with a beefy red face and large open pores and a fleshy mound of a nose. I didn't like to look at him, and when he talked, he boomed so loud I could hardly understand him. On top of all that, the smell in that place was awful: not quite as bad as the drugstore, but some ways similar to it. I kept my eyes on the menu, which was full of unfamiliar words, and tried to remember that I was hungry.

The man was shouting at me--or it was more like growling, I guess--and I couldn't make out the words at first. He said it again, and I sorted out syllables and matched them with the words on the card, and then I got it:

"Goulash is nice today, miss...."

I didn't know what goulash was, and the state my stomach was in, with the smells, I decided I'd better play safe, and ordered a glass of milk, and some vegetable soup.

The milk had a strange taste to it. Not *bad*--just *different*. But of course, this came from cows. That was all right. But the vegetable soup...!

It was quite literally putrid, made as near as I could figure out from dead animal juices, in which vegetables had been soaked and cooked till any trace of flavor or nourishment was entirely removed. I took one taste of that, and then I realized what the really nauseating part of the odor was, in the diner and the drugstore both. It was rotten meat, dead for some time, and then heated in preparation for eating.

The crackers that came with the soup were good; they had a nice salty tang. I ordered more of those, with another glass of milk, and sat back sipping slowly, trying to adjust to that smell, now that I realized I'd probably find it anywhere I could find food.

After a while, I got my insides enough in order so that I could look around a little and see the place, and the other people in it. That was when I turned around and saw Larry sitting next to me.

He was beautiful. He *is* beautiful. I know that's not what you're supposed to say about a man, and he wouldn't like it, but I can only say what I see, and of course that's partly a matter of my own training and my own feelings about myself.

At home on the ship, I always wanted to cut off my hair, because it was so black, and my skin was so white, and they didn't go together. But they wouldn't let me; they liked it that way, I guess, but *I* didn't. No child wants to feel like a freak, and nobody else had hair like that, or dead-white colorless skin, either.

Then, when I went down there, and saw all the humans, I was still a freak because I was so small.

Larry's small, too. Almost as small as I am. And he's all one color. He has hair, of course, but it's so light, and his skin is so dark (both from the sun, I found out), that he looks just about the same lovely golden color all over. Or at least as much of him as showed when I saw him that time, in the diner.

He was beautiful, and he was my size, and he didn't have ugly rough skin or big heavy hands. I stared at him, and I felt like grabbing on to him to make sure he didn't get away.

After a while I realized my mouth was half-open, and I was still holding a cracker, and I remembered that this was very bad manners. I put the cracker down and closed my mouth. He smiled. I didn't know if he was laughing at the odd way I was acting, or just being friendly, but I smiled back anyhow.

"I'm sorry," he said. "I mean, hello. How do you do, and I'm sorry if I startled you. I shouldn't have been staring."

"*You*," I said, and meant to finish, *You were staring?* But he went right on talking, so that I couldn't finish.

"I don't know what else you can expect, if you go around looking like that," he said.

"I'm sorry...." I started again.

"And you should be," he said sternly. "Anybody who walks into a place like this in the middle of a day like this looking the way you do has got to expect to get stared at a little."

The thing is, I wasn't used to the language; not used *enough*. I could communicate all right, and even understand some jokes, and I knew the spoken language, not some formal unusable version, because I learned it mostly watching those shows on the television screen. But I got confused this time, because "looking" means two different things, active and passive, and I was thinking about how I'd been *looking at* him, and....

That was my lucky day. I didn't want him to be angry at me, and the way I saw it, he was perfectly justified in scolding me, which is what I thought he was doing. But I *knew* he wasn't really angry; I'd have felt it if he was. So I said, "You're right. It was very rude of me, and I don't blame you for being annoyed. I won't do it any more."

He started laughing, and this time I knew it was friendly. Like I said, that was my lucky day; *he* thought I was being witty. And, from what he's told me since, I guess he realized then that *I* felt friendly too, because before that he'd just been bluffing it out, not knowing how to get to know me, and afraid *I*'d be sore at *him*, just for talking to me!

Which goes to show that sometimes you're better off not being *too* familiar with the local customs.

*   *   *   *   *

The trouble was there were too many things I didn't know, too many small ways to trip myself up. Things they couldn't have foreseen, or if they did, couldn't have done much about. All it took was a little caution and a lot of alertness, plus one big important item: staying in the background--not getting to know any one person too well--not giving any single individual a chance to observe too much about me.

But Larry didn't mean to let me do that. And ... I didn't want him to.

He asked questions; I tried to answer them. I did know enough at least of the conventions to realize that I didn't have to give detailed answers, or could, at any point, act offended at being questioned so much. I *didn't* know enough to realize that reluctance or irritation on my part wouldn't have made him go away. We sat on those stools at the diner for most of an hour, talking, and after a little while I found I could keep the conversation on safer ground by asking *him* about himself, and about the country thereabouts. He seemed to enjoy talking.

Eventually, he had to go back to work. As near as I could make out, he was a test-pilot, or something like it, for a small experimental aircraft plant near the city. He lived not too far from where I was staying, and he wanted to see me that evening.

I hadn't told him where the motel was, and I had at least enough caution left not to tell him, even then. I did agree to meet him at the diner, but for lunch the next day again, instead of that evening. For one thing, I had a lot to do; and for another, I'd seen enough on television shows to know that an evening date was likely to be pretty long-drawn-out, and I wasn't sure I could stand up under that much close scrutiny. I had some studying-up to do first. But the lunch-date was fine; the thought of not seeing him at all was terrifying--as if he were an old friend in a world full of strangers. That was how I felt, that first time, maybe just because he was almost as small as I. But I think it was more than that, really.

* * * * *

I drove downtown again, and found a store that seemed to sell all kinds of clothing for women. Then when I got inside, I didn't know where to start, or what to get. I thought of just buying one of everything, so as to fill up a suitcase; the things I had on seemed to be perfectly satisfactory for actual *wearing* purposes. They were quite remarkably--when you stopped to think of it--similar to what most of the women I'd seen that day were wearing, and of course they weren't subject to the same problems of dirtying and wrinkling and such as the clothes in the store were.

I walked around for a while, trying to figure out what all the different items, shapes, sizes, and colors, were for. Some racks and counters had signs, but most of them were unfamiliar words like *brunchies*, or *Bermudas* or *scuffs*; or else they seemed to be mislabeled, like *dusters* for a sort of button-down dress, and *Postage Stamp Girdles* at one section of a long counter devoted to "Foundation Garments." For half an hour or so, I wandered around in there, shaking my head every time a saleswoman came up to me, because I didn't know, and couldn't figure out, what to ask for, or how to ask for it.

The thing was, I didn't dare draw too much attention to myself by doing or saying the wrong things. I'd have to find out more about clothes, somehow, before I could do much buying.

I went out, and on the same block I found a show-window full of suitcases. That was easy. I went in and pointed to one I liked, and paid for it, and walked out with it, feeling a little braver. After all, nobody had to know there was nothing in it. On the corner, I saw some books displayed in the window of a drug store. It took all the courage I had to go in there, after my first trip into one that looked very much like it, but I wanted a dictionary. This place didn't smell quite so strong; I suppose the pharmacy was enclosed in back, and I don't believe it had a lunch counter. Anyhow, I got in and out quickly, and walked back to the car, and sat down with the dictionary.

It turned out to be entirely useless, at least as far as *brunchies* and *Bermudas* were concerned. It had "scuff, v.," with a definition; "v.," I found out, meant *verb*, so that wasn't the word I wanted, but when I remembered the slippers on the counter with the sign, it made sense in a way.

Not enough sense, though. I decided to forget about the clothes for a while. The next problem was a driver's license.

The policeman that morning had been helpful, if over-interested, and since policemen directed traffic, they ought to have the information I wanted. I found one of them standing on a streetcorner looking not too busy, and asked him, and if his hair hadn't been brown instead of reddish (and only half there) I'd have thought it was the same one I talked to before. He wanted to know how old I was, and where was I from, and what I was doing there, and did I have a car, and was I *sure* I was nineteen?

Well, of course, I wasn't sure, but they'd told me that by the local reckoning, that was my approximate age. And I almost slipped and said I *had* a car, until I realized that I didn't have a right to drive one till I had a license. After he asked that one question, I began to feel suspicious about everything else he asked, and the interest he expressed. He was helpful, but I had to remember too, that it was the police who were charged with watching for suspicious characters, and--well, it was the last time I asked a policeman for information.

He *did* tell me where I could rent a car to take my road test, though, and where to apply for the test. The Courthouse turned out to be the big building behind the square where I'd parked the car that morning, and arranging for the test turned out to be much simpler than, by then, I expected it to be. In a way, I suppose, all the questions I had to answer when I talked to the policeman had prepared me for the official session--though they didn't seem nearly so inquisitive there.

By this time, I'd come to expect that they wouldn't believe my age when I told them. The woman at the window behind the counter wanted to see a "birth certificate," and I produced the one piece of identification I had; an ancient and yellowed document they had kept for me all these years. From the information it contained, I suspected it might even *be* a birth certificate; whether or not, it apparently satisfied her, and after that all she wanted was things like my address and height and weight. Fortunately, they had taken the trouble, back on the ship, to determine these statistics for me, because things like that were always coming up on television shows, especially when people were being questioned by the police. For the address, of course, I used the motel. The rest I knew, and I guess we had the figures close enough to right so that at least the woman didn't question any of it.

I had my road test about half an hour later, in a rented car, and the examiner said I did very well. He seemed surprised, and I don't wonder, considering the way most of those people contrive to mismanage a simple mechanism like an automobile. I guess when they say Earth is still in the Mechanical Age, what they mean is that humans are just *learning* about machines.

*   *   *   *   *

The biggest single stroke of luck I had at any time came during that road test. We passed a public-looking building with a sign in front that I didn't understand.

"What's that place?" I asked the examiner, and he said, as if anyone would know what he meant, "That? Oh--the Library."

I looked it up in my dictionary as soon as I was done at the License Bureau, and when I found out what it was, everything became a great deal simpler.

There was a woman who worked there, who showed me, without any surprise at my ignorance, just how the card catalogue worked, and what the numbering system meant; she didn't ask me how old I was, or any other questions, or demand any proof of any kind to convince her I had a right to use the place. She didn't even bother me much with questions about what I was looking for. I told her there were a *lot* of things I wanted to know, and she seemed to think that was a good answer, and said if she could help me any way, not to hesitate to ask, and then she left me alone with those drawers and drawers full of letter-and-number keys to all the mysteries of an alien world.

I found a book on how to outfit your daughter for college, that started with underwear and worked its way through to jewelry and cosmetics. I also found a whole shelf full of law books, and in one of them, specific information about the motor vehicle regulations in different States. There was a wonderful book about diamonds and other precious stones, particularly fascinating because it went into the chemistry of the different stones, and gave me the best measuring-stick I found at any time to judge the general level of technology of that so-called Mechanical Age.

That was all I had time for, I couldn't believe it was so late, when the librarian came and told me they were closing up, and I guess my disappointment must have showed all over me, because she asked if I wouldn't like to have a card, so I could take books home?

I found out all I needed to get a card was identification. I was supposed to have a reference, too, but the woman said she thought perhaps it would be all right without one, in my case. And then, when I wanted to take a volume of the Encyclopedia Americana, she said they didn't usually circulate that, but if I thought I could bring it back within a day or two....

I promised to, and I never did, and out of everything that happened, that's the one thing I feel badly about. I think she must have been a very unusual and *good* sort of woman, and I wish I had kept my promise to her.

*   *   *   *   *

Some of the stores downtown were still open. I bought the things I'd be expected to have, as near as I could make out from the book on college girls: panties and a garter belt and a brassiere, and stockings. A slip and another blouse, and a coat, because even in the early evening it was beginning to get chilly. Then the salesgirl talked me into gloves and a scarf and some earrings. I was halfway back to the car when I remembered about night clothes, and went back for a gown and robe and slippers. That didn't begin to complete the college girls' list, but it seemed like a good start. I'd need a dress, too, I thought, if I ever did go out with Larry in the evening ... but that could wait.

I put everything into the suitcase, and drove back to the motel. On the way, I stopped at a food store, and bought a large container of milk, and some crackers, and some fruit--oranges and bananas and apples. Back in my room, I put everything away in the drawers, and then sat down with my book and my food, and had a wonderful time. I was hungry, and everything tasted good, away from the dead meat smells, and what with clothes in the drawers and everything, I was beginning to feel like a real Earth-girl.

I even took a bath in the bathroom.

A good long one. Next to the library, that's the thing I miss most. It would be even better, if they made the tubs bigger, so you could swim around some. But just getting wet all over like that, and splashing in the water, is fun. Of course, we could never spare enough water for that on the ship.

Altogether, it was a good evening; everything was fine until I tried to sleep in that bed. I felt as if I was being suffocated all over. The floor was almost as bad, but in a different way. And once I got to sleep, I guess I slept well enough, because I felt fine in the morning. But then, I think I must have been on a mild oxygen jag all the time I was down there; nothing seemed to bother me too much. That morning, I felt so good I worked up my courage to go into a restaurant again--a different one. The smell was beginning to be familiar, and I could manage better. I experimented with a cereal called oatmeal, which was delicious, then I went back to the motel, packed up all my new belongings, left the key on the desk--as instructed by the sign on the door-- and started out for Denver.

*　　*　　*　　*　　*

Denver, according to the Encyclopedia Americana, is more of a true metropolitan area than Colorado Springs; that means--on Earth--that it is dirtier, more crowded, far less pleasant to look at or live in, and a great deal more convenient and efficient to do business in. In Denver, and with the aid of a Colorado driver's license for casual identification, I was able to sell two of my larger diamonds fairly quickly, at two different places, for something approximating half of their full value. Then I parked the car they had given me on a side street, took my suitcase, coat, and book with me, and walked to the nearest car sales lot. I left the keys in the old car, for the convenience of anyone who might want it.

Everything went extraordinarily smoothly, with just one exception. I had found out everything I needed to know in that library, except that when dealing with humans, one must always allow for waste time. If I had realized that at the time I left Colorado Springs that morning, everything might have turned out very differently indeed--although when I try to think just what other way it *could* have turned out, I don't quite know ... and I wonder, too, how much they knew, or planned, before they sent me down there....

This much is sure: if I hadn't assumed that a 70-mile trip, with a 60-mile average speed limit, would take approximately an hour and a half, and if I had realized that buying an automobile was not the same simple process as buying a nightgown, I wouldn't have been late for my luncheon appointment. And if I'd been there on time, I'd never have made the date for that night. As it was, I started out at seven o'clock in the morning, and only by exceeding the speed limit on the last twenty miles of the return trip did I manage to pull into that diner parking space at five minutes before two.

His car was still there!

It is so easy to look back and spot the instant of recognition or of error. My relief when I saw his car ... my delight when I walked in and saw and *felt* his mixture of surprise and joy that I had come, with disappointment and frustration because it was so late, and he had to leave almost immediately. And my complete failure, in the midst of the complexities of these inter-reactions, to think logically, or to recognize that his ordinary perceptions were certainly the equivalent of my own....

At that moment, I wasn't thinking *about* any of these things. I spent a delirious sort of five minute period absorbing his feelings about me, and releasing my own at him. I hadn't planned to do it, not so soon, not till I knew much more than I did--perhaps after another week's reading and going about--but when he said that since I'd got there so late for lunch, I'd *have* to meet him for dinner, I found I agreed with him perfectly.

          *   *   *   *   *

That afternoon, I bought a dress. This, too, took a great deal of time, even more than the car, because in the one case I simply had to look at a number of component parts, and listen to the operation of the motor, and feel for the total response of the mechanism, to determine whether it was suitable or not--but in the other, I had nothing to guide me but my own untrained taste, and the dubious preferences of the salesgirl, plus what I *thought* Larry's reactions *might* be. Also, I had to determine, without seeming too ignorant, just what sort of dress might be suitable for a dinner date--and without knowing for sure just how elaborate Larry's plans for the evening might be.

I learned a lot, and was startled to find that I enjoyed myself tremendously. But I couldn't make up my mind, and bought three dresses instead of one. It was after that, emboldened by pleasure and success, that I went back to that first drugstore. The Encyclopedia volume I had taken from the library, besides containing the information I wanted on Colorado, had an article on Cosmetics. I decided powder was unnecessary, although I could understand easily enough how important it must be to the native women, with their thick skin and large pores and patchy coloring; that accounted for the fact that the men were mostly so much uglier ... and I wondered if Larry used it, and if that was why his skin looked so much better than the others'.

Most of the perfumes made me literally ill; a few were inoffensive or mildly pleasant, if you thought of them just as smells, and not as something to be mistaken for one's *own* smell. Apparently, though, from the amount of space given over to them on the counter, and the number of advertisements I had seen or heard for one brand or another, they were an essential item. I picked out a faint lavender scent, and then bought some lipstick, mascara, and eyebrow pencil. On these last purchases, it was a relief to find that I had no opportunity to display my ignorance about nuances of coloring, or the merits of one brand over another. The woman behind the counter knew exactly what I should have, and was not interested in hearing any of my opinions. She even told me how to apply the mascara, which was helpful, since the other two were obvious, and anyhow I'd seen them used on television, and the lipstick especially I had seen women use since I'd been here.

It turned out to be a little more difficult than it looked, when I tried it. Cosmetics apparently take a good deal more experience than clothing, if you want to have it look *right*. Right by *their* standards, I mean, so that your face becomes a formal design, and will register only a minimum of actual emotion or response.

I was supposed to meet Larry in the cocktail lounge of a hotel in Manitou Springs, the smaller town I'd passed through the day before on my way down from the mountain. I drove back that way now, with all my possessions in my new car, including the purse that held not only my remaining diamonds and birth certificate, but also a car registration, driver's license, wallet, money, and makeup. A little more than halfway there, I saw a motel with a "Vacancy" sign out, and an attractive clean look about it. I pulled in and got myself a room with no more concern than if I'd been doing that sort of thing all my life.

This time there was no question about my age, nor was there later on that evening, in the cocktail lounge or anywhere else. I suppose it was the lipstick that made the difference, plus a certain increase in self-confidence; apparently I wasn't too small to be an adult, provided I looked and acted like one.

The new room did not have a bathtub. There was a shower, which was fun, but not as much as the tub had been. Dressing was *not* fun, and when I was finished, the whole effect still didn't look right, in terms of my own mental image of an Earth-woman dressed for a date.

It was the shoes, of course. This kind of dress wanted high heels. I had tried a pair in the store, and promptly rejected the whole notion. Now I wondered if I'd been too hasty, but I realized I could not conceivably have added that discomfort to the already-pressing difficulties of stockings and garter belt.

This last problem got so acute when I sat down and tried to drive the car, that I did some thinking about it, and decided to take them off. It seemed to me that I'd seen a lot of bare legs with flat heels. It was only with high heels that stockings were a real necessity. Anyhow, I pulled the car over to the side on an empty stretch of road, and wriggled out of things with a great deal of difficulty. I don't believe it made much difference in my appearance. No one *seemed* to notice, and I do think the lack of heels was more important.

*   *   *   *   *

All of this has been easy to put down. The next part is harder: partly because it's so important; partly because it's personal; partly because I just don't remember it all as clearly.

Larry was waiting for me when I got to the hotel. He stood up and walked over to me, looking at me as if I were the only person in the room besides himself, or as if he'd been waiting all his life, and only just that moment saw what it was he'd been waiting for. I don't know how I looked at him, but I know how I felt all of a sudden, and I don't think I can express it very well.

It was odd, because of the barriers to communication. The way he felt and the way I did are not things to put into words, and although I couldn't help but feel the impact of *his* emotion, I had to remember that he was deaf-and-blind to mine. All I could get from him for that matter, was a sort of generalized *noise*, loud but confused, without any features or details.

He smiled, and I smiled, and he said, "I didn't know if you'd really come ..." and I said, "Am I late?" and he said, "Not much. What do you want to drink?"

I knew he meant something with alcohol in it, and I didn't dare, not till I'd experimented all alone first.

"Could I get some orange juice?" I asked.

He smiled again. "You can get anything you want. You don't drink?" He took my arm, and walked me over to a booth in the back corner, and went on without giving me a chance to answer. "No, of course you don't. Just orange juice and milk. Listen, Tina, I've been scared to ask you, but we might as well get it over with. How old are you anyhow?..." We sat down, but he still didn't give me a chance to answer. "No, that's not the right question. Who are you? What are you? What makes a girl like you exist at all? How come they let you run around on your own like this? Does your mother.... Never mind me, honey. I've got no business asking anything. Sufficient unto the moment, and all that. I'm just talking so much because I'm so nervous. I haven't felt like this since ... since I first went up for a solo in a Piper Cub. I didn't think you'd come, and you did, and you're still here in spite of me and my dumb yap. Orange juice for the lady, please," he told the waiter, "and a beer for me. Draft."

I just sat there. As long as he kept talking, I didn't have to. He looked just as beautiful as he had in the diner, only maybe more so. His skin was smoother; I suppose he'd just shaved. And he was wearing a tan suit just a shade darker than his skin, which was just a shade darker than his hair, and there was absolutely nothing I could say out loud in his language that would mean anything at all, so I waited to see if he'd start talking again.

"You're not mad at me, Tina?"

I smiled and shook my head.

"Well, *say* something then."

"It's more fun listening to you."

"You say that just like you mean it ... or do you mean *funny*?"

"No. I mean that it's hard for me to talk much. I don't know how to say a lot of the things I want to say. And most people don't say anything when they talk, and I don't like listening to their voices, but I do like yours, and ... I can't help liking what you say ... it's always so *nice*. About me, I mean. Complimentary. Flattering."

"You were right the first time. And you seem to be able to say what you mean very clearly."

Which was just the trouble. Not only able to, but unable not to. It didn't take any special planning or remembering to say or act the necessary lies to other humans. But Larry was the least alien person I'd ever known. Dishonesty to him was like lying to myself. Playing a role for him was pure schizophrenia.

Right then, I knew it was a mistake. I should never have made that date, or at least not nearly so soon. But even as I thought that, I had no more intention of cutting it short or backing out than I did of going back to the ship the next day. I just tried not to talk too much, and trusted to the certain knowledge that I was as important to him as he was to me--so perhaps whatever mistakes I made, whatever I said that sounded *wrong*, he would either accept or ignore or forgive.

But of course you can't just sit all night and say nothing. And the simplest things could trip me up. Like when he asked if I'd like to dance, and all I had to say was "No, thanks," and instead, because I *wanted* to try it, I said, "I don't know how."

Or when he said something about going to a movie, and I agreed enthusiastically, and he gave me a choice of three different ones that he wanted to see ... "Oh, anyone," I told him. "You're easy to please," he said, but he insisted on my making a choice. There was something he called "an old-Astaire-Rogers," and something else that was made in England, and one current American one with stars I'd seen on television. I wanted to see either of the others. I could have said so, or I could have named one, any one. Instead I heard myself blurting out that I'd never been to a movie.

At that point, of course, he began to ask questions in earnest. And at that point, schizoid or not, I had to lie. It was easier, though, because I'd been thoroughly briefed in my story, for just such emergencies as this--and because I could talk more or less uninterruptedly, with only pertinent questions thrown in, and without having to react so much to the emotional tensions between us.

I told him how my parents had died in an automobile accident when I was a baby; how my two uncles had claimed me at the hospital; about the old house up on the mountainside, and the convent school, and the two old men who hated the evils of the world; about the death of the first uncle, and at long last the death of the second, and the lawyers and the will and everything--the whole story, as we'd worked it out back on the ship.

It answered everything, explained everything--even the unexpected item of not being able to eat meat. My uncles were vegetarians, which was certainly a harmless eccentricity compared to most of the others I credited them with.

As a story, it was pretty far-fetched, but it hung together-- and in certain ways, it wasn't even *too* far removed from the truth. It was, anyhow, the closest thing to the truth that I could tell--and I therefore delivered it with a fair degree of conviction. Of course it wasn't designed to stand up to the close and personal inspection Larry gave it; but then he *wanted* to believe me.

He seemed to swallow it. What he did, of course, was something any man who relies, as he did, on his reflexes and responses to stay alive, learns to do very early--he filed all questions and apparent discrepancies for reference, or for thinking over when there was time, and proceeded to make the most of the current situation.

We both made the most of it. It was a wonderful evening, from that point on. We went to the Astaire-Rogers picture, and although I missed a lot of the humor, since it was contemporary stuff from a time before I had any chance to learn about Earth, the music and dancing were fun. Later on, I found that dancing was not nearly as difficult or intricate as it looked--at least not with Larry. All I had to do was give in to a natural impulse to let my body follow his. It felt wonderful, from the feet on up.

Finally, we went back to the hotel, where we'd left my car, and I started to get out of his, but he reached out an arm, and stopped me.

"There's something else I guess you never did," he said. His voice sounded different from before. He put both his hands on my shoulders, and pulled me toward him, and leaned over and kissed me.

I'd seen it, of course, on television.

I'd seen it, but I had no idea....

That first time, it was something I felt on my lips, and felt so sweetly and so strongly that the rest of me seemed to melt away entirely. I had no other sensations, except in that one place where his mouth touched mine. That was the first time.

When it stopped, the world stopped, and I began again, but I had to sort out the parts and pieces and put them all together to find out who I was. While I did this, his hands were still on my shoulders, where they'd been all along, only he was holding me at arm's distance away from him, and looking at me curiously.

"It really was, wasn't it?" he said.

"What?" I tried to say, but the sound didn't come out. I took a breath and "Was what?" I croaked.

"The first time." He smiled suddenly, and it was like the sun coming up in the morning, and then his arms went all the way around me. I don't know whether he moved over on the seat, or I did, or both of us. "Oh, baby, baby," he whispered in my ear, and then there was the second time.

The second time was like the first, and also like dancing, and some ways like the bathtub. This time none of me melted away; it was all there, and all close to him, and all warm, and all tingling with sensations. I was more completely alive right then than I had ever been before in my life.

After we stopped kissing each other, we stayed very still, holding on to each other, for a while, and then he moved away just a little, enough, to breathe better.

I didn't know what to do. I didn't want to get out of the car. I didn't even want to be separated from him by the two or three inches between us on the seat. But he was sitting next to me now, staring straight ahead, not saying anything, and I just didn't know what came next. On television, the kiss was always the end of the scene.

He started the car again.

I said, "I have to ... my car ... I...."

"We'll come back," he said. "Don't worry about it. We'll come back. Let's just drive a little...?" he pulled out past my car, and turned and looked at me for a minute. "You don't want to go now, do you? Right away?"

I shook my head, but he wasn't looking at me any more, so I took a breath and said out loud, "No."

We came off a twisty street onto the highway. "So that's how it hits you," he said. He wasn't exactly talking to me; more like thinking out loud. "Twenty-seven years a cool cat, and now it has to be a crazy little midget that gets to you." He had to stop then, for a red light--the same light I'd stopped at the first time on the way in. That seemed a long long time before.

Larry turned around and took my hand. He looked hard at my face, "I'm sorry, hon. I didn't mean that the way it sounded."

"What?" I said. "What do you mean?" I hadn't even tried to make sense out of what he was saying before; he wasn't talking to me anyhow.

"Kid," he said, "maybe that was the first time for you, but in a different way it was the first time for me too." His hand opened and closed around mine, and his mouth opened and closed too, but nothing came out. The light was green; he noticed, and started moving, but it turned red again. This time he kept watching it.

"I don't suppose anybody ever told you about the birds and the bees and the butterflies," he said.

"Told me *what* about them?" He didn't answer right away, so I thought about it. "All I can think of is they all have wings. They all fly."

"So do I. So does a fly. What I mean is ... the hell with it!" He turned off the highway, and we went up a short hill and through a sort of gateway between two enormous rocks. "Have you ever been here?" he asked.

"I don't think so...."

"They call it The Garden of the Gods. I don't know why. I like it here ... it's a good place to drive and think."

There was a lot of moonlight, and the Garden was all hills and drops and winding roads between low-growing brush, and everywhere, as if the creatures of some giant planet had dropped them, were those towering rocks, their shapes scooped out and chiseled and hollowed and twisted by wind, water and sand. Yes, it was lovely, and it was non-intrusive. Just what he said--a good place to drive and think.

Once he came to the top of a hill, and stopped the car, and we looked out over the Garden, spreading out in every direction, with the moonlight shadowed in the sagebrush, and gleaming off the great rocks. Then we turned and looked at each other, and he reached out for me and kissed me again; after which he pulled away as if the touch of me hurt him, and grabbed hold of the wheel with a savage look on his face, and raced the motor, and raised a cloud of dust on the road behind us.

I didn't understand, and I felt hurt. I wanted to stop again. I wanted to be kissed again. I didn't like sitting alone on my side of the seat, with that growl in his throat not quite coming out.

I asked him to stop again. He shook his head, and made believe to smile.

"I'll buy you a book," he said. "All about the birds and the bees and a little thing we have around here we call sex. I'll buy it tomorrow, and you can read it--you *do* know how to read, don't you?--and then we'll take another ride, and we can park if you want to. Not tonight, baby."

"But I *know*...." I started, and then had sense enough to stop. I knew about sex; but what I knew about it didn't connect with kissing or parking the car, or sitting close ... and it occurred to me that maybe it did, and maybe there was a lot I *didn't* know that wasn't on Television, and wasn't on the Ship's reference tapes either. Morals and mores, and nuances of behavior. So I shut up, and let him take me back to the hotel again, to my own car.

He leaned past me to open the door on my side, but he couldn't quite make it, and I had my fourth kiss. Then he let go again, and almost pushed me out of the car; but when I started to close the door behind me, he called out, "Tomorrow night?"

"I ... all right," I said. "Yes. Tomorrow night."

"Can I pick you up?"

There was no reason not to this time. The first time I wouldn't tell him where I lived, because I knew I'd have to change places, and I didn't know where yet. I told him the name of the motel, and where it was.

"Six o'clock," he said.

"All right."

"Good night."

"Good night."

*   *   *   *   *

I don't remember driving back to my room. I think I slept on the bed that night, without ever stopping to determine whether it was comfortable or not. And when I woke up in the morning, and looked out the window at a white-coated landscape, the miracle of snow (which I had never seen before; not many planets have as much water vapor in their atmospheres as Earth does.) in summer weather seemed trivial in comparison to what had happened to me.

Trivial, but beautiful. I was afraid it would be very cold, but it wasn't.

I had gathered, from the weather-talk in the place where I ate breakfast, that in this mountain-country (it was considered to be very high altitude there), snow at night and hot sun in the afternoon was not infrequent in the month of April, though it was unusual for May.

It was beautiful to look at, and nice to walk on, but it began melting as soon as the sun was properly up, and then it looked awful. The red dirt there is pretty, and so is the snow, but when they began merging into each other in patches and muddy spots, it was downright ugly.

Not that I cared. I ate oatmeal and drank milk and nibbled at a piece of toast, and tried to plan my activities for the day. To the library first, and take back the book they'd lent me. Book ... all right then, get a book on sex. But that was foolish; I *knew* all about sex. At least I knew ... well, what did I know? I knew their manner of reproduction, and....

Just why, at that time and place, I should have let it come through to me, I don't know. I'd managed to stay in a golden daze from the time in the Garden till that moment, refusing to think through the implications of what Larry said.

Sex. Sex is mating and reproduction. Dating and dancing and kissing are parts of the courtship procedure. And the television shows all stop with kissing, because the mating itself is taboo. Very simple. Also *very* taboo.

Of course, they didn't *say* I couldn't. They never said anything about it at all. It was just obvious. It wouldn't even work. We were *different*, after all.

Oh, technically, biologically, of course, we were probably cross-fertile, but....

The whole thing was so obviously *impossible!*

They should have warned me. I'd never have let it go this far, if I'd known.

Sex. Mating. Marriage. Tribal rites. Rituals and rigamaroles, and stay here forever. Never go back.

Never go back?

There was an instant's sheer terror, and then the comforting knowledge that they wouldn't *let* me do that. I had to go back.

Baby on a spaceship?

Well, *I* was a baby on a spaceship, but that was different. How different? I was older. I wasn't born there. Getting born is complicated. Oxygen, gravity, things like that. You can't raise a *human* baby on a spaceship.... *Human?* What's human? What am I? Never mind the labels. It would be *my* baby....

I didn't want a baby. I just wanted Larry to hold me close to him and kiss me.

*   *   *   *   *

I drove downtown and on the way to the library I passed a bookstore, so I stopped and went in there instead. That was better. I could buy what I wanted, and not have to ask permission to take it out, and if there was more than one, I could have all I wanted.

I asked the man for books about sex. He looked so startled, I realized the taboo must apply on the verbal level too.

I didn't care. He showed me where the books were, and that's all that mattered. "Non-fiction here," he said. "That what you wanted, Miss?"

Non-fiction. Definitely. I thanked him, and picked out half a dozen different books. One was a survey of sexual behavior and morals; another was a manual of techniques; one was on the psychology of sex, and there was another about abnormal sex, and one on physiology, and just to play safe, considering the state of my own ignorance, one that announced itself as giving a "clear simple explanation of the facts of life for adolescents."

I took them all to the counter, and paid for them, and the man still looked startled, but he took the money. He insisted on wrapping them up, though, before I could leave.

*   *   *   *   *

The next part of this is really Larry's story, but unable as I am, even now, to be *certain* about his unspoken thoughts, I can only tell it as I experienced it. I didn't do anything all that day, except wade through the books I'd bought, piece-meal, reading a few pages here and a chapter there. The more I read, the more confused I got. Each writer contradicted all the others, except in regard to the few basic biological facts that I already knew. The only real addition to my factual knowledge was the information in the manual of technique about contraception--and that was rather shocking, even while it was tempting.

The mechanical contrivances these people made use of were foolish, of course, and typical of the stage of culture they are going through. If I wanted to prevent conception, while engaging in an act of sexual intercourse, I could, do so, of course, but....

The shock to the glandular system wouldn't be too severe; it was the psychological repercussions I was thinking about. The idea of pursuing a course of action whose sole motivation was the procreative urge, and simultaneously to decide by an act of will to refuse to procreate....

I *could* do it, theoretically, but in practice I knew I never would.

I put the book down and went outside in the afternoon sunshine. The motel was run by a young married couple, and I watched the woman come out and put her baby in the playpen. She was laughing and talking to it; she looked happy; so did the baby.

But *I* wouldn't be. Not even if they let me. I couldn't live here and bring up a child--children?--on this primitive, almost barbaric, world. Never ever be able fully to communicate with anyone. Never, ever, be entirely honest with anyone.

Then I remembered what it was like to be in Larry's arms, and wondered what kind of communication I could want that might surpass that. Then I went inside and took a shower and began to dress for the evening.

It was too early to get dressed. I was ready too soon. I went out and got in the car, and pulled out onto the highway and started driving. I was halfway up the mountain before I knew where I was going, and then I doubled my speed.

I was scared. I ran away.

*   *   *   *   *

There was still some snow on the mountain top. Down below, it would be warm yet, but up there it was cold. The big empty house was full of dust and chill and I brought fear in with me. I wished I had known where I was going when I left my room; I wanted my coat. I wanted something to read while I waited. I remembered the library book and almost went back. Instead, I went to the dark room in back that had once been somebody's kitchen, and opened the cupboard and found the projector and yelled for help.

I didn't know where they were, how far away, whether cruising or landed somewhere, or how long it would take. All I could be sure of was that they couldn't come till after dark, full dark, and that would be, on the mountain top, at least another four hours.

There was a big round black stove in a front room, that looked as if it could burn wood safely. I went out and gathered up everything I could find nearby that looked to be combustible, and started a fire, and began to feel better. I beat the dust off a big soft chair, and pulled it over close to the stove, and curled up in it, warm and drowsy and knowing that help was on the way.

I fell asleep, and I was in the car with Larry again, in front of that hotel, every cell of my body tinglingly awake, and I woke up, and moved the chair farther back away from the fire, and watched the sun set through the window--till I fell asleep again, and dreamed again, and when I woke, the sun was gone, but the mountain top was brightly lit. I had forgotten about the moon.

I tried to remember what time it rose and when it set, but all I knew was it had shone as bright last night in the Garden of the Gods.

I walked around, and went outside, and got more wood, and when it was hot in the room again, I fell asleep, and Larry's hands were on my shoulders, but he wasn't kissing me.

He was shouting at me. He sounded furious, but I couldn't feel any anger. "You God-damn little idiot!" he shouted. "What in the name of all that's holy...? ... put you over my knee and.... For God's sake, baby," he stopped shouting, "what did you pull a dumb trick like this for?"

"I was scared. I didn't even plan to do it. I just did."

"Scared? My God, I should think you would be! Now listen, babe. I don't know yet what's going on, and I don't think I'm going to like it when I find out. I don't like it already that you told me a pack of lies last night. Just the same, God help me, I don't think it's what it sounds like. But I'm the only one who doesn't. Now you better give it to me straight, because they've got half the security personnel of this entire area out hunting for you, and nobody else is going to care much what the truth is. My God, on top of everything else, you had to *run away!* Now, give out, kid, and make it good. This one has got to stick."

I didn't understand a lot of what he said. I started trying to explain, but he wouldn't listen. He wanted something else, and I didn't know what.

Finally, he made me understand.

He'd almost believed my story the night before. Almost, but there was a detail somewhere that bothered him. He couldn't remember it at first; it kept nudging around the edge of his mind, but he didn't know what it was. He forgot about it for a while. Then, in the Garden, I made my second big mistake. (He didn't explain all of this then; he just accused, and I didn't understand this part completely until later.) I wanted him to park the car.

Any girl on Earth, no matter how sheltered, how inexperienced, would have known better than that. As he saw it, he had to decide whether I was just so carried away by the night and the mood and the moment that I didn't *care*--or whether my apparent innocence was a pose all along.

When we separated in front of the hotel that night, we both had to take the same road for a while. Larry was driving right behind me for a good three miles, before I turned off at the motel. And that was when he realized what the detail was that had been bothering him: my car.

The first time he saw me, I was driving a different make and model, with Massachusetts plates on it. He was sure of that, because he had copied it down when he left the luncheonette, the first time we met.

Larry had never told me very clearly about the kind of work he did. I knew it was something more or less "classified," having to do with aircraft--jet planes or experimental rockets, or something like that. And I knew, without his telling me, that the work--not just the *job*, but the work he did at it--was more important to him than anything else ever had been. More important, certainly, than he had ever expected any woman to be.

So, naturally, when he met me that day, and knew he wanted to see me again, but couldn't get my address or any other identifying information out of me, he had copied down the license number of my car, and turned it in, with my name, to the Security Officer on the Project. A man who has spent almost every waking moment from the age of nine planning and preparing to fit himself for a role in humanity's first big fling into space doesn't endanger his security status by risking involuntary contamination from an attractive girl. The little aircraft plant on the fringes of town was actually a top-secret key division in the Satellite project, and if you worked there, you took precautions.

The second time I met him at the luncheonette, he had been waiting so long, and had so nearly given up any hope of my coming, that he was no longer watching the road or the door when I finally got there--and when he left, he was so pleased at having gotten a dinner date with me, that he didn't notice much of anything at all. Not except out of the corner of one eye, and with only the slightest edge of subconscious recognition: just enough so that some niggling detail that was out-of-place kept bothering him thereafter; and just enough so that he made a point of stopping in the Security Office again that afternoon to add my new motel address to the information he'd given them the day before.

The three-mile drive in back of my Colorado plates was just about long enough, finally, to make the discrepancy register consciously.

Larry went home and spent a bad night. His feelings toward me, as I could hardly understand at the time, were a great deal stronger, or at least more clearly defined, than mine about him. But since he was more certain just what it was he wanted, and less certain what *I* did, every time he tried to fit my attitude in the car into the rest of what he knew, he'd come up with a different answer, and nine answers out of ten were angry and suspicious and agonizing.

"Now look, babe," he said, "you've got to see this. I trusted *you*; really, all the time, I did trust you. But I didn't trust *me*. By the time I went to work this morning, I was half-nuts. I didn't know *what* to think, that's all. And I finally sold myself on the idea that if you were what you said you were, nobody would get hurt, and--well, if you *weren't* on the level, I better find out, quick. You see that?"

"Yes," I said.

"Okay. So I told them about the license plates, and about--the other stuff."

"What other stuff?" What else was there? How stupid could I be?

"I mean, the--in the car. The way you--Listen, kid," he said, his face grim and demanding again. "It's still just as true as it was then. I *still* don't know. They called me this evening, and said when they got around to the motel to question you, you'd skipped out. They also said that Massachusetts car was stolen. And there were a couple of other things they'd picked up that they wouldn't tell me, but they've got half the National Guard and all the Boy Scouts out after you by now. They wanted me to tell them anything I could think of that might help them find this place. I couldn't think of anything while I was talking to them. Right afterwards, I remembered plenty of things--which roads you were familiar with, and what you'd seen before and what you hadn't, stuff like that, so--"

"So you--?"

"So I came out myself. I wanted to find you first. Listen, babe, I love you. Maybe I'm a sucker, and maybe I'm nuts, and maybe I-don't-know-what. But I figured maybe I could find out more, and easier on you, than they could. And honey, it better be good, because I don't think I've got what it would take to turn you in, and now I've found you--"

He let it go there, but that was plenty. He was willing to listen. He wanted to believe in me, because he wanted me. And finding me in the house I'd described, where I'd said it was, had him half-convinced. But I still had to explain those Massachusetts plates. And I couldn't.

I was psychologically incapable of telling him another lie, now, when I knew I would never see him again, that this was the last time I could ever possibly be close to him in any way. I couldn't estrange myself by lying.

*   *   *   *   *

And I was *also* psychologically incapable--I found out--of telling the truth. They'd seen to that.

It was the first time I'd ever hated them. The first time, I suppose, that I fully realized my position with them.

I could not tell the truth, and I would not tell a lie; all I could do was explain this, and hope he would believe me. I could explain, too, that I was no spy, no enemy; that those who had prevented me from telling what I wanted to tell were no menace to his government or his people.

He believed me.

It was just that simple. He believed me, because I suppose he knew, without knowing how he knew it, that it was truth. Humans are not incapable of communication; they are simply unaware of it.

I told him, also, that they were coming for me, that I had called them, and--regretfully--that he had better leave before they came.

"You said they weren't enemies or criminals. You were telling the truth, weren't you?"

"Yes, I was. They won't *harm* you. But they might...." I couldn't say it. I didn't know the words when I tried to say it. *Might take you away with them ... with us....*

"Might what?"

"Might ... oh, I don't *know*!"

Now he was suspicious again. "All right," he said. "I'll leave. You come with me."

It was just that simple. Go back with him. Let them come and not find me. What could they do? Their own rules would keep them from hunting for me. They couldn't come down among the people of Earth. Go back. Stop running.

We got into his car, and he turned around and smiled at me again, like the other time.

I smiled back, seeing him through a shiny kind of mist which must have been tears. I reached for him, and he reached for me at the same time.

When we let go, he tried to start the car, and it wouldn't work. Of course. I'd forgotten till then. I started laughing and crying at the same time in a sort of a crazy way, and took him back inside and showed him the projector. They'd forgotten to give me any commands about not doing that, I guess. Or they thought it wouldn't matter.

It did matter. Larry looked it over, and puzzled over it a little, and fooled around, and asked me some questions. I didn't have much technical knowledge, but I knew what it did, and he figured out the way it did it. Nothing with an electro-magnetic motor was going to work while that thing was turned on, not within a mile or so in any direction. And there wasn't any way to turn it off. It was a homing beam, and it was on to stay-- foolproof.

That was when he looked at me, and said slowly, "You got here three days ago, didn't you, babe?"

I nodded.

"There was--God-damn it, it's too foolish! There was a--a *flying saucer* story in the paper that day. Somebody saw it land on a hilltop somewhere. Some crackpot. Some ... how about it, kid?"

I couldn't say yes and I couldn't say no, and I did the only thing that was left, which was to get hysterical. In a big way.

He had to calm me down, of course. And I found out why the television shows stop with the kiss. The rest is very private and personal.

*   *   *   *   *

Author's note: This story was dictated to me by a five-year-old boy--word-for-word, except for a very few editorial changes of my own. He is a very charming and bright youngster who plays with my own five-year-old daughter. One day he wandered into my office, and watched me typing for a while, then asked what I was doing. I answered (somewhat irritably, because the children are supposed to stay out of the room when I'm working) that I was trying to write a story.

"What kind of a story?"

"A grown-up story."

"But what kind?"

"A science-fiction story." The next thing I was going to do was to call my daughter, and ask her to take her company back to the playroom. I had my mouth open, but I never got a syllable out. Teddy was talking.

"I don't know where they got the car," he said. "They made three or four stops before the last...." He had a funny look on his face, and his eyes were glazed-looking.

I had seen some experimental work with hypnosis and post-hypnotic performance. After the first couple of sentences, I led Teddy into the living-room, and switched on the tape-recorder. I left it on as long as he kept talking. I had to change tapes once, and missed a few more sentences. When he was done, I asked him, with the tape still running, where he had heard that story.

"What story?" he asked. He looked perfectly normal again.

"The story you just told me."

He was obviously puzzled.

"The science-fiction *story," I said.*

"I don't know where they got the car," he began; his face was set and his eyes were blank.

I kept the tape running, and picked up the parts I'd missed before. Then I sent Teddy off to the playroom, and played back the tape, and thought for a while.

There was a little more, besides what you've read. Parts of it were confused, with some strange words mixed in, and with sentences half-completed, and a feeling of ambivalence or censorship or inhibition of some kind preventing much clarity. Other parts were quite clear. Of these, the only section I have omitted so far that seems to me to belong in the story is this one:--

*   *   *   *   *

The baby will have to be born on Earth! They have decided that themselves. And for the first time, I am glad that they cannot communicate with me as perfectly as they do among themselves. I can think some things they do not know about.

We are not coming back. I do not think that I will like it on Earth for very long, and I do not know--neither does Larry--what will happen to us when the Security people find us, and we cannot answer their questions. But--

I am a woman now, and I love like a woman. Larry will not be their pet; so I cannot be. I am not sure that I am fit to be what Larry thinks of as a "human being." He says I must learn to be "my own master." I am not at all sure I could do this, if it were necessary, but fortunately, this is one of Larry's areas of semantic confusion. The feminine of *master* is *mistress*, which has various meanings.

Also, there is the distinct possibility, from what Larry says, that we will not, *either* of us, be allowed even as much liberty as we have here.

There is also the matter of gratitude. *They* brought me up, took care of me, taught me, loved me, gave me a way of life, and a knowledge of myself, infinitely richer than I could ever have had on Earth. Perhaps they even saved my life, healing me when I was quite possibly beyond the power of Earthly medical science to save. But against all this--

They caused the damage to start with. It was *their* force-field that wrecked the car and killed my parents. *They* have paid for it; *they* are paying for it yet. *They* will continue to pay, for more years than make sense in terms of a human lifetime. *They* will continue to wander from planet to planet and system to system, because *they* have broken *their* own law, and now may never go home.

But *I* can.

I am a woman, and Larry is a man. We will go home and have our baby. And perhaps the baby will be the means of our freedom, some day. If we cannot speak to save ourselves, he may some day be able to speak for us.

I do not think the blocks they set in us will penetrate my womb as my own thoughts, I hope, already have.

*   *   *   *   *

Author's note: Before writing this story--as a story--I talked with Johnny's parents. I approached them cautiously. His mother is a big woman, and a brunette. His father is a friendly fat redhead. I already knew that neither of them reads science-fiction. The word is not likely to be mentioned in their household.

They moved to town about three years ago. Nobody here knew them before that, but there are rumors that Johnny is adopted. They did not volunteer any confirmation of that information when I talked to them, and they did not pick up on any of the leads I offered about his recitation.

Johnny himself is small and fair-haired. He takes after his paternal grandmother, his mother says....

*   *   *   *   *

HELPFULLY
YOURS

BY EVELYN E. SMITH

ORIGINALLY PUBLISHED IN *GALAXY*
FEBRUARY 1955

Editor's Notes:
Helpfully Yours
By Evelyn E. Smith

Imagining how life forms might have evolved differently on other planets is a common motif in science fiction. Endowing intelligent beings with strange and unusual traits, whether done seriously or in a light hearted vein, allows an author to explore themes in a new and different way. In "Helpfully Yours," Evelyn Smith examines not only the culture clash between two species, one avian and one human, but also the clash between the sexes, all in a context reminiscent of the movie "The Front Page." Told with her typical sense of humor, the story demonstrates that we are not so different under the skin—or feathers.

You can read more stories from Evelyn E. Smith in *Evelyn E. Smith Resurrected*, published by Resurrected Press.

HELPFULLY YOURS

Tarb Morfatch had read all the information on Terrestrial customs that was available in the *Times* morgue before she'd left Fizbus. And all through the journey she'd studied her *Brief Introduction to Terrestrial Manners and Mores* avidly. Perhaps it was a bit overinspirational in spots, but it had facts in it, too.

So she knew that, since the natives were non-alate, she was not to take wing on Earth. She had, however, forgotten to correlate the knowledge of their winglessness with her own vertical habits. As a result, on leaving the tender that had ferried her down from the Moon, she looked up instead of right and narrowly escaped death at the jaws of a raging groundcar that swerved out onto the field.

She recognized it as a taxi from one of the pictures in the handbook. It was a pity, she thought sadly as she was knocked off her feet, that all those lessons she had so carefully learned were to go to waste.

But it was only the wind of the car's passage that had thrown her down. As she struggled to get up, hampered by her awkward native skirts, the door of the taxi flew open. A tall young man--a Fizbian--burst out, the soft yellowish-green down on his handsome face bristling with fright until each feather stood out separately.

"Miss Morfatch! Are you all right?"

"Just--just a little shaky," she murmured, brushing dirt from her rosy leg feathers. *Too young to be Drosmig; too good-looking to be anyone important, she thought glumly. Must be the office boy.*

To her surprise, he didn't help her up. Probably it would violate some native taboo if he did, she deduced. The handbook hadn't mentioned anything that seemed to apply, but, after all, a little book like that couldn't cover everything.

*   *   *   *   *

She could see the young man was embarrassed--his emerald crest was waving to and fro.

"I'm Stet Zarnon," he introduced himself awkwardly.

The Managing Editor! The handsome young employer of her girlish dreams! But perhaps he had a wife on Fizbus--no, the Grand Editor made a point of hiring people without families to use as a pretext for expensive vacations on the Home Planet.

As she opened her mouth to say something brilliantly witty, to show she was no ordinary female but a creature of spirit and fire and intelligence, a sudden cacophony of shrill cries and explosions arose, accompanied by bursts of light. Her feathers stood erect and she clung to her employer with both feathered legs.

"If these are the friendly diplomatic relations Earth and Fizbus are supposed to be enjoying," she said, "I'm not enjoying them one bit!"

"They're only taking pictures of you with native equipment," he explained, pulling away from her. What was the matter with him? "You're the first Fizbian woman ever to come to Terra, you know."

She certainly did know--and, what was more, she had made the semi-finals for Miss Fizbus only the year before. Perhaps he had some Terrestrial malady he didn't want her to catch. Or could it be that in the four years he had spent in voluntary exile on this planet, he had come to prefer the native females? Now it was her turn to shrink from him.

He was conversing rapidly in Terran with the chattering natives who milled about them. Although Tarb had been an honors student in Terran back at school, she found herself unable to understand more than an occasional word of what they said. Then she remembered that they were not at the world capital, Ottawa, but another community, New York. Undoubtedly they were all speaking some provincial dialect peculiar to the locality.

And nobody at all booed in appreciation, although, she told herself sternly, she really couldn't have expected them to. Standards of beauty were different in different solar systems. At least they were picking up as souvenirs some of the feathers she'd shed in her tumble, which showed they took an interest.

Stet turned back to her. "These are fellow-members of the press."

She was able to catch enough of what he said next in Terran to understand that she was being formally introduced to the aboriginal journalists. Although you could never call the natives attractive, with their squat figures and curiously atrophied vestigial wings--*arms*, she reminded herself--they were very Fizboid in appearance and, with their winglessness cloaked, could have creditably passed for singed Fizbians.

Moreover, they seemed friendly; at any rate, the sounds they uttered were welcoming. She began to make the three ritual *entrechats*, but Stat stopped her. "Just smile at them; that'll be enough."

It didn't seem like enough, but he was the boss.

*   *   *   *   *

"Thank the stars we're through with that," he sighed, as they finally were able to escape their confreres and get into the taxi. "I suppose," he added, wriggling inside the clumsy Terrestrial jacket which, cut to fit over his wings, did nothing either to improve his figure or to make him look like a native, "it was as much of an ordeal for you as for me."

"Well, I am a little bewildered by it all," Tarb admitted, settling herself as comfortably as possible on the seat cushions.

"No, don't do that!" he cried. "Here people don't crouch on seats. They sit," he explained in a kindlier tone. "Like this."

"You mean I have to bend myself in that clumsy way?"

He nodded. "In public, at least."

"But it's so hard on the wings. I'm losing feathers foot over claw."

"Yes, but you could...." He stopped. "Well, anyhow, remember we have to comply with local customs. You see, the Terrestrials have those things called arms instead of legs. That is, they have legs, but they use them only for walking."

She sighed. "I'd read about the arms, but I had no idea the natives would be so--so primitive as to actually use them."

"Considering they had no wings, it was very clever of them to make use of the vestigial appendages," he said hotly. "If you take their physical limitations into account, they've done a marvelous job with their little planet. They can't fly; they have very little sense of balance; their vision is exceedingly poor--yet, in spite of all that, they have achieved a quite remarkable degree of civilization." He gestured toward the horizontal building arrangements visible through the window. "Why, you could almost call those streets. As a matter of fact, the natives do."

At the moment, she could take an interest in Terrestrial civilization only as it affected her personally. "But I'll be able to relax in the office, won't I?"

"To a certain extent," he replied cautiously. "You see, we have to use a good deal of native help because--well, our facilities are limited...."

"Oh," she said.

Then she remembered that she was on Terra at least partly to demonstrate the pluck of Fizbian femininity. Back on Fizbus, most of the *Times* executives had been dead set against having a woman sent out as Drosmig's assistant. But Grupe, the Grand Editor, had overruled them. "Time we broke with tradition," he had said. He'd felt she could do the job, and, by the stars, she would justify his faith in her!

"Sounds like rather a lark," she said hollowly.

Stet brightened. "That's the girl!" His eyes, she noticed, were emerald shading into turquoise, like his crest. "I certainly hope you'll like it here. Very wise of Grupe to send a woman instead of a man, after all. Women," he went on quickly, "are so much better at working up the human interest angle. And Drosmig is out of commission most of the time, so it's you who'll actually be in charge of 'Helpfully Yours.'"

She herself in charge of the column that had achieved interstellar fame in three short years! Basically, it had been designed to give guidance, advice and, if necessary, comfort to those Fizbians who found themselves living on Terra, for the Fizbus *Times* had stood for public service from time immemorial. As Grupe had put it, "We don't run this paper for ourselves, Tarb, but for our readers. And the same applies to our Terrestrial edition."

With the growing development of trade and cultural relations between the two planets, the Fizbians on Earth were an ever-increasing number. But they were not the only readers of "Helpfully Yours." Reprinted in the parent paper, it was read with edification and pleasure all over Fizbus. Everyone wanted to learn more about the ancient and other-worldly Terran culture.

The handbook, *A Brief Introduction to Terrestrial Manners and Mores*, owed much of its content to "Helpfully Yours." A grateful, almost fulsome, introductory note had said so. But the column truly deserved all the praise that had been lavished upon it by the handbook. How well she had studied the thoughtful letters that filled it and the excellent and well-reasoned advice-- erring, if it erred at all, on the side of overtolerance--that had been given in return. Of course, on Earth, spiritual adjustment apparently was more important than the physical; you could tell that from the questions that were asked. A number of the letters had been reprinted in an appendix to the manual.

New York
Dear Senbot Drosmig:
When in contact with Terrestrial culture, I find myself constantly overawed and weighed down by the knowledge of my own inadequacy. I cannot seem to appreciate the local art forms as disseminated by the juke box, the comic strip, the tabloid.

How can I help myself toward a greater understanding?
Hopefully yours,
Gnurmis Plitt

*   *   *   *   *

Dear Mr. Plitt:
Remember, Orkv was not excavated in a week. It took the Terrestrials many centuries to develop their exquisite and esoteric art forms. How can you expect to comprehend them in a few short years? Expose yourself to their art. Work, study, meditate.

Understanding will come, I promise you.
Helpfully yours,
Senbot Drosmig

*   *   *   *   *

Paris
Dear Senbot Drosmig:

To think that I am enjoying the benefits of Terra while my wife and little ones are forced to remain on Fizbus makes my heart ache. Surely it is not fair that I should have so much and they so little. Imagine the inestimable advantage to the fledgling of even a short contact with Terrestrial culture!

Why cannot my loved ones come to join me so that we can share all these wonderful spiritual experiences and be enriched by them together?

Poignantly yours,
Tpooly N'Ox

*   *   *   *   *

Dear Mr. N'Ox:

After all, it has been only five years since Fizbian spaceships first came into contact with Terra. In keeping with our usual colonial policy--so inappropriate and anachronistic when applied to a well-developed civilization like Terra's--at first only males are allowed to go to the new world until it is made certain over a period of years that the planet is safe for mothers and future mothers of Fizbus.

But Stet Zarnon himself, the celebrated and capable editor of the Terran edition of *The Fizbus Times*, has taken up your cause, and I promise you that eventually your loved ones will be able to join you.

Meanwhile, work, study, meditate.

Helpfully yours,
Senbot Drosmig

*   *   *   *   *

Ottawa
Dear Senbot Drosmig:

Having just completed a two-year tour of duty on Earth as part of a diplomatic mission, I am regretfully leaving this fair planet. What books, what objects of art, what, in short, souvenirs shall I take back to Fizbus which will give our people some small idea of Earth's rich cultural heritage and, at the same time, serve as useful and appropriate gifts for my friends and relatives back Home?

Inquiringly yours,
Solgus Zagroot

* * * * *

Dear Mr. Zagroot:
Take back nothing but your memories. They will be your best souvenirs.

Out of context, any other mementos might convey little, if anything, of the true beauty and advanced spirituality of Terrestrial culture, and you might cheapen them were you to use them crassly as souvenirs. Furthermore, it is possible that you, in your ignorance, might unwittingly select some items that give a distorted and false idea of our extrafizbian friends.

The Fizbian-Earth Cultural Commission, sponsored by *The Fizbian Times*, in conjunction with the consulate, is preparing a vast program of cultural interchange. Leave it to them to do the great work, for you can be sure they will do it well.

And be sure to tell your fellow-laborers in the diplomatic vineyards that it is wiser not to send unapproved Terran souvenirs back Home. They might cause a fatal misunderstanding between the two worlds. Tell them to spend their time on Earth in working, studying and meditating, rather than shopping.
Helpfully yours,
Senbot Drosmig

* * * * *

And now she--Tarb Morfatch--herself was going to be the guiding spirit that brought enlightenment and uplift to countless thousands on Terra and millions on Fizbus. Her name wouldn't appear on the columns, but the reward of having helped should be enough. Besides, Drosmig was due to retire soon. If she proved herself competent, she would take over the column entirely and get the byline. Grupe had promised faithfully.

But what, she wondered, had put Drosmig "out of commission"?

The taxi drew up before a building with a vulgar number of floors showing above ground.

"Ah--before we--er--meet the others," Stet suggested, twitching his crest, "I was wondering whether you would care to--er--have dinner with me tonight?"

This roused Tarb from her speculations. "Oh, I'd love to!" *A date with the boss right away!*

Stet fumbled in his garments for appropriate tokens with which to pay the driver. "You--you're not engaged or anything back Home, Miss Morfatch?"

"Why, no," she said. "It so happens that I'm not."

"Splendid!" He made an abortive gesture with his leg, then let her get out of the taxi by herself. "It makes the natives stare," he explained abashedly.

"But why shouldn't they?" she asked, wondering whether to laugh or not. "How could they help but stare? We are different." *He must be joking.* She ventured a smile.

He smiled back, but made no reply.

The pavement was hard under her thinly covered soles. Now that walking looked as if it would present a problem, the ban on wing use loomed more threateningly. She had, of course, walked before--on wet days when her wings were waterlogged or in high winds or when she had surface business. However, the sidewalks on Fizbus were soft and resilient. Now she understood why the Terrestrials wore such crippling foot armor, but that didn't make her feel any better about it.

A box-shaped machine took the two Fizbians up to the twentieth story in twice the time it would have taken them to fly the same distance. Tarb supposed that the offices were in an attic instead of a basement because exchange difficulties forced the *Times* to such economy. She wondered ruefully whether her own expense account would also suffer.

But it was no time to worry about such sordid matters; most important right now was making a favorable impression on her co-workers. She did want them to like her.

Taking out her compact, she carefully polished her eyeballs. The man at the controls of the machine practically performed a ritual *entrechat*.

"Don't do that!" Stet ordered in a harsh whisper.

"But why not?" she asked, unable to restrain a trace of belligerence from her voice. He hadn't been very polite himself. "The handbook said respectable Terran women make up in public. Why shouldn't I?"

He sighed. "It'll take time for you to catch on, I suppose. There's a lot the handbook doesn't--can't--cover. You'll find the setup here rather different from on Fizbus," he went on as he kicked open the door neatly lettered *THE FIZBUS TIMES* in both Fizbian and Terran. "We've found it expedient to follow the local newspaper practice. For instance--" he indicated a small green-feathered man seated at a desk just beyond the railing that bisected the room horizontally--"we have a Copy Editor."

"What does he do?" she asked, confused.

"He copies news from the other papers, of course."

"And what are *you* doing tonight, Miss Morfatch?" the Copy Editor asked, springing up from his desk to execute the three ritual entrechats with somewhat more verve than was absolutely necessary.

"Having dinner with me," Stet said quickly.

"Pulling rank, eh, old bird? Well, we'll see whether position or sterling worth will win out in the end."

As the rest of the staff crowded around Tarb, leaping and booing as appreciatively as any girl could want, she managed to snatch a rapid look around. The place wasn't really so very much different from a Fizbian newsroom, once she got over the oddity of going across, not up and down, with the desks--queerly shaped but undeniably desks--arranged side by side instead of one over the other. There were chairs and stools, no perches, but that was to be expected in a wingless society. And it was noisy. Even though the little machines had stopped clattering when she came in, a distant roaring continued, as if, concealed somewhere close by, larger, more sinister machines continued their work. A peculiar smell hung in the air--not unpleasant, exactly, but strange.

She sniffed inquiringly.

"Ink," Stet said.

"What's that?"

"Oh, some stuff the boys in the back shop use. The feature writers," he went on quickly, before she could ask what the "back shop" was, "have private offices where they can perch in comfort."

He led the way down a corridor, opening doors. "Our drama editor." He indicated a middle-aged man with faded blue feathers, who hung head downward from his perch. "On the lobster-trick last night writing a review, so he's catching fifty-one twinkles now."

"Enchanted, Miss Morfatch," the critic said, opening one bright eye. "By a curious chance, it so happens that tonight I have two tickets to--"

"Tonight she's going out with me."

"Well, I can get tickets to any play, any night. And you haven't laughed unless you've seen a Terrestrial drama. Just say the word, chick."

Stet got Tarb out of the office and slammed the door shut. "Over here is the office of our food editor," he said, breathing hard, "whom you'll be expected to give a claw to now and then, since your jobs overlap. Can't introduce you to him right now, though, because he's in the hospital with ptomaine poisoning. And this is the office you'll share with Drosmig."

Stet opened the door.

Underneath the perch, Senbot Drosmig, dean of Fizbian journalists, lay on the rug in a sodden stupor, letters to the editor scattered thickly over his shriveled person. The whole room reeked unmistakably of caffeine.

Tarb shrank back and twined both feet around Stet's. This time he did not repulse her. "But how can a--an educated, cultured man like Senbot Drosmig sink to such depths?"

"It's hard for anyone with even the slightest inclination toward the stuff to resist it here," Stet replied somberly. "I can't deny it; the sale of caffeine is absolutely unrestricted on Earth. Coffee shops all over the place. Coffee served freely at even the best homes. And not only coffee ... caffeine is insiduously present in other of their popular beverages."

Her eyes bulged sideways. "But how can a so-called civilized people be so depraved?"

"Caffeine doesn't seem to affect them the way it does us. Their nervous systems are so very uncomplicated, one almost envies them."

Drosmig stirred restlessly under his blanket of correspondence. "Go back ... Fizbus," he muttered. "Warn you ... 'fore ... too late ... like me."

Tarb's rose-pink feathers stood on end. She looked apprehensively at Stet.

"Senbot can't go back because he's in no shape to take the interstel drive." The young editor was obviously annoyed. "He's old and he's a physical wreck. But that certainly doesn't apply to you, Miss Morfatch." He looked long and hard into her eyes.

"Few years on planet," Drosmig groaned, struggling to his wings, "'ply to anybody."

His feathers, Tarb noticed, were an ugly, darkish brown. She had never seen any one that color before, but she'd heard rumors that too much caffeine could do that to you. At least she hoped it was only the caffeine.

"For your information, he was almost as bad as this when he came!" Stet snapped. "Frankly, that's why he was sent here--to get rid of his unfortunate addiction. Grupe had no idea, when he assigned him to Earth, that there was caffeine on the planet."

The old man gave a sardonic laugh as he clumsily made his way to the perch and gripped it with quivering toes.

"That is, I don't *think* he knew," Stet said dubiously.

Tarb reached over and picked a letter off the floor. The Fizbian characters were clumsy and ill-made, as if someone had formed them with his feet. Could there be such poverty here that individuals existed who could not afford a scripto? The letter didn't read like any that had ever been printed in the column--at least none that had been picked up in the Fizbus edition:

* * * * *

New York
Dear Senbot Drosmig:
I am a subaltern clerk in the shipping department of the FizbEarth Trading Company, Inc. Although I have held this post for only three months, I have already won the respect and esteem of my superiors through my diligence and good character. My habits are exemplary: I do not gamble, sing, or take caffeine.

Earlier today, while engaged in evening meditation at my modest apartments, I was aroused by a peremptory knock at the door. I flung it open. A native stood there with a small case in his hand.

"Is the house on fire?" I asked, wondering which of my few humble possessions I should rescue first.

"No," he said. "I would like to interest you in some brushes."

"Are the offices of the FizbEarth Trading Company, Inc., on fire?"

"Not to my knowledge," he replied, opening his case. "Now I have here a very nice hairbrush--"

I wanted to give him every chance. "Have you come to tell me of any disaster relative to the FizbEarth Trading Company, to myself, or to anyone or anything else with whom or with which I am connected?"

"Why, no," he said. "I have come to sell you brushes. Now here is a little number I know you'll like. My company developed it with you folks specially in mind. It's--"

"Do you know, sir, that you have wantonly interrupted me in the midst of my meditations, which constitutes an established act of privacy violation?"

"Is that a fact? Now this little item is particularly designed for brushing the wings--"

At that point, I knocked him down and punched him into insensibility with my feet. Then I summoned the police. To my surprise, they arrested me instead of him.

I am writing this letter from jail. I do not like to ask my employers to get me out because, even though I am innocent, you know how a thing like this can leave a smudge on the record.

What shall I do?

Anxiously yours,

Fruzmus Bloxx

*   *   *   *   *

"What should he do?" Tarb asked, handing Stet the paper. "Or is the question academic by now? The letter's five days old."

Stet sighed. "I'll find out whether the consulate has been notified. Native police usually do that, you know. Very thoughtful fellows. If this Bloxx hasn't been bailed out already, I'll see that he is."

"But how will we answer his letter? Advise him to sue for false arrest?"

Stet smiled. "But he has no grounds for false arrest. He is guilty of assault. The native was entirely within his rights in trying to sell him a brush. Now--" he put out a foot--"brace yourself. Privacy violation is not a crime on Terra. It is perfectly legal. In fact, it does not exist as such!"

At that point, everything went maroon.

When Tarb came to, she found herself lying upon Drosmig's desk. A skin-faced native woman was offering her water and clucking.

"Are you all right, Tarb--Miss Morfatch?" Stet demanded anxiously.

"Yes. I--I think so," she murmured, raising herself to a crouch.

"Better ... have died," Drosmig groaned from his perch. "Fate worse ... death ... awaits you."

Tarb tried to smile. "Sorry to have been so much trouble." She stuck out her tongue at both Stet and the native.

The woman drew in her breath.

"Miss Morfatch," Stet reminded Tarb, "sticking out the tongue is not an apology on Terra; it is an insult. Fortunately, Miss Snow happens to be perhaps the only Terran who would not be offended. She has become thoroughly acquainted with us and our odd little customs. She even--" he beamed at the Terran female--"has learned to speak our language."

"Hail to thee, O visitor from the stars," Miss Snow said in Fizbian. "May thy sojourn upon Earth be an incessant delight and may peace and plenty shower their gifts in abundance upon thee."

Tarb put her hand to her aching head. "I'm very glad to meet you," she said, glad she did not have to get up to make the ritual *entrechats*.

"Miss Snow is my right foot," Stet said, "but I'm going to be noble and let her act as your secretary until you can learn to operate a typewriter."

"Secretary? Typewriter?"

"Well, you see, there are no scriptos or superscriptos on Earth and we can't import any from Home because the natives--" Miss Snow smiled--"don't have the right kind of power here to run psychic installations. All prosifying has to be done directly on prosifying machines or--" he paused--"by foot."

"Catch her!" Miss Snow exclaimed in Terran.

Everything had gone maroon for Tarb again. As she fell, she could hear a sudden thump. It was, she later discovered, Drosmig falling off his perch again--the result of insecure grip, she was given to understand, rather than excessive empathy.

*   *   *   *   *

"I didn't mean, of course, to give you the impression that we actually produce the individual copies of the papers ourselves," Stet explained over the dinner table that night. "We have native printers who do that. They've turned out some really remarkable Fizbian type fonts." "Very clever of them," Tarb said, knowing that was what she was expected to say. She glanced around the restaurant. In their low-cut evening garments, the Terrestrial females looked much less Fizboid than they had during the day. All that naked-looking skin; one would think they'd want to cover it. Probably they were sick with jealousy of her beautiful rose-colored down--what they could see of it, anyway.

"Of course, our real problem is getting proofreaders. The proofing machines won't operate here either, of course, and so we need human personnel. But what Fizbian would do such degrading work? We had thought of convict labor, but--"

"Why mustn't I take off my wrap?" Tarb interrupted. "No one else is wearing one."

Stet coughed. "You'll feel much less self-conscious about your wings if you keep it on. And try not to use your feet so conspicuously. I'm sure everyone understands you need them to eat with, but--"

"But I'm not in the least self-conscious about my wings. On Fizbus, they were considered rather nice-looking, if I do say so myself."

"It's better," he said firmly, "not to emphasize the differences between the natives and ourselves. You didn't object to wearing a Terrestrial costume, did you?"

"No, I realize I must make some concessions to native prudery, but--"

"Matter of fact, I've been thinking it would be a good idea for you to wear a stole or a cape or something in the daytime when you go to and from the office. You wouldn't want to make yourself or the *Times* conspicuous, I'm sure.... No, waiter, no coffee. We'll take champagne."

"I want to try coffee," Tarb said mutinously. "Champagne! You'd think I was a fledgling, giving me that bubbly stuff!"

He looked at her. "Now don't be silly, Miss Morfatch ... Tarb. I can't let you indulge in such rash experiments. You realize I am responsible for you."

Tarb muttered darkly into her *coupe maison.*

Stet raised his eyebrows. "What did you say?"

"I was only wondering whether you'd remembered to check on whether that young man--Bloxx--ever did get out of jail."

Stet snapped his toes. "Glad you reminded me. Completely slipped my mind. Let's go and see what happened to him, shall we?"

*　　*　　*　　*　　*

As they rose to leave, a dumpy Earthwoman rushed up to them, enthusiastically babbling in Terran. Seizing Tarb's foot, she clung to it before the Fizbian girl could do anything to prevent her. Tarb had to spread her wings wide to retain her balance. Her cloak flew off and an adjoining table of diners disappeared beneath it.

Stet and the headwaiter rushed to the rescue with profuse apologies, Stet's crest undulating as if it concealed a nest of snakes. But Tarb was too much frightened to be calmed.

"Is this a hostile attack?" she shrieked frantically at Stet. "Because the handbook never said shaking feet was an Earth custom!"

"No, no, she's a friend!" Stet yelled, leaving the diners still struggling with the cloak as he sped back to her. "And shaking feet isn't an Earth custom; she thinks it's a Fizbian one. You see.... Oh, hell, never' mind--I'll explain the whole thing to you later. But she's just greeting you, trying to put you at your ease. It's Belinda Romney, a very important Terrestrial. She owns the Solar Press--you must have heard of it even on Fizbus--biggest news service on the planet. Absolutely wouldn't do to offend her. Mrs. Romney, may I present Miss Morfatch?"

The woman beamed and continued to gush endlessly.

"Tell her to let go my foot!" Tarb demanded. "It's getting so it feels carbonated."

He smiled deprecatingly. "Now, Tarb, we mustn't be rude--"

For the first time in her life, Tarb spoke Terran to a Terrestrial. She formed the words slowly and carefully: "Sorry we must leave, but we have to go to jail."

She looked to Stet for approval ... and didn't get it. He started to explain something quickly to the woman. Every time she'd heard him speak Terran, Tarb thought, he seemed to be introducing, explaining or apologizing.

It turned out that, through some oversight, the usually thoughtful Terran police department had neglected to inform the Fizbian consul that one of his people had been incarcerated, for the young man had already been tried, found guilty of assault plus contempt of court, and sentenced to pay a large fine. However, after Stet had given his version of the circumstances to a sympathetic judge, the sum was reduced to a nominal one, which the *Times* paid.

"But I don't see why you should have paid anything at all," Bloxx protested ungratefully. "I didn't do anything wrong. You should have made an issue of it."

"According to Earth laws, you did do wrong," Stet said wearily, "and this is Earth. What's more, if we take the matter up, it will naturally get into print. You don't want your employers to hear about it, do you--even if you don't care about making Fizbians look ridiculous to Terrestrials?"

"I suppose I wouldn't like FizbEarth to find out," Bloxx conceded. "As it is, I'll have to do some fast explaining to account for my not having shown up for nearly a week. I'll say I caught some horrible Earth disease--that'll scare them so much, they'll probably beg me to take another week off. Though I do wish you fellows over at the *Times* would answer your mail sooner. I'm a regular subscriber, you know."

*   *   *   *   *

"But the same kind of thing's going to happen over and over again, isn't it, Stet?" Tarb asked as a taxi took them back to the hotel in which most of the *Times* staff was domiciled. "If privacy doesn't exist on Earth, it's bound to keep occurring."

"Eh?" Stet took his attention away from her toes with some difficulty. "Some Earth people like privacy, too, but they have to fight for it. Violations aren't legally punishable--that's the only difference."

"Then surely the Terrestrials would understand about us, wouldn't they?" she asked eagerly. "If they knew how strongly we felt about privacy, maybe they wouldn't violate it--not as much, anyway. I'm sure they're not vicious, just ignorant. And you can't just keep on getting Fizbians out of jail each time they run up against the problem. It would be too expensive, for one thing."

"Don't worry," he said, pressing her toes. "I'll take care of the whole thing."

"An article in the paper wouldn't really help much," she persisted thoughtfully, "and I suppose you must have run at least one already. It would explain to the Fizbians that Terrestrials don't regard invasion of privacy as a crime, but it wouldn't tell the Terrestrials that Fizbians do. We'll have to think of--"

"You're surely not going to tell me how to run my paper on your first day here, are you?"

He tried to take the sting out of his words by twining his toes around hers, but she felt guilty. She had been presumptuous.

Probably there were lots of things she couldn't understand yet--
like why she shouldn't polish her eyeballs in public. Stet had
finally explained to her that, while Terrestrial women did make
up in public, they didn't scour their irises, ever, and would be
startled and horrified to see someone else doing so.

"But I was horrified to see them raking their feathers in
public!" Tarb had contended.

"Combing their hair, my dear. And why not? This is their
planet."

That was always his answer. *I wonder*, she speculated,
*whether he would expect a Terrestrial visitor to Fizbus to fly ...
because, after all, Fizbus is our planet.* But she didn't dare
broach the question.

However, if it was presumptuous of her to make helpful
suggestions the first day, it was more than presumptuous of Stet
to ask her up to his rooms to see his collection of rare early
twentieth-century Terrestrial milk bottles and other antiques.
So she just told him courteously that she was tired and wanted
to go to roost. And, since the hotel had a whole section fitted up
to suit Fizbian requirements, she spent a more comfortable night
than she had expected.

She awoke the next day full of enthusiasm and ready to start
in on the great work at once. Although she might have been a
little too forward the previous night, she knew, as she took a
reassuring glance in the mirror, that Stet would forgive her.

*   *   *   *   *

In the office, she was, at first, somewhat self-conscious about
Drosmig, who hung insecurely from his perch muttering to
himself, but she soon forgot him in her preoccupation with duty.
The first letter she picked up--although again oddly unlike the
ones she'd read in the paper on Fizbus--seemed so simple that
she felt she would have no difficulty in answering it all by
herself:

> *Heidelberg*
> *Dear Senbot Drosmig:*
> *I am a professor of Fizbian History at a local university.
> Since my salary is a small one, owing to the small esteem in
> which the natives hold culture, I must economize wherever I can*

in order to make both ends meet. Accordingly, I do my own cooking and shop at the self-service supermarket around the corner, where I have found that prices are lower than in the service groceries and the food no worse.

However, the manager and a number of the customers have objected to my shopping with my feet. They don't so much mind my taking packages off the shelves with them, but they have been quite vociferous on the subject of my pinching the fruit with my toes. Unripe fruit, however, makes me ill. What shall I do?

Sincerely yours,

Grez B'Groot

Tarb dictated an unhesitating reply:

Dear Professor B'Groot:

Why don't you explain to the manager of the store that Fizbians have wings and feet rather than arms and hands?

I'm sure his attitude and the attitudes of his customers will change when they learn that your pinching the fruit with your feet is not mere pedagogical eccentricity, but the regular practice on our planet. Point out to him that your feet are covered and, therefore, more sanitary than the bare hands of his other customers.

And always put on clean socks before you go shopping.

Helpfully yours,

Senbot Drosmig

Miss Snow raised pale eyebrows.

"Is something wrong?" Tarb asked anxiously. "Should I have put in that bit about work, study, meditate? It seems inappropriate somehow."

"Oh, no, not that. It's just that your letter--well, violates Mr. Zarnon's precept that, in Rome, one must do as the Romans do."

"But this isn't Rome," Tarb replied, bewildered. "It's New York."

"He didn't make the saying up," Miss Snow replied testily. "It's a Terrestrial proverb."

"Oh," Tarb said.

She resented this creature's trying to tell her how to do her job. On the other hand, Tarb was wise enough to realize that Miss Snow, unpleasant though she might be, probably did know Stet well enough to be able to predict his reactions.

So Tarb not only was reluctant to show Stet what she had already done, but hesitated about answering another and even more urgent letter that had just been brought in by special messenger. She tried to compromise by submitting the letters to Drosmig--for, technically speaking, it was he who was her immediate superior--but he merely groaned, "Tell 'em all to drop dead," from his perch and refused to open his eyes.

In the end, Tarb had to take the letters to Stet's office. Miss Snow trailed along behind her, uninvited. And, since this was a place of business, Tarb could not claim a privacy violation. Even if it weren't a place of business, she remembered, she couldn't-- not here on Earth. Advanced spirituality, hah!

Advanced pain in the pinions!

Stet read the first letter and her answer smilingly. "Excellent, Tarb--" her hearts leaped--"for a first try, but I'd like to suggest a few changes, if I may."

"Well, of course," she said, pretending not to notice the smirk on Miss Snow's face.

"Just write this Professor B'Goot that he should do his shopping at a grocery that offers service and practice his economies elsewhere. A professor, of all people, is expected to uphold the dignity of his own race--the idea, sneering at a culture that was thousands of years old when we were still building nests! Terrestrials couldn't possibly have any respect for him if they saw him prodding kumquats with his toes."

"It's no sillier than writing with one's vestigial wings!" Tarb blazed.

"Well!" Miss Snow exclaimed in Terran. "Well, *really*!"

Tarb started to stick out her tongue, then remembered. "I didn't mean to offend you, Miss Snow. I know it's your custom. But wouldn't you understand if I typewrote with my feet?"

Miss Snow tittered.

"If you want the honest truth, hon, it would make you look like a feathered monkey."

"If you want the honest truth about what you look like to me, dearie--it's a plucked chicken!"

"Tarb, I think you should apologize to Miss Snow!"

"All right!" Tarb stuck out her tongue. Miss Snow promptly thrust out hers in return.

"Ladies, ladies!" Stet cried. "I think there has been a slight confusion of folkways!" He quickly changed the subject. "Is that another letter you have there, Tarb?"

"Yes, but I didn't try to answer it. I thought you'd better have a look at it first, since Miss Snow didn't seem to think much of the job I did with the other one."

"Miss Snow always has the *Times'* welfare at heart," Stet remarked ambiguously, and read:

Chicago

Dear Senbot Drosmig:

I am employed as translator by the extraterrestrial division of Burns and Deerhart, Inc., the well-known interstellar mail-order house. As the company employs no other Fizbians and our offices are situated in a small rural community where no others of our race reside, I find myself rather lonely. Moreover, being a bachelor, with neither chick nor child on Fizbus, I have nothing to look forward to upon my return to the Home Planet some day.

Accordingly, I decided to adopt a child to cheer my declining years. I dispatched an interstellargram to a reliable orphanage on Fizbus, outlining my hopes and requirements in some detail. After they had satisfied themselves as to my income, strength of character, etc., they sent me a fatherless and motherless egg in cold storage, which I was supposed to hatch upon arrival.

However, when the egg came to Earth, it was impounded by Customs. They say it is forbidden to import extrasolar eggs. I have tried to explain to them that it is not at all a question of importation but of adoption; however, they cannot or will not understand.

Please tell me what to do. I fear that they may not be keeping the egg at the correct Fizbian freezing point--which, as you know, is a good deal lower than Earth's. The fledgling may hatch by itself and receive a traumatic shock that might very well damage its entire psyche permanently.

Frantically yours,

Glibmus Gluyt

"Oh, for the stars' sake!" Stet exploded. "This is really too much! Viz our consul, Miss Snow. That egg must go back to Fizbus at once, before any Terrestrials hear of it! And I must notify the government back on the Home Planet to keep a close check on all egg shipments. Something like this must certainly not occur again."

"Why shouldn't the Terrestrials hear of it?" Tarb asked, outraged. "And I think it's mean of you to send back a poor little orphan egg like that when it has a chance of getting a good home."

"An egg!" Miss Snow repeated incredulously. "You mean you really...?" She gave me one mad little hoot of laughter and then stopped and strangled slightly. Her face turned purple in her efforts to restrain mirth. *Really*, Tarb thought, *she looks so much better that color.*

Stet's crest twitched violently. "I hope--" he began. "I do hope you will keep this ... knowledge to yourself, Miss Snow."

"But of course," she assured him, calming down. "I'm dreadfully sorry I was so rude. Naturally I wouldn't dream of telling a soul, Mr. Zarnon. You can trust me."

"I'm sure I can, Miss Snow."

Tarb almost choked with indignation. "You mean you've been keeping the facts of our life from Terrestrials? As if they were fledglings ... no, even fledglings are told these days."

"One could hardly blame him for it, Miss Morfatch," Miss Snow said. "You wouldn't want people to know that Fizbians laid eggs, would you?"

"And why not?"

"Tarb," Stet intervened, "you don't know what you're talking about."

"Oh, don't I? You're ashamed of the fact that we bear our children in a clean, decent, honorable way instead of--" She stopped. "I'm being as bad as you two are. Probably the Terrestrials' way of reproduction doesn't seem dirty to them-- but, since they do reproduce *that* way, they could scarcely find our way objectionable!"

"Tarb, that's not how a young girl should talk!"

"Oh, go lay an egg!" she said, knowing that she had overstepped the limits of propriety, but unable to let him get away with that. "I hope to be a wife and mother some day," she added, "and I only hope that when that time comes, I'll be able to lay good eggs."

"Miss Morfatch," Stet said, keeping control of his temper with a visible effort, "that will be enough from you. If common decency doesn't restrain you, please remember that I am your employer and that *I* set the policies on *my* paper. You'll do what you're told and keep a civil tongue in your head or you'll be sent back to Fizbus. Do I make myself clear?"

"You do, indeed," Tarb said. How could she ever have thought he was charming and handsome? Well, perhaps he still was handsome, but fine feathers do not make fine deeds. And, if it came to that, it wasn't his paper.

"We have the same thing on Terra," Miss Snow murmured sympathetically to Stet. "These young whippersnappers think they can start in running the paper the very first day. Why, Belinda Romney herself--she's a distant cousin of mine, you know--told me--"

"Miss Snow," Tarb said, "I hope for the sake of Earth that you are not a typical example of the Terrestrial species."

"And you, hon," Miss Snow retorted, "don't belong on a paper, but in a chicken coop."

"Ladies!" Stet said helplessly. "Women," he muttered, "certainly do not belong on a newspaper. Matter of fact, they don't belong anywhere; their place is in the home only because there's nowhere else to put them."

Both females glared at him.

*   *   *   *   *

During the next fortnight, Tarb gained fluency in Terran and also learned to operate a Terrestrial typewriter equipped with Fizbian type--mostly so that she could dispense with the services of the invaluable Miss Snow. She didn't like typing, though--it chipped her toenails and her temper. Besides, Drosmig kept complaining that the noise prevented him from sleeping and she preferred him to sleep rather than hang there making irrelevant and, sometimes, unpleasantly relevant remarks.

"Longing for the old scripto, eh?" one of the cameramen smiled as he lounged in the open doorway of her office. Although she was fond of fresh air, Tarb realized that she would have to keep the door shut from now on. Too many of the younger members of the staff kept booing at her as they passed, and now they had formed the habit of dropping in to offer her advice, encouragement and invitations to meals. At first, the attention had pleased her--but now she was much too busy to be bothered; she was going to turn out acceptable answers to those letters or die trying.

"Well, if the power can't be converted, it can't," she said grimly. "Griblo, I do wish you'd be a dear and flutter off. I--"

He snorted. "Who says the power can't be converted? Stet, huh?"

She took her feet off the keys and looked at him. "Why do you say 'Stet' that way?"

"Because that's a lot of birdseed he gives you about not being able to convert Earth power. Could be done all right, but he and the consul have it all fixed up to keep Fizbian technology off the planet. Consul's probably being paid off by the International Association of Manufacturers and Stet's in it for the preservation of indigenous culture--and maybe a little cash, too. After all, those rare antique collections of his cost money."

"I don't believe it!" Tarb snapped. "Griblo, please--I have so much work to get through!"

"Okay, chick, but I warn you, you're going to have your bright-eyed illusions shattered. Why don't you wake up to the truth about Stet? What you should do is maybe eschew the society of all journalists entirely, and a sordid lot they are, and devote yourself to photographers--splendid fellows, all."

"Please shut the door behind you!"

The door slammed.

Tarb gazed disconsolately at the letter before her. Would she ever be able to answer letters to Stet's satisfaction? The purpose of the whole column was service--but did she and Stet mean the same thing by the same word? Or, if they did, whom was Stet serving?

She was paying too much attention to Griblo's idle remarks. Obviously he was a sorehead--had some kind of grudge against Stet. Perhaps Stet was a bit too autocratic, perhaps he had even gone native to some extent, but you couldn't say anything worse about him than that. All in all, he wasn't a bad bird and she mustn't let herself be influenced by rumormongers like Griblo.

*   *   *   *   *

Tarb got up and took the letter to Stet. He was in his office dictating to Miss Snow. *After all,* Tarb could not repress the ugly thought, *why should he care about the scriptos? He'll never have to use a typewriter.*

And he was perfectly nice about being interrupted. The only thing he didn't like was being contradicted. *I'm getting bitter,* she told herself in surprise. *And at my age, too. I wonder what I'll be like when I'm old.*

This thought alarmed her and so she smiled very sweetly at Stet as she murmured, "Would you mind reading this?" and gave him the letter.

"Run into another little snag, eh?" he said affably, giving her foot a gentle pat with his. "Well, let's see what we can do about it."

Montreal

Dear Senbot Drosmig:

I am a chef at the Cafe Inter-stellaire, which, as everyone knows, is one of the most chic eating establishments on this not very chic planet. During my spare moments, I am a great amateur of the local form of entertainment known as television. I am especially fascinated by the native actress Ingeborg Swedenborg, who, in spite of being a Terran, compares most favorably with our own Fizbian footlight favorites.

The other day, while I am in the kitchen engaged in preparing the ragout celeste a la fizbe for which I am justly celebrated on nine planets, I hear a stir outside in the dining room. I strain my ears. I hear the cry, "It is Ingeborg Swedenborg!"

I cannot help myself. I rush to the doorway. There, behold, the incomparable Ingeborg herself! She follows the headwaiter to a choice table. She is even more ravishing in real life than on the screen. On her, it does not matter that she has no feathers save on the head--even skin looks good. Overcome by involuntary ardor, I boo at her. Whereupon I am violently assailed by a powerfully built native whom I have not previously noticed to be escorting her.

I am rescued before he can do me any permanent damage, though, if you wish the truth, it will be a long time before I can fly again. However, I am given notice by the cold-hearted management. Now I am without a job. And what is more, if on this planet one is not permitted to express one's instinctive and natural admiration for a beautiful woman, then all I have to say is that it is a lousy planet and I wiggle my toes at it. How do I go about getting deported?

  Impatiently yours,
  Rajois Sludd

"Oh, I suppose it serves him right," Tarb said quickly, before Stet could comment, "but don't you think it would be a good idea if the *Times* got up a Fizbian-Terrestrial handbook of its own? It's the only solution that I can see. The regular one, I recognize now, is more than inadequate, with all that spiritual gup--" Miss Snow drew in her breath sharply--"and not much else. All these problems are bound to arise again and again. Frankly speaking, Stet, your solutions only take care of the individual cases; they don't establish a sound intercultural basis."

He grunted.

"What's more," she went on eagerly, "we could not only give copies to every Fizbian planning to visit Earth, but also print copies in Terran for Terrestrials who are interested in learning more about Fizbus and the Fizbians. In fact, all Terrans who come in contact with us should have the book. It would help both races to understand each other so much better and--"

"Unnecessary!" Stet snapped, so violently that she stopped with her mouth open. "The standard handbook is more than adequate. Whatever limitations it may have are deliberate. Setting down in cold print all that ... stuff you want to have included would make a point of things we prefer not to stress. I wouldn't want to have the Terrestrials humor me as if I were a fledgling or a foreigner."

He leaped out of his chair and paced up and down the office. One would think he had forgotten he ever could fly.

"But you are a foreigner, Stet," Tarb said gently. "No matter what you do or say, Terrestrials and Fizbians are--well, worlds apart."

"Spiritually, I am much closer to the Terrestrials than--but you wouldn't understand." He and Miss Snow nodded sympathetically at each other. "And you might be interested to know that I happen to be the author of all that 'spiritual gup.' I wrote the handbook--as a service to Fizbus, I might point out. I wasn't paid for it."

"Oh, dear!" Tarb said. "Oh, *dear*! I really and truly am sorry, Stet."

He brushed her apologies aside. "Answer that letter. Ignore the question about deportation entirely." He ran a foot through his crest. "Just tell the fellow to see our personnel manager. We could use a chef in the company dining room. Haven't tasted a decent celestial ragout--at a price I could afford--since I left Fizbus."

"Would you want me to print that reply in the column?" she asked. "'If you lose your job because you're unfamiliar with Terrestrial customs, come to the *Times*. We'll give you another job at a much lower salary.'"

"Of course not! Send your answer directly to him. You don't think we put any of those letters you've been answering in the column, do you? Or any that come in at all, for that matter. I have to write all the letters that are printed--and answer them myself."

"I should have recognized the style," Tarb said. "So this is the service the *Times* offers to its subscribers. Nothing that would be of help. Nothing that could prevent other Fizbians from making the same mistake. Nothing that could be controversial. Nothing that would help Terrestrials to understand us. Nothing, in short, but a lot of birdseed!"

"Impertinence!" Miss Snow remarked. "You shouldn't let her talk to you like that, Mr. Zarnon."

"Tarb!" Stet roared, casting an impatient glance at Miss Snow. "How dare you talk to me in that way? And all this is none of your business, anyway."

"I'm a Fizbian," she stated, "and it certainly is my business. I'm not ashamed of having wings. I'm proud of them and sorry for people who don't have them. And, by the stars, I'm going to fly. If skirts are improper to wear for flying, then I can wear slacks. I saw them in a Terrestrial fashion magazine and they're perfectly respectable."

"Not for working hours," Miss Snow sniffed.

"I have no intention of flying during working hours," Tarb snapped back. "Even you should be able to see that the ceiling's much too low."

Stet ran a foot through his crest again. "I hate to say this, Tarb, but I don't feel you're the right person for this job. You mean well, I'm sure, but you're too--too inflexible."

"You mean I have principles," she retorted, "and you don't." Which wasn't entirely true; he had principles--it was just that they were unprincipled.

"That will be enough, Tarb," he said sternly. "You'd better go now while I think this over. I'd hate to send you back to Fizbus, because I'd--well, I'd miss you. On the other hand...."

Tarb went back to her office and drafted a long interstel to a cousin on Fizbus, explaining what she would like for a birthday present. "And send it special delivery," she concluded, "because I am having an urgent and early birthday."

*   *   *   *   *

"Tarb Morfatch!" Stet howled, a few months later. "What on Earth are you doing?"

"Dictating into my scripto," Tarb said cheerfully. "Some of the boys from the print shop helped fix it up for me. They were very nice about it, too, considering that the superscriptos will probably throw them out of work. You know, Stet, Terrestrials can be quite decent people."

"Where did you get that scripto?"

"Cousin Mylfis sent it to me for my birthday. I must have complained about wearing out my claws on a typewriter and he didn't understand that scriptos won't work on Earth. Only they do." She beamed at her employer. "All it needed was a transformer. I guess you're just not mechanically minded, Stet."

He clenched his feet. "Tarb, Terrestrials aren't ready for our technology. You've done a very unwise thing in having that scripto sent to you. And I've done a very unwise thing in keeping you here against my better judgment."

"Maybe the Terrestrials aren't ready," she said, ignoring his last remark, "but I'm not going to wear my feet to the bone if I can get a gadget that'll do the same thing with no expenditure of physical energy." She placed a foot on his. "I don't see how a thing like this could possibly corrupt the Terrestrials, Stet. It's made a better, brighter girl out of me already."

"Hear, hear!" said Drosmig hoarsely from his perch.

"Shut up, Senbot. You just don't understand, Tarb. If you'll only--"

"But I'm afraid I do understand, Stet. And I won't send my scripto back."

"May I come in?" Miss Snow tapped lightly on the door frame. "Is what I hear true?"

"About the scripto?" Tarb asked. "It certainly is. All you have to do is talk into it and the words appear on the paper. Guess that makes you obsolete, doesn't it, Miss Snow?"

"And high time, too," commented Drosmig. "Never liked the old biddy."

"Senbot...." Stet began, and stopped. "Oh, what's the use trying to talk reasonably to either of you! Tarb, come back to my office with me."

She could not refuse and so she followed. Miss Snow, torn between curiosity and the scripto, hesitated and then made after them.

"I've decided to take you off the column--for this morning, anyway--and send you on an outside assignment," Stet told Tarb. "The consul's wife is coming to Earth today. Once she heard there was another woman on Terra, nothing could stop her. Consul seems to think it's my fault, too," he added moodily. "Won't believe I had nothing to do with hiring you. I told the Home Office not to send a woman, that she'd disrupt the office, and you sure as hell have."

"But I thought you said in your letters that you were doing everything in your power to bring Fizbian womenfolk to their men on Terra!" Tarb pointed out malevolently.

"Yes," he confessed. "We must please our readers. You know that. Anyway, all that's irrelevant right now. What I want you to do is go meet the consul's wife. Nice touch, having the only other Fizbian woman here be the one to interview her. Human interest angle for the Terrestrial papers. Shouldn't be surprised if Solar Press picked it up--they like items of that kind for fillers. Take Griblo along with you and make sure he has film in his camera this time."

"Yes, sir," Tarb said. "Anything you say, sir."

He pretended not to notice her sarcasm. "I have a list of the questions you should ask her." He fixed her with his eye. "You stick to them, do you hear me? I don't want anything controversial." He rummaged among the papers on his desk. "I know I had it half an hour ago. Sit down, will you, Tarb? Stop hopping around."

"If I can't have a perch, I want a stool," Tarb said. "This is a private office and I think it's a gross affectation for you to have those silly, uncomfortable chairs in it."

"If you would have your wings clipped like Mr. Zarnon's--" Miss Snow began before Stet could stop her.

"Stet, you *didn't*!"

His crest thrashed back and forth. "They'll grow back again and it's so much more convenient this way. After all, I can't use them here and I do have to associate with Terrestrials and use their equipment. The consul has had his wings clipped also and so have several of our more prominent industrialists--"

"Oh, *Stet*!" Tarb wailed. "I was beginning to think some pretty hard things about you, but I wouldn't ever have dreamed you'd do anything as awful as that!"

"Why should I have to apologize to you?" he raged. "Who do you think you are, anyway? You're an incompetent little fool. I should have fired you that first day. I've let you get away with so much only because you have a pretty face. You've only been on Earth a couple of months; how can you presume to think you know what's good and what's bad for the Fizbians here?"

"I may not know what's good," she retorted, "but I certainly do know what's bad. And that's you, Stet--you and everything you stand for. You not only don't have the courage of your convictions, you don't even have any convictions. You're ashamed of being a Fizbian, ashamed of anything that makes Fizbians different from Terrestrials, even if it's something better, something that most Terrans would like to have. You're a damned hypocrite, Stet Zarnon, that's what you are--professing to help our people when actually you're hurting them by trying to force them into the mold of an alien species."

She brushed back her crest. "I take it I'm fired," she said more quietly. "Do you want me to interview the consul's wife first or leave right away?"

It took Stet a moment to bring his voice under control. "Interview her first. We'll talk this over when you get back."

*   *   *   *   *

It was pleasant to be away from the office, she thought as the taxi pulled toward the airfield, and doing wingwork again, even if it proved to be the first and last time on this planet. Griblo sat hunched in a corner of the seat, too preoccupied with the camera, which, even after two years, he hadn't fully mastered, to pay attention to her.

Outside, it was raining, the kind of thin drizzle that, on Fizbus or Earth, could go on for days. Tarb had brought along the native umbrella she had purchased in the hotel gift shop--a delightful contraption that was supposed to keep off the rain and didn't, and was supposed to collapse and did, but at the wrong moments. She planned to take it back with her when she returned to Fizbus. Approved souvenir or not, it was the same beautiful purple as her eyes. And, besides, who had made the ruling about approved souvenirs? Stet, of course.

"No reason why we couldn't have autofax brought from Home," Griblo suddenly grumbled.

Tarb pulled herself back from her thoughts. "I suppose Stet wouldn't let you," she said. "But now that one scripto's here," she went on somewhat complacently, "he'll have to--"

"Keep this planet charming and unspoiled, he says," Griblo interrupted ungratefully. "Its spiritual values will be corrupted by too much contact with a crass advanced technology. And, of course, he's got the local camera manufacturers solidly behind him. I wonder whether they advertise in the *Times* because he helps keep autofax off Terra or whether he keeps the autofax off Terra because they advertise in the *Times*."

"But what does he care about advertising? He may talk as if he owned the *Times*, but he doesn't."

Griblo gave a nasty laugh. "No, he doesn't, but if the Terran edition didn't show a profit, it'd fold quicker than you can flip your wings and he'd have to go back to nasty old up-to-date Fizbus as a lowly sub-editor. And he wouldn't like that one bit. Our Stet, as you may have noticed, is fond of running things to suit himself."

"But Mr. Grupe told me that the *Times* isn't interested in money. It's running this edition of the paper only as a service to--oh, I suppose all that was a lot of birdseed, too!"

"Grupe!" Griblo snorted. "The sanctimonious old buzzard! He's a big stockholder on the paper. Bet you didn't know that, did you? All they're out for is money. Fizbian money, Terrestrial money--so long as it's cash."

"Tell me, Griblo," Tarb asked, "what does 'When in Rome, do as the Romans do' mean?"

Griblo grinned sourly. "Stet's favorite motto." He moved along the seat closer to her. "I'll tell you what it means, chicken. When on Earth, don't be a Fizbian."

*   *   *   *   *

The consul's wife, an old mauve creature, did not seem overpleased to see Tarb, since the younger, prettier Fizbian definitely took the spotlight away from her. The press had, of course, seen Tarb before, but at that time they hadn't been able to communicate directly with her and they didn't, she now found out, think nearly as much of Stet as he did of them.

Tarb couldn't attempt to deviate much from Stet's questions, for the consul's wife was not very cooperative and the consul himself watched both women narrowly. He was a good friend of Stet's, Tarb knew, and apparently Stet had taken the other man into his confidence.

When the interviews were over and the consular party had left, Tarb remained to chat with the Terrestrial journalists. Despite Griblo's worried objections, she joined them in the Moonfield Restaurant, where she daringly partook of a cup of coffee and then another and another.

After that, things weren't very clear. She dimly remembered the other reporters assuring her that she shouldn't disfigure her lovely wings with a stole ... and then pirouetting in the air over the bar to prolonged applause ... and then she was in the taxi again with Griblo shaking her.

"Wake up, Tarb--we're almost at the office! Stet'll have me plucked for this!"

Tarb sat up and pushed her crest out of her eyes. The sky was growing dark. They must have been gone a long time.

"I'll never hear the end of this," Griblo moaned. "Why, if only he could get someone to fill my place, Stet would fire me like a shot! Not that I wouldn't quit if I could get another job."

"Oh, it'll be mostly me he'll be mad at." Tarb pulled out her compact. Stet had warned her not to polish her eyeballs in public, but the ground with him! Her head hurt. And her feathers, she saw in the mirror, had turned almost beige. She looked horrible. She felt horrible. And Stet would probably think she was horrible.

"When Stet's mad," Griblo prophesied darkly, "he's mad at *everybody*!"

And Stet *was* mad. He was waiting in the newsroom, his emerald-blue eyes blazing as if he had not only polished but lacquered them.

"What's the idea of taking six hours to cover a simple story!" he shouted as soon as the door began to open. "Aside from the trivial matter of a deadline to be met--Griblo, *where's Tarb*? Nothing's happened to her, has it?"

"Naaah," Griblo said, unslinging his camera. "She took a short cut, only she got held up by a terrace. Snagged her umbrella on it, I believe. I heard her yelling when I was waiting for the elevator; I didn't know nice girls knew language like that. She should be up any minute now.... There she is."

He pointed to a window, through which the lissome form of the young feature writer could be seen, tapping on the glass in order to attract attention.

"Somebody better open it for her," the cameraman suggested. "Probably not meant to open from the outside. Not many people come in that way, I guess."

*   *   *   *   *

Open-mouthed, the whole newsroom stared at the window. Finally the Copy Editor got up and let a dripping Tarb in.

"Nearly thought I wouldn't make it," she observed, shaking herself in a flurry of wet pink feathers. The rest of the staff ducked, most of them too late. "Umbrella didn't do much good," she continued, closing it. It left a little puddle on the rug. "My wings got soaked right away." She tossed her wet crest out of her eyes. "Golly, but it's good to fly again. Haven't done it for months, but it seems like years." Her eye caught Miss Snow's. "You don't know what you're missing!"

"Tarb," Stet thundered, "you've been drinking coffee! *Griblo!*" But the cameraman had nimbly sought sanctuary in the darkroom.

"You'd better go home, Tarb." When Stet's eye tufts met across his nose, he was downright ugly, she realized. "Griblo can give me the dope and I'll write up the story myself. I can fill it out with canned copy. And you and I will discuss this situation in the morning."

"Won't go home when there's work to be done. Duty calls me." Giving a brief and quite recognizable imitation of a Terrestrial trumpet, Tarb stalked down the corridor to her office.

Drosmig looked up from his perch, to which he was still miraculously clinging at that hour. "So it got you, too?... Sorry ... nice girl."

"It hasn't got me," Tarb replied, picking up a letter marked *Urgent*. "I've got it." She scanned the letter, then made hastily for Stet's office.

He sat drumming on his desk with the antique stainless steel spatula he used as a paperknife.

"Read this!" she demanded, thrusting the letter into his face. "Read this, you traitor--sacrificing our whole civilization to what's most expedient for you! Hypocrite! Cad!"

"Tarb, listen to me! I'm--"

"Read it!" She slapped the letter down in front of him. "Read it and see what you've done to us! Sure, we Fizbians keep to ourselves and so the only people who know anything about us are the ones who want to sell us brushes, while the people who want to help us don't know a damn thing about us and--"

"Oh, all right! I'll read it if you'll only keep quiet!" He turned the letter right-side up.

Johannesburg

Dear Senbot Drosmig:

I represent the Dzoglian Publishing Company, Inc., of which I know you have heard, since your paper has seen fit to give our books some of the most unjust reviews on record. However, be that as it may, I have opened an office on Earth with the laudable purpose of effecting an interchange of respective literatures, to see which Terrestrial books might most profitably be translated into Fizbian, and which of the authors on our own list might have potential appeal for the Earth reader.

Dealing with authors is, of course, a nerve-racking business and I soon found myself in dire need of mental treatment. What was my horror to find that this primitive, although charming, planet had no neurotones, no psychoscopes, not even any cerebrophones--in fact, no psychiatric machines at all! The very knowledge of this brought me several degrees closer to a breakdown.

Perhaps I should have consulted you at this juncture, but I admit I was a bit of a snob. "What sort of advice can a mere journalist give me," I thought, "that I could not give myself?" So, more for amusement than anything else, I determined to consult a native practitioner. "After all," I said to myself, "a good laugh is a step forward on the road to recovery."

Accordingly, I went to see this native fellow. They work entirely without machines, I understand, using something like witchcraft. At the same time, I thought I might pick up some material for a jolly little book on primitive customs which I could get some unknown writer to throw together inexpensively. Strong human interest items like that always have great reader-appeal.

The native chap--doctor, he calls himself--was most cordial, which he should have been at the price I was paying him. One thing I must say about these natives--backward they may be, but they have a very shrewd commercial sense. You can't even imagine the trouble I had getting those authors to sign even remotely reasonable contracts ... which in part accounts for my mental disturbance, I suppose.

Well, anyway, I handed the native a privacy waiver carefully filled out in Terran. He took it, smiled and said, "We'll discuss this afterward. My contact lenses have disappeared; I suppose one of my patients has stolen them again. Can't see a thing without them."

So we sat down and had a bit of a chat. He seemed remarkably intelligent for a native; never interrupted me once.

"You are definitely in great trouble," he told me when I'd finished. "You need to be psycho-analyzed."

"Good, good," I said. "I see I've come to the right shop."

"Now just lie down and make yourself comfortable."

"Lie down?" I repeated, puzzled. I have an excellent command of Terran, but every now and then an idiom will throw me. "I tell the truth, sir, and when I am required by force of circumstances to lie, I lie up."

"No," he said, "not that kind of lying. You know, the kind you do at night when you go to sleep."

"Oh, I get you," I said idiomatically. Without further ado, I flung off my ulster and flew up to a thingummy hanging from the ceiling--chandelier, I believe, is the native term--flipped upside down, and hung from it by my toes. Wasn't the Presidential Perch, by any means, but it wasn't bad at all. "What do I do next?" I inquired affably.

"My dear fellow," the chap said, whipping out a notebook from the recesses of his costume, "how long have you had this delusion that you are a bird--or is it a bat?"

"Sir," I said as haughtily as my position permitted, "I am neither a bird nor a bat. I am a Fizbian. Surely you have heard of Fizbians?"

"Yes, yes, of course. They come from another country or planet or something. Frankly, politics is a bit outside my sphere. All I'm interested in is people--and Fizbians are people, aren't they?"

"Yes, certainly. If anything, it's you who.... Yes, they are people."

"Well, tell me then, Mr. Liznig, when was it you first started thinking you were a bat or a bird?"

I tried to control myself. "I am neither a bird nor a bat! I am a Fizbian! I have wings! See?" I fluttered them.

He peered at me. "I wish I could," he said regretfully. "Without my glasses, though, I'm as blind as a bat--or a bird."

Well, the long and the short of it is that the natives are planning to certify me as insane and incarcerate me, pending the doctor's decision as to whether my delusion is that I am a bird or a bat. They are using my privacy waiver as commitment papers.

Save me, Senbot Drosmig, for I feel that if I have to wait for the doctor's glasses to be delivered, I shall indeed go mad.

> *Distractedly yours,*
> *Tgos Liznig*

"I'll handle this myself," Stet said crisply. "I'll tell the consul to advise the Terran State Department that this man should be deported as an undesirable alien. That'll solve the problem neatly. We can't have this contaminating the pure stream of Terrestrial literature with--"

"But aren't you going to explain to them that he's perfectly sane?" Tarb gasped.

"No need to bother. He'll be grateful enough to get off the planet. Besides, how do I know he is perfectly sane?"

"Stet Zarnon, you're perfectly horrid!"

"And you, Tarb Morfatch, are disgustingly drunk. Now you go right home and sleep it off. I know I was too harsh with you-- my fault for letting you go out alone with Griblo in the first place when you've been here only a few months. Might have known those Terran journalists would lead you astray. Nice fellows, but irresponsible." He flicked out his tongue. "There, I've apologized. Now will you go home?"

"Home!" Tarb shrieked. "Home when there's work to be done and--"

"--and you're not going to be the one to do it. Tarb," he said, attempting to seize her foot, which she pulled away, "I was going to tell you tomorrow, but you might as well know tonight. I've taken you off the column for good. I have a better job for you."

She looked at him. "A better job? Are you being sarcastic? What as?"

"As my wife." He got up and came over to her. She stood still, almost stunned. "That solves the whole problem tidily. An office is no place for you, darling--you're really a simple home-girl at heart. Newspaper work is too strenuous for you; it upsets you and makes you nervous and irritable. I want you to stay home and take care of our house and hatch our eggs--unostentatiously, of course."

"Why, you--" she spluttered.

He put his foot over her mouth. "Don't give me your answer now. You're in no condition to think. Tell me tomorrow."

*   *   *   *   *

It rained all night and continued on into the morning. Tarb's head ached, but she had to make an appearance at the office. First she vizzed an acquaintance she had made the day before; then she took her umbrella and set forth.

As she kicked open the door to the newsroom, all sound ceased. Voices stopped abruptly. Typewriters halted in mid-click. Even the roar of the presses downstairs suddenly seemed to mute. Every head turned to look at Tarb.

Humph, she thought, removing her plastic oversocks, *so suppose I was a little oblique yesterday. They needn't stare at me. They never stare at Drosmig. Just because I'm a woman, I suppose!* The gate crashed loudly behind her.

"Oh, Miss Morfatch," Miss Snow called. "Mr. Zarnon said he wanted to see you as soon as you came in. It's urgent." And she giggled.

"Really?" Tarb said. "Well, he'll just have to wait until I've wrung out my wings." Sooner or later, she would have to face Stet, but she wanted to put it off as long as possible.

She opened the door to her office and halted in amazement. For, seated on a stool behind the desk, haggard but vertical, was Senbot Drosmig, busily reading letters and blue-penciling comments on them with his feet.

"Good morning, my dear," he said, giving her a wan smile. "Surprised to see me functioning again, eh?"

"Well--yes." She opened her dripping umbrella mechanically and stood it in a corner. "How--"

"I realized last night that all that happened to you was my fault. You were my responsibility and I failed you."

"Oh, don't be melodramatic, Senbot. I wasn't your responsibility and you didn't fail me. Not that I'm not glad to see you up and doing again, but--"

"But I did fail you!" the aged journalist insisted. "And, in the same way, I failed my people. I shouldn't have given in. I should have fought Zarnon as you, my dear, tried to do. But it isn't too late!" The fire of the crusader lit up in his watery old eyes. "I can still fight him and his sacred crows--his Earthlings! If I have to, I can go over his head to Grupe. Grupe may not understand Stet's moral failings, but he certainly will comprehend his commercial ones. Grupe owns stock in other Fizbian enterprises besides the *Times.* Autofax, for example."

"Oh, Senbot!" Tarb wailed. "The whole thing's such an awful mess!"

"I don't think it'll be necessary to threaten that far," he comforted her. "Stet is no fool. He knows which side of his breadnut is peeled."

"I'm sure you'll do a wonderful job," she exclaimed, impulsively giving a ritual *entrechat.* "And I wish I could stay and help you, but...."

"I know, my dear."

"You do?" She was puzzled. "But how did the news get around so quickly?"

He shrugged. "The Terrestrial grapevine is almost as efficient as the Fizbian. Didn't you notice any change in the--ah--atmosphere when you came in?"

"Oh, was that the reason?" Tarb laughed merrily. "Somehow it never occurred to me that they could have heard so soon."

"But the morning editions have been out for hours."

The door to the office was flung open. Stet stormed in, bristling with a most unloverlike rage.

"Miss Morfatch--" he waved a crumpled copy of the *Terrestrial Tribune* at her--"when I give an order, I expect to be obeyed! Didn't Miss Snow tell you to report directly to my office the instant you came in? Although that's a question I don't have to ask; I know Miss Snow, at least, is someone I can trust."

"I was coming to see you, Stet," Tarb said soothingly. "Right away."

"Oh, you were, were you? And have you seen this?" Stet fairly threw the paper at her. Smack in the middle of the front page was a picture of herself in full flight over the airfield bar. Not a very good picture, but what could you expect with Terrestrial equipment? When the autofax came, perhaps she would be done justice.

FIZBIAN NEWSHEN GIVES EARTH A FLUTTER

"Though No Mammal, I Pack a Lot of Uplift," Says Beautiful Fizbian Gal Reporter

"I feel that you Terrans and we Fizbians can get along much better," lovely Tarb Morfatch, Fizbus *Times* feature writer, told her fellow-reporters yesterday at the Moonfield Restaurant, "if we learn to understand each other's differences as well as appreciate our similarities.

"With commerce between the two planets expanding as rapidly as it has been," Miss Morfatch went on, "it becomes increasingly important that we make sure there is no clash of mores between us. Where adaptation is impossible, we must both adjust. 'When in Rome, do as the Romans do' is an outmoded concept in the complex interstellar civilization of today. The Romans must learn to accept us as we are, and vice versa.

"Forgive me if I've offended you by my frankness," she said, sticking out her tongue in the charming gesture of apology that is acquiring such a vogue on Earth, Belinda Romney and many other socialites having enthusiastically adopted it, "but you've violated our privacy so many times, I feel I'm entitled to hurt your feelings just a teeny-weeny bit...."

"Those Terran journalists," Tarb said admiringly. "Never miss a trick, do they? Am I in all the other papers too, Stet? Same cheesecake?"

"You've made an ovulating circus out of us--that's what you've done!"

"Nonsense. Good strong human interest stuff; it'll make us lovable as chicks all over the planet. Gee--" she read on--"did I say all that while I was caffeinated? I ought to turn out some pretty terrific copy sober."

"And to think you, the woman I had asked to make my wife, did this to me."

"Oh, that's all right, Stet," Tarb said without looking up from the paper. "I wasn't going to accept you, anyway."

"Good for you, Tarb," Drosmig approved.

"You're going back to Fizbus on the next liner--do you hear me?" Stet raged.

She smiled sunnily. "Oh, but I'm not, Stet. I'm going to stay right here on Earth. I like it. You might say the spiritual aura got me."

He snorted. "How can you possibly stay? You don't have an independent income and this is an expensive planet. Besides, I won't let you stay on Earth. I have considerable influence, you know!"

"Poor Stet." She smiled at him again. "I'm afraid the Fizbian press--the Fizbian consul even--are pretty small pullets beside the Solar Press Syndicate. You see, I came in this morning only to resign."

He stared at her.

"Yesterday," she informed him, "I was offered another position--as feature writer for the SP. I hadn't decided whether or not to accept when I reported back last evening, but you made up my mind for me, so I called them this morning and took the job. My work will be to explain Fizbians to Terrans and Terrans to Fizbians--as I wanted to do for the *Times*, Stet, only you wouldn't let me."

"It's no use saying anything to you about loyalty, I suppose?"

"None whatsoever," she said. "I owe the *Times* no loyalty and I'm doing what I do out of loyalty to Fizbus ... plus, of course, a much higher salary."

"I'm glad for you, Tarb," Drosmig said sincerely.

"Be glad for yourself, Senbot, because Stet will have to let you conduct the column your way from now on. Either it'll supplement my work in the Terrestrial papers or he'll look like a fool. And you do hate looking like a fool, don't you, Stet?"

He didn't answer.

"Better give up, Stet." She turned to Drosmig. "Well, good-by, Senbot--or, rather, so long. I'm sure we'll be seeing each other again. Good-by, Stet. No hard feelings, I hope?"

He neither moved nor spoke.

"Well ... good-by, then," she said.

The door closed. Stet stared after her. The forgotten umbrella dripped forlornly in the corner.

Time Enough At Last
By Lyn Venable

Originally Published in *If Worlds of Science Fiction*
January 1953

Editor's Notes:
Time Enough At Last
By Lyn Venable

Lyn Venable achieved a sort of science fiction immortality when the story "Time Enough At Last" was adapted for the television series "Twilight Zone" in an episode staring Burgess Meredith. Over the years it has been seen by countless millions in reruns making her one of the most visible authors in the book. The story addresses one of the themes current during the era, the aftermath of a nuclear war.

During the 50's Venable had seven stories published. As an author, she was more concerned with the reactions of people to events rather than the events themselves. Her first story was published in 1952 and the last in 1957. By the time of the "Twilight Zone" adaptation she appears to have stopped writing.

Lyn Venable's full name was Marilyn Venable. Other than the existence of the seven published stories there is no other biographical information available.

TIME ENOUGH AT LAST

For a long time, Henry Bemis had had an ambition. To read a book. Not just the title or the preface, or a page somewhere in the middle. He wanted to read the whole thing, all the way through from beginning to end. A simple ambition perhaps, but in the cluttered life of Henry Bemis, an impossibility.

Henry had no time of his own. There was his wife, Agnes who owned that part of it that his employer, Mr. Carsville, did not buy. Henry was allowed enough to get to and from work--that in itself being quite a concession on Agnes' part.

Also, nature had conspired against Henry by handing him with a pair of hopelessly myopic eyes. Poor Henry literally couldn't see his hand in front of his face. For a while, when he was very young, his parents had thought him an idiot. When they realized it was his eyes, they got glasses for him. He was never quite able to catch up. There was never enough time. It looked as though Henry's ambition would never be realized. Then something happened which changed all that.

Henry was down in the vault of the Eastside Bank & Trust when it happened. He had stolen a few moments from the duties of his teller's cage to try to read a few pages of the magazine he had bought that morning. He'd made an excuse to Mr. Carsville about needing bills in large denominations for a certain customer, and then, safe inside the dim recesses of the vault he had pulled from inside his coat the pocket size magazine.

He had just started a picture article cheerfully entitled "The New Weapons and What They'll Do To YOU", when all the noise in the world crashed in upon his ear-drums. It seemed to be inside of him and outside of him all at once. Then the concrete floor was rising up at him and the ceiling came slanting down toward him, and for a fleeting second Henry thought of a story he had started to read once called "The Pit and The Pendulum". He regretted in that insane moment that he had never had time to finish that story to see how it came out. Then all was darkness and quiet and unconsciousness.

*   *   *   *   *

When Henry came to, he knew that something was desperately wrong with the Eastside Bank & Trust. The heavy steel door of the vault was buckled and twisted and the floor tilted up at a dizzy angle, while the ceiling dipped crazily toward it. Henry gingerly got to his feet, moving arms and legs experimentally. Assured that nothing was broken, he tenderly raised a hand to his eyes. His precious glasses were intact, thank God! He would never have been able to find his way out of the shattered vault without them.

He made a mental note to write Dr. Torrance to have a spare pair made and mailed to him. Blasted nuisance not having his prescription on file locally, but Henry trusted no-one but Dr. Torrance to grind those thick lenses into his own complicated prescription. Henry removed the heavy glasses from his face. Instantly the room dissolved into a neutral blur. Henry saw a pink splash that he knew was his hand, and a white blob come up to meet the pink as he withdrew his pocket handkerchief and carefully dusted the lenses. As he replaced the glasses, they slipped down on the bridge of his nose a little. He had been meaning to have them tightened for some time.

He suddenly realized, without the realization actually entering his conscious thoughts, that something momentous had happened, something worse than the boiler blowing up, something worse than a gas main exploding, something worse than anything that had ever happened before. He felt that way because it was so quiet. There was no whine of sirens, no shouting, no running, just an ominous and all pervading silence.

*   *   *   *   *

Henry walked across the slanting floor. Slipping and stumbling on the uneven surface, he made his way to the elevator. The car lay crumpled at the foot of the shaft like a discarded accordian. There was something inside of it that

Henry could not look at, something that had once been a person, or perhaps several people, it was impossible to tell now.

Feeling sick, Henry staggered toward the stairway. The steps were still there, but so jumbled and piled back upon one another that it was more like climbing the side of a mountain than mounting a stairway. It was quiet in the huge chamber that had been the lobby of the bank. It looked strangely cheerful with the sunlight shining through the girders where the ceiling had fallen. The dappled sunlight glinted across the silent lobby, and everywhere there were huddled lumps of unpleasantness that made Henry sick as he tried not to look at them.

"Mr. Carsville," he called. It was very quiet. Something had to be done, of course. This was terrible, right in the middle of a Monday, too. Mr. Carsville would know what to do. He called again, more loudly, and his voice cracked hoarsely, "Mr. Carrrrsville!" And then he saw an arm and shoulder extending out from under a huge fallen block of marble ceiling. In the buttonhole was the white carnation Mr. Carsville had worn to work that morning, and on the third finger of that hand was a massive signet ring, also belonging to Mr. Carsville. Numbly, Henry realized that the rest of Mr. Carsville was under that block of marble.

Henry felt a pang of real sorrow. Mr. Carsville was gone, and so was the rest of the staff--Mr. Wilkinson and Mr. Emory and Mr. Prithard, and the same with Pete and Ralph and Jenkins and Hunter and Pat the guard and Willie the doorman. There was no one to say what was to be done about the Eastside Bank & Trust except Henry Bemis, and Henry wasn't worried about the bank, there was something he wanted to do.

He climbed carefully over piles of fallen masonry. Once he stepped down into something that crunched and squashed beneath his feet and he set his teeth on edge to keep from retching. The street was not much different from the inside, bright sunlight and so much concrete to crawl over, but the unpleasantness was much, much worse. Everywhere there were strange, motionless lumps that Henry could not look at.

Suddenly, he remembered Agnes. He should be trying to get to Agnes, shouldn't he? He remembered a poster he had seen that said, "In event of emergency do not use the telephone, your loved ones are as safe as you." He wondered about Agnes. He looked at the smashed automobiles, some with their four wheels pointing skyward like the stiffened legs of dead animals. He couldn't get to Agnes now anyway, if she was safe, then, she was safe, otherwise ... of course, Henry knew Agnes wasn't safe. He had a feeling that there wasn't anyone safe for a long, long way, maybe not in the whole state or the whole country, or the whole world. No, that was a thought Henry didn't want to think, he forced it from his mind and turned his thoughts back to Agnes.

*   *   *   *   *

She had been a pretty good wife, now that it was all said and done. It wasn't exactly her fault if people didn't have time to read nowadays. It was just that there was the house, and the bank, and the yard. There were the Jones' for bridge and the Graysons' for canasta and charades with the Bryants. And the television, the television Agnes loved to watch, but would never watch alone. He never had time to read even a newspaper. He started thinking about last night, that business about the newspaper.

Henry had settled into his chair, quietly, afraid that a creaking spring might call to Agnes' attention the fact that he was momentarily unoccupied. He had unfolded the newspaper slowly and carefully, the sharp crackle of the paper would have been a clarion call to Agnes. He had glanced at the headlines of the first page. "Collapse Of Conference Imminent." He didn't have time to read the article. He turned to the second page. "Solon Predicts War Only Days Away." He flipped through the pages faster, reading brief snatches here and there, afraid to spend too much time on any one item. On a back page was a brief article entitled, "Prehistoric Artifacts Unearthed In Yucatan". Henry smiled to himself and carefully folded the sheet of paper into fourths. That would be interesting, he would read all of it. Then it came, Agnes' voice. "Henrrreee!" And then she was upon him. She lightly flicked the paper out of his hands and into the fireplace. He saw the flames lick up and curl possessively around the unread article. Agnes continued, "Henry, tonight is the Jones' bridge night. They'll be here in thirty minutes and I'm not dressed yet, and here you are ... *reading*." She had emphasized the last word as though it were an unclean act. "Hurry and shave, you know how smooth Jasper Jones' chin always looks, and then straighten up this room." She glanced regretfully toward the fireplace. "Oh dear, that paper, the television schedule ... oh well, after the Jones leave there won't be time for anything but the late-late movie and.... Don't just sit there, Henry, hurrreeee!"

Henry was hurrying now, but hurrying too much. He cut his leg on a twisted piece of metal that had once been an automobile fender. He thought about things like lock-jaw and gangrene and his hand trembled as he tied his pocket-handkerchief around the wound. In his mind, he saw the fire again, licking across the face of last night's newspaper. He thought that now he would have time to read all the newspapers he wanted to, only now there wouldn't be any more. That heap of rubble across the street had been the Gazette Building. It was terrible to think there would never be another up to date newspaper. Agnes would have been very upset, no television schedule. But then, of course, no television. He wanted to laugh but he didn't. That wouldn't have been fitting, not at all.

He could see the building he was looking for now, but the silhouette was strangely changed. The great circular dome was now a ragged semi-circle, half of it gone, and one of the great wings of the building had fallen in upon itself. A sudden panic gripped Henry Bemis. What if they were all ruined, destroyed, every one of them? What if there wasn't a single one left? Tears of helplessness welled in his eyes as he painfully fought his way over and through the twisted fragments of the city.

* * * * *

He thought of the building when it had been whole. He remembered the many nights he had paused outside its wide and welcoming doors. He thought of the warm nights when the doors had been thrown open and he could see the people inside, see them sitting at the plain wooden tables with the stacks of books beside them. He used to think then, what a wonderful thing a public library was, a place where anybody, anybody at all could go in and read.

He had been tempted to enter many times. He had watched the people through the open doors, the man in greasy work clothes who sat near the door, night after night, laboriously studying, a technical journal perhaps, difficult for him, but promising a brighter future. There had been an aged, scholarly gentleman who sat on the other side of the door, leisurely paging, moving his lips a little as he did so, a man having little time left, but rich in time because he could do with it as he chose.

Henry had never gone in. He had started up the steps once, got almost to the door, but then he remembered Agnes, her questions and shouting, and he had turned away.

He was going in now though, almost crawling, his breath coming in stabbing gasps, his hands torn and bleeding. His trouser leg was sticky red where the wound in his leg had soaked through the handkerchief. It was throbbing badly but Henry didn't care. He had reached his destination.

Part of the inscription was still there, over the now doorless entrance. P-U-B--C L-I-B-R---. The rest had been torn away. The place was in shambles. The shelves were overturned, broken, smashed, tilted, their precious contents spilled in disorder upon the floor. A lot of the books, Henry noted gleefully, were still intact, still whole, still readable. He was literally knee deep in them, he wallowed in books. He picked one up. The title was "Collected Works of William Shakespeare." Yes, he must read that, sometime. He laid it aside carefully. He picked up another. Spinoza. He tossed it away, seized another, and another, and still another. Which to read first ... there were so many.

He had been conducting himself a little like a starving man in a delicatessen--grabbing a little of this and a little of that in a frenzy of enjoyment.

But now he steadied away. From the pile about him, he selected one volume, sat comfortably down on an overturned shelf, and opened the book.

Henry Bemis smiled.

There was the rumble of complaining stone. Minute in comparison which the epic complaints following the fall of the bomb. This one occurred under one corner of the shelf upon which Henry sat. The shelf moved; threw him off balance. The glasses slipped from his nose and fell with a tinkle.

He bent down, clawing blindly and found, finally, their smashed remains. A minor, indirect destruction stemming from the sudden, wholesale smashing of a city. But the only one that greatly interested Henry Bemis.

He stared down at the blurred page before him.

He began to cry.

A MATTER OF PROPORTION
BY ANN WALKER

ORIGINALLY PUBLISHED IN *ASTOUNDING SCIENCE FICTION*
AUGUST 1959

Editor's Notes:
A Matter of Proportion
By Ann Walker

Of all the stories in this collection, this seems in many ways to be the least dated. The idea of a brain transplant, of course, is not a new one. It has been dealt with varying degrees of seriousness in since *Frankenstein*, but here it serves merely as a vehicle for a deeper theme, that of the everyday struggles of paraplegics. Given the level of trauma being suffered daily in military actions and the increased ability to keep people alive in the aftermath, this story seems particularly timely.

Other than the publication of two stories, "A Matter of Proportion" in 1959 and "The Oversight of Dirty-Jets Ryan" there is no biographical information available.

A Matter of Proportion

In the dark, our glider chutes zeroed neatly on target--only Art Benjamin missed the edge of the gorge. When we were sure Invader hadn't heard the crashing of bushes, I climbed down after him. The climb, and what I found, left me shaken. A Special Corps squad leader is not expendable--by order. Clyde Esterbrook, my second and ICEG mate, would have to mine the viaduct while my nerve and glycogen stabilized.

We timed the patrols. Clyde said, "Have to wait till a train's coming. No time otherwise." Well, it was his show. When the next pair of burly-coated men came over at a trot, he breathed, "Now!" and ghosted out almost before they were clear.

I switched on the ICEG--inter-cortical encephalograph-- planted in my temporal bone. My own senses could hear young Ferd breathing, feel and smell the mat of pine needles under me. Through Clyde's, I could hear the blind whuffle of wind in the girders, feel the crude wood of ties and the iron-cold molding of rails in the star-dark. I could feel, too, an odd, lilting elation in his mind, as if this savage universe were a good thing to take on- -spray guns, cold, and all.

We wanted to set the mine so the wreckage would clobber a trail below, one like they'd built in Burma and Japan, where you wouldn't think a monkey could go; but it probably carried more supplies than the viaduct itself. So Clyde made adjustments precisely, just as we'd figured it with the model back at base. It was a tricky, slow job in the bitter dark.

I began to figure: If he armed it for this train, and ran, she'd go off while we were on location and we'd be drenched in searchlights and spray guns. Already, through his fingers, I felt the hum in the rails that every tank-town-reared kid knows. I turned up my ICEG. "All right, Clyde, get back. Arm it when she's gone past, for the next one."

I felt him grin, felt his lips form words: "I'll do better than that, Willie. Look, Daddy-o, no hands!" He slid over the edge and rested elbows and ribs on the raw tie ends.

We're all acrobats in the Corps. But I didn't like this act one little bit. Even if he could hang by his hands, the heavy train would jolt him off. But I swallowed my thoughts.

He groped with his foot, contacted a sloping beam, and brought his other foot in. I felt a dull, scraping slither under his moccasin soles. "Frost," he thought calmly, rubbed a clear patch with the edge of his foot, put his weight on it, and transferred his hands to the beam with a twist we hadn't learned in Corps school. My heart did a double-take; one slip and he'd be off into the gorge, and the frost stung, melting under his bare fingers. He lay in the trough of the massive H-beam, slid down about twenty feet to where it made an angle with an upright, and wedged himself there. It took all of twenty seconds, really. But I let out a breath as if I'd been holding it for minutes.

As he settled, searchlights began skimming the bridge. If he'd been running, he'd have been shot to a sieve. As it was, they'd never see him in the mingled glare and black.

His heart hadn't even speeded up beyond what was required by exertion. The train roared around a shoulder and onto the viaduct, shaking it like an angry hand. But as the boxcars thunder-clattered above his head, he was peering into the gulf at a string of feeble lights threading the bottom. "There's the flywalk, Willie. They know their stuff. But we'll get it." Then, as the caboose careened over and the searchlights cut off, "Well, that gives us ten minutes before the patrol comes back."

*　　*　　*　　*　　*

He levered onto his side, a joint at a time, and began to climb the beam. Never again for me, even by proxy! You just *couldn't* climb that thing nohow! The slope was too steep. The beam was too massive to shinny, yet too narrow to lie inside and elbow up. The metal was too smooth, and scummed with frost. His fingers were beginning to numb. And--he *was* climbing!

In each fin of the beam, every foot or so, was a round hole. He'd get one finger into a hole and pull, inching his body against the beam. He timed himself to some striding music I didn't know, not fast but no waste motion, even the pauses rhythmic.

I tell you. I was sweating under my leathers. Maybe I should have switched the ICEG off, for my own sake if not to avoid distracting Clyde. But I was hypnotized, climbing.

In the old days, when you were risking your neck, you were supposed to think great solemn thoughts. Recently, you're supposed to think about something silly like a singing commercial. Clyde's mind was neither posturing in front of his mental mirror nor running in some feverish little circle. He faced terror as big as the darkness from gorge bottom to stars, and he was just simply as big as it was--sheer life exulting in defying the dark, the frost and wind and the zombie grip of Invader. I envied him.

Then his rhythm checked. Five feet from the top, he reached confidently for a finger hole ... No hole.

He had already reached as high as he could without shifting his purchase and risking a skid--and even his wrestler's muscles wouldn't make the climb again. My stomach quaked: Never see sunlight in the trees any more, just cling till dawn picked you out like a crow's nest in a dead tree; or drop ...

Not Clyde. His flame of life crouched in anger. Not only the malice of nature and the rage of enemies, but human shiftlessness against him too? Good! He'd take it on.

Shoulder, thigh, knee, foot scraped off frost. He jammed his jaw against the wet iron. His right hand never let go, but it crawled up the fin of the strut like a blind animal, while the load on his points of purchase mounted--watchmaker co-ordination where you'd normally think in boilermaker terms. The flame sank to a spark as he focused, but it never blinked out. This was not the anticipated, warded danger, but the trick punch from nowhere. This was It. A sneak squall buffeted him. I cursed thinly. But he sensed an extra purchase from its pressure, and reached the last four inches with a swift glide. The next hole was there.

He waited five heartbeats, and pulled. He began at the muscular disadvantage of aligned joints. He had to make it the first time; if you can't do it with a dollar, you won't do it with the change. But as elbow and shoulder bent, the flame soared again: Score one more for life!

A minute later, he hooked his arm over the butt of a tie, his chin, his other arm, and hung a moment. He didn't throw a knee up, just rolled and lay between the rails. Even as he relaxed, he glanced at his watch: three minutes to spare. Leisurely, he armed the mine and jogged back to me and Ferd.

As I broke ICEG contact, his flame had sunk to an ember glow of anticipation.

*   *   *   *   *

We had almost reached the cave pricked on our map, when we heard the slam of the mine, wee and far-off. We were lying doggo looking out at the snow peaks incandescent in dawn when the first Invader patrols trailed by below. Our equipment was a miracle of hot food and basic medication. Not pastimes, though; and by the second day of hiding, I was thinking too much. There was Clyde, an Inca chief with a thread of black mustache and incongruous hazel eyes, my friend and ICEG mate--what made him tick? Where did he get his delight in the bright eyes of danger? How did he gear his daredevil valor, not to the icy iron and obligatory killing, but to the big music and stars over the gorge? But in the Corps, we don't ask questions and, above all, never eavesdrop on ICEG.

Young Ferd wasn't so inhibited. Benjamin's death had shaken him--losing your ICEG mate is like losing an eye. He began fly-fishing Clyde: How had Clyde figured that stunt, in the dark, with the few minutes he'd had?

"There's always a way, Ferd, if you're fighting for what you really want."

"Well, I want to throw out Invader, all right, but--"

"That's the start, of course, but beyond that--" He changed the subject: perhaps only I knew of his dream about a stronghold for rebels far in these mountains. He smiled. "I guess you get used to calculated risks. Except for imagination, you're as safe walking a ledge twenty stories up, as down on the sidewalk."

"Not if you trip."

"That's the calculated risk. If you climb, you get used to it."

"Well, how did you *get* used to it? Were you a mountaineer or an acrobat?"

"In a way, both." Clyde smiled again, a trifle bitterly and switched the topic. "Anyway, I've been in action for the duration except some time in hospital."

Ferd was onto that boner like an infielder. To get into SC you have to be not only championship fit, but have no history of injury that could crop up to haywire you in a pinch. So, "Hospital? You sure don't show it now."

Clyde was certainly below par. To cover his slip he backed into a bigger, if less obvious, one. "Oh, I was in that Operation Armada at Golden Gate. Had to be patched up."

He must have figured, Ferd had been a kid then, and I hadn't been too old. Odds were, we'd recall the episode, and no more. Unfortunately, I'd been a ham operator and I'd been in the corps that beamed those fireships onto the Invader supply fleet in the dense fog. The whole episode was burned into my brain. It had been kamikaze stuff, though there'd been a theoretical chance of the thirty men escaping, to justify sending them out. Actually, one escape boat did get back with three men.

I'd learned about those men, out of morbid, conscience-scalded curiosity. Their leader was Edwin Scott, a medical student. At the very start he'd been shot through the lower spine. So, his companions put him in the escape boat while they clinched their prey. But as the escape boat sheered off, the blast of enemy fire killed three and disabled two.

Scott must have been some boy. He'd already doctored himself with hemostatics and local anaesthetics but, from the hips down, he was dead as salt pork, and his visceral reflexes must have been reacting like a worm cut with a hoe. Yet somehow, he doctored the two others and got that boat home.

The other two had died, but Scott lived as sole survivor of Operation Armada. And he hadn't been a big, bronze, Latin-Indian with incongruous hazel eyes, but a snub-nosed redhead. And he'd been wheel-chaired for life. They'd patched him up, decorated him, sent him to a base hospital in Wisconsin where he could live in whatever comfort was available. So, he dropped out of sight. And now, this!

Clyde was lying, of course. He'd picked the episode at random. Except that so much else about him didn't square. Including his name compared to his physique, now I thought about it.

                              *   *   *   *   *

I tabled it during our odyssey home. But during post-mission
leave, it kept bothering me. I checked, and came up with what
I'd already known: Scott *had* been sole survivor, and the others
were certified dead. But about Scott, I got a runaround. He'd
apparently vanished. Oh, they'd check for me, but that could
take years. Which didn't lull my curiosity any. Into Clyde's past I
was sworn not to pry.

We were training for our next assignment, when word came
through of the surrender at Kelowna. It was a flare of sunlight
through a black sky. The end was suddenly close.

Clyde and I were in Victoria, British Columbia. Not
subscribing to the folkway that prescribes seasick intoxication as
an expression of joy, we did the town with discrimination. At
midnight we found ourselves strolling along the waterfront in
that fine, Vancouver-Island mist, with just enough drink taken
to be moving through a dream. At one point, we leaned on a rail
to watch the mainland lights twinkling dimly like the hope of a
new world--blackout being lifted.

Suddenly, Clyde said, "What's fraying you recently, Will?
When we were taking our ICEG reconditioning, it came through
strong as garlic, though you wouldn't notice it normally."

Why be coy about an opening like that? "Clyde, what do you
know about Edwin Scott?" That let him spin any yarn he chose--
if he chose.

He did the cigarette-lighting routine, and said quietly, "Well,
I *was* Edwin Scott, Will." Then, as I waited, "Yes, really me, the
real me talking to you. This," he held out a powerful, coppery
hand, "once belonged to a man called Marco da Sanhao ... You've
heard of transplanting limbs?"

I had. But this man was no transplant job. And if a spinal
cord is cut, transplanting legs from Ippalovsky, the primo
ballerino, is worthless. I said, "What about it?"

"I was the first--successful--brain transplant in man."

For a moment, it queered me, but only a moment. Hell, you
read in fairy tales and fantasy magazines about one man's mind
in another man's body, and it's marvelous, not horrible. But--

By curiosity, I know a bit about such things. A big surgery journal, back in the '40s, had published a visionary article on grafting a whole limb, with colored plates as if for a real procedure[A]. Then they'd developed techniques for acclimating a graft to the host's serum, so it would not react as a foreign body. First, they'd transplanted hunks of ear and such; then, in the '60s, fingers, feet, and whole arms in fact.

But a brain is another story. A cut nerve can grow together; every fiber has an insulating sheath which survives the cut and guides growing stumps back to their stations. In the brain and spinal cord, no sheaths; growing fibers have about the chance of restoring contact that you'd have of traversing the Amazon jungle on foot without a map. I said so.

"I know," he said, "I learned all I could, and as near as I can put it, it's like this: When you cut your finger, it can heal in two ways. Usually it bleeds, scabs, and skin grows under the scab, taking a week or so. But if you align the edges exactly, at once, they may join almost immediately healing by First Intent. Likewise in the brain, if they line up cut nerve fibers before the cut-off bit degenerates, it'll join up with the stump. So, take a serum-conditioned brain and fit it to the stem of another brain so that the big fiber bundles are properly fitted together, fast enough, and you can get better than ninety per cent recovery."

*   *   *   *   *

"Sure," I said, parading my own knowledge, "but what about injury to the masses of nerve cells? And you'd have to shear off the nerves growing out of the brain."

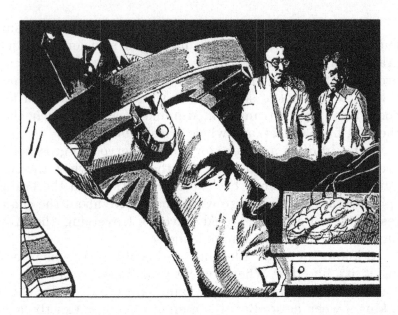

"There's always a way, Willie. There's a place in the brain stem called the isthmus, no cell masses, just bundles of fibers running up and down. Almost all the nerves come off below that point; and the few that don't can be spliced together, except the smell nerves and optic nerve. Ever notice I can't smell, Willie? And they transplanted my eyes with the brain--biggest trick of the whole job."

It figured. But, "I'd still hate to go through with it."

"What could I lose? Some paraplegics seem to live a fuller life than ever. Me, I was going mad. And I'd seen the dogs this research team at my hospital was working on--old dogs' brains in whelps' bodies, spry as natural.

"Then came the chance. Da Sanhao was a Brazilian wrestler stranded here by the war. Not his war, he said; but he did have the decency to volunteer as medical orderly. But he got conscripted by a bomb that took a corner off the hospital and one off his head. They got him into chemical stasis quicker than it'd ever been done before, but he was dead as a human being--no brain worth salvaging above the isthmus. So, the big guns at the hospital saw a chance to try their game on human material, superb body and lower nervous system in ideal condition, waiting for a brain. Only, whose?

"Naturally, some big-shot's near the end of his rope and willing to gamble. But *I* decided it would be a forgotten little-shot, name of Edwin Scott. I already knew the surgeons from being a guinea pig on ICEG. Of course, when I sounded them out, they gave me a kindly brush-off: The matter was out of the their hands. However, I knew whose hands it *was* in. And I waited for my chance--a big job that needed somebody expendable. Then I'd make a deal, writing my own ticket because they'd figure I'd never collect. Did you hear about Operation Seed-corn?"

That was the underground railway that ran thousands of farmers out of occupied territory. Manpower was what finally broke Invader, improbable as it seems. Epidemics, desertions, over-extended lines, thinned that overwhelming combat strength; and every farmer spirited out of their hands equalled ten casualties. I nodded.

"Well, I planned that with myself as director. And sold it to Filipson."

I contemplated him: just a big man in a trench coat and droop-brimmed hat silhouetted against the lamp-lit mist. I said, "You directed Seed-corn out of a wheel chair in enemy territory, and came back to get transplanted into another body? Man, you didn't tell Ferd a word of a lie when you said you were used to walking up to death." (But there was more: Besides that dour Scot's fortitude, where did he come by that high-hearted valor?)

He shrugged. "You do what you can with what you've got. *Those* weren't the big adventures I was thinking about when I said that. I had a team behind me in those--"

I could only josh. "I'd sure like to hear the capperoo then."

He toed out his cigarette. "You're the only person who's equipped for it. Maybe you'd get it, Willie."

"How do you mean?"

"I kept an ICEG record. Not that I knew it was going to happen, just wanted proof if they gave me a deal and I pulled it off. Filipson wouldn't renege, but generals were expendable. No one knew I had that transmitter in my temporal bone, and I rigged it to get a tape on my home receiver. Like to hear it?"

I said what anyone would, and steered him back to quarters before he'd think better of it. This would be something!

*   *   *   *   *

On the way, he filled in background. Scott had been living
out of hospital in a small apartment, enjoying as much liberty as
he could manage. He had equipment so he could stump around,
and an antique car specially equipped. He wasn't complimentary
about them. Orthopedic products had to be: unreliable, hard to
service, unsightly, intricate, and uncomfortable. If they also
squeaked and cut your clothes, fine!

Having to plan every move with an eye on weather and a
dozen other factors, he developed in uncanny foresight. Yet he
had to improvise at a moment's notice. With life a continuous
high-wire act, he trained every surviving fiber to precision,
dexterity, and tenacity. Finally, he avoided help. Not pride, self-
preservation; the compulsively helpful have rarely the wit to ask
before rushing in to knock you on your face, so he learned to bide
his time till the horizon was clear of beaming simpletons. Also,
he found an interest in how far he could go.

These qualities, and the time he had for thinking, begot
Seed-corn. When he had it convincing, he applied to see General
Filipson, head of Regional Intelligence, a man with both insight
and authority to make the deal--but also as tough as his post
demanded. Scott got an appointment two weeks ahead.

That put it early in April, which decreased the weather
hazard--a major consideration in even a trip to the Supermarket.
What was Scott's grim consternation, then, when he woke on D-
day to find his windows plastered with snow under a driving
wind--not mentioned in last night's forecast of course.

He could concoct a plausible excuse for postponement--which
Filipson was just the man to see through; or call help to get him
to HQ--and have Filipson bark, "Man, you can't even make it
across town on your own power because of a little snow." No,
come hell or blizzard, he'd have to go solo. Besides, when he
faced the inevitable unexpected behind Invader lines, he couldn't
afford a precedent of having flinched now.

He dressed and breakfasted with all the petty foresights that
can mean the shaving of clearance in a tight squeeze, and got off
with all the margin of time he could muster. In the apartment
court, he had a parking space by the basement exit and, for a
wonder, no free-wheeling nincompoop had done him out of it last

night. Even so, getting to the car door illustrated the ordeal ahead; the snow was the damp, heavy stuff that packs and glares. The streets were nasty, but he had the advantage of having learned restraint and foresight.

HQ had been the post office, a ponderous red-stone building filling a whole block. He had scouted it thoroughly in advance, outside and in, and scheduled his route to the general's office, allowing for minor hazards. Now, he had half an hour extra for the unscheduled major hazard.

But on arriving, he could hardly believe his luck. No car was yet parked in front of the building, and the walk was scraped clean and salted to kill the still falling flakes. No problems. He parked and began to unload himself quickly, to forestall the elderly MP who hurried towards him. But, as Scott prepared to thank him off, the man said, "Sorry, Mac, no one can park there this morning."

Scott felt the chill of nemesis. Knowing it was useless, he protested his identity and mission.

But, "Sorry, major. But you'll have to park around back. They're bringing in the big computer. General himself can't park here. Them's orders."

He could ask the sergeant to park the car. But the man couldn't leave his post, would make a to-do calling someone--and that was Filipson's suite overlooking the scene. No dice. Go see what might be possible.

But side and back parking were jammed with refugees from the computer, and so was the other side. And he came around to the front again. Five minutes wasted. He thought searchingly.

He could drive to a taxi lot, park there, and be driven back by taxi, disembark on the clean walk, and there you were. Of course, he could hear Filipson's "Thought you drove your own car, ha?" and his own damaging excuses. But even Out Yonder, you'd cut corners in emergency. It was all such a comfortable Out, he relaxed. And, relaxing, saw his alternative.

*   *   *   *   *

He was driving around the block again, and noted the back entrance. This was not ground level, because of the slope of ground; it faced a broad landing, reached by a double flight of steps. These began on each side at right-angles to the building and then turned up to the landing along the face of the wall. Normally, they were negotiable; but now, even had he found parking near them, he hadn't the chance of the celluloid cat in hell of even crossing the ten feet of uncleaned sidewalk. You might as well climb an eighty-degree, fifty-foot wall of rotten ice. But there was always a way, and he saw it.

The unpassable walk itself was an avenue of approach. He swung his car onto it at the corner, and drove along it to the steps to park in the angle between steps and wall--and discovered a new shut-out. He'd expected the steps to be a mean job in the raw wind that favored this face of the building; but a wartime janitor had swept them sketchily only down the middle, far from the balustrades he must use. By the balustrades, early feet had packed a semi-ice far more treacherous than the untouched snow; and, the two bottom steps curved out beyond the balustrade. So ... a sufficiently reckless alpinist might assay a cliff in a sleet storm and gale, but he couldn't even try if it began with an overhang.

Still time for the taxi. And so, again Scott saw the way that was always there: Set the car so he could use its hood to heft up those first steps.

Suddenly, his thinking metamorphosed: He faced, not a miserable, unwarranted forlorn hope, but the universe as it was. Titanic pressure suit against the hurricanes of Jupiter, and against a gutter freshet, life was always outclassed--and always fought back. Proportions didn't matter, only mood.

He switched on his ICEG to record what might happen. I auditioned it, but I can't disentangle it from what he told me. For example, in his words: Multiply distances by five, heights by ten, and slickness by twenty. And in the playback: Thirty chin-high ledges loaded with soft lard, and only finger holds and toe holds. And you did it on stilts that began, not at your heels, at your hips. Add the hazard of Helpful Hosea: "Here, lemme giveya hand, Mac!", grabbing the key arm, and crashing down the precipice on top of you.

Switching on the ICEG took his mind back to the snug apartment where its receiver stood, the armchair, books, desk of diverting work. It looked awful good, but ... life fought back, and always it found a way.

*   *   *   *   *

He shucked his windbreaker because it would be more encumbrance than help in the showdown. He checked, shoelaces, and strapped on the cleats he had made for what they were worth. He vetoed the bag of sand and salt he kept for minor difficulties--far too slow. He got out of the car.

This could be the last job he'd have to do incognito--Seed-corn, he'd get credit for. Therefore, he cherished it: triumph for its own sake. Alternatively, he'd end at the bottom in a burlesque clutter of chrom-alum splints and sticks, with maybe a broken bone to clinch the decision. For some men, death is literally more tolerable than defeat in humiliation.

Eighteen shallow steps to the turn, twelve to the top. Once, he'd have cleared it in three heartbeats. Now, he had to make it to a twenty-minute deadline, without rope or alpenstock, a Moon-man adapted to a fraction of Earth gravity.

With the help of the car hood, the first two pitches were easy. For the next four or five, wind had swept the top of the balustrade, providing damp, gritty handhold. Before the going got tougher, he developed a technic, a rhythm and system of thrusts proportioned to heights and widths, a way of scraping holds where ice was not malignantly welded to stone, an appreciation of snow texture and depth, an economy of effort.

He was enjoying a premature elation when, on the twelfth step, a cleat strap gave. Luckily, he was able to take his lurch with a firm grip on the balustrade; but he felt depth yawning behind him. Dourly, he took thirty seconds to retrieve the cleat; stitching had been sawed through by a metal edge--just as he'd told the cocksure workman it would be. Oh, to have a world where imbecility wasn't entrenched! Well--he was fighting here and now for the resources to found one. He resumed the escalade, his rhythm knocked cockeyed.

Things even out. Years back, an Invader bomber had scored a near miss on the building, and minor damage to stonework was unrepaired. Crevices gave fingerhold, chipped-out hollows gave barely perceptible purchase to the heel of his hand. Salutes to the random effects of unlikely causes!

He reached the turn, considered swiftly. His fresh strength was blunted; his muscles, especially in his thumbs, were stiffening with chill. Now: He could continue up the left side, by the building, which was tougher and hazardous with frozen drippings, or by the outside, right-hand rail, which was easier but meant crossing the open, half-swept wide step and recrossing the landing up top. Damn! Why hadn't he foreseen that? Oh, you can't think of everything. Get going, left side.

*   *   *   *   *

The wall of the building was rough-hewn and ornamented with surplus carvings. Cheers for the 1890s architect!

Qualified cheers. The first three lifts were easy, with handholds in a frieze of lotus. For the next, he had to heft with his side-jaw against a boss of stone. A window ledge made the next three facile. The final five stared, an open gap without recourse. He made two by grace of the janitor's having swabbed his broom a little closer to the wall. His muscles began to wobble and waver: in his proportions, he'd made two-hundred feet of almost vertical ascent.

But, climbing a real ice-fall, you'd unleash the last convulsive effort because you had to. Here, when you came down to it, you could always sit and bump yourself down to the car which was, in that context, a mere safe forty feet away. So he went on because he had to.

He got the rubber tip off one stick. The bare metal tube would bore into the snow pack. It might hold, *if* he bore down just right, and swung his weight just so, and got just the right sliding purchase on the wall, and the snow didn't give underfoot or undercane. And if it didn't work--it didn't work.

Beyond the landing, westwards, the sky had broken into April blue, far away over Iowa and Kansas, over Operation Seedcorn, over the refuge for rebels that lay at the end of all his roads....

He got set ... and lifted. A thousand miles nearer the refuge! Got set ... and lifted, balanced over plunging gulfs. His reach found a round pilaster at the top, a perfect grip for a hand. He drew himself up, and this time his cleated foot cut through snow to stone, and slipped, but his hold was too good. And there he was.

No salutes, no cheers, only one more victory for life.

Even in victory, unlife gave you no respite. The doorstep was three feet wide, hollowed by eighty years of traffic, and filled with frozen drippings from its pseudo-Norman arch. He had to tilt across it and catch the brass knob--like snatching a ring in a high dive.

No danger now, except sitting down in a growing puddle till someone came along to hoist him under the armpits, and then arriving at the general's late, with his seat black-wet.... You unhorse your foeman, curvet up to the royal box to receive the victor's chaplet, swing from your saddle, and fall flat on your face.

But, he cogitated on the bench inside, getting his other cleat off and the tip back on his stick, things do even out. No hearty helper had intervened, no snot-nosed, gaping child had twitched his attention, nobody's secretary--pretty of course--had scurried to helpfully knock him down with the door. They were all out front superintending arrival of the computer.

*   *   *   *   *

The general said only, if tartly, "Oh yes, major, come in. You're late, a'n't you?"

"It's still icy," said Ed Scott. "Had to drive carefully, you know."

In fact, he *had* lost minutes that way, enough to have saved his exact deadline. And that excuse, being in proportion to Filipson's standard dimension, was fair game.

*   *   *   *   *

I wondered what dimension Clyde would go on to, now that the challenge of war was past. To his rebels refuge at last maybe? Does it matter? Whatever it is, life will be outclassed, and Scott-Esterbrook's brand of life will fight back.

THE END

FOOTNOTES:

[A] Hall, "Whole Upper Extremity Transplant for Human Beings." Annals of Surgery 1944, #120, p. 12.

THE HERO
BY ELAINE WILBER

ORIGINALLY PUBLISHED IN *If Worlds of Science Fiction*
FEBRUARY 1958

Editor's Notes:
The Hero
By Elaine Wilber

Stories describing contact with alien species were popular during this period, if not always terribly realistic. This was especially true when the aliens are more or less human and the subject of "fraternization" arose. Wilber presents a light hearted view of one such Earth expedition and the crews attempts to avoid boredom.

Other than the existence of the single story "The Hero" there is no biographical information available.

THE HERO

Two months after the landing, Ship UXB-69311 was rigged out with most things needed to make life bearable, if not interesting, for the crew. Perched on the manicured, blue-green sod of the planet Engraham, its inner parts were transformed and refitted for the many months of the Exploration. No effort and no flight of imagination had been spared to make the ship resemble more a country club than a barracks. With the permission of Colonel Mondrain, the crew's bunkroom had been completely rearranged, and a segment thereof made into a quietly elegant bar. Plans for this eventual rejuvenation had been fomenting throughout the very tiresome and very monotonous journey.

When they first landed, the natives fled, and thus it was easy to liberate furnishings from the adjacent village. When the inhabitants returned, after the purposes of the visiting Earthman were acknowledged to be harmless, they proved to be too courteous to carp about a few missing articles.

The chairs, of a very advanced design and most comfortable, were made of a light and durable metal alloy thus far unknown to Earth. The bar (which was probably not its purpose on Engraham, no one knew or cared what its function had been) was of a design so futuristic that it would have turned a modern artist mad. The utensils, also liberated, were unbelievably delicate, yet strong and easy to wash. At first, since the Earth had not intended the Exploration to resemble the type that Texas-stationed servicemen like to run in Matamoros, there was nothing to drink in the utensils. But hardly six weeks had passed before the first hero of the Exploration, a man named O'Connors, discovered a palatable fruit growing on nearby bushes. By means of a system of improvised pipes (also liberated) it was no time at all before tasty beverages, somewhat strident but quite effective, were being run off and consumed in quantities. The machine known as O'Connors Joy-Juicer was concealed behind the bar, and all that was ever seen on the bar when Colonel Mondrain or the Doctors were around was an innocuous fruit juice.

The Earth Command had stocked the ship with reading material, most of it of a disgustingly educational nature, in photostatic cards: and the second hero of the Exploration was a man named Kosalowsky, who discovered in the psychology sections the works of Freud and Krafft-Ebing. After this discovery, a few interesting discussions arose.

After these changes had been made, there was very little to do.

The Earth Command had assumed that the natives of Engraham would resent the Explorations (most planets did), and so had sent along the crew of thirty men for protection. All had labored mightily to become part of this special crew, chosen for endurance and known war-like qualities. For once they got back to Earth, all were slated to be mustered out of service immediately, decorated to the ears, and awarded full, life-time pensions. Many already had contracts to appear on television and one man, Blunt, hinted at a long term Hollywood contract.

But once they got there, there was little to do after all. A guard was posted; instruments were checked; and, although the necessity seemed slight, the ship was kept primed for instantaneous emergency take-off. On the day corresponding to Earth's Saturday, the ship was G. I.'d from stem to stern. The maintenance crew made sure that no parts deteriorated or got liberated by enterprising natives. But the natives were not an inventive race. It was discovered by the Doctors (Anker, Frank, Pelham and Flandeau) that the natives literally did not know how to steal. They were backward. Dr. Flandeau, who was making great strides with the language, reported that there was some evidence that the Engrahamites had once possessed this skill, along with murder, mayhem, bad faith, and politics, but had lost it, through a deterioration of the species.

Thus, once the ship had been transformed into a place worthy of human dwelling, and the beverage question had been solved, and utter, imbecilic boredom circumvented by the timely discoveries of Freud and Krafft-Ebing, the men found time hanging heavily on their hands; and the more the doctors discovered about the Engrahamites, the more dismal the situation became. The doctors, growing more and more fascinated by their tasks, left the ship bright and early each day, returning around nightfall to reduce their growing stacks of data to points of Earthly relevance. The Colonel was also out most of the time. He paid many social calls on the natives, who, being courteous, received him, and was often returned at night in a chauffeured native Hop-Hop. Life in the bunkroom became a sullen round of poker, reading of Krafft-Ebing, and gab: and Earth currency changed hands daily in the never-ending crap game.

For there was one great lack in their lives. This lack, and the inability to do anything about it, absorbed many hours of conversation. At first, complaints only occurred at intervals; but as weeks passed, the lamentations became so fervent, so constant, and so heart-rending, that Dr. Flandeau observed to Dr. Frank that more stirring passages had not been made since the Jeremiad. For Dr. Flandeau, although aging, was in his off hours a poet, and a Frenchman always.

Dr. Frank said, "Yes, well, poor bastards."

At first, nostalgically, the crew harked back to happier times on Earth. Soon not one young lady of their collective acquaintance had escaped the most minute analysis. They were young men--the oldest, Blunt, was only twenty-six--and several of them had married young, greatly limiting their activities so that even their cumulative memories could not last forever. After several weeks, repetition began to set in. Once all successes had been lovingly remembered, down to the last, exquisite detail, they began recalling their failures. The master strategist, the unofficial referee of these seminars, was Dick Blunt.

"Now where you went wrong there," he would tell a fledgling reporting complete zero with a YWCA resident, "was in making her feel that you were interested. Your line with a girl like that should be one of charity. Pure charity. You impress on her that you're doing her a terrific favor. You offer to bring to her dull life romance, adventure, tenderness."

"I couldn't even get my hands on her," complained the reproved failure, Herbert Banks.

"I've always found that type the easiest ones of all," Blunt said indifferently. "Dull, of course."

The testiness, the self-pity, the shortness of temper and the near-riots over stolen packages of cigarettes, were not improved after the Doctors, having surveyed the situation thoroughly, decided that it would do no harm to let the men of the crew go out on Liberty.

Fraternizing with natives was, of course, strictly forbidden. They were not to drink off premises. (Nor on, for that matter.) They were exhorted not to steal, not to engage in fights.

Still, they could walk around, take pictures of the strange pink houses and the dazzling cities. They could watch a covey of children swim in the municipal pools. They could look at the fountains, the so-called "miraculous fountains of Engraham", or climb the strange, glassy mountains. The natives, although shy of them, were most polite, and some smiled enchantingly-- especially the women.

*   *   *   *   *

This was the worst rub of all: there were women, and they were gorgeous. A little smaller than most Earth women, with bright eyes, and high, arched eyebrows, looking forever as if they had heard the most priceless joke. Their faces conformed to the most rigid standards of Caucasian beauty. Their legs, so delicate, so tapering, so fantastically small of ankle, were breath-taking. Their clothes, which would have driven a Parisian designer to suicide, were draped carelessly over the most exquisite figures. True, they were a little deficient in one department, and this was explained, before they were granted liberty, by Dr. Flandeau. The women of Engraham, he said, did not bear children.

This announcement was not received with special gloom, for until then, none of the crew had seen an Engrahamite woman. But Willy Lanham, a dark-haired, skinny boy from Tennessee, asked, unhappily, "Don't they even go in for games or nothin'?"

Flandeau understood instantly. He shook his head sadly. "I should think not. It has been a long time since they have observed the normal functions. The women are mainly for decoration, although it is said that some are also created for brains. They are a most strange people."

After this--granted these agonizing liberties, and able to see that which was biologically unattainable--the crew became so demoralized that not even Kosalowsky's discovery of the works of Wilhelm Reik relieved the deep gloom.

However, they had reckoned without the superior genius of Dick Blunt. Blunt received Flandeau's news as unhappily as the others, and, like the rest, was made miserable by the sight of the glorious damozels. But he was a reasonable man and he put his reasoning powers to work. Soon he alone was cheerful. He went around with the absorbed, other-world look of a physicist grappling with a problem in ionospheric mathematics without the use of an IBM calculator. One day he went on Liberty alone. He did not return until the fall of night, and when he came in his elation was so immoderate that the others thought there must be bars on Engraham after all.

"I have found the answer to our question," he said.

No one needed to ask what question. O'Connors hurried to pour Blunt a drink.

"I have spent the day pursuing this answer logically," said Blunt. "I have done what any thoughtful man would do. I have read up on it."

"How?" cried Henderson.

"At the library."

Blunt then described his day: finding his way to the library by means of pantomime; and finding at last, that file of photographs--photographs of an utterly self-explanatory nature. And these he pulled from his pocket, for ignoring all discipline, he had stolen them.

The pictures passed from hand to hand. O'Connors passed them on to Pane, and suddenly felt the need to open the window behind him. It was Willy Lanham, the boy from Tennessee, who voiced those exultant words that rose to the throats of all:

He said, "Hey! They're made just like the Earth girls."

The conversation, at this intensely interesting point, was cut short by the arrival of the Colonel. He alighted from the native Hop-Hop--waved cheerily to its driver, and began coming up. The bottle and glasses vanished, and Kosalowsky began to read aloud from a book especially reserved for these occasions. The men maintained looks of studious interest as the officer went through. He went up the ladder to his own quarters, there to write in his growing volume, THE COMING OCCUPATION AND GOVERNMENT OF ENGRAHAM. They listened until his door clicked.

The conversation was resumed in more subdued tones.

"Do you think," said Pane shakily, "They still *could?*"

"Not a question of it," Blunt said. "These pictures prove it. It's what you might call a lost art. Once upon a time, as with all the fortunate parts of the galaxy, this art was known to the Engrahamites. Through some terrific foul-up, they lost it. Probably a combination of the science of incubation, and the reign of some ghastly square, like Queen Victoria. Thus were the girls of Engraham deprived of the pleasures of love."

"The men, too," said Willy. All glared at him reproachfully. To care about the happiness of the Engrahamite men was thought not quite patriotic.

"Gradually," Blunt went on, "they must have begun to lose interest. Probably there was some taboo. In the end they probably all thought, oh, to hell with it, and began serving on committees."

A long sigh went up.

"It is for us," Blunt said softly, treasuring each word, "to restore these unhappy maidens to their original human rights.

"But it isn't going to be easy," Blunt went on. His voice dropped even lower. "Think what would happen if it went sour. Those Doctors would get wind of it. We'd be stuck in the Ship for the rest of the Exploration."

There was a sober pause. Finally Banks cleared his throat and said, "Well, how do you think it should be handled, Blunt?"

"Well, every beachhead needs an invasion," Blunt said, casually holding out his glass. O'Connors leapt to fill it. "One guy has got to lay the groundwork. Let him enlighten one quail. Explain things to her." He took a long, leisurely drink, and sighed. "This quail will rush around telling the others. Pretty soon there'll be so many hanging around the ship that--"

There was a general rush for cooling beverages.

"Right," someone said, when the faculty of speech was recovered.

"And necessarily," said Blunt, "this has to be the guy with the most savvy. The one who knows the score. The one most likely to succeed. Check?"

All knew what this was leading up to. Martin said unhappily, "Check, Blunt, You're our boy."

*   *   *   *   *

Blunt was scheduled to stand guard the next day, but Willy Lanham, eager to assist the cause, volunteered to take over for him. The hours seemed to creep by. His air was swaggering and cool when he returned, and all gathered round with eager curiosity--all but Lanham, who had not recovered from standing guard.

Blunt sauntered to the bar, accepted a drink, sipped it, lighted a cigarette, and took a long, pensive drag. Finally he said reminiscently, "What a doll!"

Pane, never a subtle man, cried in anguish, "Well, how'd you make out?"

Blunt smiled smugly. He began his recital. He was walking along the street and he met this gorgeous creature. A full description followed (broken by the arrival of the Colonel and two paragraphs of the DECLINE AND FALL) making it clear that this was the dish of dishes, the most beautiful of the beautiful, the most charming, and the most intelligent. She allowed herself to be addressed in Blunt's few words of Engrahamic and, smiling ever patiently, sat with him for several hours. Their talk took place in a secluded bower, in one of the many parks. She was agreeable and charmed and promised to see him again. He even managed, through terrific feats of pantomime, to impress on her the need of secrecy in future meetings.

"That was all?" someone said, when he finished.

"For the first meeting, I think I did wonders," said Blunt. "After all, sex hasn't been known here since a time corresponding to our Stone Age."

Later, when the nightly poker game was beginning, Willy Lanham said, "Why didn't you just make a grab for her?"

"That's the hill-billy approach," Blunt said disdainfully. "These girls are civilized--very, very civilized. It's important not to shock them."

*   *   *   *   *

Blunt's next gambit was to set about learning the language. For this he went not to Flandeau, who best knew it, but to Ankers, who was a pure scientist in every sense of the word, and not so likely to suspect his motives. The girl proved very cultured. She took him to art galleries, to symphonies, and mountain climbing, for scrambling up and down the glassy hills was a favorite Engrahamic sport. As he advanced in the language, he learned that her name was Catataphinaria, which meant "she will attain relative wisdom". He found that she worked for the Eleven who, while not rulers, offered general suggestions which the populace more or less followed.

Although his slow progress inevitably bored the crew, still, it offered that one precious ray of hope, and they became so tractable that even the Doctors noticed it. They laid it to the secret ingredient that Dr. Frank had introduced into the drinking water.

The summer wore on, becoming hotter each day. By the end of the second month of his courtship, Blunt began to speak to her of love.

She laughed. She said that she had little curiosity on the subject, although it was now and then mentioned by the students of antiquity. Assured that it was pleasurable, she said that she heard that barbarians also enjoyed murdering people and making them butts of jokes.

Willy Lanham said, "Don't listen to what a girl *says*. Just make a grab for her."

This suggestion was laughed to scorn.

Weeks passed, the summer began to wane. Tempers again began to shorten. Flandeau said to Frank, "The men are worse again."

"Yes, perhaps we should increase the dosage."

The fruits for the Joy-Juicer grew thin on the silvery bushes, and men ranged far and wide, putting in supplies for the winter.

*   *   *   *   *

One night, when Blunt had won at poker, all the men lay in their bunks, too dispirited to drink, to shoot craps, almost too miserable even for speech. Blunt again began talking of

Catataphinaria. Drowsily Lanham said, "I think you're going at it the wrong way, Dick. Try some real rough stuff. You know-- kiss her. She might like it."

Before Blunt could defend his strategy, Kosalowsky sat up in his bunk. "Yes, for cripes sake," he said, "Move in for the kill. Or shut up about it. You're driving us all nuts."

"Would you like to try?" Blunt suggested softly.

"Sure I'll try," Kosalowsky said. He turned on the light over his bunk. "Give me a crack at her. I could have managed it weeks ago. All you've done is talk to the quail."

"Yah, Dick, maybe you're using the wrong approach on this one," O'Connors suggested.

"It's the damn places you take her," Kosalowsky said. "Art galleries. Anybody ever seduce a girl in an art gallery? Symphonies. Popping around in her damn Hop-Hop. Can't you ever get her alone?"

"She lives with ten other girls," Blunt said sulkily. "They're all home all the time."

"Well, bring her here, then," Pane suggested. "We'll all take a powder."

"Where?"

There was no answer. They could not all, by day, desert the ship, and it was getting too chilly for the crew to hide in adjacent shrubbery. "We could put up a wall," Pane said suddenly, "between the bunks and the bar."

"With what?"

"I know," Banks said eagerly, "where there's a whole pile of stuff. It's nice thin metal, just lying there getting rusty."

"I think you're premature--"

"Premature!" Kosalowsky shouted. "Six months you've been chasing this tomato. You call that premature?"

"Only four by Engrahamic time," Blunt said, insulted.

"Listen," Kosalowsky said, "that wall goes up tomorrow. And you're smuggling her in tomorrow night. Or else," he said, glaring at Blunt, "after that it's every man for himself. Check?"

Blunt, only slightly seen in the light from Kosalowsky's bunk, was white with rage. "All right, guys," he said stonily. "I've been trying to do right by this frail. Nothing abrupt or hillbilly. Nothing to hurt her delicate feelings or her fine mind. But if this is how you want it--Okay!"

*   *   *   *   *

The next day the wall went up.

Hardly a word was said as it was hammered in place. Once up, the place was G. I.'d thoroughly. The ash trays were washed, the floor vacuumed, and the lights adjusted to achieve the most tellingly seductive effect. Blunt went out at two, thin-lipped and silent.

"The jerk," Kosalowsky said, "I think he's a lot of hot air. That's what *I* think."

The Colonel came in at nightfall and asked about the wall. They told him that it was to cut off the recreation section from the sleeping quarters, for the protection of those who wanted more sleep to prepare for the grueling winter watches.

"Very good idea men," the Colonel said, and went upstairs to write another chapter in his book.

At nine the men disappeared into their bunks. O'Connors won the responsible job of peering through the narrow slit in the wall. Behind him could be heard the labored breathing of twenty-seven distraught men. One man snored. "Wake up, you stupid ass," Pane told Lanham. "You'll wreck the show."

At last the door opened and Blunt came in--with the girl.

She was breath-taking. She wore, O'Connors reported, a dress cut to here--and her hair was piled high on her patrician head. Blunt had not lied. She was even prettier than the usual run of Engraham girls.

"He's offering her a drink," O'Connors whispered.

"She take it?"

"No--she's sitting at the bar. He's having one, though. He's turning on the hi-fi."

He did not have to tell them, since all could hear the soft music. They had selected a program of melodies considered sure-fire.

"He's talking to her--putting his arm around her waist. Oh-oh. She knocked it off. She's laughing, though."

In the silence they all heard her laugh. Several men moved uncomfortably. "He's leading her toward the couch--oh-oh--she stopped to look at the radar screen."

It was the auxiliary radar, not the important one in the control room. "What's he doing?"

"Telling her--he's edging her to the couch again--now she's asking about the Bassett Blaster. They're fooling around with the gun. He's showing her how it works--trying to put his hands--!"

This last was lost, for there was a sudden, resounding blast. Their bunks, the entire ship, trembled.

The meaning was clear to all. They flattened to their bunks, and waited tensely. They heard a sound, the sound of a foot kicking a body. A hand scratched tentatively along the wall.

No one moved. "She killed him." O'Connors voice was no more than a slight whisper. "Lay low--lay low."'

Then a woman's voice said, in perfect English, "All right, you men. Come out of there."

The door was found and flung open. Catataphinaria stood in the dim light--still holding the Blaster. She said again, more sharply, "I said, Come out of there!"

Clumsily, they came down from their bunks.

"Now," she said, as she had them all against the wall, "call down the others."

But this was unnecessary, for the Doctors and the Colonel were already descending the ladder. They turned quite white at the sight of her. Wordlessly, she indicated that they were to join the others. The Doctors found it harder to adjust to a purely military sort of emergency. Ankers asked clearly, "What on earth is this nonsense?"

"No nonsense," the girl said. "Just do as I say. First, surrender all your papers."

"Our papers?"

"Your research. Your conclusions. Everything."

Henderson said, "I'll go get it, Ma'am."

"I would also like the Colonel's amusing work on the coming occupation."

"I know where it is, sir," Martin said swiftly. "I'll get it."

The Colonel's expression was stony. He nodded to Martin to get it, and it occurred to him that the girl was one of those whom he had personally selected as the most promising for the puppet governments. But when he asked about her identity, she cut him off without a word.

"Then, may I ask where you learned such flawless English?"

"All of us know English," she said. "It is a very stupid language."

Martin and Henderson returned with the papers. Gingerly they approached her, handed the papers to her, and darted back to their places in the line. She placed the stack on the bar, leafed through it, all the while keeping them covered with the Blaster, and remarked on finishing, "It is exactly what one would expect barbarians to find interesting."

Flandeau, however, remained a scientist to the last.

"We find ourselves unhappily deceived," he said. "We were certain--that you were utterly without defenses. We were told that you did not know *how* to lie, cheat, dissemble, or fight."

"Only not with each other." she said. "It was, so to speak, a lost art." She glanced at Blunt. Several men squirmed. "But it is one that we have regained," she said.

"And what will you do with us?" Flandeau asked.

"We have decided to let you go," she said. "Now that we possess this weapon,"--she brandished the Blaster--"which we can copy, we think we can prevent more Explorations. At least this is the opinion of the Eleven. So I am instructed to let you leave--at once, of course."

"You are most charming," said Flandeau.

"At once," she repeated.

"Yes, of course. Men! Prepare for blastoff!"

*   *   *   *   *

The way back was tedious--the floating around, the boredom, the unending blackness of space--but at least it was going home. After the first weeks of space-sickness, things returned to near normal, and the Doctors conferred with the Colonel. It was decided that the best report should be that Engraham was uninviting, bleak, and of no interest to Earthmen. The reputations of all were at stake (the doctors found themselves, stripped of their papers, unable to recollect enough, and the Colonel desperately feared a court-martial) and the crew was thus advised. All agreed to keep their mouths shut. Thus their honorable discharges, medals, and life-time pensions would be safe.

So, with all this decided, and Earth only a few months away, relative cheerfulness reigned. Only Willy Lanham continued to mope.

"What's biting you?" Kosalowsky asked, one day as they lay strapped in adjacent bunks. "Your face is as long as this ship."

"I just feel bad," Willy said. "I can feel bad if I want to, can't I?"

"What the hell, we'll soon be home. We can really raise some hell, then."

"I miss my girl," Willy blurted out.

"You'll see her pretty soon."

"I mean my girl on Engraham."

It happened that just then several other men, bored with lying still, were floating past. They gripped the edges of Willy's bunk.

"You mean you had," Kosalowsky said cunningly, "a girl on Engraham?"

"Sure I did," said Willy defensively. "Didn't all you guys?"

More and more men joined the knot of bodies around Willy's bunk. The atmosphere became distinctly menacing.

"You mean you didn't?" Willy said. "You mean it wasn't a gag we were pulling on Blunt?"

They were silent. One pair of floating hands neared Willy's throat.

"Honest," he said. "I didn't think you were that dumb. I thought you were just letting Blunt make an ass of himself. I thought that--well, it was so easy. I even told Dick a couple of times. You just had to make a grab for 'em."

Pane suddenly let out a harsh sound, like the cry of a wounded bull.

"So who was this frail?" Kosalowsky asked heavily.

"Yeah!" echoed the others.

"Well, she was just a frail, I guess," Willy said. "I used to see her around the ship. On guard duty. I used to see her all the time. What the hell," he said, "You think I'm dumb or something? Why'd you think I was willing to stand guard all the time?"

LONGEVITY
BY THERESE WINDSER

ORIGINALLY PUBLISHED IN *AMAZING SCIENCE FICTION STORIES*
MAY 1960

Editor's Notes:
Longevity
By Therese Windser

This story deals with another common theme in science fiction of the period, that of a civilization rebuilding after some undescribed apocalypse that happened in the dim past.

Other than the existence of the single story "Longevity" there is no biographical information available.

Longevity

Legend had it, that many thousands of years ago, right after the Great Horror, the whole continent of the west had slowly sunk beneath the West Water, and that once every century it arose during a full moon. Still, Captain Hinrik clung to the hope that the legend would not be borne out by truth. Perhaps the west continent still existed; perhaps, dare he hope, with civilization. The crew of the Semilunis thought him quite mad. After all, hadn't the east and south continents been completely annihilated from the great sky fires; and wasn't it said that they had suffered but a fraction of what the west continent had endured?

The Semilunis anchored at the mouth of a great river. The months of fear and doubt were at end. Here, at last, was the west continent. A small party of scouts was sent ashore with many cautions to be alert for luminescent areas which meant certain death for those who remained too long in its vicinity. Armed with bow and arrow, the party made its way slowly up the great river. Nowhere was to be seen the color green, only dull browns and greys. And no sign of life, save for an occasional patch of lichen on a rock.

After several days of rowing, the food and water supply was almost half depleted and still no evidence of either past or present habitation. It was time to turn back, to travel all the weary months across the West Water, the journey all in vain. What a small reward for such an arduous trip ... just proof of the existence of a barren land mass, ugly and useless.

On the second day of the return to the Semilunis, the scouting party decided to stop and investigate a huge opening in the rocky mountainside. How suspiciously regular and even it looked, particularly in comparison to the rest of the countryside which was jagged and chaotic.

They entered the cave apprehensively, torches aflare and weapons in hand. But all was darkness and quiet. Still, the regularity of the cave walls led them on. Some creature, man or otherwise, must have planned and built this ... but to what end? Now the cave divided into three forks. The torches gave only a hint of the immensity of the chambers that lay at the end of each. They selected the center chamber, approaching cautiously, breath caught in awe and excitement. The torches reflected on a dull black surface which was divided into many, many little squares. The sameness of them stretched for uncountable yards in all directions. What were these ungodly looking edifices? The black surface was cold and smooth to the touch and quite regular except for a strange little hole at the bottom of each square and a curious row of pictures along the top.

They would copy these strange pictures. Perhaps back home there would be a scholar who would understand the meaning behind these last remains of the people of the west continent. The leader took out his slate and painstakingly copied:

Safeguard your valuables at
ALLEGHANY MOUNTAIN VAULTS
Box #4544356782

HOMO INFERIOR
BY MARI WOLF

ORIGINALLY PUBLISHED IN *IF WORLDS OF SCIENCE FICTION*
NOVEMBER 1953

Editor's Notes:
Homo Inferior
By Mari Wolf

Homo Inferior is Mari Wolf's take on what it would be like to be a normal human when most of the race has evolved into something else. It is not a unique theme, nor is its resolution that novel, but the telling of the story is well done. The seven stories she had published in during the period show great talent and promise. and she could write with both emotion and humor.

Mari Wolf is probably known more for her participation in the West Coast science fiction fan scene than for her writing. She seems to have been fondly remembered by many of those she met during those years as an attractive, friendly young woman. She also seems to have been responsible for introducing people to each other at the many conventions she attended. Some of the reminiscences also indicate that she was involved in the design of wind tunnels and amateur rocketry.

The seven stories she had published have been collected in *Mari Wolf Resurrected*.

Mari Wolf was born August 27, 1927 and grew up in Laguna Beach, California. In the early 50's she was active in the science fiction fan scene and for a number of years wrote a column for *Imagination* magazine called "Fandora's Box." She also had a number of short stories published during this period and in 1961 a novel *The Golden Frame* came out. She was married to fellow science fiction author and fan columnist Roger Phillips Graham.

Homo Inferior

The starship waited. Cylindrical walls enclosed it, and a transparent plastic dome held it back from the sky and the stars. It waited, while night changed to day and back again, while the seasons merged one into another, and the years, and the centuries. It towered as gleaming and as uncorroded as it had when it was first built, long ago, when men had bustled about it and in it, their shouting and their laughter and the sound of their tools ringing against the metallic plates.

Now few men ever came to it. And those who did come merely looked with quiet faces for a few minutes, and then went away again.

The generations kaleidoscoped by. The Starship waited.

*   *   *   *   *

Eric met the other children when he was four years old. They were out in the country, and he'd slipped away from his parents and started wading along the edge of a tiny stream, kicking at the water spiders.

His feet were soaked, and his knees were streaked with mud where he'd knelt down to play. His father wouldn't like it later, but right now it didn't matter. It was fun to be off by himself, splashing along the stream, feeling the sun hot on his back and the water icy against his feet.

A water spider scooted past him, heading for the tangled moss along the bank. He bent down, scooped his hand through the water to catch it. For a moment he had it, then it slipped over his fingers and darted away, out of his reach.

As he stood up, disappointed, he saw them: two boys and a girl, not much older than he. They were standing at the edge of the trees, watching him.

He'd seen children before, but he'd never met any of them. His parents kept him away from them--and from all strangers.

He stood still, watching them, waiting for them to say something. He felt excited and uncomfortable at the same time.

They didn't say anything. They just watched him, very intently.

He felt even more uncomfortable.

The bigger boy laughed. He pointed at Eric and laughed again and looked over at his companions. They shook their heads.

Eric waded up out of the water. He didn't know whether to go over to them or run away, back to his mother. He didn't understand the way they were looking at him.

"Hello," he said.

The big boy laughed again. "See?" he said, pointing at Eric. "He can't."

"Can't what?" Eric said.

The three looked at him, not saying anything. Then they all burst out laughing. They pointed at him, jumped up and down and clapped their hands together.

"What's funny?" Eric said, backing away from them, wishing his mother would come, and yet afraid to turn around and run.

"You," the girl said. "You're funny. Funny, funny, funny! You're stu-pid."

The others took it up. "Stu-pid, stu-pid. You can't talk to us, you're too stu-pid...."

They skipped down the bank toward him, laughing and calling. They jumped up and down and pointed at him, crowded closer and closer.

"Silly, silly. Can't talk. Silly, silly. Can't talk...."

Eric backed away from them. He tried to run, but he couldn't. His knees shook too much. He could hardly move his legs at all. He began to cry.

They crowded still closer around him. "Stu-pid." Their laughter was terrible. He couldn't get away from them. He cried louder.

"Eric!" His mother's voice. He twisted around, saw her coming, running toward him along the bank.

"Mama!" He could move again. He stumbled toward her.

"He wants his mama," the big boy said. "Funny baby."

His mother was looking past him, at the other children. They stopped laughing abruptly. They looked back at her for a moment, scuffing their feet in the dirt and not saying anything. Suddenly the big boy turned and ran, up over the bank and out of sight. The other boy followed him.

The girl started to run, and then she looked at Eric's mother again and stopped. She looked back at Eric. "I'm sorry," she said sulkily, and then she turned and fled after the others.

Eric's mother picked him up. "It's all right," she said. "Mother's here. It's all right."

He clung to her, clutching her convulsively, his whole body shaking. "Why, Mama? Why?"

"You're all right, dear."

She was warm and her arms were tight around him. He was home again, and safe. He relaxed, slowly.

"Don't leave me, Mama."

"I won't, dear."

She crooned to him, softly, and he relaxed still more. His head drooped on her shoulder and after a while he fell asleep.

But it wasn't the same as it had been. It wouldn't ever be quite the same again. He knew he was different now.

*   *   *   *   *

That night Eric lay asleep. He was curled on his side, one chubby hand under his cheek, the other still holding his favorite animal, the wooly lamb his mother had given him for his birthday. He stirred in his sleep, threshing restlessly, and whimpered.

His mother's face lifted mutely to her husband's.

"Myron, the things those children said. It must have been terrible for him. I'm glad at least that he couldn't perceive what they were thinking."

Myron sighed. He put his arm about her shoulders and drew her close against him. "Don't torture yourself, Gwin. You can't make it easier for him. There's no way."

"But we'll have to tell him something."

He stroked her hair. The four years of their shared sorrow lay heavily between them as he looked down over her head at his son.

"Poor devil. Let him keep his childhood while he can, Gwin. He'll know he's all alone soon enough."

She nodded, burying her face against his chest. "I know...."

Eric whimpered again, and his hands clenched into fists and came up to protect his face.

Instinctively Gwin reached out to him, and then she drew back. She couldn't reach his emotions. There was no perception. There was no way she could enter his dreams and rearrange them and comfort him.

"Poor devil," his father said again. "He's got his whole life to be lonely in."

*   *   *   *   *

The summer passed, and another winter and another summer. Eric spent more and more time by himself. He liked to sit on the glassed-in sunporch, bouncing his ball up and down and talking to it, aloud, pretending that it answered him back. He liked to lie on his stomach close to the wall and look out at the garden with its riotous mass of flowers and the insects that flew among them. Some flew quickly, their wings moving so fast that they were just blurs. Others flew slowly, swooping on outspread bright-colored wings from petal to petal. He liked these slow-flying ones the best. He could wiggle his shoulder blades in time with their wings and pretend that he was flying too.

Sometimes other children came by on the outside of the wall. He could look out at them without worrying, because they couldn't see him. The wall wasn't transparent from the outside. He liked it when three or four of them came by together, laughing and chasing each other through the garden. Usually, though, they didn't stay long. After they had played a few minutes his father or his mother went out and looked at them, and then they went away.

Eric was playing by himself when the old man came out to the sunporch doorway and stood there, saying nothing, making no effort to interrupt or to speak. He was so quiet that after a while Eric almost didn't mind his being there.

The old man turned back to Myron and Gwin.

"Of course the boy can learn. He's not stupid."

Eric bounced the ball, flung it against the transparent glass, caught it, bounced it again.

"But how, Walden?" Gwin shook her head. "You offer to teach him, but--"

Walden smiled. "Remember *these*?"

... Walden's study. The familiar curtains drawn aside, and the shelves behind them. The rows of bright-backed, box-like objects, most of them old and spotted, quite unhygienic ...

Gwin shook her head at the perception, but Myron nodded.

"Books. I didn't know there were any outside the museums."

Walden smiled again. "Only mine. Books are fascinating things. All the knowledge of a race, gathered together on a few shelves...."

"Knowledge?" Myron shrugged. "Imagine storing knowledge in those--boxes. What are they? What's in them? Just words...."

The books faded as Walden sighed. "You'd be surprised what the old race did, with just those--boxes."

He looked across at Eric, who was now bouncing his ball and counting, out loud, up to three, and then going back and starting again.

"The boy can learn what's in those books. Just as if he'd gone to school back in the old times."

Myron and Gwin looked doubtfully at each other, and then over at the corner where Eric played unheeding. Perhaps Walden could help. Perhaps....

"Eric," Gwin said aloud.

"Yes, mother?"

"We've decided you're going to go to school, the way you want to. Mr. Walden here is going to be your teacher. Isn't that nice?"

Eric looked at her and then at the old man. Strangers didn't often come out on the sunporch. Strangers usually left him alone.

He bounced the ball again without answering.

"Say something, Eric," his mother commanded.

Eric looked back at Walden. "He can't teach me to be like other children, can he?"

"No," Walden said. "I can't."

"Then I don't want to go to school." Eric threw the ball across the room as hard as he could.

"But there once were other people like *you*," Walden said. "Lots of them. And you can learn about them, if you want to."

"Other people like me? Where?"

Myron and Gwin looked helplessly at each other and at the old man. Gwin began to cry and Myron cursed softly, on the perception level so that Eric wouldn't hear them.

But Walden's face was gentle and understanding as he answered, so understanding that Eric couldn't help wanting desperately to believe him.

"Everyone was like you once," Walden said. "A long time ago."

*   *   *   *   *

It was a new life for Eric. Every day he would go over to Walden's and the two of them would pull back the curtains in the study and Walden would lift down some of the books. It was as if Walden was giving him the past, all of it, as fast as he could grasp it.

"I'm really like the old race, Walden?"

"Yes, Eric. You'll see just how much like them...."

Identity. Here in the past, in the books he was learning to read, in the pictures, the pages and pages of scenes and portraits. Strange scenes, far removed from the gardens and the quiet houses and the wordless smile of friend to friend.

Great buildings and small. The Parthenon in the moonlight, not too many pages beyond the cave, with its smoky fire and first crude wall drawings. Cities bright with a million neon lights, and still later, caves again--the underground stations of the Moon colonies. All unreal, and yet--

They were his people, these men in the pictures. Strange men, violent men: the barbarian trampling his enemy to death beneath his horse's hooves, the knight in armor marching to the Crusade, the spaceman. And the quieter men: the farmer, the artisan, the poet--they too were his people, and far easier to understand than the others.

The skill of reading mastered, and the long, sweeping vistas of the past. Their histories. Their wars. "Why did they fight, Walden?" And Walden's sigh. "I don't know, Eric, but they did."

So much to learn. So much to understand. Their art and music and literature and religion. Patterns of life that ebbed and flowed and ebbed again, but never in quite the same way. "Why did they change so much, Walden?" And the answer, "You probably know that better than I, Eric...."

Perhaps he did. For he went on to the books that Walden ignored. Their mathematics, their science. The apple's fall, and the orbits of planets. The sudden spiral of analysis, theory, technology. The machines--steamships, airplanes, spaceships....

And the searching loneliness that carried the old race from the caves of Earth to the stars. The searching, common to the violent man and the quiet man, to the doer and the dreaming poet.

Why do we hunger, who own the Moon and trample the shifting dust   of Mars?

Why aren't we content with the worlds we've won? Why don't we   rest, with the system ours?

We have cast off the planets like outgrown toys, and now we want   the stars....

"Have you ever been to the stars, Walden?"

Walden stared at him. Then he laughed. "Of course not, Eric. Nobody goes there now. None of our race has ever gone. Why should we?"

There was no explaining. Walden had never been lonely.

And then one day, while he was reading some fiction from the middle period of the race, Eric found the fantasy. Speculation about the future, about their future.... About the new race!

He read on, his heart pounding, until the same old pattern came clear. They had foreseen conflict, struggle between old race and new, suspicion and hatred and tragedy. The happy ending was superficial. Everyone was motivated as they had been motivated.

He shut the book and sat there, wanting to reach back across the years to the old race writers who had been so right and yet so terribly, blindly wrong. The writers who had seen in the new only a continuation of the old, of themselves, of their own fears and their own hungers.

"Why did they die, Walden?" He didn't expect an answer.

"Why does any race die, Eric?"

His own people, forever removed from him, linked to him only through the books, the pictures, and his own backward-reaching emotions.

"Walden, hasn't there *ever* been anyone else like me, since they died?"

Silence. Then, slowly, Walden nodded.

"I wondered how long it would be before you asked that. Yes, there have been others. Sometimes three or four in a generation."

"Then, perhaps...."

"No," Walden said. "There aren't any others now. We'd know it if there were." He turned away from Eric, to the plastic wall that looked out across the garden and the children playing and the long, level, flower-carpeted plain.

"Sometimes, when there's more than one of them, they go out there away from us, out to the hills where it's wild. But they're found, of course. Found, and brought back." He sighed. "The last of them died when I was a boy."

Others like him. Within Walden's lifetime, others, cut off from their own race, lonely and rootless in the midst of the new. Others like him, but not now, in his lifetime. For him there were only the books.

The old race was gone, gone with all its conflicts, all its violence, its stupidity--and its flaming rockets in the void and its Parthenon in the moonlight.

*   *   *   *   *

Eric came into the study and stopped. The room was filled with strangers. There were half a dozen men besides Walden, most of them fairly old, white-haired and studious looking. They all turned to look at him, watched him gravely without speaking.

"Well, there he is." Walden looked from face to face. "Are you still worried? Do you still think that one small boy constitutes a threat to the race? What about you, Abbot?"

"I don't know. I still think he should have been institutionalized in the beginning."

"Why? So you could study the brain processes of the lower animals?" Walden's thoughts were as sarcastic as he could send them.

"No, of course not. But don't you see what you've done, by teaching him to read? You've started him thinking of the old race. Don't deny it."

"I don't."

The thin man, Drew, broke in angrily. "He's not full grown yet. Just fourteen, isn't he? How can you be sure what he'll be like later? He'll be a problem. They've always been problems."

They were afraid. That was what was the matter with them. Walden sighed. "Tell them what you've been studying, Eric," he said aloud.

For a minute Eric was too tongue-tied to answer. He stood motionless, waiting for them to laugh at him.

"Go on. Tell them."

"I've been reading about the old race," Eric said. "All about the stars. About the people who went off in the starships and explored our whole galaxy."

"What's a galaxy?" the thin man said. Walden could perceive that he really didn't know.

Eric's fear lessened. These men weren't laughing at him. They weren't being just polite, either. They were interested. He smiled at them, shyly, and told them about the books and the wonderful, strange tales of the past that the books told. The men listened, nodding from time to time. But he knew that they didn't understand. The world of the books was his alone....

"Well?" Walden looked at the others. They looked back. Their emotions were a welter of doubt, of indecision.

"You've heard the boy," Walden said quietly, thrusting his own uneasiness down, out of his thoughts.

"Yes." Abbot hesitated. "He seems bright enough--quite different from what I'd expected. At least he's not like the ones who grew up wild in the hills. This boy isn't a savage."

Walden shrugged. "Maybe they weren't savages either," he suggested. "After all, it's been fifty years since the last of them died. And a lot of legends can spring up in fifty years."

"Perhaps we have been worrying unnecessarily." Abbot got up to go, but his eyes still held Walden's. "But," he added, "it's up to you to watch him. If he reverts, becomes dangerous in any way, he'll have to be locked up. That's final."

The others nodded.

"I'll watch him," Walden told them. "Just stop worrying."

He stood at the door and waited until they were out of sight. Then and only then did he allow himself to sigh and taste the fear he'd kept hidden. The old men, the men with authority, were the dangerous ones.

Walden snorted. Even with perception, men could be fools.

*   *   *   *   *

The summer that Eric was sixteen Walden took him to the museum. The aircar made the trip in just a few hours--but it was farther than Eric had ever traveled in his life, and farther than most people ever bothered traveling.

The museum lay on an open plain where there weren't many houses. At first glance it was far from impressive. Just a few big buildings, housing the artifacts, and a few old ruins of ancient constructions, leveled now and half buried in the sands.

"It's nothing." Eric looked down at it, disappointed. "Nothing at all."

"What did you expect?" Walden set the aircar down between the two largest buildings. "You knew it wouldn't be like the pictures in the books. You knew that none of the old race's cities are left."

"I know," Eric said. "But I expected more than this."

He got out of the car and followed Walden around to the door of the first building. Another man, almost as old as Walden, came toward them smiling. The two men shook hands and stood happily perceiving each other.

"This is Eric," Walden said aloud. "Eric, this is Prior, the caretaker here. He was one of my schoolmates."

"It's been years since we've perceived short range," Prior said. "Years. But I suppose the boy wants to look around inside?"

Eric nodded, although he didn't care too much. He was too disappointed to care. There was nothing here that he hadn't seen a hundred times before.

They went inside, past some scale models of the old cities. The same models, though a bit bigger, that Eric had seen in the three-dimensional view-books. Then they went into another room, lined with thousands of books, some very old, many the tiny microfilmed ones from the middle periods of the old race.

"How do you like it, Eric?" the caretaker said.

"It's fine," he said flatly, not really meaning it. He was angry at himself for feeling disappointment. Walden had told him what to expect. And yet he'd kept thinking that he'd walk into one of the old cities and be able to imagine that it was ten thousand years ago and others were around him. Others like him....

Ruins. Ruins covered by dirt, and no one of the present race would even bother about uncovering them.

Prior and Walden looked at each other and smiled. "Did you tell him?" the caretaker telepathed.

"No. I thought we'd surprise him. I knew all the rest would disappoint him."

"Eric," the caretaker said aloud. "Come this way. There's another room I want to show you."

He followed them downstairs, down a long winding ramp that spiraled underground so far that he lost track of the distance they had descended. He didn't much care anyway. Ahead of him, the other two were communicating, leaving him alone.

"Through here," Prior said, stepping off the ramp.

They entered a room that was like the bottom of a well, with smooth stone sides and far, far above them a glass roof, with clouds apparently drifting across its surface. But it wasn't a well. It was a vault, forever preserving the thing that had been the old race's masterpiece.

It rested in the center of the room, its nose pointing up at the sky. It was like the pictures, and unlike them. It was big, far bigger than Eric had ever visualized it. It was tall and smooth and as new looking as if its builders had just stepped outside for a minute and would be back in another minute to blast off for the stars.

"A starship," Walden said. "One of the last types."

"There aren't many left," Prior said. "We're lucky to have this one in our museum."

Eric wasn't listening. He was looking at the ship. The old race's ship. His ship.

"The old race built strange things," Prior said. "This is one of the strangest." He shook his head. "Imagine the time they put in on it.... And for what?"

Eric didn't try to answer him. He couldn't explain why the old ones had built it. But he knew. He would have built it himself, if he'd lived then. *We have cast off the planets like outgrown toys, and now we want the stars....*

His people. His ship. His dream.

                    *   *   *   *   *

The old caretaker showed him around the museum and then left him alone to explore by himself. He had all the time he wanted.

He studied. He worked hard all day long, scarcely ever leaving the museum grounds. He studied the subjects that now were the most fascinating to him of all the old race's knowledge-- the subjects that related to the starships. Astronomy, physics, navigation, and the complex charts of distant stars, distant planets, worlds he'd never heard of before. Worlds that to the new race were only pin-pricks of light in the night sky.

All day long he studied. But in the evening he would go down the winding ramp to the ship. The well was lighted with a softer, more diffuse illumination than that of the houses. In the soft glow the walls and the glass-domed roof seemed to disappear and the ship looked free, pointing up at the stars.

He didn't try to tell the caretaker what he thought. He just went back to his books and his studies. There was so much he had to learn. And now there was a reason for his learning. Someday, when he was fully grown and strong and had mastered all he needed from the books, he was going to fly the ship. He was going to look for his people, the ones who had left Earth before the new race came....

He told no one. But Walden watched him, and sighed.

"They'll never let you do it, Eric. It's a mad dream."

"What are you talking about?"

"The ship. You want to go to the stars, don't you?"

Eric stared at him, more surprised than he'd been in years. He had said nothing. There was no way for Walden to know. Unless he'd perceived it--and Eric couldn't be perceived, any more than he could perceive other people....

Walden shook his head. "It wasn't telepathy that told me. It was your eyes. The way you look at the ship. And besides, I've known you for years now. And I've wondered how long it would be before you thought of this answer."

"Well, why not?" Eric looked across at the ship, and his throat caught, choking him, the way it always did. "I'm lonely here. My people are gone. Why shouldn't I go?"

"You'd be lonelier inside that ship, by yourself, away from Earth, away from everything, and with no assurance you'd ever find anyone at all, old race or new or alien...."

Eric didn't answer. He looked back at the ship, thinking of the books, trying to think of it as a prison, a weightless prison carrying him forever into the unknown, with no one to talk to, no one to see.

Walden was right. He would be too much alone in the ship. He'd have to postpone his dream.

He'd wait until he was old, and take the ship and die in it....

Eric smiled at the thought. He was seventeen, old enough to know that his idea was adolescent and melodramatic. He knew, suddenly, that he'd never fly the ship.

*　　*　　*　　*　　*

The years passed. Eric spent most of his time at the museum. He had his own aircar now, and sometimes he flew it home and visited with his parents. They liked to have him come. They liked it much better than having to travel all the way to the museum to visit him.

Yet, though he wasn't dependent on other people any more, and could fly the aircar as he chose, he didn't do much exploring. He didn't have any desire to meet strangers. And there were always the books.

"You're sure you're all right?" his mother said. "You don't need anything?"

"No. I'm fine."

He smiled, looking out through the sunporch wall into the garden. It seemed years and years since he'd pressed his nose to the glass, watching the butterflies. It had been a long time.

"I've got to get going," he said. "I want to be back at the museum by dark."

"Well, if you're sure you won't stay...."

They said goodbye and he went out and got into the aircar and started back. He flew slowly, close to the ground, because he really had plenty of time and he felt lazy. He skimmed along over a valley and heard laughter and dipped lower. A group of children was playing. Young ones--they even talked aloud sometimes as they played. Children.... There were so many children, always in groups, laughing....

He flew on, quickly, until he was in a part of the country where he didn't see any houses. Just a stream and a grove of trees and bright flowers. He dropped lower, stopped, got out and walked down to the stream.

It was by another stream that he'd met the children who had laughed at him, years ago. He smiled, sadly.

He felt alone, but in a different sense from his usual isolation. He felt free, away from people, away even from the books and their unspoken insistence that their writers were dead and almost forgotten. He stood by the edge of the stream, watching water spiders scoot across the rippled surface.

This was the same. This stream had probably been here when the old race was here, maybe even before the old race had even come into existence.

Water spiders. Compared to man, their race was immortal....

The sun was low when he turned away from the stream and walked back to where he had parked the aircar. He scarcely looked about him as he walked. He was sure he was alone, and he felt no caution, no need to watch and listen.

But as he turned toward the car he saw the people. Two. Young, about his own age. A boy and a girl, smiling at each other, holding hands.

They weren't a dozen feet in front of him. But they didn't notice him. They were conscious of no one but each other. As Eric watched, standing frozen, unwilling to draw attention to himself by even moving or backing up, the two leaned closer together. Their arms went around each other, tightly, and they kissed.

They said nothing. They kissed, and then stood apart and went on looking at each other. Even without being able to perceive, Eric could feel their emotion.

Then they turned, slowly, toward him. In a moment they would be aware of him. He didn't want them to think he was spying on them, so he went toward them, making no effort to be quiet, and as he moved they stepped still farther apart and looked at him, startled.

They looked at each other as he passed, even more startled, and the girl's hand went up to her mouth in surprise.

They know, Eric thought bitterly. They know I'm different.

He didn't want to go back to the museum. He flew blindly, not looking down at the neat domed houses and the gardens and the people, but ahead, to the eastern sky and the upthrust scarp of the hills. The hills, where people like him had fled, for a little while.

The occasional aircars disappeared. The gardens dropped away, and the ordered color, and there was grass and bare dirt and, ahead, the scraggly trees and out-thrust rocks of the foothills. No people. Only the birds circling, crying to each other, curious about the car. Only the scurrying animals of the underbrush below.

A little of the tension drained from him as he climbed. Perhaps in these very hills men like him had walked, not many generations ago. Perhaps they would walk there again, amid the disorder of tree and canyon and tumbled rock. Amid the wildness, the beauty that was neither that of the gardens nor that of the old race's cities, but older, more enduring than either.

Below him were other streams, but these were swift-flowing, violent, sparkling like prismed sunlight as they cascaded over the rocks. Their wildness called to him, soothed him as the starship soothed him, as the gardens and the neat domed houses never could.

He knew why his kind had fled to the hills, for whatever little time they had. He knew too that he would come again.

Searching. Looking for his own kind.

That was what he was doing. That was what he had always intended to do, ever since he had heard of the others like

himself, the men who had come here before him. He realized his
motive suddenly, and realized too the futility of it. But futile or
not, he would come again.

For he was of the old race. He shared their hungering.

*   *   *   *   *

Walden was reading in his study when the council members
arrived. They came without advance warning and filed in
ceremoniously, responding rather coolly to his greeting.

"We're here about the boy," Abbot began abruptly. "He's at
the museum now, isn't he?"

Walden nodded. "He's been spending most of his time there
lately."

"Do you think it's wise, letting him wander around alone?"

Trouble. Always trouble. Just because there was one young
boy, Eric, asking only to be let alone. And the old council
members wouldn't rest until they had managed to find an excuse
to put him in an institution somewhere, where his actions could
be watched, where there wouldn't be any more uncertainty.

"Eric's all right."

"Is he? Prior tells me he leaves the museum every day. He
doesn't come here. He doesn't visit his family."

The thin man, Drew, broke in. "He goes to the hills. Just like
the others did. Did you know that, Walden?"

Walden's mouth tightened. It wouldn't do to let them read
his hostility to their prying. It would be even worse to let them
know that they worried him.

"Besides," Drew added, "he's old enough to be thinking about
women now. There's always a chance he'll--"

"Are you crazy?" Walden shouted the words aloud. "Eric's not
an animal."

"Isn't he?" Abbot answered quietly. "Weren't all the old race
just animals?"

Walden turned away from them, closing his mind to their
thoughts. He mustn't show anger. If he did, they'd probably
decide he was too emotional, not to be trusted. They'd take Eric
away, to some institution. Cage him....

"What do you want to do with the boy?" Walden forced his thoughts to come quietly. "Do you want to put him in a zoo with the other animals?"

The sarcasm hurt them. They wanted to be fair. Abbot especially prided himself on his fairness.

"Of course not."

They hesitated. They weren't going to do anything. Not this time. They stood around and made a little polite conversation, about other things, and then Abbot turned toward the door.

"We just wanted to be sure you knew what was going on." Abbot paused. "You'll keep an eye on the boy, won't you?"

"Am I his keeper?" Walden asked softly.

They didn't answer him. Their thoughts were confused and a bit irritated as they went out to the aircar that had brought them. But he knew they'd be back. And they would keep track of Eric. Prior, the caretaker, would help them. Prior was old too, and worried....

Walden walked back into his study, slowly. His legs were trembling. He hadn't realized how upset he had been. He smiled at the intensity of his emotions, realizing something he'd always kept hidden, even from himself.

He was as fond of Eric as if the boy had been his own son.

*   *   *   *   *

Eric pushed the books away, impatiently. He didn't feel like studying. The equations were meaningless. He was tired of books, and history, and all the facts about the old race.

He wanted to be outdoors, exploring, walking along the hillsides, looking for his own kind.

But he had already explored the hills. He had flown for miles, and walked for miles, and searched dozens of caves in dozens of gorges. He had found no one. He was sure that if there had been anyone he would have discovered some sign.

He opened the book again, but he couldn't concentrate on it.

Beyond those hills, across another valley, there were even higher mountains. He had often looked across at them, wondering what they held. They were probably as desolate as the ones he'd searched. Still, he would rather be out in them, looking, than sitting here, fretting, almost hating the old race because it had somehow bequeathed him a heritage of loneliness.

He got up abruptly and went outside to the aircar.

It was a long way to the second range of mountains. He flew there directly, skimming over the nearer hills, the ones he had spent weeks exploring. He dropped low over the intervening valley, passing over the houses and towns, looking down at the gardens. The new race filled all the valleys.

He came into the foothills and swung the car upward, climbing over the steep mountainsides. Within a mile from the valley's edge he was in wild country. He'd thought the other hills were wild, but here the terrain was jagged and rock-strewn, with boulders flung about as if by some giant hand. There were a hundred narrow canyons, opening into each other, steep-sloped, overgrown with brambles and almost impenetrable, a maze with the hills rising around them and cutting off all view of the surrounding country.

Eric dropped down into one of the larger canyons. Immediately he realized how easy it would be to get lost in those hills. There were no landmarks that were not like a hundred jutting others. Without the aircar he would be lost in a few minutes. He wondered suddenly if anyone, old race or new, had ever been here before him.

He set the aircar down on the valley floor and got out and walked away from it, upstream, following the little creek that tumbled past him over the rocks. By the time he had gone a hundred paces the car was out of sight.

It was quiet. Far away birds called to each other, and insects buzzed around him, but other than these sounds there was nothing but his own footsteps and the creek rapids. He relaxed, walking more slowly, looking about him idly, no longer searching for anything.

He rounded another bend, climbed up over a rock that blocked his path and dropped down on the other side of it. Then he froze, staring.

Not ten feet ahead of him lay the ashes of a campfire, still smoldering, still sending a thin wisp of smoke up into the air.

He saw no one. Nothing moved. No tracks showed in the rocky ground. Except for the fire, the gorge looked as uninhabited as any of the others.

Slowly Eric walked toward the campfire and knelt down and held his hand over the embers. Heat rose about him. The fire hadn't been out for very long.

He turned quickly, glancing about him, but there was no sudden motion anywhere, no indication that anyone was hiding nearby. Perhaps there was nobody near. Perhaps whoever had built the fire had left it some time before, and was miles away by now....

He didn't think so. He had a feeling that eyes were watching him. It was a strange feeling, almost as if he could perceive. Wishful thinking, he told himself. Unreal, untrue....

But *someone* had been here. Someone had built the fire. And it was probably, almost certainly, someone without perception. Someone like himself.

His knees were shaking. His hands trembled, and sweat broke out on the palms. Yet his thoughts seemed calm, icily calm. It was just a nervous reaction, he knew that. A reaction to the sudden knowledge that people *were* here, out in these hills where he had searched for them but never, deep down, expected to find them. They were probably watching him right now, hidden up among the trees somewhere, afraid to move because then he would see them and start out to capture them.

If there were people here, they must think that he was one of the normal ones. That he could perceive. So they would keep quiet, because a person with perception couldn't possibly perceive a person who lacked it. They would remain motionless, hoping to stay hidden, waiting for him to leave so that they could flee deeper into the hills.

They couldn't know that he was one of them.

He felt helpless, suddenly. So near, so near--and yet he couldn't reach them. The people who lived here in the wild mountain gorges could elude him forever.

No motion. No sound. Only the embers, smoking....

"Listen," he called aloud. "Can you hear me?"

The canyon walls caught his voice, sent it echoing back, fainter and fainter. "... can you hear me can you hear me can you...."

No one answered.

"I'm your friend," he called. "I can't perceive. I'm one of you."

Over and over it echoed. "... one of you one of you one of you...."

"Answer me. I've run away from them too. Answer me!"

"Answer me answer me answer me...."

The echoes died away and it was quiet, too quiet. No sound. Even if they heard him, they wouldn't answer.

He couldn't track them. If they had homes that were easy to find they would have left them by now. He was helpless.

The heat from the fire rose about him, and he tasted smoke and coughed. Nothing moved. Finally he stood up, turned away from the fire and walked on past it, up the stream.

No one. No tracks. No sign. Only the feeling that other eyes watched him as he walked along, other ears listened for the sound of his passing.

He turned back, retraced his steps to the fire. The embers had blackened. The wisp of smoke that curled upward was very thin now. Otherwise everything was the same as it had been.

He couldn't give up and fly back to the museum. If he did he might never find them again. But even if he didn't, he might never find them.

"Listen!" He screamed the word, so loudly that they could have heard it miles away. "I'm one of you. I can't perceive. Believe me! You've got to believe me!"

"Believe me believe me believe me...."

Nothing. The tension went out of him suddenly and he began to tremble again, and his throat choked up, wanting to cry. He stumbled away from the embers, back in the direction of the aircar.

"Believe me...." This time the words were little more than a whisper, and there was no echo.

"I believe you," a voice said quietly.

*   *   *   *   *

He swung about, trying to place it, and saw the woman. She stood at the edge of the trees, above the campfire, half hidden in the undergrowth. She looked down at him warily, a rock clenched in her hand. She wasn't an attractive sight.

Illustration]

She looked old, with a leathery skin and gnarled arms and legs. Her grey-white hair was matted, pulled back into a snarled bun behind her head. She wore a shapeless dress of some roughwoven material that hung limply from her shoulders, torn, dirty, ancient. He'd never seen an animal as dirty as she.

"So you can't perceive," the woman cackled. "I believe it, boy. You don't have that look about you."

"I didn't know," Eric said softly. "I never knew until today that there were any others."

She laughed, a high-pitched laugh that broke off into a choking cough. "There aren't many of us, boy. Not many. Me and Nell--but she's an old, old woman. And Lisa, of course...."

She cackled again, nodding. "I always told Lisa to wait," she said firmly. "I told her that there'd be another young one along."

"Who are you?" Eric said.

"Me? Call me Mag. Come on, boy. Come on. What are you waiting for?"

She turned and started off up the hill, walking so fast that she was almost out of sight among the trees before Eric recovered enough to follow her. He stumbled after her, clawing his way up the steep slope, slipping and grabbing the branches with his hands and hauling himself up the rocks.

"You're a slow one." The old woman paused and waited for him to catch up. "Where've you been all your life? You don't act like a mountain boy."

"I'm not," Eric said. "I'm from the valley...."

He stopped talking. He realized, suddenly, the futility of trying to explain his life to her. If she had ever known the towns, it would have been years ago. She was too old, and tattered, and so dirty that her smell wasn't even a good clean animal smell.

"Hurry up, boy!"

He felt unreal, as if this were a dream, as if he would awaken suddenly and be back at the museum. He almost wished that he would. He couldn't believe that he had found another like himself and was now following her, scrambling up a mountain as if he were a goat.

A goat. Smells. The dirty old woman in front of him. He wrinkled his nose in disgust and then was furious with himself, with his reactions, with the sudden knowledge that he had glamorized his kind and had hoped to find them noble and brilliant.

This tattered old woman with her cackling laugh and leathery, toothless face and dirt encrusted clothing couldn't be like him. He couldn't accept it....

Mag led him up the slope and then over some heaped boulders, and suddenly they were on level ground again. They had come out into a tiny canyon, a blind pocket recessed into the mountain, almost completely surrounded by walls that rose sharply upward. Back across the gorge, huddled against the face of the mountain, was a tiny hut.

It was primitive, like those in the prehistoric sections of the old history books. It was made of branches lashed together, with sides that leaned crookedly against each other and a matted roof that looked as if it would slide off at any minute. It was like a twig house that a child might make with sticks and grass.

"Our home," Mag said. Her voice was proud.

He didn't answer. He followed her across toward it, past the mounds of refuse, the fruit rinds and bones and skins that were flung carelessly beside the trail. He smelled the scent of decay and rottenness and turned his head away, feeling sick.

"Lisa! Lisa!" Mag shouted, the words echoing and re-echoing.

A figure moved just inside the hut doorway. "She's not here," a voice called. "She's out hunting."

"Well, come on out, Nell, and see what I've found."

The figure moved slowly out from the gloom of the hut, bending to get through the low door, half straightening up outside, and Eric saw that it was an old, old woman. She couldn't straighten very far. She was too old, bent and twisted and brittle, feebler looking than anyone Eric had ever seen before. She hobbled toward him slowly, teetering from side to side as she walked, her hands held out in front of her, her eyes on the ground.

"What is it, Mag?" Her voice was as twisted as her body.

"A boy. Valley boy. Just the age for our Lisa, too."

Eric felt his face redden and he opened his mouth to protest, to say something, anything, but Mag went right on talking, ignoring him.

"The boy came in an aircar. I thought he was one of the normals--but he's not. Hasn't their ways. Good looking boy, too."

"Is he?" Nell had reached them. She stopped and looked up, right into Eric's face, and for the first time he realized that she was blind. Her eyes were milky white, without pupils, without irises. Against the brown leather of her skin they looked moist and dead.

"Speak, boy," she croaked. "Let me hear your voice."

"Hello," Eric said, feeling utterly foolish and utterly confused. "I'm Eric."

"Eric...." Nell reached out, touched his arm with her hand, ran her fingers up over his shoulders, over his chest.

"It's been a long time since I've heard a man's voice," she said. "Not since Mag here was a little girl."

"Have you been--here--all that time?" Eric asked, looking around him at the hut, and the meat hanging to dry, covered with flies, and the leather water bags, and the mounds of refuse, the huge, heaped mounds that he couldn't stop smelling.

"Yes," Nell said. "I've been here longer than I want to remember, boy. We came here from the other mountains when Mag was only a baby."

*   *   *   *   *

They walked toward the hut, and as they neared it he smelled a new smell, that of stale smoke and stale sweat overlying the general odor of decay.

"Let's talk out here," he said, not wanting to go inside.

They sat down on the hard earth and the two women turned their faces toward him, Mag watching him intently, Nell listening, her head cocked to one side like an old crippled bird's.

"I always thought I was the only one like me," Eric said. "The people don't know of any others. They don't know you exist. They wouldn't believe it."

"That's the way we want it," Mag said. "That's the only way it can be."

Nell nodded. "I was a girl in the other hills," she said, nodding toward the west, toward the museum. "There were several of us then. There had been families of us in my father's time, and in his father's time, and maybe before that even. But when I was a girl there was only my father and my mother and another wife of my father's, and a lot of children...."

She paused, still looking toward the west, facing a horizon she could no longer see. "The normal ones came. We'd hidden from them before. But this time we had no chance to hide. I was hunting, with the boy who was my father's nephew.

"They surrounded the hut. They didn't make any sound. They don't have to. I was in the forest when I heard my mother scream."

"Did they kill her?" Eric cried out. "They wouldn't do that."

"No, they didn't kill any of them. They dragged them off to the aircars, all of them. My father, my mother and the other woman, the children. We watched from the trees and saw them dragged off, tied with ropes, like wild animals. The cars flew away. Our people never came back."

She stopped, sunken in revery. Mag took up the story. Her voice was matter-of-fact, completely casual about those long ago events.

"A bear killed my father. That was after we came back here. Nell was sick. I did the hunting. We almost starved, for a while, but there's lots of game in the hills. It's a good life here. But I've been sorry for Lisa. She's a woman now. She needs a man. I'm glad you came. I would have hated to send her out looking for a normal one."

"But--" Eric stopped, his head whirling. He didn't know what to say. Anything at all would sound wrong, cruel.

"It's dangerous," Mag went on, "taking up with the normals. They think it's wrong. They think we're animals. One of us has to pick a man who's stupid--a farmer, maybe--and even then it's like being a pet. A beast."

It took a moment for Eric to realize what she was saying, and when he did realize, the thought horrified him.

"Lisa's father was stupid," Mag said. "He took me in when I came down from the hills. He didn't send for the others. Not then. He kept me and fed me and treated me kindly, and I thought I was safe. I thought our kind and theirs could live together."

She laughed. Deep, bitter lines creased her mouth. "A week later the aircar came. They sneaked up to the garden where I was. He was with them. He was leading them."

She laughed again. "Their kindness means nothing. Their love means nothing. To them, we're animals."

The old woman, Nell, rocked back and forth, her face still in revery. Flies crawled over her bare arms, unheeded.

"I got away," Mag said. "I saw them coming. They can't run fast, and I knew the hiding places. I never went back to the valleys. Nell would have starved without me. And there was Lisa to care for, later...."

The flies settled on Eric's hands and he brushed them away, shivering.

Mag smiled. The bitterness left her face. "I'm glad I don't have to send Lisa down to the valley."

She got up before he could answer, before he could even think of anything to say or do. Crossing over to the pole where the dried meat hung, she pulled a piece of it loose and brought it back to where they sat. Some she gave to the old woman and some she kept for herself and the rest, most of it, she tossed to Eric.

"You must be hungry, boy."

It was filthy. Dirt clung to it--dust and pollen and grime--and the flies had flown off in clouds when she lifted it down.

The old woman raised her piece and put the edge of it in her mouth and started to chew, slowly, eating her way up the strip. Mag tore hers with her teeth, rending it and swallowing it quickly, watching Eric all the time.

"Eat."

It was unreal. He couldn't be here. These women couldn't exist.

He lifted the meat, feeling his stomach knot with disgust, wanting to fling it from him and run, blindly, down the hill to the aircar. But he didn't. He had searched too long to flee now. Shuddering, he closed his mind to the flies and the smell and the filth and bit into the meat and chewed it and swallowed it. And all the time, Mag watched him.

The sun passed overhead and began to dip toward the west. The shadows, which had shortened as they sat in front of the hut, lengthened again, until they themselves were half in the shadow of the trees lining the gorge. Still Lisa did not come. It was very quiet. The only sounds that broke the silence were their own voices and the buzzing of the flies.

They talked, but communication was difficult between them. Eric tried to accept their ideas, their way of life, but he couldn't. The things they said were strange to him. Their whole pattern of life was strange to him. He could understand it at all only because he had studied the primitive peoples of the old race. But he couldn't imagine himself as one of them. He couldn't think of himself as having grown up among them, in the hills, living only to hunt and gather berries and store food for the wintertime. He couldn't think of himself hiding, creeping through the gorges like a hunted animal, flattening himself in the underbrush whenever an aircar passed by.

He sat and listened to them talk, and his amazement grew. Their beliefs were so different. He listened to their superstitious accounts of the old race, and the way it had been "in the beginning."

He listened to their legends of the old gods who flew through the air and were a mighty people, but who were destroyed by a new race of devils. He listened as they told him of their own ancestors, children of the gods, who had fled to the hills to await the gods' return. They had no conception at all of the thousands of years that had elapsed between the old race's passing and their own forefathers' flight into the hills. And when he tried to explain, they shook their heads and wouldn't believe him.

He didn't hear Lisa come. One minute the far end of the clearing was empty and still and the next minute the girl was walking across it toward them, a bow in one hand and a pair of rabbits dangling from the other.

She saw him and stopped, the rabbits dropping from her hand.

"Here's your young man, Lisa," Mag said. "Valley boy. His name's Eric."

He stared back at her, more in curiosity than in surprise. She wasn't nearly as unattractive as he had thought she would be. She wouldn't be bad looking at all, he thought, if she were clean. She was fairly tall and lean, too skinny really, with thin muscular arms instead of the softly rounded arms the valley girls had. She was too brown, but her skin hadn't turned leathery yet, and there was still a little life in the lank brown hair that fell matted about her shoulders.

"Hello, Lisa," he said.

"Hello." Her eyes never left him. She stared at him, her lips trembling, her whole body tensed. She looked as if she were going to turn and run at any moment, as if only his quietness kept her from fleeing.

With a sudden shock Eric realized that she too was afraid-- afraid of him. His own hesitation fell away and he smiled at her.

Mag got up and went over to the girl and put her arm around Lisa's shoulders. "Don't be afraid of him, child," Mag said. "He's a nice boy. Not like one of *them*."

Lisa trembled.

Eric watched her, pitying her. She was as helpless as he before the calm assumption of the older women. More helpless, because she had probably never thought of defying them, of escaping the pattern of their lives.

"Don't worry, Lisa," he said. "I won't hurt you."

Slowly she walked toward him, poised, waiting for a hostile move. She came within a few feet of him and then sank to her haunches, still watching him, still poised.

She was as savage as the others. A graceful, dirty savage.

"You're really one of us?" she said. "You can't perceive?"

"No," he said. "I can't perceive."

"He's not like them," Mag said flatly. "If you'd ever been among them, you'd know their ways."

"I've never seen a man before, up close," Lisa said.

Her eyes pleaded with him, and suddenly he knew why he pitied her. It was because she felt helpless before him, and begged him not to harm her, and thought of him as something above her, more powerful than she, and dangerous. He looked across at her and felt protective, and it was a new feeling to him, absolutely new. Because always before, around the normals, even around his own parents and Walden, he had been the helpless one.

He liked this new feeling, and wished it could last. But it couldn't. He couldn't do as the old women expected him to, leave the valley and his parents, leave the books and the museum and the ship, just to hide in the hills like a beast with them.

He had come to find his people, but these three were not they.

"You two go on off and talk," Mag said. "We're old. We don't matter now. You've got things to settle between you."

She cackled again and got up and went into the hut and old Nell got up also and followed her.

The girl shivered. She drew back a little, away from him. Her eyes never left his face.

"Don't be afraid, Lisa," he said gently. "I won't hurt you. I won't even touch you. But I would like to talk to you."

"All right," she said.

They got up and walked to the end of the gorge, the girl keeping always a few feet from him. At the boulders she stopped and faced him, her back against a rock, her thin body still trembling.

"Lisa," he said. "I want to be your friend."

Her eyes widened. "How can you?" she said. "Men are friends. Women are friends. But you're a man and I'm a woman and it's different."

He shook his head helplessly, trying to think of a way to explain things to her. He couldn't say that he found her dirty and unattractive and almost another species. He couldn't say that he'd searched the hills, often thinking of the relationship between man and woman, but that she wasn't the woman, that she never could be the woman for him. He couldn't tell her that he pitied her in perhaps the same way that the normals pitied him.

Still, he wanted to talk to her. He wanted to be her friend. Because he was sure now that he could search the mountains forever, and perhaps find other people, even if those he found were like her, and Mag and Nell.

"Listen, Lisa," he said. "I can't live up here. I live in the valley. I came in an aircar, and it's down in the canyon below here. I have to go back--soon. Before it gets completely dark."

"Why?"

"If I don't the normals will come looking for me. They'll find the aircar and then they'll find us. And you and your family will be taken away. Don't you understand?"

"You're going?" Lisa said.

"In a little while. I must."

She looked at him, strangely. She looked at his clothes, at his face, at his body. Then she looked at her own hands and touched her own coarse dress, and she nodded.

"You won't come back," she said. "You don't like me. I'm not what you were searching for."

He couldn't answer. Her words hurt him. The very fact that she could recognize their difference from each other hurt him. He pitied her still more.

"I'll come back," he said, "Of course I will. As often as I can. You're the only other people I've ever known who didn't perceive."

She looked up into his face again. Her eyes were very large. They were the only beautiful thing about her.

"Even if you do come back, you won't want me."

There wasn't any answer at all.

*   *   *   *   *

It was dusk when Eric got back to the museum. He landed the aircar and climbed out and walked across to the building, still feeling unreal, still not believing that the events of this day had actually happened.

He nodded to Prior and the old caretaker nodded back and then stood staring at him, troubled and curious. Eric didn't notice the other's expression, nor the fact that Prior followed him to the top of the spiral ramp and remained there for a while, watching.

Eric stood at the bottom of the well where he had so often stood before, staring across at the ship, then looking up, up, up its sleek length to where its nose pointed yearningly toward the night sky. But tonight he found no comfort in the sight, no sense of kinship with its builders. Tonight the ship was a dead and empty thing.

"*You won't want me--*" Her voice, her eyes, came between him and the stars.

He had thought of finding his people and sharing with them their common heritage from the past, the knowledge of the old race and its thoughts and its science and its philosophy. He had thought of sharing with them the old desire for the stars, the old hunger, the old loneliness that the new race could never understand. He had been wrong.

His people.... He pushed the thought away.

He looked up at the stars that were merely pin-pricks of light at the top of the well and wondered if anyone, old race or new or something different from either, lived among them now. And he felt small, and even the ship was small, and his own problems and his own search were unimportant. He sat down and leaned back against the smooth wall and closed his eyes, blotting out the ship and the stars, and finally, even Lisa's face before him.

The old caretaker found him sleeping there, and sighed, and went away again, still frowning. Eric slept on, unheeding. When he awoke it was late morning and the stars were gone and clouds drifted across the mouth of the well.

There was no answer here. The starship would never fly.

And Eric went back to the mountains.

*   *   *   *   *

It was two weeks later that the councilmen stood facing Walden across the great museum table. They had come together, Abbot and Drew and the others, and they faced him together, frowning. Their thoughts were hidden. Walden could catch only glimpses of what lay beneath their worry.

"Every day." Abbot's eyes were hard, unyielding. "Why, Walden? Why does he go there every day?"

"Does it matter?"

"Perhaps. Perhaps not. We can't tell--yet."

The ring of faces, of buried perceptions, of fear, anxiety, and a worry that could no longer be shrugged off. And Eric away, as he was every day now, somewhere in the distant hills.

"The boy's all right." Walden checked his own rush of worry.

"Is he?"

The worry in the open now, the fear uncontained, and no more vacillation. Their thoughts hidden from Walden, their plans hidden, and nothing he could do, no way to warn Eric, yet.

Abbot smiled, humorlessly. "The boy had better be all right...."

*   *   *   *   *

Eric landed in the canyon and made sure that the aircar was hidden under a ledge, with branches drawn about it so that no one could spot it from above. Then he turned and started for the slope, and as he reached it Lisa ran down to meet him.

"You're late," she called.

"Am I? Have you really been waiting for me?"

"Of course." She came over to meet him, laughing, openly glad that he had come.

He smiled back at her and walked along beside her, having to take long strides to match her skipping ones, and he too was glad that he'd come. Lately he felt like this every day. It was a feeling he couldn't analyze. Nothing had changed. The girl was still too thin and too brown and too dirty, although now she had begun to wash her dress and her body in the mountain stream and to comb the snarls from her hair. But it didn't make her attractive to him. It only made her less unattractive.

"Will you always have to go away every night?" she asked guilelessly.

"I suppose so."

He looked down at her and smiled, wondering why he came. There was still an air of unreality about the whole situation. He felt numb. He had felt that way ever since the first day, and the feeling had grown, until now he moved and spoke and smiled and ate and it was as if he were someone else and the person he had been was gone completely. He liked coming here. But there was no triumph in being with these people, no sense of having found his own kind, no purpose, nothing but a vague contentment and an unwillingness to search any farther.

"You're very quiet," Lisa said.

"I know. I was thinking."

She reached out and touched his arm, her fingers strong and muscular. He smiled at her but made no move toward her, and after a moment she sighed and took her hand away.

"Why are you so different, Eric?"

"Perhaps because I was raised by the others, the normal ones. Perhaps just because I've read so many books about the old race...."

They came up to the boulders that blocked the entrance of the little gorge where the hut was. Lisa started toward them, then stopped abruptly.

"Let's go on up the hill. I want to talk to you, without them."

"All right."

He followed her without speaking, concentrating all his effort on scrambling over the rougher spots in the trail. She didn't say anything more until they had come out on a high ledge that overlooked the whole canyon and she had sat down and motioned for him to sit down too.

"Whew," he panted. "You're a mountain goat, Lisa."

She didn't smile. "I've liked your coming to see us," she said. "I like to listen to you talk. I like the tales you tell of the old ones. But Mag and Nell are upset."

He knew what was coming. His eyes met hers, and then he looked away and reddened and felt sorry for her and what he would have to tell her. This was a subject they had managed to avoid ever since that first day, although the older women brought it up whenever he saw them.

"Mag says I must have a man," Lisa said. Her voice was tight. He couldn't tell if she was crying because he couldn't bear to look at her. He could only stare out over the canyon and listen and wait.

"She says if it isn't you I'll have to find someone else, later on, but she says it ought to be you. Because *they're* dangerous, and besides, if it's you our children will be sure to be like us."

"What?" He swung around, startled. "Do you mean that if one parent were normal the child might be too?"

"Yes," she said. "It might. They say that's happened. Sometimes. No one knows why we're born. No one knows why some are one way and some another."

"Lisa...." He stopped.

"I know. You don't want me. I've known that all the time."

"It isn't just that."

He tried to find the words to express what he felt, but anything he might say would be cold and cruel and not quite true. He felt the contentment drain out of him, and he felt annoyed, because he didn't want to have to think about her problem, or about anything.

"Why do they want you to have a child?" he said roughly. "Why do they want our kind to go on, living here like animals, or taken to the valleys and separated from each other and put into institutions until we die? Why don't they admit that we've lost, that the normals own the Earth? Why don't they stop breeding and let us die?"

"Your parents were normal, Eric. If all of us died, others would be born, someday."

He nodded and then he closed his eyes and fought against the despair that rose suddenly within him and blotted out the last of the contentment and the unreality. He fought against it and lost. And suddenly Lisa was very real, more real even than the books had ever been. And the dirty old women were suddenly people--individuals, not savages. He tried to pity them, to retreat into his pity and his loneliness, but he couldn't even do that.

The people he had looked for were imaginary. He would never find them, because Mag and Nell and Lisa were his people. They were like him, and the only difference between him and them was one of luck. They were dirty and ignorant. They had been born in the mountains and hunted like beasts. He was more fortunate; he had been born in the valley.

He was a snob. He had looked down on them, when all the time he was one of them. If he had been born among them, he would have been as they were. And, if Lisa had lived in another age, she too would have sought the stars.

Eric sat very still and fought until a little of the turmoil quieted inside of him. Then he opened his eyes again and stared across the canyon, at the rock slides and the trees growing out from the slopes at twisting, precarious angles, and he saw everything in a new light. He saw the old race as it had been far earlier than the age of space-travel, and he knew that it had conquered many environments on Earth before it had gained a chance to try for those of space. He felt humble, suddenly, and proud at the same time.

Lisa sat beside him, not speaking, drawing away from him and letting him be by himself, as if she knew the conflicts within him and knew enough not to interrupt. He was grateful both for her presence there beside him and for her silence.

Much later, when afternoon shadows had crept well out from the rocks, she turned to him. "Will you take me to the valley someday, Eric?"

"Maybe. But no one must know about you. You know what would happen if any of them found out you even existed."

"Yes," she said. "We'd have to be careful, all right. But you could take me for a ride in the aircar sometime and show me things."

Before, he would have shrugged off her words and forgotten them. Now he couldn't. Decision crystalized quickly in his mind.

"Come on, Lisa," he said, getting to his feet and reaching down to help her up also. "I'll take you to the valley right now."

She looked up at him, unable to speak, her eyes shining, and then she was running ahead of him, down the slope toward the aircar.

*   *   *   *   *

The car climbed swiftly away from the valley floor, up between the canyon walls and above them, over the crest of the hills. He circled it for a moment, banking it over on its side so that she could look down at the gorge and the rocks and the cascading stream.

"How do you like it, Lisa?"

"I don't know." She smiled, rather weakly, her body braced against the seat. "It feels so strange."

He smiled back and straightened the car, turning away from the mountains until the great, gardened valley stretched out before them, all the way to the foot of the western hills.

"I'll show you the museum," he said. "I only wish I could take you inside."

She moved away from him, nearer to the window, and looked down at the scattered houses that lay below them, at the people moving in the gardens, at the children.

"I never dreamed it was like this," she said. "I never could picture it before."

There was a longing in her face he'd never noticed before. He stared at her, and she was different suddenly, and her thin muscular body was different too.

Pioneer--that was the word he wanted.

The girls of the new race could never be pioneers.

"Look, Eric. Over there. Aircars."

The words broke in on his thoughts and he looked away from her, following her gaze incuriously, not much interested. And then his fingers stiffened on the controls and the peacefulness fell away from him as if it had never been.

"Lots of them," she said.

Aircars. Eight or ten of them, more than he had ever seen at one time, spread out in a line and flying eastward, straight toward him.

They mustn't see Lisa. They mustn't get close enough to realize who he was.

He swung away from them, perpendicular to their course, angling so that he would be out of perception range, and then he circled, close to the ground, as they swept by, undeviating, purposeful, toward the mountains.

Toward the mountains.

Fear. Sudden, numbing fear and the realization of his own carelessness.

"What's the matter, Eric?"

He had swung about and now followed them, far behind them and off to one side, much too far away for them to try to perceive him. Perhaps, he thought, perhaps they don't know. But all the time he remembered his own trips to the canyon, taken so openly.

"Oh, Eric, they're not--"

He swung up over the last ridge and looked down, and her words choked off in her throat. Below them lay the canyon, and in it, the long line of aircars, landed now, cutting off the gorge, the light reflecting off them, bronze in the sunset. And the tiny figures of men were even now spreading out from the cars.

"What'll we do, Eric?"

Panic. In her voice and in her eyes and in her fingers that bit into his arm, hurting him, steadying him against his own fear and the twisting realization of his betraying lack of caution.

"Run. What else can we do?"

Down back over the ridge, out of sight of the aircars and into the foothills, and all the while knowing that there was nowhere to run to now.

"No, Eric! We've got to go back. We've got to find Mag and Nell--" Her voice rose in anguish, then broke, and she was crying.

"We can't help them by going back," he said harshly. "Maybe they got away. Maybe they didn't. But the others would catch us for sure if they got near us."

Run. It was all they could do, now. Run to other hills and leave the aircar and hide, and live as Lisa had lived, as others of their kind had lived.

"We've got to think of ourselves, Lisa. It's all we can do, now."

Down through the foothills, toward the open valley, and the future, the long blind race to other mountains, and no choice left, no alternative, and the books lost and the starship left behind, forever....

Lisa cried, and her fingers bit into his arm. Ahead of him, too close to flee or deceive, was another line of aircars, flying in from the valley, their formation breaking as they veered toward him.

"Land, Eric. Land and run!"

"We can't, Lisa. There's not enough time."

Everything was lost now--even the hills.

Unless ... one chance. The only chance, and it was nearly hopeless.

"Get in the back, Lisa," he said. "Climb over the seat and hide in that storage compartment. And stay there."

The two nearest cars had swung about now and paralleled his course, flanking him, drifting in nearer and nearer.

"Why?" Lisa clung to him. "What are you going to do?"

"They don't know you're with me. They probably don't even know I went back to the canyon. They think I'll land at the museum, not suspecting anything's wrong. So I'll do just what they expect me to. Go back, and pretend I don't know a thing."

"You're mad."

"It's our only chance, Lisa. If only they don't lock me up tonight...."

She clung to him for still another minute and then she climbed over the seat and he heard the luggage compartment panel slide open and, a moment later, shut.

The nearest aircar drifted still closer to him, escorting him west-ward, toward the museum. Behind him, other cars closed in.

*   *   *   *   *

Walden and Prior were waiting for him at the entrance of the main building, just as they had waited so often before. He greeted them casually, trying to act exactly as he usually did, but their greetings to him were far from casual. They stared at him oddly, Prior even drawing back a little as he approached. Walden looked at him for a long moment, very seriously, as if trying to tell him something, but what it was Eric didn't know. Both men were worried, their anxiety showing in their manner, and Eric wondered if he himself showed the fear that gripped him.

They must know what had happened. By now probably every normal person within a hundred miles of the museum must know.

At the entrance he glanced back idly and saw that one of the aircars that had followed him had landed and that the others were angling off again, leaving. It was too dark to see how many men got out of the car, but Walden and Prior were facing in that direction, communicating, and Eric knew that they knew. Everything.

It was like a trap around him, with each of their minds a strand of the net, and he was unable to see which strands were about to entangle him, unable to see if there were any holes through which he might escape. All he could do was pretend that he didn't even know the net existed, and wait.

Half a dozen men came up to Prior and Walden. One of them was Abbot. His face was very stern, and when he glanced over at where Eric stood in the building entrance his face grew even sterner.

Eric watched them for a moment; then he went inside, the way he usually did when there were lots of people around. He wished he knew what they were saying. He wished he knew what was going to happen.

He went on into the library and pulled out a book at random and sat down and started turning the pages. He couldn't read. He kept waiting for them to come in, for one of them to lay a hand on his shoulder and tell him to come along, that they knew he had found other people like himself and that he was a danger to their race and that they were going to lock him up somewhere.

What would happen to Lisa? They'd find her, of course. She could never escape alone, on foot, to the hills.

What had happened to Mag and Nell?

No one came. He knew that their perceptions lay all around him, but he could sense no emotions, no thoughts but his own.

He sat and waited, his eyes focused on the book but not seeing it. It seemed hours before anyone came. Then Prior and Abbot and Walden were in the archway, looking across at him. Prior's face was still worried, Abbot's stern, Walden's reassuring....

Eric forced himself to smile at them and then turn another page and pretend to go on reading. After a moment he heard their footsteps retreating, and when he looked up again they were gone.

He sat a while longer and then he got up and walked down the ramp and stood for a few minutes looking at the ship, because that too would be expected of him. He felt nothing. The ship was a world away now, mocking him, for his future no longer lay in the past, with the old race, but out in the hills. If he had a future at all....

He went up the ramp again, toward his own room. No one else was in sight. They had all gone to bed, perhaps. They wouldn't expect him to try to run away now.

He began to walk, as aimlessly as he could, in the direction of the aircar. He saw no one. Perhaps it wasn't even guarded. He circled around it, still seeing no one; then, feeling more secure suddenly, he went directly toward it and reached up to open the panel and climb in.

"Is that you, Eric?"

Walden's voice. Quiet as always. And it came from inside the car.

* * * * *

Eric stood frozen, looking up at the ship, trying to see Walden's face and unable to find it in the darkness. He didn't answer--couldn't answer. He listened, and heard nothing except Walden, there above him, moving on the seat.

Where was Lisa?

"I thought you'd come back here," Walden said. He climbed down out of the aircar and stood facing Eric, his body a dim shadow.

"Why are you here?" Eric whispered.

"I wanted to see you. Without the others knowing it. I was sure you'd come here tonight."

Walden. Always Walden. First his teacher and then his friend, and now the one man who stood between him and freedom. For a second Eric felt his muscles tense and he stiffened, ready to leap upon the older man and knock him down and take the ship and run. Then he relaxed. It was a senseless impulse, primitive and useless.

"The others don't know you have any idea what's happened, Eric. But I could tell. It was written all over you."

"What did they find, Walden?"

The old man sighed, and when he spoke his voice was very tired. "They found two women. They tried to capture them, but the women ran out on a ledge. The older one slipped and fell and the other tried to catch her and she fell too. They were dead when the men reached them."

Eric listened, and slowly his tension relaxed, replaced by a dull ache of mourning. But he knew that he was glad to hear that they were dead and not captured, not dragged away from the hills to be bathed and well fed and imprisoned forever under the eyes of the new race.

"The old one was blind," Walden said. "It may have been her blindness that caused her to fall."

"It wasn't."

"No, Eric, it probably wasn't."

They were silent for a moment, and there was no sound at all except for their own breathing. Eric wondered if Lisa still hid in the aircar, if she was listening to them, afraid and hopeless and crying over the death of her people.

"Why did you come out here, Walden?"

"To see you. I came today, when I realized how suspicious the council had grown. I was going to warn you, to tell you to keep away from the hills, that they wanted an excuse to lock you up. I was too late."

"I was careless, Walden." He felt guilt twist inside of him.

"No. You didn't know the danger. I should have warned you sooner. But I never dreamed you would find anyone in the hills, Eric. I never dreamed there were any more without perception, this generation."

Eric moved nearer the car and leaned against it, the cold plastic next to his body cooling him a little, steadying him against the feverish trembling that shook his legs and sent sweat down over him and made him too weak, suddenly, to want to struggle further.

"Let me go, Walden. Let me take the car and go."

Walden didn't move. He stood quietly, a tall thin shape in the darkness.

"There are other people the searchers didn't find, aren't there? And you're going to them."

Eric didn't answer. He looked past Walden, at the car, wishing he could somehow call to Lisa, wishing they could perceive so that he could reassure her and promise her that somehow he'd still take her to freedom. But it would be an empty promise....

"I've warned you too late. You've found your people, but it won't do you any good. They'll hunt you through the hills, and I won't be able to help you any more."

Eric looked back at him, hearing the sadness in his voice. It was real sadness, real emotion. He thought of the years he had spent with Walden, learning, absorbing the old race knowledge, and he remembered that all through those years Walden had never once made him feel uncomfortable because of the difference between them.

He looked at the old man for a long time, wishing that it was day so he could read the other's expression, wondering how he had managed to take this man for granted for so long.

"Why?" he whispered. "Why are you helping me? Why aren't you like the others?"

"I never had a son, Eric. Perhaps that's the reason."

Eric thought of Myron and shook his head. "No, it isn't that. My father doesn't feel the way you do. He can't forget that I'm not normal. With him, I'm always aware of the difference."

"And you're not with me?"

"No," Eric said. "I'm not. Why?" And he wondered why he had never asked that question before.

"The final question," Walden said softly. "I wondered how long it would be before you asked it. I wondered if you'd ever ask it.

"Haven't you ever thought about why I never married, Eric? Haven't you ever asked yourself why I alone learned to read, and collected books, and studied the old race?"

"No," Eric admitted. "I just accepted you."

"Even though I can perceive and you can't." Walden paused and Eric waited, not knowing what was coming and yet sure that nothing could surprise him now.

"My father was normal," Walden said slowly. "But I never saw him. My mother was like you. So was my brother. We lived in the hills and I was the only one who could perceive. I learned what it was to be different."

Eric stared. He couldn't stop staring. And yet he should have realized, long ago, that Walden was different too, in his own way.

Walden smiled back, his face, shadowed in moonlight, as quiet and as understanding as ever. For a moment neither spoke, and there was only the faraway sound of crickets chirping and the rustling of the wind in the gardens.

And then, from within the aircar, there was a different rustling, that of a person moving.

"Lisa!"

Eric pushed the compartment panel back. The soft light came on automatically, framing her where she curled against the far wall.

"You heard us?"

She nodded. Tears had dried on her cheeks. Her eyes were huge in her thin face.

"We'd better go, Lisa."

He reached in to help her out.

They didn't see the aircar dropping in for a landing until it was almost upon them, until its lights arced down over the museum walls.

"Hide, Eric. In here--" Lisa pulled him forward.

Behind them, Walden's voice, suddenly tired in the darkness. "It's too late. They know I'm here. And they're wondering why."

The three of them stood frozen, watching each other, while the dark shape of the car settled to the ground some thirty yards away.

"It's Abbot," Walden said. He paused, intent for a moment, and added, "He doesn't know about you. Get out of sight somewhere, both of you, away from here--"

"Come on, Lisa--" Eric swung away from the car, toward the shelter of the building and whatever hiding place there might be. "Hurry!"

They ran, and the museum rose in front of them, and the door was open. They were through it and into the dim corridor, and there was no one around; Walden's figure was lost in the night outside. Beyond the libraries the great ramp spiraled downward.

"This way, Lisa!"

They came out into the bottom of the well and there in front of them the starship rested. Still reaching upward. Still waiting, as it had waited for so many uncounted years.

Their ship--if only it could be their ship....

"Oh, Eric!"

Side by side they stood staring at it, and Eric wished that they could get into it and go, right now, while they were still free and there was no one to stop them. But they couldn't. There was no food in the ship, no plant tanks, none of the many provisions the books listed.

Besides, if they took off now they would destroy the museum and all the people in it, and probably kill themselves as well.

"Eric! We know you're down there!" It wasn't Walden's voice.

Lisa moved closer. Eric put his arm around her and held her while footsteps hurried toward them down the ramp. The council. Abbot and Drew and the others. Prior, shaking his head. Walden.

"Let us go," Eric cried. "Why won't you let us go?"

Walden turned to the others. His eyes pleaded with them. His lips moved and his hands were expressive, gesturing. But the others stood without moving, without expression.

Then Abbot pushed Walden aside and started forward, his face hard and determined and unchangeable.

"You won't let us go," Eric said.

"No. You're fools, both of you."

There was one answer, only one answer, and with it, a hot violence in his blood as the old race pattern came into focus, as the fear and the futility fell away.

It was only a few steps to the ship. Eric caught Lisa's arm and pulled her after him and ran toward it, reaching up to the door. In one motion he flung it open and lifted her through it, then he swung about to face the others.

"Let us go!" he shouted. "Promise to let us go, or we'll take off anyway and if we die at least you'll die too!"

Abbot stopped. He looked back at Walden, his face scornful. "You see?" he said aloud. "They're mad. And you let this happen."

He turned away, dismissing Walden, and came toward the ship. The others followed him.

Eric waited. He stood with his back to the door, waiting, as Abbot strode toward him, ahead of the other councilmen, alone and unprotected.

"You're the fool!" Eric said. He laughed as he leaped forward.

Abbot's eyes went wide suddenly; he tried to dodge, gave a little grunt, and went limp in Eric's grasp.

Eric laughed again, swung Abbot into the ship and leaped in himself. The old race and its violence had never been nearer.

He slammed the door shut, bolted it, and turned back to where the councilman was struggling to his feet.

"Now will you let us go?" Eric said softly. "Or must we take off now, with you--for the stars?"

For a long moment Abbot looked at him, and then his lips trembled and his whole body went slack in defeat.

"The ship is yours," he whispered. "Just let me go."

Outside the ship, Walden chuckled wryly.

*   *   *   *   *

The Vacuum Suit was strange against Eric's body, as strange as the straps that bound him to the couch. He looked over at Lisa and she too was unrecognizable, a great bloated slug tied down beside him. Only her face, frightened behind the helmet, looked human.

He reached for the controls, then paused, glancing down through the view screens at the ground, at the people two hundred feet below, tiny ants scurrying away from the ship, running to shelter but still looking up at him. He couldn't see his parents or Walden.

His fingers closed about the control lever but still he stared down. Everything that had been familiar all his life stood out sharply now, because he was leaving and it would never be there again for him. And he had to remember what it was like....

Then he looked up. The sky was blue and cloudless above him, and there were no stars at all. But he knew that beyond the sky the stars were shining.

And perhaps, somewhere amid the stars, the old race waited.

He turned to Lisa. "This may be goodbye, darling."

"It may be. But it doesn't matter, really."

They had each other. It was enough. Even though they could never be as close to each other as the new race was close. They were separate, with a gulf always between their inmost thoughts, but they could bridge that gulf, sometimes.

He turned back to the controls and his fingers tightened. The last line of the poem shouted in his mind, and he laughed, for he knew finally what the poet had meant, what the old race had lived for. *We have cast off the planets like outgrown toys, and now we want the stars....*

He pulled the lever back and the ship sprang free. A terrible weight pressed against him, crushing him, stifling him. But still he laughed, because he was one of the old race, and he was happy.

And the meaning of his life lay in the search itself.

$$* \quad * \quad * \quad * \quad *$$

They stood staring up at the ship until it was only a tiny speck in the sky, and then they looked away from it, at each other. A wave of perception swept among them, drawing them closer to each other in the face of something they couldn't understand.

"Why did they go?" Abbot asked, in his mind.

"Why did any of the old race go?" Walden answered.

The sunlight flashed off the ship, and then it was gone.

"It's not surprising that the old race died," Abbot said. "They were brilliant, in their way, and yet they did such strange things. Their lives seemed so completely meaningless...."

Walden didn't answer for a moment. His eyes searched the sky for a last glimpse of the ship, but there was nothing at all. He sighed, and he looked at Abbot, and then past him, at all the others.

"I wonder," he said, "how long it will be before some other race says the same thing about us."

No one answered. He turned and walked away from them, across the trampled flowers, toward the museum and the great empty vault where the starship had waited for so long.

Also From Resurrected Press
SCIENCE FICTION AUTHORS RESURRECTED

FYFE RESURRECTED - THE STORIES OF H. B. FYFE
Stories from the Golden Age of Science Fiction by the author of D-99. dealing with the interaction of humans and aliens on far off worlds in ways that were as creative as they were imaginative.

SCHMITZ RESURRECTED - SELECTED STORIES OF JAMES H. SCHMITZ
Includes "An Incident on Route 12", "Watch the Sky", "The Other Likeness", "The Star Hyacinths", "Oneness", "The Winds of Time", "Ham Sandwich" and "Gone Fishing".

SHECKLY RESURRECTED - THE EARLY STORIES OF ROBERT SHECKLEY
Resurrected Press has collected some of the best of these from the 50's including "Warrior Race", "The Leech", "Watchbird", "Warm", "Diplomatic Immunity", "The Hour of Battle", "Besides Still Waters", "Keep Your Shape", "One Man's Poison", 'Ask a Foolish Question", "Cost of Living", "Death Wish Forever".

DICK RESURRECTED - THE EARLY STORIES OF PHILIP K. DICK
Early stories from the author of the novels that inspired "Blade Runner," "Total Recall," and "A Scanner Darkly".

HAMILTON RESURRECTED - CLASSIC STORIES OF EDMOND HAMILTON
Edmond Hamilton was one of the most popular writers during the 30's and 40's, the period that saw the first flowering of modern science fiction.

SMITH RESURRECTED - SELECTED STORIES OF EVELYN E. SMITH
During an era when women rarely appeared in science fiction magazines, Evelyn E. Smith appeared regularly in the pages of Galaxy and Fantastic Universe. Resurrected Press is proud to return these stories to print.

OTHER CLASSIC SCIENCE FICTION NOVELS

TALENTS, INCORPORATED - BY MURRAY LEINSTER
When a Mekinese fleet conquers his home planet, Captain Bors turns to Talents, Incorporated for help using their collection of individuals with unusual abilities to defeat the enemy and save the galaxy.

THE PIRATES OF ERSATZ - BY MURRAY LEINSTER
Bran Hodden just wanted to be an electronic engineer and marry a delightful girl. But when he's framed by the powers on Walden he's forced to turn back to his family's trade, piracy. Also published as The Pirates of Zan.

EMPIRE - BY CLIFFORD SIMAK
Spencer Chambers and Interplanetary Power owned the Solar System because they controlled the source of power. It fell to Russell Page and Harry Wilson to challenge that control if they had to cross the universe to do it.

NIGHT OF THE LONG KNIVES - THE CREATURE FROM THE CLEVELAND DEPTHS - BY FRITZ LEIBER
Two classic novellas set in the not too distant future from a classic master of science fiction.

ARMAGEDDON - 2419 A.D. - THE AIR LORDS OF HAN - BY PHILLIP FRANCIS NOWLAN
The two novels that introduced the world to that intrepid hero of the 25th Century, Buck Rogers. Buck Rogers must save the world from the clutches of the insidious Han.

Resurrected Press Fiction by Randall Garrett

Anything You Can Do...

What do you do when an alien with exceptional physical abilities crash lands on Earth and leaves a path of death and destruction in its wake? You use biological modification to create an enhanced human able to match the alien in strength and speed. But is the result still human?

Unwise Child

After two unsuccessful and seemingly random attempts on his life in the space of as many hours, Michael Raphael Gabriel finds himself called on to act as engineering officer on a new type of spacecraft designed for one mission only, to carry a giant computer to a distant destination before it can destroy the Earth. But once under way he discovers there is a murderer on board and the computer has gone crazy.

By Randall Garrett and Laurence Janifer

Pagan Passions

The Gods and Goddesses of the Ancient Greece and Rome have returned to rule Earth. William Forrester, a mortal teacher, dedicated to the pleasures of the mind, finds himself caught up in the power struggles of the immortals and seduced by the pleasures of the flesh.

The Fictional Detective
by Greg Fowlkes

Who killed Ezekial O. Handler?

A beautiful dame, a hard-boiled private eye – and a dead body.

It started like any other case. When a famous writer dies in a mysterious car crash, private detective Frank Slade is called in to find answers, but all he finds is more questions. Who killed Ezekial Handler? Who is Janet Nielsen and why is she so interested in finding out? Who is leaving the neatly typed clues? And as Slade tries to find answers to these questions he starts to wonder if the ultimate answer will threaten his very existence.

Read about it in
The Fictional Detective

Visit www.thefictionaldetective.com

About Resurrected Press

A division of Intrepid Ink, LLC, Resurrected Press is dedicated to bringing high quality, vintage books back into publication. See our entire catalogue and find out more at www.ResurrectedPress.com.

About Intrepid Ink, LLC

Intrepid Ink, LLC provides full publishing services to authors of fiction and non-fiction books, eBooks and websites. From editing to formatting, from publishing to marketing, Intrepid Ink gets your creative works into the hands of the people who want to read them. Find out more at www.IntrepidInk.com.

Made in the USA
Coppell, TX
21 January 2025